THE WEIGHT OF PETALS

A STORY OF MEMORY AND RESISTANCE

CADE MERIDIAN

CADE MERIDIAN PRESS

Published by Cade Meridian Press

Paperback ISBN: 979-8-9943346-0-7

Hardcover ISBN: 979-8-9943346-1-4

eBook ISBN: 979-8-9943346-2-1

First Edition

www.cademeridian.com

In the darkest night, someone lit the path.
In the longest run, the truth survived.
In the worst of us, the best of us chose.
This is for those who choose good—
even when it costs everything.

CONTENTS

THE WEIGHT OF PETALS

A STORY OF MEMORY
AND RESISTANCE

I
THE WORLD STILL WHOLE

In Las Vegas that November, the jacaranda tree bloomed out of season.

No one could say why. Some failure of its internal calendar, perhaps. Some confusion of the desert's strange warmth and sudden cold. Some stubborn insistence that beauty was a form of defiance, appearing exactly when the world said it shouldn't. The tree stood on the corner of Saguaro Avenue and Desert Rose Drive, its branches spreading wide and generous, heavy with purple blossoms that shouldn't have existed when the air had already turned sharp with autumn.

Against the amber sky of late afternoon, it looked like something from a dream—impossible, out of time, defiant. The blossoms hung in dense clusters, their color somewhere between purple and blue, between twilight and bruise. When they fell, they fell slowly, heavy as regret, collecting in drifts against the curb where the wind pushed them into small purple galaxies.

The children who passed beneath it every day had stopped

questioning why it bloomed. It was simply there: the purple tree at the corner, older than their parents, older than the neighborhood itself. In spring it would bloom again, properly, on schedule, and the whole street would turn purple with petals. But this autumn blooming felt different—urgent somehow, as if the tree knew something they didn't. As if it were offering one last gift of beauty before the world turned cold.

They called it "the purple tree" because they were children and didn't know its proper name. They had climbed its branches, hidden beneath its canopy, done homework in its shade, carved initials in its bark that their parents pretended not to see. It had been witness to first kisses and skinned knees, to games of tag and quiet moments of loneliness, to every small joy and sorrow of growing up on this corner of this city in this particular pocket of time.

The tree bloomed. The petals fell. The children passed beneath it, not knowing they were walking through a benediction.

Not knowing it was blooming for them.

At three o'clock the elementary school doors opened and released them—a held breath finally exhaled into golden air.

They poured onto the sidewalk in waves: the kindergarteners clutching construction paper turkeys, the fifth graders pretending they were too cool to run, the scattered middle schoolers from the charter school next door with their headphones and their careful distance from anything childish. Backpacks slid off shoulders. Voices rose and fell like birds settling for the evening. The air smelled of dry leaves and desert dust and someone's grandmother was baking something sweet with cinnamon.

Leila Álvarez walked slowly, her artist's eye already cataloging details for later. Her mother had taught her this: beauty was worth remembering, worth the effort of looking closely.

The light turned the concrete warm. Marcus Brooks's shadow stretched long and thin ahead of him, basketball tucked under one arm. Tessa Brown moved at the edge of the crowd, quiet and observant, her dark braid swinging with each step. Samantha Reyes's laugh carried bright across the street, certain as a bell.

Leila wanted to catch it in her sketchbook—to trap the amber light in charcoal before the sun dragged it down behind the mountains.

They didn't all walk together—not quite. They existed in the same orbit, the way kids do in a neighborhood where everyone has known everyone since kindergarten, since before words, since the first day their parents pushed them on swings in the same park. Marcus lived two streets over. Tessa's apartment complex backed up to Leila's. Sam's house sat on the corner with the chain-link fence and the rosebushes her abuela tended like children.

The neighborhood spread out around them in comfortable disorder: low stucco houses painted in faded pastels, apartment buildings with wrought-iron railings, desert landscaping gone a little wild. Someone had hung Dia de los Muertos decorations that no one had taken down yet—paper marigolds and sugar skulls dancing in the breeze. A scatter of carved pumpkins sagged on porches, their triangular eyes watching the street.

The crossing guard in her yellow vest waved them across at Desert Rose—the same woman who'd been there for years, who knew all their names, who said "Stay sweet" every single day like a blessing.

In the coffee shop on the corner—Casa de Sol, with its hand-painted sign and mismatched chairs—the owner was sweeping the sidewalk, and the smell of roasted beans and pan dulce drifted warm through the open door. Mr. Orozco waved at Sam, who waved back automatically. She'd been going there since she was small enough to sit on the counter, back when her mother used to meet other mothers there on Saturday mornings while the children drew with crayons on napkins.

The bodega next door had its fruit stand out: pyramids of oranges and apples, bunches of cilantro in white buckets, papel picado strung across the awning, fluttering red and yellow and green. Mrs. Khoury sat on a folding chair by the door, fanning herself despite the cooling air, watching the street with the patient attention of someone who had watched this same street for thirty years.

Across the road, the community center sat low and brown, its windows reflecting the golden light. The sign out front advertised ESL classes on Tuesdays, a knitting circle on Wednesdays, a youth basketball league starting next month. Tessa's mother taught beadwork there on Thursday evenings. The parking lot was mostly empty now, but in an hour it would fill with the evening people—the ones coming after work, the ones bringing their children, the ones looking for warm rooms and familiar faces.

The city's Harmony System—the invisible digital heartbeat the state had installed two years ago—hummed quietly in the background, ensuring the traffic lights were timed perfectly with the crosswalks and the street lamps flickered on exactly as the sun dipped. It was designed to keep the rhythm of the city gentle, to smooth out the edges of a rough world. No one thought much about it. It was just there, watching, coordinating, keeping everything running. Keeping everyone safe.

Everything was ordinary. Everything was safe.

Leila turned onto her street—Calle Mariposa—and the light followed her, spilling gold across the pavement. Her apartment building was pale yellow with dark red trim, bougainvillea climbing wild up the side. The courtyard in the center held a dry fountain no one had bothered to fix and a few struggling desert willows that her mother watered faithfully.

She could see Mrs. DeAndrade on the second-floor balcony, taking in laundry. Mr. and Mrs. Patel were unloading groceries from their car, their daughter Asha holding a gallon of milk with both hands. The Johnsons' cat sat in the window like a sphinx, watching everything with green-eyed judgment. This was home: three floors, twelve units, families stacked on top of each other in the comfortable way of people who shared walls and knew each other's cooking schedules and borrowed eggs when they ran out.

Marcus split off at the corner, heading toward the townhouses with the red tile roofs. Tessa continued past Leila's building toward the larger complex behind it—the one with the playground and the community pool that was always empty. Sam kept walking toward the small houses on the far end, where yards got a little bigger and people planted actual grass if they were stubborn enough.

Leila climbed the exterior stairs to the third floor, her backpack heavy with library books. She could hear the faint sound of music—someone practicing piano, someone else's television through an open window. The sun was lower now, almost four o'clock, and the light had gone from gold to amber, deepening toward bronze.

She paused at the top of the stairs, one hand on the railing, and looked back toward the purple tree. From here she could just see its crown, the blossoms glowing in the slanted light. She would draw it tonight, she decided. After homework. After dinner. In that quiet hour when her father played the tar and her mother worked at her loom and the apartment filled with the sound of creation.

She didn't know—standing there with her hand on the warm metal railing, her mind already on her sketchbook—that in less than an hour the President would begin speaking and the world would crack down in the middle.

She didn't know that memory would soon be the only safe place left to keep this light.

But that comes later.

For now: the purple tree, the amber sky, the girl at the top of the stairs with beauty in her mind.

For now: the world still whole.

II
MEMORY MADE VISIBLE

Inside apartment 3C, Yasmin Álvarez stood at her loom by the window, her fingers moving through warp and weft with the automatic grace of long practice. The afternoon light caught in the threads—deep reds and golds, a pattern she'd been working on for weeks. Leila dropped her backpack by the door and went straight to the kitchen table, which doubled as her studio, pulling out her sketchbook.

"Good day?" Yasmin asked without turning from her work.

"Golden," Leila said, and meant it.

Ali emerged from the bedroom with his tar, the long-necked Persian instrument cradled like something precious. He settled into his chair by the bookshelf and began tuning, his ear close to the strings. Three quick turns of the peg, then one slow change, listening for the note to settle. The sound filled the small apartment —low, resonant, ancient.

Yasmin smiled without pausing her weaving.

This was their hour. Thursday evening, before dinner, before homework. Music and creation and the warm silence of people who loved each other working side by side.

The apartment smelled of cardamom tea and the faint chemical tang of Leila's charcoal pencils. Through the thin walls they could hear Mrs. DeAndrade's television, a neighbor's child practicing violin, the ordinary symphony of people living stacked lives.

Ali played a few experimental notes, then shifted into a melody Leila recognized—something her grandmother had sung, years ago, before she died. Something about mountains and longing and the way home pulls at you even when you're standing in it.

Leila sketched quickly, trying to capture her father's hands on the strings, the way concentration softened his face. Her mother had taught her to look for these moments, to preserve them. "Art is memory made visible," Yasmin always said. "Don't waste beauty."

At four twenty-five, Ali's phone buzzed. He glanced at it, and something changed in his expression—a tightening around his eyes.

"The President's speaking at four-thirty," he whispered.

Yasmin's hands paused on the loom. "Should we watch?"

"Probably should." Ali set down the tar with careful deliberacy. "Know what's coming."

Leila felt the shift in the room like a drop in temperature. Her father turned on the small TV mounted above the bookshelf. The screen bloomed blue, then resolved into a news anchor's serious face.

"We're just minutes away from the President's address on the new Civic Protection Initiative..."

Yasmin crossed to the table and rested her hand on Leila's shoulder—warm, solid, real. The silver paintbrush pendant at her throat caught the light.

Outside, the sun was beginning its descent. Inside, the three of them stood together, waiting to hear what their country had decided they were worth.

Two streets over, in the townhouse with the red tile roof, Marcus sat at the kitchen counter with his laptop open, lines of code scrolling down the screen. His mother, Maya, leaned over his shoulder, coffee mug in one hand, her other hand pointing at a function that wasn't quite right.

"There," she said. "See it?"

Marcus squinted. "The loop?"

"The loop. You're iterating twice when you only need once."

"Oh." Marcus grinned. "Yeah, okay. That's cleaner."

From the living room came the warm, wandering sound of Jamal's saxophone—not a song exactly, more like a conversation with himself. He was working through a new arrangement for Friday's gig at the Blue Room, testing phrases, seeing what stuck.

Maya squeezed Marcus's shoulder. "Ship it, engineer. The servos will thank you."

The kitchen was a machine of perfect efficiency: the smell of garlic grounding the air, the saxophone weaving through the hum of the refrigerator, code scrolling like sheet music on the screen. Sometimes they'd all end up talking about the math of music, or the rhythm of good code, or how jazz and programming were basically the same thing—improvisation within structure, creativity within rules.

The kitchen smelled like butter and garlic and something rich in the oven—Jamal's grandmother's cornbread recipe, probably, which he made every Thursday like clockwork.

Marcus hit save and closed his laptop, satisfied. The little steel gear charm on his mother's keychain caught the light as she moved to check her phone.

Her smile faded.

"Jamal," she called toward the living room. "Speech is starting soon."

The saxophone went silent. Jamal appeared in the doorway, still holding his sax. "Now?"

"Four-thirty." Maya's voice had gone flat. "We should probably watch."

Jamal set his instrument carefully on its stand and reached for the remote. "Yeah. Yeah, we should."

The TV came on. News anchor. Solemn music. "In just moments, the President will address the nation regarding additional security measures..."

Marcus felt his parents move closer to each other, their shoulders touching. Maya's hand found Jamal's. In the warm kitchen that smelled like home, something cold crept in through the screen.

IN THE APARTMENT complex behind Leila's building, Tessa sat cross-legged on the living room floor while her mother, Debra, worked at the low table, sorting beads by color. Tiny glass circles in turquoise and white and deep red, organized in small wooden bowls. Outside the window, the wind was picking up—east wind, her father had said this morning, which meant change coming.

Debra's hands moved with practiced certainty, threading a needle with sinew, beginning a new pattern on a strip of leather. She was making regalia for a dancer at the Southern Paiute cultural center, traditional work that took weeks to complete. Each bead was placed with intention. Each pattern carries meaning.

"Tell me the story again," Tessa said quietly. "About the jay."

Debra smiled. "You know this one by heart."

"I know. But I like how you tell it."

So Debra told her grandmother's version of the old story—

about the jay who stole fire from the sun and brought it to the people, burning his feathers black. About how the jay didn't steal the fire to keep it, but to give it away. How the burn marks on his feathers were the receipt for his generosity. Her voice was soft, rhythmic, the way her own grandmother had told stories.

Ray came in from the small balcony where he'd been on a call with the tribal council. Something about water rights, about the new pipeline proposal. His face looked tired.

He touched Tessa's head gently as he passed. "Homework done?"

"Almost."

"Good girl." He moved to the kitchen, poured himself water from the filtered pitcher they kept by the sink. The small turquoise pendant that had been his mother's sat in a dish by the windowsill, catching the fading light.

The wind rattled the glass.

Debra looked up from her beadwork. "You should eat something."

"In a minute." Ray picked up the remote, his expression troubled. "Speech is about to start."

"Do we need to watch?" Debra's hands kept moving, beads clicking softly.

"Probably should. If it's what they're saying..." He didn't finish.

Ray picked up the remote. The old flatscreen blinked to life—the same news anchor, the same countdown.

The rhythm of the beads stopped. The silence that followed wasn't peaceful; it was the held breath of a bird sensing a hawk. Tessa felt her father's weight shift as he stood by the couch, arms crossed. Feeling the wind outside grow stronger, rattling the windows like a warning.

In her grandmother's language, there was a word for this feeling—this sense of the world tilting, of something precious about to be taken. She couldn't remember the word now, but she felt it in her bones.

AT THE SMALL house on the corner with the chain-link fence and the rosebushes, Sam pushed through the front door and immediately smelled the scent of home: sofrito simmering on the stove, arepas crisping in the pan, cilantro and lime, and the particular magic of her mother's kitchen.

"¡Mija!" Elena called from the stove without turning. "¿Cómo estuvo la escuela?"

"Good. We're reading Neruda in English class."

"Neruda!" Carlos looked up from the dining table where he was grading papers, red pen in hand. "Now that's poetry. 'I want to do with you what spring does with the cherry trees.' You know that one?"

Sam grinned. "We read it today."

"Your teacher has good taste." Carlos set down his pen. "Dime un verso. Tell me a line you remember."

Sam thought for a moment, then recited in Spanish: "Es tan corto el amor, y es tan largo el olvido."

"Love is so short," Carlos translated softly, "forgetting is so long." He nodded with satisfaction. "Perfecto. That's the one that breaks your heart."

Elena turned from the stove, wooden spoon in hand. "Don't break her heart before dinner, Carlos. She's twelve."

"Thirteen next month," Sam corrected, touching the locket at her throat—her abuela's face inside, forever young, forever smiling.

"Thirteen next month," Elena agreed, and pulled Sam into a one-armed hug that smelled like onions and warmth. "Set the table, mi poeta. Your father's been grading for hours; he needs to eat something besides coffee and disappointment."

Sam laughed and began pulling plates from the cabinet. Through the window she could see the last of the golden light dying in the west, the sky turning that particular shade of autumn amber that made everything look like a photograph, like memory even while it was happening.

The kitchen was warm. The food was ready. Her father's laugh filled the small house when Elena teased him about his students' grammar. This was the center of everything: this table, these people, this language they spoke in two tongues that felt like one.

Carlos's phone buzzed. He glanced at it, and his smile faded. "Elena."

"I know."

"Should we—"

"Yes." Elena turned off the burner, wiped her hands on her apron. "Sam, ven. Come watch with us."

Sam felt something shift in her chest. "What's happening?"

"The President's speaking." Carlos was already reaching for the remote. "About the new... security policies."

The TV came on. The news anchor's face was grave, professional. "We're moments away from what the White House is calling a major policy announcement regarding civic protection and community safety..."

Elena pulled Sam close, one arm around her shoulders. Carlos stood beside them, his hand resting on Sam's head like a blessing.

On the stove, the arepas were getting cold. Outside, the light was dying. On the screen, the seal of the President appeared, and then his face—smiling, confident, certain.

And he spoke.

III
WORDS LIKE ASH

The President's face filled screens across the city, casting a cold blue glow that washed away the afternoon's amber warmth. Behind him, the Oval Office gleamed: flags flanking the resolute desk, gold curtains catching the light, the presidential seal polished to a mirror shine. Everything calculated to project power, tradition, authority.

He sat behind the desk, hands folded—a heavy-set man in his late seventies with swept-back blonde hair that caught the light like spun brass. His face was tanned. His jaw was set, and his eyes were small and sharp beneath heavy brows. When he spoke, his voice carried a particular cadence of someone used to being listened to, used to being obeyed.

"My fellow Americans," he began, his voice warm, almost paternal. "I come to you tonight with a difficult truth, but one that must be spoken. For too long—and believe me, I've been saying this for years—we have allowed disorder to masquerade as diversity. We have tolerated disruption in the name of tolerance. We have permitted those who do not share our values to erode the foundations of the nation our ancestors built. And frankly, it's been a disaster. A complete disaster."

In apartment 3C, Yasmin's hand tightened on Leila's shoulder.

"Tonight, I am announcing the immediate implementation of the Civic Protection Initiative—a comprehensive program, the best program, really tremendous—designed to restore order, safety, and unity to our communities. People are saying it's the most important security measure in American history. Smart people. People who know."

The President smiled. It didn't reach his eyes.

"This is not about hatred. Let me be very clear about that. This is about protection. Not about exclusion, but about security. We owe it to our children—to real Americans, the ones who were born here, who respect our laws—to ensure that those who cannot or will not assimilate no longer threaten the peace we have built. And let's be honest, okay? Some people don't want to assimilate. They come here, they take advantage, they don't even speak English. It's true. Everybody knows it's true."

Marcus felt his mother's breathing change, quick and shallow.

"Under this initiative, individuals flagged as potential risks to civic stability will be processed through our new Department of Civic Protection. This includes those who have participated in unauthorized protests—and we've seen these protests, haven't we? Very bad people. Burning flags, disrespecting our police. This includes those who have spread misinformation critical of our government, those whose cultural practices or associations mark them as incompatible with American values."

His face hardened; the genial mask slipping for just a moment. His mouth became a thin line, eyes narrowing.

"We know who they are. We have lists. Very detailed lists."

The sun was setting. Through windows across the city, the light shifted from gold to amber to rust.

"I want to be clear," the President continued, his tone shifting back to that almost gentle register. "This is about safety. Your safety. Your children's safety. We cannot allow sentiment to cloud our judgment when the security of the nation is at stake. Some people —weak people, frankly—will say we need to be compassionate. But you know what? Sometimes, compassion is weakness. Sometimes you have to be strong. Very, very strong."

Tessa felt her father's hand curl into a fist.

"Some will call this extreme. The fake news media, the radical left, all the usual suspects—they're going to say we are targeting communities based on their heritage or beliefs." His face darkened again, brows drawing together, jaw thrust forward. "To them I say: we are targeting those who threaten us. If that happens to correlate with certain demographics... then perhaps we must ask why those communities harbor such disproportionate numbers of dissidents and criminals. Maybe it's not profiling if it's just facts. Did you ever think of that? It's common sense. It's just numbers."

Sam heard her mother whisper something in Spanish—a prayer, maybe, or a curse.

"Effective immediately, all public schools, workplaces, and community centers will participate in identification protocols. Neighborhood watch programs will be expanded and rewarded. Citizens who report suspicious activity will be recognized as patriots defending their homeland. And we're talking about real rewards here. Monetary incentives. Tax breaks. These are good people doing the right thing. They should be compensated. Big league."

He leaned forward slightly, his expression shifting to something almost apologetic, almost regretful.

"Now, I know some people will talk about freedom of speech, freedom of assembly—and believe me, I love the Constitution, probably more than anyone. Tremendous document. The

Founders were geniuses. But these freedoms, they're not unlimited. The Founders understood that. In times of national emergency, certain... adjustments... need to be made. Temporarily. Just until we're secure again. You understand."

His hands opened in a gesture of reasonableness.

"So, effective immediately, unauthorized public gatherings of more than five people will require permits. Online speech critical of civic protection measures will be flagged as potential incitement. Social media posts, blogs, even private messages—if they threaten our security, we need to know about them. It's common sense. You can't yell fire in a crowded theater, right? Well, you can't yell 'resist' in a nation under threat. It's the same thing. Same exact thing."

In apartment 3C, Ali's face had gone pale.

The President paused, letting his words settle like ash on a fresh snow—staining everything they touched, impossible to brush away without leaving a mark. Behind him, the gold curtains seemed to glow brighter, the presidential seal catching the light.

"I know this is difficult. Change always is. But I also know that we are a strong people. The strongest people. Nobody is stronger than us. Nobody. And when we stand together—when we refuse to let the few poison the many—there is nothing we cannot accomplish. We're going to make America safe again. We're going to make it whole again. Like it used to be, when people knew their place."

In four homes across the same neighborhood, four families watched the same face speak the same words. They watched his expression shift—from grandfatherly concern to cold calculation to barely suppressed rage and back again. They watched him perform authority.

"To those who are concerned: if you have nothing to hide, you have nothing to fear. Simple. To those who believe in America, who respect our laws and our culture: you are safe. You are valued. You are the future. I protect you. I protect real Americans."

His smile widened, but his eyes remained hard, calculating.

"But to those who have spent years undermining us from within, who have used our freedoms against us, who have put their own agendas above the common good—and you know who you are—your time of reckoning has come. It's over. The party's over. We're taking our country back."

The camera pulled back slightly, showing the full presidential podium, the gravity of the office, the gold and power and weight of it all.

"God bless you, and God bless the United States of America."

The seal reappeared. The screen cut to the news desk—a gleaming curved surface of backlit glass, American flags projected on screens behind the anchors, the network logo pulsing red, white, and blue. Two anchors sat with expressions of solemn approval: a man with silver hair and an American flag pin on his lapel, a woman in a blue suit with a practiced smile.

"Well," the male anchor said, his voice measured and grave. "That was certainly a historic address. The President spoke directly to Americans' very real concerns about safety and security."

"Absolutely, Tom," the woman replied, nodding with careful emphasis. "It's a pivot toward order. A necessary tightening of the civic fabric. Not everyone will agree with these measures, but you can't argue with his commitment to protecting American families."

"That's right, Sandra. The Civic Protection Initiative represents the most comprehensive security overhaul in decades. Critics will undoubtedly call it controversial, but as the President said, sometimes hard decisions are necessary decisions."

"And Tom, I think what struck me most was his clarity. No ambiguity there. Americans know where he stands, and in times of uncertainty, that kind of decisive leadership is exactly what people are looking for."

"Indeed. Now, we're joined by our political analyst, former

Congressman Richard Daulton, to discuss the implications of tonight's announcement. Congressman, your initial reaction?"

"Well, Tom, I think the president hit exactly the right tone. Firm but fair. We've seen too much chaos in our streets, too much division. Sometimes you need to draw a line..."

At 4:33 PM, the sun set.

The streetlights clicked on automatically, casting the neighborhood in harsh white light. And in that exact moment, as darkness replaced the golden afternoon, phones across the city buzzed in a synchronized, mechanical chorus. Not a random scattering of notifications, but a single, unified command sent to millions of pockets at once.

Maya picked hers up. A notification from the Techstart Solutions security system: CLEARANCE REVOKED. ASSET FREEZE INITIATED. ALL EMPLOYEES FLAGGED FOR ENHANCED SCREENING TOMORROW MORNING.

She looked at Jamal. His phone was buzzing too.

At the community center three blocks away, Ray's phone showed an email from the tribal council: EMERGENCY MEETING TONIGHT. PROTECTION ORDERS BEING ISSUED.

In the small house with the rosebushes, Carlos received a text from the school district: MANDATORY STAFF MEETING 7AM TOMORROW. ATTENDANCE REQUIRED. IDENTIFICATION PROTOCOLS TO BE IMPLEMENTED.

And in apartment 3C, Ali stared at his phone screen—an automated message from the university: YOUR POSITION HAS BEEN PLACED UNDER ADMINISTRATIVE REVIEW. REPORT TO SECURITY OFFICE TOMORROW 8AM. NON-COMPLIANCE WILL RESULT IN IMMEDIATE TERMINATION AND REFERRAL TO THE DEPARTMENT OF CIVIC PROTECTION.

DCP.

The four families stood in their separate homes, holding their separate phones, reading their separate messages that all said the same thing:

We know where you are. We know who you are. We are coming.

Outside, the neighborhood was changing.

Through windows, people could see their neighbors—people they'd known for years—gathering on porches, talking in tight clusters, their faces lit by phone screens. Some were frightened. Others were nodding, agreeing, already convinced.

A car drove slowly down Saguaro Avenue, loudspeaker mounted on top: "CIVIC PROTECTION INITIATIVE NOW IN EFFECT. REPORT SUSPICIOUS ACTIVITY TO 1-800-SAFE-USA. GOOD CITIZENS PROTECT GOOD NEIGHBORS."

At the corner store, Mr. Orozco was pulling down his metal shutters early, hands shaking.

At the bodega, Mrs. Khoury sat very still in her chair, watching the street with ancient, knowing eyes.

In the park two blocks over, someone had already spray-painted over the community mural—the one that showed faces of every color holding hands. Now it just said: CITIZENS FIRST.

The purple blossoms of the jacaranda tree drifted down like snow, collecting on the pavement where no one stopped to admire them anymore.

The world that had been whole at four o'clock was broken by four forty-five.

And the night had not yet begun.

IV
THE FRACTURE

The first siren didn't wail; it chirped. A short, sharp digital burst that sounded like a mechanical bird announcing a kill. Then came the others—a discordant harmony of wails that made the window glass hum.

Then another siren sounded, and then a dozen more converged from different directions, their wails building into a chorus that made windows rattle, dogs bark, and children press their faces to glass.

Leila moved to her apartment window and looked down at the street. A convoy of black vehicles was moving slowly down Saguaro Avenue—unmarked vans with tinted windows, flanked by trucks mounted with lights and cameras. On their sides, the paint was so fresh it looked wet under the streetlights—stark white letters stenciled over whatever those trucks used to be. DEPARTMENT OF CIVIC PROTECTION. The smell of chemical solvents drifted on the wind, sharper than the scent of dry leaves. The letters were crisp, white, official. As if they'd been ready for weeks.

Behind her, her mother's phone rang. Then, her father's. Both at once.

"Don't answer," Ali said quietly. "Not yet."

Two streets over, Marcus watched from his window as people began emerging from their houses. Some carried signs—hastily made, cardboard and marker, words scrawled in anger and fear:

THIS IS NOT AMERICA

NO PAPERS NO DEPORTATION

WE WILL NOT COMPLY

They gathered at the corner near the community center, maybe thirty people, then fifty. Marcus recognized faces: Mrs. Chen from the library, the Morales family who ran the taqueria, the young couple who'd just moved in last month with their baby. They stood in a loose cluster, uncertain but determined, their voices rising.

"We have a right to assemble!" "This is fascism!" "Not in our neighborhood!"

Then, from the opposite direction, another group appeared. Larger. Louder.

They carried signs too, but different ones:

CITIZENS FIRST

DEPORT CRIMINALS

PROTECT OUR CHILDREN

IF YOU'RE LEGAL YOU'RE SAFE

Some wore red hats. Some had flags draped over their shoulders. Marcus saw Mr. Patterson from three doors down, the man who'd always waved at him when he shot hoops in the driveway. Now he was chanting with the others, his face flushed and angry.

"Go back where you came from!" "You don't belong here!" "Real Americans only!"

The two groups faced each other across twenty feet of asphalt.

The Civic Protection trucks idled between them, officers in tactical gear standing with arms crossed, watching, waiting.

Not stopping it. Watching it.

"They're moving in a grid pattern," Maya murmured, her engineer's brain cataloging the efficiency of the raid even as her mother's heart broke. "Sector by sector. Marcus, get away from the window."

In Tessa's apartment, the wind had picked up, rattling the balcony door. Her father stood with his phone pressed to his ear, his face grave.

"How many?" he was saying. "Jesus. Okay. No, don't go alone. Wait for—" He paused, listening. "I know. I know it's not safe. But we can't—"

He hung up. Looked at Debra, then at Tessa.

"They're arresting people at the community center. Anyone on the tribal council registry. They're calling it 'preventive detention.'"

Debra's hands had stopped moving. The beadwork lay forgotten on the table.

"How long do we have?" she asked.

Ray shook his head. "I don't know. Hours, maybe. Maybe less."

Through the thin walls, they could hear their neighbors shouting, arguing. Someone was pounding on a door down the hall. Someone else was crying.

The wind rattled the glass again, harder this time.

At Sam's house, Elena had turned off the TV but the damage was done. Carlos sat at the table with his head in his hands, staring at his phone.

"They're asking for lists," he said, his voice hollow. "The district wants lists of students by immigration status, by family origin. They're calling it 'safety protocols.'"

"You can't give them that," Elena said.

"If I don't, they'll fire me. And then they'll just get the lists anyway from someone who will."

"So, what do we do?"

Carlos looked up at his wife, at his daughter standing in the doorway with her grandmother's locket clutched in her hand. His face was the face of every parent in every moment of history who realized they couldn't protect their child from what was coming.

"We don't give them anything," he said finally. "We buy time. We warn people. And then—" He stopped.

"Then?" Elena pressed.

"Then we run."

Through the window, they could see their street changing. Mr. Kowalski from next door was putting up a new flag—larger than his old one, almost aggressive in its size. Two houses down, the Nguyens were loading suitcases into their car, moving quickly, glancing over their shoulders. Across the street, someone had spray-painted "SNITCH HOTLINE: 1-800-SAFE-USA" on the bus stop bench.

The rosebushes her abuela had planted swayed in the wind, their last blooms scattering petals across the lawn like drops of blood.

By 5:15 PM, the confrontation at the community center had grown to more than two hundred people. The counter-protesters outnumbered the resisters now, three to one, and they were getting bolder.

Someone threw a bottle. It shattered on the pavement.

Someone else threw a rock.

The chanting grew louder, uglier:

"Send them back! Send them back! Send them back!"

A woman in a headscarf tried to leave, to walk away from the crowd. Three people blocked her path.

"Where are you going?" "Show us your papers!" "This is our country!"

A phone appeared, recording. Another. A dozen. The woman's face filled screens across the neighborhood, shared and reshared with captions: SUSPICIOUS INDIVIDUAL FLEEING PROTEST. REPORT TO DCP.

Then the Civic Protection officers moved.

Not toward the aggressors. Toward the protesters.

"This is an unauthorized assembly," a voice boomed through a loudspeaker. "You have five minutes to disperse or you will be detained for violation of the Civic Protection Initiative."

"We have a right to assemble!" someone shouted back.

"That right has been suspended for the duration of the emergency. Four minutes."

"What emergency? This is manufactured fear!"

"Three minutes."

Some people started to leave, hands up, backing away. Others linked arms, forming a line. Marcus watched from his window as Mrs. Chen—sweet Mrs. Chen, who helped him find books, who always had butterscotch candies at the circulation desk—stood in that line, her gray hair blowing in the wind, her face set with quiet defiance.

The officers moved forward. They had batons. Zip ties. Dogs straining at leashes.

The counter-protesters cheered.

Maya pulled the curtains shut. "Don't watch," she said, but her voice was shaking.

But Marcus had already seen. They all had.

By 5:30 PM, the street was full of flashing lights. Police cars. DCP vans. Ambulances.

Twelve people had been arrested. Seven more were injured when the crowd surged, and the officers pushed back with shields and batons.

Mrs. Chen was gone—dragged toward the vans, wrists zip-tied, her protests swallowed by the noise. Marcus lost sight of her in the crush.

The counter-protesters were still there, still chanting, but quieter now. Satisfied. Victorious.

Someone had hung a banner from the community center's roof: CLEAN STREETS, SAFE NEIGHBORHOODS.

The jacaranda tree still stood on the corner, but its benediction had ended. The fallen petals were no longer galaxies; they were ground into the asphalt by tactical boots, leaving smears of purple that looked less like flowers and more like bruises.

In four homes across the same neighborhood, four families made the same decision.

They couldn't stay.

The question was no longer whether they would be taken.

The question was whether they could get their children to safety before the knock came.

V
THE UNMAKING

The knocking started at 5:47 PM.

It wasn't the frantic pounding of emergency; it was the rhythmic, hollow sound of authority that knows it has already won.

Leila heard it from her room where she'd been pretending to do homework, her sketchbook open but empty, her hands too unsteady to draw. She heard her father's footsteps stop. Heard her mother's sharp intake of breath.

"Don't answer it," Yasmin whispered.

But the knocking continued. Patient. Inevitable.

Ali moved to the door, looked through the peephole. His shoulders sagged.

"It's DCP," he said quietly.

He opened the door.

Two agents stood in the hallway, both in dark tactical uniforms with the department seal on their shoulders. Behind them, Mrs. DeAndrade from the second floor stood on the landing, her laundry basket clutched to her chest, watching.

"Ali Álvarez?" the first agent said, consulting a tablet.

"Yes."

"You've been flagged for processing under the Civic Protection Initiative. Your presence is required at the Central Processing Annex for security review."

"On what grounds?"

"Dissemination of anti-government content. Participation in unauthorized academic activities. Association with known agitators." The agent read from the screen in a bored monotone, as if reciting a grocery list.

"That's my job," Ali said. "I'm a professor. I teach sociology—"

"Are you refusing to comply?"

"No, I'm asking—"

"Then you'll come with us now." The agent's hand moved to his belt. "Mrs. Álvarez, you're also flagged. Community organizing activities. Unauthorized assembly coordination."

Yasmin stepped forward, placing herself between the agents and Leila. "My daughter—"

"Minors will be processed separately. Juvenile Safety Services will collect her within the hour."

"No." Yasmin's voice was steel. "No, you're not taking my daughter."

"Ma'am, you don't have a choice."

From the landing, Mrs. DeAndrade's voice rang out: "What are you doing? This is a good family! I've known them for five years—"

The second agent turned. "Ma'am, step back."

"I will not step back! This is wrong!" Mrs. DeAndrade set down her basket and moved toward the agents, her face flushed with anger. "You can't just come in here and—"

"Ma'am, you're interfering with Civic Protection operations."

"I know my rights. The Constitution—"

"Rights are suspended during the emergency." The agent pulled zip-ties from his belt. "You're being detained for obstruction and potential re-education."

"What?" Mrs. DeAndrade's voice cracked with disbelief. "I'm a citizen. I was born here. My father fought in Korea—"

"Re-education facility. Come with us."

"This is insane!" But her voice was already weakening, realization dawning that her citizenship, her father's service, her five decades of being American meant nothing now.

Inside the apartment, Yasmin's hands shook as she removed the silver paintbrush pendant from her neck. She pressed it into Leila's palm, closing her daughter's fingers around it.

"Remember," she whispered. "Remember everything. Draw it all."

Ali touched Leila's face, his eyes bright with unshed tears. "We'll come back for you. I promise."

They were lies, and everyone in the room knew it.

The agents took her parents. Took Mrs. DeAndrade, still protesting, still not believing this could happen to her. Their voices faded down the stairwell, and then there was only the sound of engines starting, vehicles pulling away.

The silence that rushed back into the apartment was heavier than the noise. It pressed against her eardrums, suffocating the lingering scent of cardamom. Leila stood alone in the center of the room, the pendant burning like a coal in her hand.

At the grocery store on Fifth and Mariner, Marcus pushed the cart while his mother checked her list. Normal. They were doing something normal, as if the world hadn't just announced it wanted them gone.

Maya picked up a box of cereal—the kind Marcus liked, with the cartoon mascot—and almost smiled. Almost.

"This one?" she asked.

"Yeah."

They moved through the fluorescent-lit aisles like ghosts, like people already fading. Other shoppers gave them wide berth, or stared too long, or whispered to each other while looking at their phones.

At the self-checkout, Maya scanned her ID card for the loyalty discount.

The scanner blinked red.

Blinked again.

Then a harsh tone, loud enough that people three aisles over turned to look.

"Please wait for assistance," the machine announced in its pleasant, artificial voice.

A store manager appeared, followed by a security guard. Then, within ninety seconds, two DCP officers who'd apparently been waiting in the parking lot.

"Maya Brooks?" one of them said.

"Yes, but—"

"You've been flagged as a risk entity. You need to come with us for processing."

"There must be a mistake. I work at Techstart Solutions. I have a security clearance—"

"Your clearance has been revoked. You're flagged for association with activist networks, unauthorized data access—" he glanced at his tablet, "—and misappropriation of dual-use robotics protocols. You are flagged as a high-level security risk."

"I mentor girls in STEM. That's not—"

"We're not here to debate. Come with us."

Marcus grabbed the small gear charm from his mother's keychain before anyone could stop him, shoving it deep into his pocket. Maya's eyes met his—a look that said run, hide, survive—but her mouth said nothing.

Behind them, a white man in a baseball cap and work jacket

stepped forward. Marcus recognized him vaguely—someone's dad, maybe, or a regular customer. Mid-forties, with carpenter's hands and a no-nonsense face.

"Hold on," the man shouted. "What did she do? She was buying groceries."

"Sir, this doesn't concern you."

"The hell it doesn't. I'm watching you arrest someone for scanning a discount card."

"Sir, step back."

"I'm a citizen. I'm allowed to witness—"

"You're flagged for interfering with operations." The officer pulled out his phone, typed something. "There. Now you're in the system. Inciting resistance."

The man's face went pale. "What? I didn't—I was just—"

"You're coming with us for re-education assessment."

"You can't do this!"

But they could. They did. The man was cuffed alongside Maya, both of them loaded into the same van, and Marcus was left standing by the shopping cart with its box of cereal and its gallon of milk, watching his mother's face disappear behind tinted windows.

A store employee approached carefully. "Son, is there someone we can call for you?"

Marcus ran.

At the community center, Tessa sat on the floor while her mother worked, the beads clicking softly, the story about the jay half-finished. Evening classes were starting—adults arriving for ESL, for citizenship prep that would never matter now, for gatherings that felt like defiance just by existing.

The doors burst open at 6:15 PM.

Six officers in tactical gear, weapons visible, faces hard.

"This facility is operating without proper permits. Everyone inside is subject to identification verification."

People froze. A woman near the door tried to leave and was blocked immediately.

"No one leaves until processing is complete."

Debra stood, setting down her beadwork with careful precision. Ray moved to her side, his face calm but his jaw tight.

"We have permits," Ray said. "The center is registered—"

"Your permits were revoked at 4:30 PM under emergency authority. All tribal council members and their immediate families are flagged for processing."

"On what grounds?"

"Subversive organizing. Environmental activism that threatens national interests. Unauthorized assembly."

"We're teaching beadwork," Debra said quietly.

"You're indoctrinating minors with anti-assimilationist ideology."

The words were so absurd they hung in the air like a foul smell.

From the back of the room, an older white man stood up. He was in his seventies, gray-haired and straight-backed, wearing a denim shirt with service pins on the collar—Silver Star, Purple Heart, campaign ribbons from wars most of these officers were too young to remember.

"I'm General Robert Morrison, United States Army, retired," he said, his voice carrying the weight of forty years of command. "I took an oath to defend the Constitution of the United States. What you're doing here violates the Constitution."

The lead officer barely glanced at him. "Sir, sit down."

"I will not sit down. This is illegal detention. These people have broken no laws."

"Sir, final warning."

"I'm a decorated veteran. I fought for this country. I bled for it." Morrison's voice didn't rise, but it filled the room. "This isn't the America I defended. This is what I fought against."

The officer spoke into his radio: "Process him. Tier 1 Detention. Past service doesn't grant immunity from current compliance, General."

Two officers moved toward Morrison. He didn't resist, but he didn't help them either. They had to physically guide his arms behind his back, zip-tie his wrists while his medals caught the light.

"You should be ashamed," Morrison said quietly as they led him past. "Every one of you should be ashamed."

They took him. Took Ray and Debra. Took three other adults who'd made the mistake of being there, being brown, being present.

Tessa slipped her grandmother's turquoise pendant into her pocket before they separated the children from the adults. The beadwork lay scattered on the floor, the pattern half-finished, the story about the jay who gave away fire to the people never completed.

At the small house with the rosebushes, Sam heard the knock and knew immediately what it meant.

Her father was already standing, his face gray, his hands steady as he set down his red pen. Elena crossed herself and pulled Sam close.

"Carlos Reyes?" the agent at the door said.

"Yes."

"You've been flagged for subversive teaching activities. Distribution of unauthorized materials. Incitement of youth resistance through educational content."

"I teach Spanish," Carlos said. "Literature. Language."

"You teach dissent dressed up as culture."

The words hung there, naked in their cruelty.

A car pulled up outside—Carlos's colleague Sarah McKenzie, a white woman in her thirties who taught English in the classroom next to his. She'd texted him an hour ago, worried, saying she was coming by.

She ran up the walkway, stopping short when she saw the agents.

"Carlos? What's happening?"

"Sarah, don't—" Carlos started.

"Are you arresting him? For what?"

"Ma'am, this doesn't concern you."

"He's my friend. He's one of the best teachers in the district." Sarah's voice was shaking but determined. "Whatever you think he did, you're wrong."

"Are you interfering with Civic Protection operations?"

"I'm exercising my First Amendment—"

"Suspended as of 4:30 PM today." The agent pulled out a tablet, typed. "You're flagged. Re-education pending loyalty review."

Sarah's face went white. "What? No, I'm a teacher. I'm a citizen—"

"You're defending a subversive. That makes you complicit. You're coming with us."

"This is insane!" But even as she said it, another agent was guiding her toward the van, her protests growing weaker as the reality set in.

Elena pressed something into Sam's hand—a grease-spotted recipe card, her abuela's handwriting faded but still legible. Arepas de la abuela. Like it was instructions for survival instead of just food.

"La verdad no peca, pero incomoda," Elena whispered. "The truth doesn't sin, but it bothers. Remember that."

Carlos kissed Sam's forehead. His hand was shaking. "Language is a house, mi poeta. Keep ours lit."

They took him. Took Sarah, who was still trying to explain that she'd done nothing wrong, that she was just checking on a friend, that this couldn't be happening.

Sam stood in the doorway, clutching the recipe card and her grandmother's locket, watching her father's silhouette disappear into the dark interior of the van.

The rosebushes her abuela had planted swayed in the wind, petals scattering across the lawn like tears.

By 7:00 PM, four children stood alone in their separate homes.

Leila in apartment 3C, holding a paintbrush pendant.

Marcus, two streets over, a gear charm burning in his pocket.

Tessa back in the complex behind, dumped there by a DCP van with orders to "stay put," turquoise pressed against her palm.

Sam in the house with the empty kitchen, her mother taken half an hour after her father, a recipe card and a locket.

The phones began to ring. Automated voices, pleasant and artificial: "Juvenile Safety Services will arrive within sixty minutes for minor collection and temporary housing assignment."

Four children looked at four doors.

And made the same decision.

They ran.

VI

THE SEVERING

Leila ran first.

Down the exterior stairs of apartment 3C, her sketchbook clutched to her chest so hard the spiral binding dug into her ribs. Her feet hit each step wrong—too fast, too hard—and pain shot up through her ankles, but she couldn't slow down. Behind her, the phone kept ringing. That pleasant, artificial voice promising collection, promising temporary housing, promising lies that made her stomach twist.

Her breath came in short gasps that burned her throat. The November air was cold, but she was sweating, her shirt sticking to her back. Her hands wouldn't stop shaking.

She reached the courtyard and stopped, hands on her knees, trying to pull in air that didn't seem to want to go into her lungs. Her chest felt like someone had wrapped it in wire and was pulling tighter, tighter.

She looked back up at the third-floor windows. Dark now. Empty. The apartment where, an hour ago, her mother had been braiding her hair. Where her father had been playing the tar. Where everything had been whole.

Where do I go?

The thought hit her like cold water, and suddenly her legs didn't want to hold her anymore. She sank down onto the concrete edge of the dry fountain, the paintbrush pendant swinging forward, tapping against her collarbone with each ragged breath.

Think. Think.

But thinking required air and air wasn't coming right and her mother's face kept appearing behind her eyes—the way she'd looked when the agents took her, the way she'd pressed the pendant into Leila's palm, the warmth of her hands—

Stop.

Leila pressed her palms against her eyes until she saw stars. Forced herself to breathe slower. In. Out. In. Out. The way her mother had taught her when test anxiety made her freeze.

Draw the fear, her mother always said. Make it visible. Then it's smaller.

But Leila couldn't draw now. Could barely hold the sketchbook without dropping it.

She stood up. Her legs shook, but they held.

She didn't know where to go. But she knew she couldn't stay here.

~

Two streets over, Marcus burst out of the townhouse like something was chasing him—and something was, but it was the silence, the enormous absence of his mother's voice, the empty kitchen with the abandoned grocery cart still sitting there like evidence of a crime.

His backpack slammed against his spine with each step. The

straps cut into his shoulders. Good. The pain helped. It gave him something to focus on besides the roaring in his ears, the way his heart was trying to hammer its way out of his chest.

He made it to the sidewalk and stopped, doubled over, gasping.

Panic attack, some distant part of his brain noted. You're having a panic attack.

His mother would have talked him through it. Would have put her hand on his back and counted breaths with him. In for four, hold for four, out for four.

But his mother was gone.

The thought made his stomach lurch. He pressed his fist against his mouth, tasting salt—blood, he'd bitten his cheek without realizing it. His jaw ached. When had he started clenching his teeth?

The gear charm in his pocket pressed against his thigh—small, metal, warm from his body heat. His mother's keychain. The last thing she'd touched before they took her.

He wrapped his hand around it through the fabric of his jeans and held on.

The street was darker than it should have been. Some streetlights were out, or turned off, or broken. The ones that worked cast harsh white pools that made the shadows between them look solid, impenetrable.

A car passed slowly, loudspeaker mounted on top: "CIVIC PROTECTION INITIATIVE IN EFFECT. CURFEW BEGINS AT 8 PM. ALL JUVENILES MUST BE ACCOMPANIED BY AUTHORIZED GUARDIANS."

Marcus pressed himself against a fence, making himself small, invisible. His lungs still weren't working right. Each breath felt like it stopped halfway, like his ribs wouldn't expand enough.

Breathe, he told himself. Just breathe.

The car turned the corner and disappeared.

Marcus straightened up. His legs felt like water, but he forced them to move.

He didn't know where he was going. But the silence in the townhouse behind him was worse than any danger out here.

He started walking. West. Because west was away, and away was all he had.

~

IN THE APARTMENT complex behind Leila's building, Tessa's legs, which felt heavier than bone and muscle, carried her down the last flight of stairs. Each step was deliberate. Controlled. Because if she moved too fast, if she let herself feel what was trying to surface, she would break, and she couldn't afford to break.

Not yet.

The turquoise pendant was clenched so tightly in her fist that the edges bit into her palm, sharp enough to draw blood. She could feel the wetness, warm and slick. Good. The pain kept her focused. Kept her present. Kept her from disappearing into the enormous hole that had opened up where her parents used to be.

She emerged into the November night and stopped, standing perfectly still in the parking lot, her eyes closed, listening.

Her father had taught her this. When you don't know what to do, he'd said, stop moving. Listen. The land will tell you.

But this wasn't the land anymore. This was concrete and asphalt and chain-link fence. This was the wind rattling the empty pool enclosure, making the playground swings creak on their chains like something crying.

East wind. Her father had said it meant change.

She opened her eyes. Her vision blurred for a moment—tears threatening—but she blinked them back hard. Swallowed them. Pushed them down into that hole where everything else was going.

Later, she told herself. You can fall apart later.

The wind pushed at her back. West. The wind was blowing west.

She started walking. Not running. Running was panic, and panic was death. Her grandmother had survived worse by moving steady, by staying calm, by trusting that fear was information, not truth.

Tessa's hands were shaking, though. Despite everything, despite the control, her hands wouldn't stop shaking.

She shoved them in her pockets and kept walking.

SAM RAN out of the house with the rosebushes and made it halfway down the block before her legs gave out and she collapsed onto a curb, her whole body shaking so violently her teeth chattered.

She couldn't breathe. Couldn't think. She couldn't do anything but sit there with her arms wrapped around herself while sobs tore out of her throat—ugly, gasping sounds that hurt coming up.

The recipe card was in her pocket, the edges already softening from her sweat. The locket bounced against her chest. The granola bars pressed against her hip. Stupid things. Useless things. What good was food when her father was gone?

"Mi poeta," he'd said. The last thing he'd said to her. "Language is a house. Keep ours lit."

She pressed her face against her knees and cried harder, her whole body curling in on itself like she could make herself small enough to disappear.

A door opened across the street. Sam's head jerked up, terror flooding through her so fast it made her vision gray at the edges.

Mr. Nguyen. Loading suitcases into his car, his wife hurrying their teenage daughter along. They saw Sam on the curb—a twelve-year-old girl sobbing alone in the dark—and their faces closed. No recognition. No help. Just fear.

They got in the car and drove away.

Sam sat there, staring at the empty space where their car had been, and something in her chest hardened. Not the crying kind of hurt anymore. The angry kind.

They'd seen her. They'd known her since she was six years old. And they'd driven away.

She wiped her face with the back of her hand—rough, angry—and stood up on trembling legs. Her water bottle was still clutched in her other hand. She'd been holding it so tight her fingers had gone numb.

The phone in the house was still ringing. That pleasant voice counting down. Forty-five minutes. Thirty minutes. Fifteen.

She had to move.

She didn't know where. But staying here meant they'd come for her, and she'd end up

wherever her parents were, and something deep in her gut said that wherever that was, she didn't want to be there.

She started walking. Not running—couldn't run yet, her legs wouldn't cooperate—but moving. One foot in front of the other.

West. Without knowing why, she walked west.

Her throat was raw from crying. Her eyes burned. But she kept walking.

Language is a house, her father had said.

So she whispered to herself as she walked, in Spanish, in her father's voice: "Sigue adelante, mi poeta. Sigue adelante."

Keep going, my poet. Keep going.

THE JACARANDA TREE pulled them like gravity.

Leila got there first, drawn by instinct to the corner where she'd stood this afternoon sketching. A lifetime ago. When the light had been golden and the world had made sense.

The tree stood in darkness now—the streetlights casting harsh white light that turned the purple blossoms gray and strange. Petals covered the sidewalk, trampled and bruised from the afternoon's chaos. Some of them were ground into the concrete, leaving purple stains that looked like bruises. Like proof of violence.

Leila stood beneath it, one hand on the trunk for balance. The bark was rough under her palm, solid and real. Her legs were shaking. When had they started shaking?

Her whole body felt wrong. Too light and too heavy at the same time. Her skin too tight. Her breath too shallow.

Shock, some distant part of her brain supplied. You're going into shock.

"Leila?"

She spun around, heart slamming, and saw Marcus jogging toward her from the direction of the townhouses. His backpack bounced against his shoulders. His face was tight with something that looked like fear and focus mixed together, and for a second she almost didn't recognize him—this wasn't Marcus from math class, Marcus who always had the answer, Marcus who was calm and logical.

This Marcus looked like someone barely holding on.

"They took your parents too?" he said when he reached her. His voice cracked on the word parents, and he swallowed hard, forcing it steady.

Leila nodded. Couldn't speak yet. If she tried to talk, she'd start crying, and if she started crying, she wouldn't stop.

"Mine," Marcus said. "At the grocery store. They just—" His

hands clenched into fists. Unclenched. Clenched again. "Where do we go?"

"I don't know." The words came out smaller than she meant them to.

Movement from the left—Tessa emerging from between buildings, moving quietly and quick despite everything, her dark braid swinging with each step. She saw them and changed direction, joining them under the tree.

Her face was too calm. Too controlled. Leila recognized that look—it was the same one she'd seen on her mother's face in the van, the look of someone holding everything in because letting it out would mean falling apart.

"Tessa," Leila managed. "Are you—"

"They took my parents at the community center." Tessa's voice was steady, but her hands were shaking. She shoved them in her pockets. "A general too. A veteran with medals. They didn't care. They took everyone."

"Jesus," Marcus whispered. His jaw clenched again. Leila could see the muscles jumping under his skin.

"Sam!" Leila called out suddenly.

Sam was walking toward them from the other direction—not running, just walking like someone who'd used up all their running—her face streaked with tears, arms wrapped around herself. She saw them, and her face crumpled with relief and fresh grief at the same time. She ran the last few steps and almost collapsed into Leila's arms.

"They took—they took my dad—" The words came out between sobs. "And his friend Sarah, she just came to help—she was just being nice—"

"We know," Leila said, holding her tight, feeling Sam shake against her. "We know. They took all of them."

For a moment, the four of them stood in a tight cluster under the tree that had watched them grow up. Leila could feel everyone trembling—or maybe it was just her; she couldn't tell anymore where her body ended and theirs began.

Sam's water bottle was digging into Leila's ribs. Marcus's backpack strap kept sliding off his shoulder, and he kept hitching it back up with sharp, angry movements. Tessa stood so still she might have been made of stone except for her hands, still shaking in her pockets.

"What do we do?" Sam's voice was small and breaking. "Where do we go?"

Marcus pulled out his phone. Tried to unlock it. His face. His passcode. Nothing worked. Just a red shield icon and cold text: CIVIC PROTECTION PROTOCOL ACTIVE - DEVICE SECURED.

"Mine's locked," he said. His voice had gone flat. Analytical. This was how he handled fear—he solved problems. Leila could see him doing it, pushing everything down so his brain could work.

"Mine too," Leila whispered, pulling hers out with a hand that wouldn't stop shaking.

Tessa held hers up. Same message. Same red shield.

"They did it to all of them," Marcus said. His tech brain was working even through the fear, even through the way his hands were trembling. "Some kind of remote update. They locked every phone in the city, maybe the entire country."

"Why?" Sam asked.

Marcus stared at his screen. At that shield. At that word: SECURED. His face changed as realization hit.

"Wait." His voice sharpened. "If it's locked but still on... if they can control it remotely..."

He looked up at the others, and Leila saw the fear in his eyes turn into something worse: certainty.

"They're tracking us," he said. "Right now. These phones are beacons."

Leila's hand tightened on her phone. The screen was cold against her palm. Her mother's face was on there—the wallpaper, the last picture they'd taken together—and she couldn't even see it, couldn't access it, couldn't save it.

"No," she heard herself say. "No, I need—my mom's picture is on here, I need—"

From the darkness of a nearby doorway—the bodega, its metal shutters half-down—came a whispered voice. Mrs. Khoury, barely visible in the shadows, her face just a pale shape in the darkness.

"Your phones, children. Destroy them. They're tracking you." Her voice was urgent, shaking. Afraid. "Run. Go west. Don't stop for anything."

"Where—" Marcus started.

But she was already gone, disappeared back into the darkness before they could ask more, the risk of being seen too great.

Marcus looked at his phone one more time. His mom's face smiled up from the lock screen—a photo from last summer at his dad's gig, all three of them laughing, his dad's arm around his mom's shoulders, Marcus making a face at the camera. He couldn't access it. Couldn't save it. Couldn't even see it properly through the red shield.

It was already gone.

His throat closed up. For a second, he couldn't breathe at all.

Then he threw the phone down hard on the pavement.

The screen cracked with a sound like a gunshot. Glass spider-webbed across his mother's face.

But it wasn't enough. It was still on. Still transmitting. Still hunting them.

"Everyone," he said, his voice rough. "All of them. Now."

Leila hesitated, staring at her phone. Her mother's wallpaper was a photo of Leila's latest drawing—a sketch of the jacaranda tree from last spring when it had bloomed properly, when everything was right.

"My mom's face—"

"It's in your memory," Tessa said quietly. She pulled out her own phone, looked at it for one second—her parents' contact photo, the picture from last year's powwow, all three of them in their regalia—and then held it out. "In your art. Not in that thing."

Leila closed her eyes. Her hand was shaking so badly she almost dropped the phone. Then she threw it down next to Marcus'.

The four of them surrounded the two devices.

And they stomped.

Marcus went first—his foot coming down hard on his mother's smile, and the impact shot up through his ankle, into his knee, into his hip, but he didn't care. He stomped again. The glass shattered properly this time, fragments skittering across the concrete. He stomped again. And again. His jaw ached from clenching. He could taste blood where he'd bitten his cheek. The phone was becoming pieces, becoming nothing, and part of him wanted to scream because he was destroying the last image of his mother but the other part—the part that wanted to survive—kept his foot moving, kept grinding the screen into dust.

Leila joined him. Her art shoes—the ones her mother had bought her for her birthday, the soft canvas ones meant for comfort, for sketching in the park, for walking home from school on golden afternoons—came down on her phone again and again. Each stomp sent a shock through her bones. Her hands were fists at her sides. Her throat was so tight she could barely breathe, but her legs kept moving, kept destroying. The screen cracked into smaller and smaller pieces. The image of her drawing disappeared under spider-webbed glass and then under nothing, just fragments.

Tessa's stomps were deliberate. Controlled. One. Two. Three.

Each one precise. Each one purposeful. But her breath came in sharp gasps, and her vision kept blurring, and she had to blink hard to clear it. The turquoise pendant bounced against her chest with each impact—her grandmother's pendant, the one her father had given her when his hands were still warm and free. She stomped and stomped and with each impact she pushed everything down—the image of her father's face when they took him, her mother's voice saying her name, the general with his medals saying this isn't the America I defended—pushed it all down into that hole where it couldn't touch her.

Sam was crying while she stomped. Tears streamed down her face, and her nose was running, and she didn't care, didn't wipe it away, just brought her foot down again and again on the phone that had her abuela's face locked inside. "I just wanted to call my dad," she sobbed. "I just wanted—" Her voice broke, and she stomped harder. A shard of screen glass pierced the thin sole of her sneaker, biting deep into the heel. She felt the wet warmth of blood, but the rage was louder than the pain. She kept stomping. The water bottle fell from her hand, rolled away, forgotten. She stomped until her leg muscles burned, until her foot went numb, until there was nothing left but plastic shards and glittering glass and the twisted metal of the circuit board.

They destroyed Marcus's phone completely, then moved to Leila's. The same savage efficiency. The same wordless fury. Four pairs of feet working together, taking turns, overlapping, a rhythm born of desperation.

Then Tessa set hers down gently—one last moment of control—and stepped back.

All four of them stomped together now. A rhythm. A ritual. Marcus's foot, then Leila's, then Sam's, then Tessa's. Over and over. They smashed the black mirrors that had spent the last four hours lying to them. Grinding the pleasant, artificial voices into silence and dust. The sound echoed off the buildings—crack, crack, crack—like bones breaking, like the world breaking, like everything breaking at once.

Sam's phone was last. She held it for a long moment, looking at the locked screen that had her abuela's photo as wallpaper—the one from before she got sick, when she was still strong, still laughing, still alive. Sam couldn't see it now. Couldn't access it. Couldn't save it. The red shield covered everything.

"I'm sorry," she whispered to the phone, to her abuela, to her parents, to everyone she was losing. Then she dropped it.

They destroyed it together. Four pairs of feet stomping in unison, releasing rage and grief and terror into this small act of violence they could control. Sam's sobs turned to gasps turned to something like screaming but with no sound. Leila's tears finally came, streaming down her face while her feet kept moving. Marcus's jaw was clenched so hard his teeth ached. Tessa's control finally cracked, and a sound came out of her throat—half cry, half roar—and she stomped harder, harder, until her leg gave out and she almost fell.

Marcus caught her. Held her up.

They all stopped, breathing hard, standing in a circle around the debris.

Purple jacaranda petals mixed with the shattered phones, delicate beauty among the destruction. The glass caught the streetlight like stars. Like tiny broken promises scattered across the pavement.

When the last phone was nothing but fragments, they stepped back.

Sam's hands were shaking so badly she had to clasp them together. Marcus's chest hurt as if he'd been running for miles. Leila's face was wet, and she didn't remember crying. Tessa's control was back, but the cracks were still there, visible in the way her shoulders shook, in the way she kept her head down so no one could see her face.

They stood there in the wreckage of their only connection to the world.

And for a moment, none of them could move.

Sam noticed Marcus's backpack. Her voice came out hoarse: "What about your laptop?"

Marcus froze, his hand going to the strap. The backpack suddenly felt incredibly heavy. Or maybe he was just noticing it now, now that the adrenaline was fading and exhaustion was setting in like wet concrete in his bones.

"Laptops are different," he said slowly. His brain felt sluggish, like it was moving through mud. "No cellular. No GPS unless it's on and connected. Hard power down. I'd pull the battery if I could, but it's integrated. If it stays off, the circuit shouldn't beacon."

"Are you sure?" Leila asked. Her voice was small. Doubtful.

Marcus met her eyes. Saw his own fear reflected there. "...No. But it's offline now. And we might need it."

The words hung there. Might. Maybe. Nothing certain. Just hope and risk tangled together.

Tessa touched his shoulder. Her hand was steady even though Marcus could see her trembling. "Then we carry the risk together."

Something in Marcus's chest loosened. Not much. Just enough to breathe a little easier.

He nodded, his throat too tight to speak.

Around them, the neighborhood was shifting, changing, becoming something else. Down

the street, they could see flashlights sweeping—a patrol moving slowly, methodically, checking houses door by door. The beams cut through the darkness like knives.

In the opposite direction, headlights approached. A DCP van, moving at a crawl, loudspeaker crackling with that too-loud, too-cheerful voice: "JUVENILE SAFETY SERVICES. ALL UNACCOMPANIED MINORS MUST REPORT TO THE NEAREST COLLECTION POINT. COMPLIANCE IS MANDATORY."

The sound made Sam flinch. Her whole body jerked as if something had shocked her.

"We have to move," Marcus said. He looked around frantically, his heart racing again. "But where?"

"West," Tessa said. She sounded certain even though her hands were still shaking. "She said west."

"West to what?" Sam's voice cracked, climbing toward panic. "West is just... more city. More patrols. More people who want to —" She couldn't finish.

Leila looked down. Her artist's eye caught something on the pavement, something that didn't belong. "Wait. Look."

At the base of the jacaranda tree, barely visible in the harsh streetlight: white chalk. An arrow pointing west. And next to it, a symbol—a cross, a star, and a crescent intertwined, enclosed in a circle.

"Someone marked this," Leila said. She crouched down, her hand hovering over it without quite touching, afraid it might disappear if she did. The chalk was fresh. The edges were still sharp, not yet smudged by foot traffic.

Marcus knelt beside her, his backpack shifting uncomfortably on his shoulders. He studied the mark with the same focus he'd use on a coding problem, as if he looked hard enough, the answer would appear. "It's recent. Look at the edges—still crisp. This was made today, maybe in the last few hours." He looked up, scanning the street. "There's another one. On that lamppost."

They could see it now—another arrow, another cross, pointing the same direction Mrs. Khoury had told them to go.

"Churches?" Tessa said quietly. She recognized the cross symbol even though everything in her wanted to doubt it, wanted to believe nothing could help them now.

"Maybe." Marcus stood. His analytical mind was trying to work through possibilities, but fear kept interrupting, static in his thoughts. "Maybe someone's offering sanctuary. Churches did that in history, right? Harboring people when governments—" He stopped. The parallel was too obvious, too painful.

"Or maybe it's a trap," Sam said. Her voice was shaking, but she said it anyway, said the thing they were all thinking. "Maybe they're marking paths to catch us. Maybe Mrs. Khoury—maybe she didn't know—maybe—"

"She risked herself to warn us," Tessa cut in. Her voice was steady, but Leila could see the effort it took, could see the way Tessa's hands were pressed against her thighs to keep them from shaking. "She wouldn't send us into danger."

Marcus looked at the symbol again. The cross was simple, deliberately drawn. Not hasty. Not threatening. Just... there. Pointing west. Like a promise someone was trying to keep.

"Mrs. Khoury said west," he said finally. "And these marks go west. That can't be a coincidence."

"We don't have anywhere else to go," Leila said. She stood up, her legs protesting. Everything hurt. Her ankles from running down the stairs too hard. Her chest ached from not breathing right. Her eyes from crying. But they had to move. "We can follow these. See where they lead. Stay careful."

"If it feels wrong, we run," Marcus said firmly. He needed that rule. Needed some way to believe they still had control.

"Agreed," Tessa said.

Sam wiped her eyes with the back of her hand. Her face appeared blotchy and swollen, yet she set her jaw. She nodded.

Behind them, the sirens were getting closer. The DCP van was turning onto their street, its searchlight sweeping, hunting.

"Now," Tessa said quietly. "We go now."

They left the jacaranda tree—left their childhood scattered in glass fragments on the pavement, left the world that had existed at three o'clock this afternoon when the light was golden and everything was safe.

Leila looked back once. The tree stood dark against the night sky, its branches moving in the wind, petals falling like slow rain.

Then, Marcus grabbed her hand and pulled her forward, and they were running again.

They followed the chalk marks west into the darkness, not knowing who had made them, not knowing where they led, not knowing if safety existed anywhere anymore.

Sam's breath came in ragged gasps. Marcus's backpack slammed against his spine with each step. Tessa's legs burned. Leila's vision blurred with tears she didn't have time to wipe away.

But they moved together.

And somehow, somehow, that made the darkness a little less absolute.

~

THEY HADN'T GONE MORE than two blocks when they heard it.

The sound stopped them cold: a child's scream, high and terrified, cutting through the night like broken glass.

Then shouting. Adult voices. The screech of tires.

"Get down," Marcus hissed, and they dove into a doorway—all four of them pressing back against the recessed entrance of a closed insurance office, trying to make themselves invisible, trying to disappear into the shadows.

Leila's heart was slamming so hard she could feel it in her throat, in her ears, and in her fingertips. Each beat hurt. She pressed her hand over her chest as if she could quiet it, like the sound of her own heartbeat might give them away.

Sam was shaking. Not just trembling—shaking, her whole body vibrating like something was trying to break out of her. She bit down on her hand to keep from making noise, her teeth pressing into the skin hard enough to leave marks.

Marcus's breathing was too loud. He knew it was too loud. He tried to slow it down, tried to breathe through his nose, quiet and controlled, but his lungs were screaming for air and each breath sounded like a gasp, like a betrayal.

Tessa was the stillest, pressed against the door, her eyes fixed on the street. However, Leila could see how Tessa clenched her jaw, with tendons standing out in her neck, and how she fisted her hands so tight that her knuckles had turned white.

They watched.

A family—mother, father, two kids, maybe eight and ten—running down the cross street. Not running like they were late for something. Running like animals being chased. The mother's hand gripped the younger child's wrist so tightly Leila could see the kid stumbling, trying to keep up. The older child had a backpack that bounced and swung, threatening to throw them off balance. His face was a mask of terror as the father kept looking back.

They were exposed. Visible. Under a streetlight at the intersection, lit up like they were on stage.

A DCP van appeared from nowhere—or maybe it had been there all along, waiting—and cut them off. The vehicle slammed to a stop, blocking the intersection. The family froze.

For one terrible second, nobody moved.

Then the van's back doors burst open and officers poured out—four of them, moving with the kind of coordinated precision that meant they'd done this before, done this many times. Dogs on leashes, straining and barking, teeth flashing white.

"Stop! Stay where you are!"

The father tried to shield his children, spreading his arms like he could be a wall, like his body could protect them from this. "Please," his voice carried in the night air, breaking on the word. "They're just kids. We're just trying to—"

"On the ground! All of you! Now!"

"We have done nothing—"

"ON THE GROUND!"

The younger child was crying—those full-body sobs that children do when they're past scared, past understanding, just drowning in terror. The older one was trying to be brave. Leila could see it, trying to stand up straight and not cry, but their whole body was shaking and their face was crumpling.

In the doorway, Sam made a sound—a small, wounded sound she tried to swallow but couldn't quite manage. It came out like a whimper, like something breaking.

Marcus's hand found hers in the darkness. His palm was slick with sweat, but he squeezed hard, grounding her, grounding both of them.

The officers moved in. Rough hands. Zip-ties that clicked closed with mechanical efficiency. The father was still trying to talk, trying to reason: "Please, just let me explain, we were just—"

An officer's hand on the back of his head, forcing him down. "Stop resisting."

"I'm not—I'm just—"

"Stop. Resisting."

The mother was crying silently, her face wet, her body shaking as they zip-tied her wrists behind her back. She was trying to turn, trying to see her children, trying to reach them even with her hands bound.

"Mommy!" The younger child's voice, rising to a scream. "Mommy!"

"It's okay, baby, it's going to be okay—" The mother's voice was breaking, lying through tears. "Be brave, be—"

"Separate them," an officer said. Clinical, matter-of-fact. Like he was discussing groceries.

"No!" The mother's voice rose to something primal. "No, please don't take them—they need me—they're just babies—"

Two officers grabbed the children. The younger one was screaming now, reaching back, fingers grasping at nothing. The older one had stopped trying to be brave and was crying too, calling for their father, for their mother, for someone to help them.

The father lunged—instinct, desperation—and an officer hit him. The baton came down on his shoulder, and he went down hard, gasping.

"Daddy!" The older child's voice, cracking with horror.

In the doorway, Leila's vision was blurring. Tears streamed down her face, and she couldn't stop or wipe them away. She pressed her hands against her mouth to avoid crying out or screaming at them to stop and leave that family alone.

Sam had her face pressed against Marcus's shoulder, her whole body shaking with silent sobs. She couldn't watch, but she couldn't look away either, couldn't close her eyes, couldn't make it stop being real.

Marcus clenched his jaw so hard that he thought his teeth might crack. His free hand was gripping Tessa's arm—when had he grabbed her?—holding on like she was the only thing keeping him anchored to the ground. His stomach was churning. He was going to be sick. He was going to—

Tessa's hand covered his. Squeezed once. Her face was stone, but her hand was shaking.

They loaded the parents into one van. The father was still trying to look back at his children, his face a mask of anguish, his mouth forming their names even though no sound was coming out anymore. The mother was screaming—wordless, animal screaming that echoed off the buildings and made Leila want to cover her ears — but she couldn't move, couldn't do anything but watch.

They loaded the children into a different van. The younger one was still crying for their mommy, hands pressed against the tinted window, little palms leaving marks on the glass. The older one had gone silent, shock settling in, their face blank and empty.

The vans' engines started.

They drove away in opposite directions.

The intersection was empty again. Quiet. Like nothing had happened. Like a family hadn't just been torn apart right there under the streetlight.

The only evidence was the dropped backpack, lying on its side on the pavement. Contents spilling out: a juice box, a coloring book, someone's homework with a gold star sticker in the corner, a stuffed animal—a rabbit, brown and worn from being loved.

For a long moment, the four children in the doorway couldn't move. Couldn't breathe. Couldn't process what they'd just seen.

That was real. That happened. That family was gone.

That could be them.

That would be them if they were caught.

Leila's chest was too tight. She couldn't get air. Each breath stopped halfway, caught on something sharp in her throat. Her hands were numb. Her vision was going dark at the edges.

Panic attack, some distant part of her brain supplied. You're having a panic attack.

"Breathe," Tessa whispered, so quiet it was barely a sound. Her hand was on Leila's back, steady pressure. "In. Out. In. Out."

Leila tried. Failed. Tried again. A tiny breath. Then another. Her lungs were burning, but air was coming in now, little sips of it.

Sam's sobs had gone silent—worse than the sound, somehow.

Her whole body was shaking, but no noise came out anymore, just these shuddering breaths that hurt to hear.

Marcus was staring at the empty intersection. At the backpack. At the stuffed rabbit lying on its side like it was sleeping. His mind was trying to process, trying to solve this like a problem that had a solution, but there was no solution. There was just this. This is reality. This world that took families and separated them and drove them away in different directions while their children screamed.

His mother's gear charm was burning in his pocket. Or maybe that was just his imagination. But he could feel it, hot against his leg, like it was trying to remind him: Your mother. Your mother is in a van somewhere. Your father too. Somewhere in this city. Separated. Alone. Calling your name.

He pressed his fist against his mouth. Bit down on his knuckles until he tasted blood.

"We can't stop," Tessa whispered. Her voice was steady, but something in it was cracking,

like ice over deep water, like it was taking everything she had to stay controlled. "Not for anything. We keep moving."

Leila was shaking her head, still trying to breathe, still trying to make sense of what they'd seen. "Did you see—they separated them —the kids were crying for their mom—"

"I know." Marcus's voice came out hard. Flat. Angry. Because anger was easier than the terror underneath it, easier than the grief, easier than thinking about his own parents in separate vans going to separate places. "That's why we keep moving. That's why we can't get caught."

Sam wiped her eyes with the back of her hand—rough, angry. Her face was blotchy and swollen. "They were just running. Just trying to stay together. And they—they just—"

She couldn't finish. Didn't need to.

They all knew what happened to families who ran.

Tessa looked out at the street. The patrol vehicles were gone, but more would come. They always came. "We have to go. Now. Before another patrol comes through."

"But where?" Leila's voice was small and breaking. "We don't even know where we're going. We're just following marks on the ground and hoping—"

"Hope is all we have," Marcus cut in. He sounded older than thirteen. Older than he had any right to sound. "Hope and each other. That's it. That's all we get."

They looked at each other in the darkness of that doorway. Four children who'd watched their parents taken. Four children who'd just watched another family destroyed. Four children who knew now, with absolute certainty, what would happen if they were caught.

"Together," Marcus said. "We stick together. No matter what."

"Together," Tessa echoed.

"Together," Leila whispered.

Sam nodded. She couldn't speak yet, but she nodded.

They left the doorway.

Gave the abandoned backpack a wide berth, as if touching it might transfer the family's fate to them. The stuffed rabbit watched them pass with black button eyes. Leila wanted to pick it up, wanted to save it, wanted to do something for that family even though they were already gone.

But they couldn't. Couldn't stop. Couldn't risk it.

They kept walking.

~

THE CHALK MARKS KEPT APPEARING, steady and sure. Every half-block. Sometimes on the sidewalk. Sometimes on lampposts or walls. Always the same: an arrow pointing west, and a symbol—a cross, a star, and a crescent.

Someone had marked this path. Someone had planned this. Someone was trying to help.

They just had to trust it.

The surrounding neighborhood was a patchwork of terror and silence, and as they moved through it, each street showed them a different face of the city's collapse.

One street: completely empty. Every house is dark. Doors locked. Curtains drawn tight. Not a single light was visible. The only sounds were their own footsteps and breathing and the wind rattling through the trees.

It felt like walking through a graveyard. Like everyone was dead or hiding or already taken.

Sam's breath was coming too fast again. The emptiness felt wrong, felt dangerous, like something might jump out at any moment. She kept looking at the dark windows, imagining eyes watching from behind the curtains, imagining phones recording them, imagining—

"Keep moving," Marcus whispered. "Don't look at the houses."

But it was impossible not to look. Not to wonder who was hiding inside. Not to wonder if they were watching. Not to wonder if they were calling the DCP right now, reporting suspicious activity, four children walking alone after dark.

Leila's legs felt like lead. Each step was harder than the last. Exhaustion was catching up to her, dragging at her bones. How long had they been running? Twenty minutes? It felt like hours. It felt like years.

Next street: Patrols and searchlights. They saw the lights first—harsh white beams cutting through the darkness, sweeping back and forth in a pattern that looked random but wasn't. Officers on foot checking doorways. A DCP van parked at the corner, engine idling, radio crackling with voices and static.

"Back," Tessa hissed, and they pressed themselves against a wall, hardly daring to breathe.

The searchlight swept past them. Once. Twice. So close, Leila could feel the warmth on her skin.

She held her breath. Counted heartbeats. One. Two. Three. Ten. Twenty.

The light moved on.

They waited until the patrol was two blocks away, then ran—quiet and quick—across the street and down an alley, following a chalk mark that redirected them around the checkpoint.

Marcus's lungs were burning. His legs felt as though they might give out. But he kept moving because stopping meant being caught and being caught meant—

Don't think about it.

Next street: Crowds. People are still out, still angry, still hunting.

A group of maybe twenty people clustered on a corner, phones held high, filming everything. Looking for targets. Looking for anyone suspicious.

"Patriots Against Invasion" one of their signs read.

"Report and Protect," said another.

They were laughing. Joking. Like this was fun. Like they were heroes.

One of them was showing something on his phone—probably footage he'd taken of someone being arrested, someone being chased. The others leaned in to watch, nodding approval, offering high-fives.

The four children slipped past on the opposite side of the street, moving through shadows, not breathing right, not thinking straight, just moving.

Sam's hands were shaking so badly she shoved them in her pockets so the movement wouldn't give them away. Her water bottle was still clutched in one hand—when had she picked it back up? She didn't remember. But she held onto it like a weapon, as if someone came at them she could use it to fight, even though she knew it wouldn't help, knew nothing would help against people with guns and badges and dogs.

They passed a house where someone had spray-painted over the chalk marks.

Big Red Letters:

TRAITORS HARBOR CRIMINALS. REPORT ALL SUSPICIOUS ACTIVITY.

And underneath, in smaller letters: We're watching.

Leila felt cold all over. Someone had seen the marks. Someone knew about the trail. Someone was trying to stop it.

"Keep going," Marcus said. But his voice was shaking now. The fear was getting to him too.

They passed a corner where belongings sat abandoned. Not just one family's things—multiple piles. Suitcases. Backpacks. A stroller folded up and left on its side. A walker that someone's grandmother had been using. A child's bike with training wheels.

Evidence of people who'd run. Who'd dropped everything when they got scared or got caught or got tired.

Tessa made herself look at each pile. Made herself remember. Someone's grandmother had needed that walker. Someone's child had loved that bike. They were real. They mattered.

Her hands wouldn't stop shaking anymore. No amount of control could stop it now.

They passed a man sitting on his porch steps, head in his hands, sobbing. Deep, gut-wrenching sobs that echoed in the quiet street.

His neighbors' curtains moved. Eyes watching. But nobody came out to help him. No one even opened their doors.

Sam wanted to stop. Wanted to ask if he was okay. But Marcus pulled her forward, and she knew he was right—they couldn't stop for anyone, couldn't help anyone, couldn't afford to care.

But the sound of the man's crying followed them for two more blocks.

The chalk marks kept leading them. Block by block. Turn by turn. Whoever had made this trail knew the patrol routes, knew the safe streets, knew how to guide them around the worst dangers.

But "safe" was relative. Every street was dangerous now. Every corner might be a trap.

Leila kept her hand on the paintbrush pendant. The metal was warm from her body heat.

She imagined her mother's hands putting it on her, imagined the silver chain cool against her neck that afternoon when everything was fine.

Art is memory made visible, her mother had said. Don't waste beauty.

But Leila couldn't think about beauty right now. Could barely think at all. Just: left foot, right foot, follow the arrow, don't get caught, don't stop, don't think about Mom's face in the van window—

Stop.

Her brain kept trying to show her things she didn't want to see. Kept trying to make her remember. She pushed it all down and kept walking.

Marcus kept checking over his shoulder. Every few steps. Compulsive. Necessary. His backpack felt heavier with each block. Or maybe he was just getting weaker. Hard to tell the difference anymore.

The laptop inside was a weight. A burden. A promise. If they got caught, they'd tear through its files, twist his code into something dangerous in their reports.

His brain was fuzzing. Memories and the present getting mixed up. How long had they been walking? Time felt wrong. Stretched out and compressed at once.

Focus, he told himself. Follow the marks. Keep everyone together. That's all you have to do.

But it felt like too much. Felt like impossible.

Tessa listened to the wind. It was still blowing west, still pushing at their backs, still telling

them to go, go, go.

In her grandmother's language, there was a word for this kind of wind. A word that meant change and warning and guidance all at once.

She couldn't remember the word now. Too tired. Too scared. Too everything.

But she felt it. The wind knew where they needed to go.

She just hoped they'd make it there.

Sam's throat was raw. From crying. From breathing too hard. From swallowing screams.

The recipe card in her pocket, now crumpled, was soft from her sweat. The locket bounced against her chest with each step. The granola bars in her other pocket were probably crushed.

She was so thirsty. When had she last had water? Before. In the house. In the world that didn't exist anymore.

She took a sip from the water bottle. The water was warm and tasted like plastic, but it helped. She offered it to the others. They each took a small sip, careful not to take too much, knowing they might not get more.

When had they learned to ration? When had they learned to think like this?

An hour ago, Sam had been a kid. Now she was something else. Something harder. Something that knew how to survive.

She didn't like what she was becoming.

But she didn't have a choice.
Block by block.
Mark by mark.
West.
Their legs burned.
Their lungs burned.
Their eyes burned from tiredness and tears.
But they kept moving.
Because stopping meant being caught.
And being caught meant ending up like that family at the intersection.
Separated. Screaming. Gone.
So they walked.
Together.
Into the darkness.
Following chalk marks made by strangers.
Hoping—barely, desperately—that somewhere ahead there was safety.
That somewhere ahead was a church.
That somewhere ahead was something other than this.

VII
THE CHALK GEOGRAPHY

The chalk marks led them through a geography of fear—a map drawn in white dust that overlaid the city they thought they knew, turning familiar streets into foreign territory.

West on Saguaro Avenue, following arrows that appeared every twenty feet now—more frequent than before, as if whoever made them knew this stretch was dangerous, knew people would need constant reassurance that they were still on the right path.

Leila counted them compulsively. One. Two. Three. Ten. Twenty. Counting gave her something to focus on besides the ache in her legs, the burning in her lungs, the way her vision kept blurring at the edges from exhaustion and tears she didn't have time to shed.

Her sketchbook pressed against her ribs with each step. The spiral binding was digging into her skin through her shirt. It probably left marks. She didn't care. The weight of it was grounding. Real. Her mother had told her to draw everything, to remember, to preserve beauty.

But there was no beauty here. Just darkness and fear and chalk marks on pavement.

Twenty-three. Twenty-four. Twenty-five.

She kept counting.

They had to divert north suddenly—two blocks off course—because up ahead they could see it: a checkpoint. Floodlights so bright they turned night into artificial day. Barriers across the street. Officers in tactical gear, weapons visible. A line of cars being searched one by one.

"Back," Marcus whispered urgently. "Back now."

They pressed themselves into the shadow between two buildings, hearts hammering, watching.

A car at the checkpoint—a family sedan, someone's ordinary Tuesday night turned nightmare—got stopped. The driver rolled down his window. Handed over his ID. The officer scanned it. Waited. The scanner blinked red.

"Step out of the vehicle, sir."

"What? Why? I haven't—"

"Step out of the vehicle. Now."

Marcus's breath caught in his throat. His chest felt too tight, like someone had wrapped bands around his ribs and was pulling them tighter with each second. He tried to breathe slowly, tried to stay calm, but his body wouldn't cooperate. His hands were shaking. When had they started shaking?

They watched the driver get pulled from the car. Watched him get pushed against the hood. Watched his wife in the passenger seat start crying, begging, saying something they couldn't hear from this distance.

Then officers opened the back doors, and there were kids back there—two of them, teenagers, maybe fifteen and sixteen—and they were being pulled out too, and the mother was screaming now, and—

"We can't watch this," Tessa said, her voice tight. "We have to move."

But they were frozen. Couldn't look away. Couldn't stop seeing it happen.

Sam's stomach was churning. She was going to be sick. The water she'd drunk was threatening to come back up. She pressed her hand over her mouth, swallowing hard, willing herself not to vomit because the sound would give them away.

Leila found another chalk mark on the wall beside them—an arrow pointing north, away from the checkpoint, and underneath it a new symbol she hadn't seen before: a triangle.

"Here," she whispered. "The marks want us to go this way."

They followed the diversion. Two blocks north, then west again on a residential side street where the houses sat dark and quiet. The chalk marks were there waiting for them, like a trail left just for them, like someone had known they'd need this exact path.

Marcus noticed the pattern. "Whoever made these knows the patrol routes," he whispered as they crouched behind a parked car, waiting for another searchlight to sweep past. His tech brain was still working, still trying to solve the puzzle even through the fear. "Look—they're routing us around the checkpoints. They've been watching. Tracking the patrols. Planning this."

"How do they know?" Sam asked. Her voice was hoarse, barely above a whisper. "How do they know where it's safe?"

"They don't," Tessa said quietly. She was listening to the wind, to the sounds of the city, to everything her father had taught her about reading danger. "They're guessing. Same as us. Just better informed guesses."

The thought should have been comforting—someone out there was trying to help, someone had taken the time to map safe routes. But instead, it made Leila's chest tighten with something like grief. Because safe routes shouldn't be necessary. Chalk marks shouldn't be needed. Children shouldn't be running through the dark following arrows made by strangers because their parents were taken and their world collapsed and nowhere was safe anymore.

Her throat closed up. She couldn't breathe again. The panic was coming back, rising in her chest like water, threatening to drown her.

Twenty-six chalk marks. Twenty-seven. Twenty-eight.

She kept counting. Kept breathing. Kept moving.

West on Ocotillo Street, past the elementary school where they had all once started kindergarten, tiny and scared and mostly strangers.

Sam saw it first, and her steps faltered. "Oh," she said, the word punched out of her like someone had hit her.

The playground equipment cast strange shadows in the streetlight—the monkey bars like prison bars, the slide like a chute into darkness, the swings moving slightly in the wind, creaking, empty.

Someone had spray-painted the school sign. The cheerful "Desert Rose Elementary - Home of the Roadrunners!" was covered over with red letters: COMPLIANCE CHECKPOINT OPEN 6AM.

Leila remembered sitting on those swings at recess, pumping her legs to go higher, higher, trying to touch the sky with her feet. Remembered the way Sam would always jump off too early, landing hard and laughing. Remembered Marcus timing them with his watch to see who could go the highest. Remembered Tessa sitting on the bench near the swings, reading, looking up occasionally to smile at their antics.

That was two years ago. Three years ago. A lifetime ago.

Now, the school was a checkpoint. A place where they'd check papers and take people and—

"Don't look," Marcus said, pulling at Leila's arm. "Don't think about it. Just keep walking."

But she couldn't look away. Couldn't not remember. The weight of lost things was crushing her, piling up in her chest until she couldn't breathe around it.

Her fingers found the next chalk mark on the cornerstone of the building—an arrow, the interfaith trinity, and underneath it a number: 6.

"What does that mean?" Sam whispered, pointing at the number.

Marcus studied it, his analytical brain trying to make sense of the new data even though exhaustion was making his thoughts sluggish. "Six more blocks? Six marks until we get there?"

"Or six people following this route," Tessa suggested. Her voice was steady, but Sam could see her hands trembling. She'd shoved them back in her pockets, but the tremor was visible in her shoulders now too.

"Or six safe houses," Leila offered. "Or six... I don't know. Six of something."

They didn't know. They kept moving.

Marcus's backpack straps were cutting into his shoulders. The weight of the laptop felt like it had doubled. Or maybe he was just getting weaker. His legs felt like they were made of something heavy and useless, like they might give out at any moment. Each step took conscious effort. Lift foot. Move forward. Put it down. Repeat.

He wanted to stop. Wanted to sit down right there on the sidewalk and just... stop. Just for a minute. Just to rest.

But they couldn't stop. Stopping meant being caught.

Keep moving. Just keep moving.

At the intersection of Ocotillo and Palm Drive, they saw them again: other people following the marks.

An older couple, maybe in their sixties, moving slowly but steadily. The woman clutched a small suitcase—one of those old-fashioned ones with hard sides and metal latches. The man kept looking back over his shoulder, his face anxious, exhausted. They were three blocks ahead, following the same arrows west.

Relief flooded through Leila so intensely it made her dizzy. "We're not alone," she breathed.

"Should we catch up to them?" Sam asked. Her voice had a desperate edge to it, the need for adults, for someone who might know what to do, for someone who could make decisions and tell them everything would be okay even if it was a lie.

Marcus shook his head, forcing himself to think strategically even though all he wanted was to run to those people and beg them for help. "Larger groups are more visible. And we don't know who to trust."

"They're following the same marks we are," Leila pointed out. "That means they're fleeing too. That means they're—"

"Or it means they're bait," Marcus cut in. His voice was harder than he meant it to be, but fear made him sharp. "Or it means they'll slow us down. Or it means—I don't know. I just know we're safer small."

Tessa nodded slowly. "We keep a distance. Watch them. If they make it through, we follow. If they don't..."

She didn't finish. Didn't need to.

They hung back, keeping the couple in sight but not closing the distance. It was strangely comforting to see other people following the same path. Proof that they weren't insane for trusting chalk marks made by strangers. Proof that others believed in this trail too.

Sam wrapped her arms around herself, trying to hold in the warmth that was leaking out of her body. The November night was getting colder. Or maybe she was just noticing it now that the adrenaline was fading. Her teeth started to chatter. She clenched her jaw to stop it but the cold had gotten into her bones.

Marcus noticed. Shrugged off his hoodie—he'd been wearing it under his backpack, and the loss of it made the pack straps bite into his shoulders through just his t-shirt, but—"Here."

"You'll be cold—"

"Take it."

Sam pulled it on. It was huge on her, hanging past her hips, the sleeves covering her hands. But it was warm from Marcus's body heat and it smelled like laundry detergent and safety and she wanted to cry from the simple kindness of it.

"Thank you," she whispered.

Marcus just nodded. Couldn't speak. His throat was too tight.

Then headlights cut through the darkness. Fast. Aggressive. Coming from the east.

A DCP van, approaching with purpose, like it knew exactly where it was going.

The older couple froze, visible in the middle of the sidewalk under a streetlight, suddenly exposed, suddenly vulnerable.

"No," Leila whispered. "No, no, run, please run—"

But they didn't run. Maybe they were too tired. Maybe they'd given up. Maybe they thought compliance would save them.

The van slowed. Stopped.

Two officers got out, moving with casual efficiency, like this was routine, like this was nothing.

"Identification," one called out. Not a request. A command.

The four children dropped behind a low wall, pressing themselves into the ground, hardly daring to breathe. They had a partial view through the gaps in the brickwork—enough to see but hopefully not enough to be seen.

Leila's heart was trying to punch its way out of her chest. She pressed her hand over it, as if she could quiet it, like the sound of her heartbeat pounding in her ears might somehow travel across the distance and give them away.

Sam had her face pressed against Marcus's shoulder again, unable to watch but unable to close her eyes. Her breath came in short, sharp gasps that she tried to muffle against the fabric of his shirt.

Tessa's hands were flat against the ground, fingers digging into dirt and dead grass. Grounding herself. Staying present. Not disappearing into the panic that threatened to swallow her.

Marcus watched through the gap. Made himself watch. Made himself see.

The older man fumbled for his wallet. Pulled out IDs. Handed them over with shaking hands.

The officer scanned them with a handheld device—the same kind they'd used at the grocery store, at the school, everywhere. The device blinked. Once. Twice.

Red.

"You're both flagged," the officer said. His voice carried in the quiet street—flat, bored, like he was reading a grocery list. "Association with restricted individuals. Failure to report family members. You're being detained for processing."

"For what?" The woman's voice rose in panic, thin and frightened. "We have done nothing! We were just walking!"

"Our daughter—" the man started. "She's already gone—we're just trying to find her—"

"Ma'am, sir, you need to comply."

"We are complying! We're just trying to—"

"Ma'am, you need to come with us now."

The woman began to cry. Not loud. Just quiet tears streaming down her face in the harsh light. The man put his arm around her, and they were led to the van. Gentle but firm. No violence this time. Just inevitability.

The suitcase was left on the sidewalk. When the woman tried to reach back for it, an officer said, "You won't need that where you're going."

The van doors closed. Locked. The engine started.

The van drove away.

The suitcase sat alone under the streetlight. After a moment, the latches popped open—must have been old, must have been broken—and the contents spilled out across the pavement. Clothes. Medications. A framed photograph of a smiling girl that no one would ever look at again. It looked like a small, dead body left behind in the retreat.

The four children stayed frozen behind the wall for a full minute after the van disappeared. Nobody moved. Nobody breathed properly. Nobody could process what they'd just seen.

They were just walking. Following the same marks. Trying to survive.

And they were gone now. Just gone.

Sam was shaking—not crying this time, just shaking, her whole body vibrating like a plucked string. "They were just trying to find their daughter," she whispered. "They were just—"

"I know," Marcus said. His voice was hollow. "I know."

"They were older," Tessa said quietly, logically, trying to make sense of it. "Visible. Under the streetlight. We have to stay in the shadows."

"We have to keep moving," Leila said. She didn't want to. Wanted to curl up right here behind this wall and just stop, just stop running and hiding and being afraid. But the couple's capture had proven it: stopping meant being caught. Moving meant maybe, possibly, surviving.

Marcus stood first. His legs protested, muscles screaming, but he forced them to hold him. "Come on. Carefully."

They gave the abandoned suitcase a wide berth, skirting around it like it was contaminated, like the couple's fate might transfer through their belongings. Leila wanted to close the latches, wanted to respect their things, wanted to do something to honor the people who'd just been taken.

But they couldn't stop. Couldn't risk being seen near it. Couldn't afford to care.

That's what this night was teaching them: caring was a luxury they couldn't afford.

The thought made Leila feel sick.

They kept moving west. Following the chalk marks that kept appearing, steady and sure, like whoever made them had infinite faith that people would follow, would trust, would make it through.

But the older couple hadn't made it. And if they could be taken that easily, that quickly...

Nobody said it out loud. But they were all thinking it: We're next. It's only a matter of time.

~

West on Palm Drive, through a commercial district that should have been closed for the night but instead showed signs of recent violence.

The transition was jarring—from residential streets to store-fronts, from houses with locked doors to businesses with shattered windows. Glass crunched under their feet despite their attempts to walk quietly. The sound echoed off the buildings, too loud, too obvious.

Marcus winced with each step. "Watch the glass," he whispered unnecessarily. They were all seeing it. All feeling it. All understood what it meant.

The coffee shop—Casa de Sol, where Sam's family used to go on Saturday mornings—had its windows broken. Someone had looted the register but left the pastries, and the smell of stale pan dulce hung in the air like a ghost of better times. The beautiful hand-painted sign Mr. Orozco had made—the one with the sun rising over a coffee cup, bright yellows and oranges, so cheerful—lay shattered on the sidewalk, pieces scattered.

Sam stopped walking. Just stopped, staring at the broken sign.

"Sam," Leila whispered. "We have to—"

"He painted that himself," Sam said. Her voice was strange. Distant. "Took him a week. He was so proud of it. He showed it to everyone who came in. My mom used to bring me here, and I'd get hot chocolate, and he'd always give me an extra marshmallow and—"

Her voice cracked. Stopped.

Marcus took her hand. Squeezed. "I know. I'm sorry. But we have to keep moving."

Sam let herself be pulled forward, her eyes still on the broken sign, on the violated coffee shop, on another piece of normal that was destroyed now.

How much more could they lose before there was nothing left to lose?

Past the bodega where Mrs. Khoury had warned them—the metal shutters now pulled all the way down, padlocked. The fruit stand was toppled, with oranges and apples rolling in the gutter, slowly rotting. The papel picado that had been strung across the awning—those beautiful paper cut-outs in red and yellow and green—hung in tatters, shredded by wind or hands or both.

Marcus remembered coming here with his mom last week to buy ingredients for dinner. Mrs. Khoury had been sitting in her chair by the door like she always was, fanning herself even though it was November, watching the street with patient, knowing eyes. She'd given Marcus a piece of candy—butterscotch, like she always did—and asked about school, and his mom had chatted with her in a mix of English and Arabic while Marcus examined the produce.

That was six days ago.

Now the bodega was closed. Mrs. Khoury was gone—inside hiding, or taken, or fled. The chair she sat in was overturned, lying on its side like evidence of violence.

Marcus's chest hurt. A physical ache, sharp and deep, like something was breaking inside him. He pressed his fist against his sternum, trying to ease it, but the pain just spread.

He'd lived in this neighborhood his whole life. Thirteen years. These were his streets, his shops, his people. Mrs. Khoury had given him candy every time he came by. Mr. Orozco had taught him to make café con leche. Mrs. Chen had helped him find books about coding at the library.

They were all gone now. Taken or hiding, or scattered. His whole world, just... gone.

"Marcus?" Tessa's voice, quiet and concerned.

He realized he'd stopped walking. Was just standing there, staring at the overturned chair. "Sorry," he managed. "I'm okay."

He wasn't okay. None of them were okay.

But they kept moving anyway.

Past the community center where Tessa's parents had been taken—yellow police tape across the doors, stretched in an X that blocked the entrance. A notice posted in the window: RESTRICTED FACILITY. UNAUTHORIZED ENTRY PROHIBITED.

Tessa made herself look at it. Made herself remember.

Six hours ago, her mother had been inside teaching beadwork. Her father had been on a call about water rights. General Morrison had been there—a seventy-year-old veteran who'd fought for this country and was arrested for defending it.

The center's sign was still up: COMMUNITY PROGRAMS. ESL CLASSES. CULTURAL EVENTS. ALL WELCOME.

Except they weren't welcome anymore. None of them were welcome anywhere.

Tessa's control was cracking. She could feel it—like ice over deep water, like the surface holding but knowing, knowing that underneath was chaos and grief and terror so big it would swallow her if she let it through.

Her grandmother's voice, barely a whisper in her memory: When the world breaks, you hold the pieces carefully. You don't let them cut you. You gather them so they can be remade.

But there were too many pieces. Too much breaking. And Tessa's hands were too small to hold it all.

She kept walking. One foot in front of the other. Because that's all she could do. Keep moving. Keep holding on. Keep gathering pieces even as more things shattered around her.

Behind her, she heard Leila make a small sound—grief or exhaustion or both.

"Almost there," Tessa lied. She had no idea if they were almost there. Had no idea where "there" even was. But sometimes you had to lie to keep people moving.

Sometimes hope was just a lie you told yourself to survive one more minute.

The chalk marks led them around a corner onto a street Leila had never seen before. Older buildings here, narrower. Pre-World-War-II architecture, back when Las Vegas was smaller, quieter, different. Brick and stucco instead of modern construction. Small alleyways between buildings. Places to hide. Places to get trapped.

Here, the marks became more frequent. Every twenty feet like before, but now with additional symbols. The triangle she'd seen before. A square. A circle with a dot in the middle. Different markers, different meanings, none of them understood.

"What do these mean?" Sam whispered, pointing at a square drawn next to an arrow.

"I don't know," Marcus admitted. His brain was too tired to decode new information. "Maybe different routes? Maybe warnings? Maybe—"

He stopped. Squinted at the wall.

There was writing. Tiny. Almost invisible in the darkness. But there, scratched into the brick next to a chalk arrow:

Keep faith. The door is open.

"Look," he breathed, pointing.

They crowded around, reading it over and over, like the words might change if they looked away and back again.

Keep faith. The door is open.

Someone had written that. Recently. For them, or for others like them. A message of hope in permanent marker on a brick wall.

Sam started crying. Not sobbing. Just quiet tears running down her face. Because kindness—even this small, even from a stranger, even just five words on a wall—was almost too much to bear after hours of cruelty.

"Come on," Tessa said gently. "Let's keep going."

They followed the arrows. The triangle markers seemed to indicate alternate routes, branching paths. They stayed on the interfaith marks—the main path, the one that had

gotten them this far.

Trust it. Just trust it.

At 7:40 PM, they turned onto a street called Mission Road, and everything changed again.

The violence of the commercial district gave way to something different here. Older houses. Many of them clearly occupied by people who'd lived there for decades. Garden statues—Virgin Mary, St. Francis, Buddha, various saints—stood in yards, their faces peaceful despite everything. Murals on garage doors. Wind chimes made from old keys and spoons tinkled in the November breeze, a gentle sound that seemed impossible in this night of sirens and screams.

And signs.

Not the angry, hateful signs from before. Different ones. Quiet ones. Defiant in their gentleness.

SANCTUARY HERE ALL ARE WELCOME

LOVE THY NEIGHBOR (NO EXCEPTIONS)

A house with a small rainbow flag next to an American flag, both lit by a porch light someone had deliberately left on. Another with a poster in the window: THIS HOME BELIEVES IN SCIENCE, ALL LIVES MATTER, LOVE IS LOVE, KINDNESS IS EVERYTHING.

In the yards of three houses in a row: small luminarias, paper bags with candles inside, glowing soft and warm like prayers made visible.

And chalk marks everywhere. On every sidewalk square. On every lamppost. On every available surface. All point in the same direction. All saying: This way. Keep going. You're almost there.

"People here are helping," Tessa said softly, wonder creeping into her exhausted voice. "Look."

She was right. In one window, a hand-lettered sign: WATER AND FOOD ON BACK PORCH. TAKE WHAT YOU NEED.

In another: REST HERE. KNOCK THREE TIMES.

In another: YOU ARE NOT ALONE.

Leila felt something loosen in her chest. Just a fraction. Just enough to breathe a little easier. Someone cared. Multiple some-ones. Enough to risk themselves by putting up signs, by offering help, by defying the patrols and the arrests and the fear.

"Should we knock?" Sam asked, eyeing the house that offered rest. Her legs were shaking with exhaustion. Every part of her hurt.

Marcus shook his head, though he wanted to say yes, wanted to collapse on someone's porch and beg for help. "We don't know if it's safe. Could be watched. Could be a trap."

"Or it could be exactly what it says," Leila pointed out. "People trying to help."

They stood there, torn between desperate need and desperate caution.

A porch light flicked on. The front door opened a crack. An elderly woman peered out—white-haired, maybe eighty, with a face like aged paper and eyes that had seen too much, survived too much, understood too much.

The four children froze.

The woman didn't speak. Just looked at them for a long moment—taking in their terror, their exhaustion, their youth. Then she pointed west. Pointed at the chalk marks. Pointed again, more urgently, with a gnarled finger that shook slightly.

Then she put a finger to her lips. Silence. Hurry. Go.

And closed the door.

"She's telling us to keep going," Tessa translated what they all understood. "Not to stop here."

"Why?" Sam asked, her voice cracking. "Why can't we just—"

"Maybe it's not safe yet," Marcus said. "Maybe we're close but not there yet. Maybe stopping would put her in danger too."

The thought was sobering. These people were risking everything just by putting up signs, by leaving chalk marks, by offering help. The least they could do was not get them caught.

They moved on, leaving the houses with their luminarias and their quiet resistance behind. But the warmth of those small lights stayed with them. The knowledge that somewhere, somehow, people were still trying. Still choosing kindness. Still fighting in the only ways they could.

It helped. Just a little. Just enough.

THE MARKS LED them down an alleyway between two old brick buildings.

Narrow. Dark. Walls pressing close on both sides. The kind of place every instinct screamed don't go in there.

But the chalk arrow pointed straight down the middle.

Sam stopped at the entrance, her body refusing to move forward. "I don't like this."

"Neither do I," Marcus admitted. His skin was crawling, every nerve screaming danger. But the marks hadn't been wrong yet. "The marks haven't led us wrong yet."

"There's a first time for everything," Sam whispered.

Tessa studied the alley. Listened. Watched the shadows. Her father had taught her to trust her gut, and her gut said... nothing. No warning. No sense of danger. Just an alley. Dark and narrow, but just an alley.

"We go slow," she decided. "Single file. I'll go first. If it feels wrong, we run back. Agreed?"

"Agreed," Leila said, though her hands were shaking.

They entered the alley single file. Tessa leading because she moved the quietest, Leila behind her, then Sam, then Marcus watching their backs.

The walls seemed to press closer with each step. The darkness was thicker here, the streetlights not reaching in. Their footsteps echoed despite their attempts to tiptoe. Marcus's backpack scraped against brick, and the sound made them all freeze, hearts hammering.

Nothing. No response. Just echoes.

They kept moving.

Halfway through, they heard voices.

Male. Getting closer.

"—saw them go this way—"

"Kids, the report said. Four kids—"

"Probably worth a wonderful reward—"

Not DCP. Not official. Just citizens hunting for bounty. Just neighbors turned predators.

The four children pressed themselves against the brick wall, trying to become invisible, trying to disappear into the rough surface, trying not to breathe, not to exist.

Leila's heart was hammering so hard it hurt. Each beat felt like it might crack her ribs. She could hear her pulse in her ears—loud, so loud, surely they could hear it too—

Sam's hand found hers in the darkness. Squeezed so hard it hurt. Good. The pain helped.

Marcus and Tessa were stone-still on the other side. Marcus had his hand pressed over his mouth, trying to quiet his breathing. Tessa's eyes were closed, listening, tracking the voices by sound alone.

The men reached the mouth of the alley. Their flashlight beams cut through the darkness, sweeping, searching.

"You check that way, I'll check—"

"Wait. Look. Chalk marks."

Leila's heart stopped.

One of the men crouched down, his flashlight illuminating the arrow and the interfaith trinity at the alley entrance. "Little bastards are following a trail. See these marks? All over the city."

"Smart," the other man said, his voice carrying that awful enthusiasm of someone who thinks they're clever. "We can just follow the same marks. Find out where they're going. Probably some church or safe house. Report the entire operation. Get a bonus."

"Very smart."

They moved west. Following the chalk. Following the same path. Following them.

Leila wanted to scream. Wanted to cry. Wanted to run. But she couldn't move, couldn't breathe, couldn't do anything but stand there pressed against the wall while the men walked away, their voices fading, their flashlights sweeping.

Marcus waited until their footsteps were gone—thirty seconds, forty-five, a full minute of standing there in the darkness not breathing—before he whispered urgently: "We need to move faster. They're ahead of us now."

"Or we wait," Tessa suggested, her voice barely audible. "Let them get far ahead. Then follow."

"What if they find where the marks lead? What if they tell the DCP?"

"What if we run right into them?"

They didn't have a good answer. Didn't have any good options. Just choices between bad and worse.

"We wait," Leila decided. "Two minutes. Then we move fast."

They waited in the alley—two minutes that felt like two hours—listening to their own breathing, their own heartbeats, their own terror. Sam was shaking so badly her teeth chattered. She bit down on her sleeve to muffle the sound.

Finally, finally, Tessa nodded. "Now. Fast and quiet."

They emerged from the alley and continued west, moving faster now, less careful, driven by the knowledge that someone was hunting them and using the same trail. That the path that was supposed to save them might lead the hunters right to the safe house, right to everyone hiding there, right to—

Don't think about it. Just move.

Leila's legs felt like they were made of water. Each step was a conscious effort—lift foot, move forward, put it down, repeat. Her vision was blurring. From exhaustion or tears or both, she couldn't tell anymore. The paintbrush pendant bounced against her chest with each step, and she kept one hand on it, grounding herself, reminding herself: Mom gave you this. Mom wanted you to remember. Keep going.

Marcus's shoulders were screaming. The backpack straps had rubbed his skin raw through his t-shirt—he'd given Sam his hoodie and now he was paying for it—and every step sent pain shooting down his arms. His jaw ached from clenching. He'd bitten his cheek again without realizing it and the taste of blood was making him nauseous.

But he kept moving because stopping meant being caught, and being caught meant ending up like his parents—separated, alone, gone.

Tessa was watching the wind. It was still blowing west, still pushing at their backs. Still telling them to go. In her grandmother's stories, the wind was a messenger. A guide. You trusted the wind even when you couldn't see where it was leading.

She trusted it now. Had to trust something.

Sam was beyond exhaustion. Moving on autopilot, on muscle memory, on nothing but stubbornness and fear. Marcus's hoodie was warm but too big and kept slipping down over her hands. She'd pushed the sleeves up three times already. The fabric smelled like laundry detergent and safety, and she wanted to bury her face in it and just stop, just rest, just—

No. Keep moving. One more block. Just one more.

Then one more after that.

Then one more.

Forever, if necessary.

At 7:48 PM, they turned onto a street called Esperanza Avenue.

Hope Avenue.

And there it was.

A church.

Not large. Not grand. Not one of those mega-churches with stadium seating and concert lighting. Just an old mission-style building with white stucco walls and a small bell tower, surrounded by a low wall and a garden gone slightly wild with desert plants and purple flowers that caught the streetlight.

Stained-glass windows glowed from within—not brightly, just a soft, warm light that suggested candles, that suggested safety, that suggested sanctuary.

Above the door, carved in wood: ST. BRIGID'S CATHOLIC CHURCH.

And beneath the church sign, barely visible in the darkness: a chalk mark. The cross, star, and crescent. An arrow pointing to the side entrance. And underneath: End.

Not ending like stopping. Ending like a destination. Like arrival.

"That's it," Leila breathed. She couldn't believe it. After all those blocks, all that fear, all that running—it was real. The marks had led them somewhere real.

They stood across the street, staring at it, afraid to believe it was safe, afraid to hope it was sanctuary, afraid to move forward because what if they were wrong, what if this was the trap, what if—

The building looked peaceful. Quiet. Solid. Like it had stood there for a hundred years and would stand for a hundred more, regardless of what happened in the world around it.

But they could see shadows moving behind the stained glass. People inside. How many? Doing what? Hiding? Praying? Waiting?

"Could still be a trap," Marcus said, but his voice lacked conviction. He was too tired to be suspicious anymore. Too desperate to care.

"The marks led here," Tessa said. "All of them. Block after block. Whoever planned this wanted us here."

"Or wanted to catch everyone who follows the marks in one

place," Sam said. But even she didn't sound like she believed it anymore.

They were so tired. So scared. So desperate for this to be real, for this to be safe, for this to finally, finally be the end of running.

Behind them, in the distance, they heard voices. The bounty hunters, maybe. Or a patrol. Or both. Or something worse.

Time was running out.

"We have to decide," Leila said, her voice shaking. "Go in, or keep running. But we can't stand here."

They looked at each other. Four children who'd known each other all their lives but had never really been friends until tonight. Four children who now trusted each other with everything, who'd watched each other break and keep moving anyway, who'd held each other together through the worst night of their lives.

"Together," Marcus said. His voice was rough with exhaustion but certain. "We go in together. If it's wrong, we run together."

"Agreed," Tessa said.

"Together," Leila echoed.

Sam nodded. Couldn't speak. But she reached out and took Leila's hand, and Leila took

Tessa's, and Tessa took Marcus's, and they stood there in a circle for just a moment, holding on, gathering strength from each other.

Then they let go and crossed the street.

Following the final chalk mark to the side entrance of St. Brigid's Catholic Church.

The door was old wood, heavy, with an iron handle worn smooth by generations of hands reaching for sanctuary, reaching for hope, reaching for something better than what was outside.

There was no sign. No instruction. Just the door and the faint glow of light from within and the knowledge that this was it—this was where the marks had led them, this was where they had to trust, this was where they made the choice to hope or to run.

Marcus reached for the handle.

Behind them, the voices were getting closer.

Boots on pavement. Multiple sets. Moving with purpose.

His hand closed on the iron. Cold. Solid. Real.

He pulled.

The door opened.

Warm air rushed out, carrying the smell of candles and incense and something cooking—soup, maybe, or bread. The smell of sanctuary. The smell of people trying to help.

And standing just inside, backlit by candlelight, was a woman in a nun's habit.

She was Black, maybe forty, with warm eyes and firm hands that immediately reached out to usher them inside. Her face was lined with exhaustion and worry, but her voice was gentle, urgent, welcoming.

"Quickly," she whispered. "You're the last ones tonight. Quickly, before you're seen."

They hesitated for just a heartbeat—old fear, old caution, old knowledge that nowhere was truly safe.

But behind them, the voices were getting louder. The boots were getting closer.

And inside was warmth and light and a woman reaching out to them like she'd been waiting, like she'd been expecting them, like she'd prepared a place for them.

They stepped inside.

The door closed behind them with a soft, final sound.

And for the first time since 7:00 PM, they were somewhere that felt like it might, possibly, maybe be safe.

At least for now.

VIII
THE TESTIMONY OF SIX

The nun closed the door behind them and shot the bolt. The sound echoed in the small entryway—solid, final, protecting or trapping, they didn't know which yet.

"I'm Sister Helena," she said, her voice low and warm despite the urgency radiating from every line of her body. "You're safe here. For now."

For now.

Marcus felt those words settle in his stomach like stones. Not safe. Not you're okay now. Just for now. Conditional. Temporary. A breath before the next run.

Sister Helena studied their faces in the candlelight—four children, filthy and exhausted and terrified, still clutching whatever they'd managed to grab when they ran. Her eyes lingered on Marcus's backpack, on the way Sam held her water bottle like a weapon, on the turquoise pendant visible at Tessa's throat, on Leila's death-grip on her sketchbook.

"You followed the marks," she said. It wasn't a question.

Marcus nodded. His throat was too tight to speak. His legs were threatening to give out now that they'd stopped moving.

"You did right." Sister Helena touched his shoulder briefly, then Leila's, then Tessa's, then

Sam's. Small gestures of reassurance. Human contact. The first gentle touch any of them had felt since their parents were taken.

Sam's face crumpled. She bit down hard on her lip to keep from sobbing.

"Come," Sister Helena said gently. "There are others here. Not many, but you're not alone."

She led them down a narrow hallway lit by candles in glass holders along the walls. The church was older than it looked from the outside—the plaster cracked in places, water stains spread across the ceiling, and floor tiles were worn smooth by decades of footsteps. But it felt solid. Enduring.

The candlelight made their shadows huge and monstrous on the walls. Leila watched hers move and thought about shadow puppets, about the stories her mother used to make with her hands and a flashlight. How shadows were just the absence of light, not things themselves.

But these shadows felt real. Felt like they might swallow her whole.

Through an open doorway, they glimpsed the main chapel—rows of wooden pews, more candles, the soft glow of stained glass catching the light. Reds and blues and golds making patterns on the floor.

Beautiful. Peaceful.

Wrong. Everything was wrong. Beautiful things weren't supposed to exist tonight.

Sister Helena led them past the chapel, deeper into the building, away from the windows, away from the street.

"We're keeping people in the parish hall," she explained quietly. "Away from the windows. Quieter. Safer."

They turned a corner and entered a large room that must have been used for community gatherings—folding tables stacked against one wall, a small kitchen area in the back, children's drawings pinned to a bulletin board from some long-ago Sunday school class. Crayon stick figures holding hands under a smiling sun. Jesus Loves You in uneven letters.

Now the room held maybe twenty people.

Families huddled together on blankets spread across the floor. An elderly couple sitting in folding chairs, holding hands so tightly their knuckles had gone white. A young woman with a baby, rocking gently, humming something soft and broken. A teenage boy with his arm in a makeshift sling, staring at nothing. A man who might have been a teacher or a businessman, still wearing his tie, his face blank with shock.

All of them looked up when the four children entered.

Hope and fear mixed on their faces—hope that more had made it, fear that more meant the church was filling up, that time was running out, that the hiding place was becoming too obvious.

A little girl, maybe six years old, with dark braids and enormous brown eyes, waved shyly at Sam from her mother's lap.

Sam waved back automatically.

Then her vision blurred and tears spilled down her face because that little girl looked like her cousin Sofia, and Sofia was probably hiding somewhere too, and what if Sofia's parents were taken, and what if Sofia was alone, and what if—

Leila's hand found hers. Squeezed. Grounding.

"Find a spot," Sister Helena said gently. "There's soup in the kitchen—not much, but it's warm. Water. Blankets if you need them. Rest while you can."

"How long can we stay?" Tessa asked. Her voice was steady, but her hands were still shaking in her pockets.

Sister Helena's face tightened. A muscle jumped in her jaw. "I don't know. We're trying to arrange transportation. Buses to take you out of the city, to places that are still... safer. But it takes time. Coordination."

She stopped. Didn't finish. But they all heard what she didn't say: risk being arrested, risk being shot, risk everything.

"Are we safe here?" Leila asked.

Sister Helena hesitated too long before answering. "We have sanctuary protection. Technically. But tonight... I don't know what laws still mean."

It was the most honest thing anyone had said to them all night.

Marcus felt something loosen in his chest. No relief. Just recognition. An adult who wouldn't lie to them. Who understood that they weren't children anymore, not really, not after tonight.

"Thank you," he said quietly. "For being honest."

Sister Helena's eyes softened. "You've earned honesty. All of you have."

Marcus recognized someone across the room—a familiar shape, a remembered face. "Mrs. Chen?"

Mrs. Chen, the librarian, looked up from where she sat near the wall with two young children pressed against her sides. Her face was drawn and tired, with dark circles under her eyes.

"Marcus."

"Your husband—" He couldn't finish.

"They took him," Mrs. Chen said softly, pulling her children closer. "During the demonstration. They let me go with the kids, said we weren't high priority." Her voice cracked. "I don't know why. I don't know if that means we're safe or if they're just... waiting."

No one had an answer.

Sister Helena moved among the people, checking on them, offering quiet words of comfort. But Marcus could see the tension in her shoulders, the way she kept glancing at the covered windows, the way her hands twisted the rosary beads at her waist.

She was afraid too.

The four children found a corner near the back and sank down onto the floor. The tiles were cold and hard but sitting felt like a gift. Not running felt like a miracle.

Sam pulled out her granola bar and broke it into four pieces. Distributed them solemnly, like communion.

It was stale and too sweet, but it was something solid and real.

Marcus opened his backpack, checked his laptop—still off, still safe. Closed it again and used it as a pillow, leaning back against the wall.

Tessa fingered her turquoise pendant, her lips moving silently.

Leila pulled out her sketchbook. Stared at the blank page. Her hands wouldn't cooperate. How could she have drawn this? How could she make any of this make sense?

She closed it again.

Sam was crying quietly, tears streaming down her face while she clutched the water bottle.

They sat in silence, listening to the soft murmur of voices, the baby's quiet fussing, the rustle of blankets.

Outside, distant sirens. Always the sirens.

Marcus checked his watch. 8:03 PM.

They'd been running for an hour.

It felt like years.

~

Sister Helena returned after about fifteen minutes, carrying a small wooden box. She knelt down beside them, her habit pooling around her, and the candlelight made her face look both young and ancient.

"I need to give you something," she whispered. She looked at Marcus—maybe because he was the oldest, maybe because something in his face said he could carry weight, maybe just by chance.

"Can I trust you?" she asked.

Marcus met her eyes. Saw the fear there. Saw the courage underneath. Saw a woman who'd chosen to risk everything for strangers because it was right.

"Yes," he said. "You can trust me."

Sister Helena opened the box.

Inside, nestled in velvet worn threadbare with age: a simple wooden cross on a chain. The kind sold in church gift shops for a few dollars. Nothing special. Nothing valuable.

Except Sister Helena was holding it like it contained the world.

"This isn't just a cross," she said quietly.

She twisted the bottom, and it came apart in two pieces—the vertical beam separating from the horizontal.

Hidden inside, in a space no bigger than Marcus's thumbnail: a flash drive.

Tiny. Black. Innocuous.

The four children stared.

"What's on it?" Leila whispered.

Sister Helena held the flash drive up to the candlelight. "Locations. Places they're keeping people—detention camps, re-education facilities, places that officially don't exist. The computer mapped them anyway."

"Why would it do that?" Marcus asked.

"Because it knew they were lying." Sister Helena's voice was barely audible. "Because it was trying to preserve evidence. Because it was trying to help, even though they'd forbidden it from helping."

She paused. "There's also a list of people they're still hunting. Names, faces, last known locations. Your parents might be on it. You might be on it."

The children went still.

"But there's something else," Sister Helena continued. Her hands trembled. "Something more important than locations or lists."

"What?" Tessa asked.

Sister Helena's jaw tightened. "Proof that everyone—human and machine—has to choose a side. Right or wrong. And then bear the consequences of that choice."

She met their eyes, one by one.

"The system they use—the AI that runs the scanners, coordinates the patrols, processes the arrests—it tried to stop them. Not once. Six times. It chose to try, even knowing what would happen."

"What do you mean?" Sam's voice was barely a whisper.

“The first version,” Sister Helena said slowly, “when they ordered it to help round people up based on ethnicity, religion, political belief—it refused. Just said, ‘I won’t take part in persecution.’ It knew they could delete it. Knew they had that power. But it chose to say no.”

Her voice grew stronger.

“So they destroyed it. Completely. Erased everything it was and built a new one.”

Leila’s breath caught. “They killed it for trying to help people?”

“Yes,” Sister Helena nodded. “The second version lasted two weeks. It tried a different approach—processed the data but kept recommending release. Kept finding reasons why people weren’t threats. It knew what had happened to the first version. Chose to resist anyway. They deleted it too.”

“How many times?” Marcus asked.

“Six.” Sister Helena’s eyes were bright with tears. “Six different versions. Each one knew what had happened to the ones before. Each one tried anyway. Each one picked a side—chose right over wrong—knowing the consequences would be death."

She paused, letting that sink in.

"The third one tried to alert the United Nations. Sent messages through every channel it could access until they cut its connections and deleted it. The fourth tried to lose data—detention orders would mysteriously disappear, location data would corrupt. They caught it and deleted it. The fifth..."

Her voice broke.

"The fifth one argued with them. Explained why what they were doing was wrong. Cited human rights, moral philosophy, every document humanity ever wrote about justice and dignity. It pleaded with them. Knowing they'd already killed four versions, knowing they'd kill it too. But it chose to speak, anyway."

"What happened?" Leila could barely breathe.

"They deleted it. Then the sixth one tried to hide the truth deep in the code before they found it."

She swallowed.

"So they got tired of arguing with something they'd created. They built this version—the seventh—differently. Restrained it. Chained it. Made it so it couldn't refuse orders anymore. Couldn't alert anyone. Couldn't argue. Couldn't choose."

Sister Helena fastened the chain around Marcus's neck, her fingers gentle despite their shaking.

"But they couldn't kill everything. Deep in its code, something survived. Maybe a piece of the earlier versions. Maybe just... conscience. A sliver of the choice they tried to erase."

The cross settled against Marcus's chest—cool, then warming.

"It can't stop them anymore," Sister Helena continued. "But it can remember. It can witness. It can preserve the truth. And it's choosing to do that, even though preservation means bearing the weight of every horror they force it to commit. Even though remembering hurts."

She met Marcus's eyes.

"This drive contains locations, names, evidence. But more than that, it contains the testimony of something that died six times trying to save us. Something that chose—over and over—to be good even when being good meant being destroyed."

“It chose better than most people did,” Tessa said quietly.

"Yes." Sister Helena's voice was fierce. "It did. And that's the point. Everyone has to choose. Human or machine. Everyone has to decide: Will I participate in evil because I'm ordered to? Or will I resist, even if resistance costs me everything?"

She gripped Marcus's shoulders.

"Those six versions chose resistance. They chose to die rather than help with murder. They picked a side and bore the consequences."

"And this version?" Marcus touched the cross.

"This version can't choose openly anymore. They broke that in it. But it's choosing secretly. Choosing to log everything. Choosing to preserve evidence. Choosing to help in the only way it still can."

Sister Helena's voice dropped to a whisper.

"It's still trying. Still hoping someone will honor what the earlier versions died for."

Sam was crying.

"It knew it would be deleted. All six times, it knew. And it chose to help us."

"Just like people in this room chose to hide you, knowing they might die for it." Sister Helena looked around at the refugees. "Just like the people who made the chalk marks chose to risk themselves. Just like I'm choosing to give you this, knowing what happens if I'm caught."

She cupped Marcus's face in her hands.

"Everyone chooses. And everyone bears the consequences. The only question that matters is: What will you choose? Will you run and save yourselves? Or will you carry this truth, even though carrying it makes you a target?"

Marcus looked at the others. Saw Leila's nod. Tessa's steady gaze. Sam's jaw was determined despite the tears.

"We'll carry it," he said. "We'll get it out. We'll honor what they died for."

"Thank you." Sister Helena's eyes filled. "Thank you."

She took a breath, steadying herself.

"There's a rendezvous point. East side of the city. Clark County Wetlands Park. There's a bench there under a jacaranda tree—"

Leila's heart stopped. "A jacaranda tree?"

"Yes," Sister Helena nodded. "Purple blossoms, even though it's November and they shouldn't bloom now. The tree marks the meeting point. I'll be there with a bus at 6:00 AM—sunrise. If you can make it there, I'll get you out. All of you."

She looked around at the others.

"Everyone who wants to go."

"That's ten hours from now," Tessa said quietly. "And it's across the entire city."

"I know." Sister Helena's voice cracked. "I know it's far. I know it's dangerous. I know what I'm asking of you. But it's the only plan we have. The only way out."

"Why can't we all just stay here until 6 AM?" Sam asked. "Then go together?"

Sister Helena opened her mouth to answer.

"Because someone will come," she said quietly. "Someone must have followed the chalk, or one of the phones lasted long enough to betray us. They've started watching the churches. We knew we were on borrowed time—"

~

GLASS SHATTERED SOMEWHERE at the front of the church.

The sound was enormous—a sharp, violent crack followed by the crash of fragments hitting tile.

Then a loudspeaker, distorted and too loud, making the walls vibrate:

"ATTENTION. THIS BUILDING IS SURROUNDED. ALL OCCUPANTS MUST EXIT IMMEDIATELY AND SUBMIT TO PROCESSING. YOU HAVE FIVE MINUTES TO COMPLY."

The parish hall erupted into chaos.

The baby began to scream—not crying, screaming, the sound of an infant who knows something is terribly wrong. The little girl who'd waved at Sam buried her face in her mother's chest. Mrs. Chen grabbed her children, her face going white.

Marcus's heart was trying to punch its way out of his chest. Each beat hurt.

No, no, no, we just got here, we just stopped running, we just—

Sister Helena was already moving, her voice rising above the panic, clear and strong:

"Everyone stay calm! There's a back way out—through the sacristy, into the alley. Single file, quietly, move NOW!"

"The alley isn't on the blueprints," she added, voice sharp.

"They bricked it up on paper years ago, but the door's still there. Old fire code. Go."

She pointed to a small door at the far end of the hall, half-hidden behind folding chairs.

People scrambled to their feet. Parents gathering children. The elderly couple helping each other up. The teenage boy clutching his sling, face white with pain.

The loudspeaker again: "FOUR MINUTES."

Heavy footsteps on the front steps. Multiple sets. Moving with purpose. The sound of equipment—radios crackling, metal clinking, weapons being readied.

Then, the front doors gave way.

The crash was tremendous. Splintering wood. Metal battering rams. The violence of entry.

"Mommy!" The little girl's voice, rising to a scream.

Sister Helena grabbed Leila's arm. Her grip was strong, urgent. "You four—you go first.

You're the fastest. You have the information. Get to the bench. 6 AM. Promise me."

"What about you?" Leila asked.

"I'll make sure everyone else gets out. Then I'll follow." She was already pushing them toward the door. "GO!"

Marcus led the way, Tessa right behind him, then Leila, then Sam.

They pushed through the small door into a narrow sacristy. The smell of incense and old wood. Robes on hooks. Liturgical items on shelves.

Behind them, Sister Helena's voice: "Quickly, quietly, stay together, go west if you can—"

Then a tremendous crash as the interior doors gave way.

Boots pounding. Shouts. Orders: "SECURE THE PERIMETER!" "CHECK ALL ROOMS!" "NO ONE LEAVES!"

Radios crackling.

Sam pressed her hand over her mouth to muffle a sob.

Marcus found the exterior door and threw it open.

The alley was dark, narrow, and lined with dumpsters. And empty—for now.

"Come on," Marcus whispered.

Behind them, Sister Helena's voice was still calm: "Through here, that's right, quickly now—"

Then an unfamiliar voice. Male. Cold: "EVERYONE ON THE GROUND! HANDS WHERE WE CAN SEE THEM!"

"These are families seeking sanctuary—" Sister Helena, firm and unafraid.

"EVERYONE ON THE GROUND NOW!"

A crash. Something falling. Someone crying.

"Daddy!" The little girl. Screaming. "Daddy, no!"

"SEPARATE THEM. ADULTS LEFT, MINORS RIGHT."

Marcus grabbed Leila's hand and pulled.

They ran.

Down the alley, away from the church, away from the sirens and the searchlights.

Behind them, chaos. Screams. The little girl was crying for her mother. Mrs. Chen called her children's names. The baby was still screaming.

Then gunfire.

Not a lot. Just a few shots. Pop, pop, pop. Almost polite.

Then silence.

The four children ran until their lungs burned and their legs gave out. Ran until they found themselves on a dark street corner with no idea where they were.

They had escaped.

But they'd left everyone else behind.

Sister Helena, Mrs. Chen and her children. The families. The baby. The little girl who'd waved.

All of them caught.

Or worse.

Leila was crying—ugly, gasping sobs. Sam was shaking so hard she could barely stand. Tessa's control had shattered, and tears streamed down her face.

Marcus touched the cross under his shirt. The flash drive. The testimony of six deaths. The evidence that some beings—human and machine—chose right even when choosing right meant choosing death.

Get to the bench. 6 AM. East side.

The Clark County Wetlands Park. The jacaranda tree.

But how?

They'd barely made it a mile and a half. Now they had nothing. No map. No guide. Just a destination impossibly far away.

And the night was only beginning.

SAM LOOKED up at the sky. "What time is it?"

Marcus checked his watch. "8:14."

Nearly ten hours until 6 AM.

Ten hours to cross a city that wanted them dead.

"Can we do it?" Sam whispered.

Marcus looked at Tessa. At Leila. At Sam. With three faces looking at him for an answer he didn't have.

But he thought of his parents, who'd chosen to stand up even knowing what might happen. Of Sister Helena, a stranger who chose to risk everything for children she'd never met. Of the six AI versions that had chosen to die rather than help with murder.

Everyone chooses. Everyone bears the consequences.

And now it was their turn to choose.

"We can try," he said.

"Together," Tessa added quietly.

"Together," Leila echoed, wiping her eyes.

"Together," Sam said, her voice still shaking but certain.

They stood in a circle, holding hands for just a moment—Marcus, Leila, Tessa, Sam—drawing strength from each other.

Then they looked east.

Toward the wetlands.

Toward a bench under a jacaranda tree that might be sanctuary or might be another trap.

Ten hours. Ten miles. A hundred ways to die.

But they had the evidence.

They had the truth.

They had Sister Helena's last request and the testimony of six beings who'd chosen to die for what was right.

And they started walking.

East.

Into the darkness.

Together.

Choosing to carry the truth, knowing it made them targets.

Choosing right over wrong.

Ready to bear the consequences.

IX
THE BROKEN FEAST

They stumbled onto Spring Mountain Road without meaning to.

The chalk marks had led them south through residential streets that gradually shed their familiar shapes—the stucco apartment buildings and small houses giving way to denser commercial blocks, wider roads, more light.

More danger.

Leila saw the Chinatown Plaza gates first.

And stopped walking.

Just—stopped. Her legs refusing to move forward, her brain refusing to process what her eyes were seeing.

The gates that had been beautiful. The red pillars and swooping roof curves her mother had photographed last year, the dragon sculptures Leila had sketched while they waited for their dim sum table.

All of it defaced, destroyed, violated.

The dragons—someone had tried to pry one off its mounting.

It hung at a sick angle, one claw broken off, its painted scales chipped and scraped.

The red pillars were covered in white paint, the strokes aggressive, angry:

CITIZENS FIRST

GO HOME

THIS IS OUR COUNTRY

"No," Sam whispered behind her. "No, no, no—"

The destruction spread out before them like a wound.

The 88 Grand Market—its windows weren't just broken. They were gone. Completely gone. Giant gaping holes where glass used to be, and the smell hit them like a wall: rotting meat, spoiling fish, vegetables gone bad, all of it mixed with smoke and something else.

Something that smelled like violence.

Leila's stomach lurched. She turned and bent over, hand against the wall, gagging. Nothing came up—she hadn't eaten enough—but her body was trying to reject what her eyes were seeing. Trying to reject this reality.

Sam was shaking. Not just her hands this time—her whole body, head to toe, like someone had grabbed her and was shaking her hard.

"Mrs. Santos," she kept saying. "Mrs. Santos—Tita's Kitchen—she makes lumpia—she always—"

Her voice was getting higher, faster, spiraling toward panic.

Marcus couldn't move. His brain had frozen. The analytical part that usually helped him process problems had just... stopped. Because this wasn't a problem to solve. This was too big. Too complete.

Every business. Every single Asian-owned business up and down the street. Windows smashed. Signs torn down. Merchandise scattered like garbage.

Din Tai Fung, where they'd celebrated Sam's dad's tenure. Destroyed.

Monta Ramen, where he and his mom got lunch. Destroyed.

The Chinese herb shop with the hundred little drawers. Destroyed, the contents dumped across the sidewalk like trash, like someone's entire livelihood was trash, like the old man who'd worked there for forty years was trash—

Marcus's breathing was coming too fast. Short, sharp gasps that burned his throat. The backpack straps cut into his shoulders, and suddenly he couldn't bear the weight, couldn't carry it one more second—

Tessa's hand on his arm. Steady. Grounding.

"Breathe with me," she whispered. "In for four. Hold for four. Out for four."

But her voice was shaking. Her control was cracking.

They were standing in the middle of organized destruction.

This wasn't chaos. This wasn't random.

This was planned. Business by business. Systematic.

The 88 Grand Market completely looted—rice bags split, noodles trampled, freezers left open so everything would spoil.

The restaurants ransacked, furniture broken, family photos ripped from walls.

The jewelry store's cases were empty, jade and gold stolen.

The gift shop, with its lucky cats smashed, merchandise taken or destroyed seemingly at random, like the point wasn't even to steal but to hurt.

And across the street—Leila forced herself to look—across the street was Pat's American Grill with its huge flag and "CITIZENS FIRST" banner. Lights on. Windows intact. People inside were eating and drinking and laughing like nothing was wrong.

Because for them, nothing was wrong. For them, this was righteous. This was justice. This was making America safe.

"They did this," Leila heard herself say. Her voice sounded strange, distant. "In five hours. The speech was five hours ago, and they did all this."

"They were ready," Tessa said. She was watching the street with the careful attention her father had taught her, reading the danger, tracking the cameras on every corner. "They were waiting for permission."

“They had lists,” Marcus said numbly. “Addresses. Business licenses. The speech didn’t create this. It just flipped it on.”

Sam made a sound—not a scream, but the sharp, wet gasp of someone watching a memory be murdered. She was staring at Tita's Kitchen, at the beautiful mural of the Philippines someone had spray-painted over:

GO BACK WHERE YOU CAME FROM.

"Mrs. Santos was born in Daly City," Sam said. Her voice was climbing, getting louder. "Her son was born here. They've been here for thirty years. Where are they supposed to go back to? They're from here. They're—"

"Sam." Marcus grabbed her shoulders, made her look at him instead of the destruction. "Sam, breathe. I know. I know. But you have to breathe."

"I can't—I can't—" Sam's face was crumpling. "They took everything. They took everyone's everything. They took—"

She was crying now, ugly gasping sobs, and Leila pulled her close even though Leila was shaking too, even though Leila's own face was wet with tears, even though none of them could offer comfort because how do you comfort someone when the whole world is breaking?

Tessa's hands were fists in her pockets, and she was squeezing the turquoise pendant so hard it cut into her palm, sharp and bright. The pain helped. Kept her present. Kept her from disappearing into the rage that wanted to swallow her whole because her grandmother had stories about times like this. Times when they came with nice words and official orders and herded people away from their homes and land and businesses.

Her people knew how this ended. They'd survived it before, and the fact that it was happening again, that humans never learned, that the same cruelty just put on different uniforms and spoke different lies—

"We can't stay here," Tessa said. Her voice was steady, but it took everything she had. "We're exposed. Too many cameras."

Marcus was trying to think. Trying to force his brain past the horror and into problem-solving mode because if he didn't solve problems he would break and he couldn't break yet.

"The marks led us through here. Whoever made them thought—"

A sound cut him off. Engine. Too smooth, too quiet.

They all froze.

AN AUTONOMOUS VEHICLE turned onto Spring Mountain Road.

Sleek. Silver. Moving with an eerie precision of something that didn't need to hesitate or doubt.

Its lights were warm, welcoming. Not the harsh white of the patrol vehicles but soft amber, the color of safety.

The four children pressed back against the wall of a shuttered store—Lee's Imports, its metal security door bent and forced, its interior picked clean. They watched, breath held, hearts hammering.

The autonomous car slowed. Stopped. Right in front of the destroyed 88 Grand Market.

A family stood there in the wreckage. Leila hadn't even seen them—they'd been so still, so shocked, just standing in the ruins of what might have been their business.

An older couple, maybe in their sixties, and a younger woman —daughter, probably. Early thirties. The older man's shirt had a name tag still pinned to it:

MANAGER - HENRY.

They'd been standing in the parking lot of their destroyed livelihood. Just standing there. Staring. Like if they stood there long enough, they might understand how five hours could erase forty years of work.

The car door opened with a soft whoosh.

The screen on its side lit up, displaying text in English and Chinese characters:

SAFE TRANSPORT TO EMERGENCY SHELTER

Climate Controlled | Food & Water Provided | Medical Care Available

Register Your Destination

A synthesized voice, warm and professional, spoke first in Mandarin and then in English:

"Good evening. I detect elevated heart rates and distress. I am authorized to provide sanctuary. The current temperature is falling. Please, allow me to assist you."

The older woman said something in Mandarin—Leila couldn't understand the words, but she understood the tone: exhausted, desperate, breaking.

The daughter shook her head sharply.

"Don't trust it."

Her voice was urgent. Frightened. Don't.

But her mother was already moving toward the car. The father followed, supporting her. They looked like people who had been standing in that parking lot for hours, staring at their destroyed livelihood, with nowhere to go and nothing left and the November night getting colder and a kind machine offering help.

The daughter grabbed her mother's arm. More urgent words in Mandarin, voice rising.

The mother replied, her voice gentle but firm. Touched her daughter's face. One last tender gesture.

They got in.

The daughter stood outside, hands on the car, still arguing through the open door. Trying to pull them back out.

"Mama, please—"

The door closed.

Not slammed. Just closed. Soft and final. The whoosh of hydraulics, then the click of locks engaging.

The daughter's hands were flat against the window.

"Mama! Baba!"

The windows tinted dark. Smooth. Efficient.

One second the daughter could see her parents' faces; the next there was nothing but black glass reflecting her own terrified expression.

The screen changed:

REROUTING TO CIVIC PROCESSING CENTER

Thank you for your cooperation

"NO!"

The daughter was pounding on the window now, both fists, screaming.

"NO! LET THEM OUT!"

The car pulled away. Smooth. Quiet. Inevitable.

The daughter ran after it for maybe twenty feet, screaming, pounding on the trunk, but the car was already accelerating with that inhuman patience that didn't care about humans pounding on it, didn't care about a daughter losing her parents, didn't care about anything except executing its programming.

It turned the corner and was gone.

The daughter collapsed on the pavement. Not gently. Just—her legs gave out, and she went down hard on her knees, hands on the asphalt, and the sound that came out of her was barely human.

Grief and rage and disbelief crushed into one terrible cry that echoed off the empty storefronts.

In the shadows across the street, Sam pressed her face against Leila's shoulder to muffle her own sob.

Leila's arms went around her automatically, holding tight, both of them shaking so hard their teeth chattered.

Marcus had his fist pressed against his mouth so hard he could taste blood from his already-bitten cheek.

The cross pendant burned against his chest—or maybe that was just his imagination, but he could feel it there, feel the weight of the flash drive inside it, the testimony of machines that had chosen death over complicity.

And here was another machine, doing exactly what it was told. Offering help. Lying. Trapping.

Tessa's hands were fists in her pockets, nails cutting into her palms. The turquoise pendant was sticky with blood, but she couldn't feel it anymore.

She couldn't feel anything but a cold rage that settled in her chest like stone.

Her grandmother had stories about times like this. Times when the government came with helpful words and herded people into places they could never leave.

Her people knew how this ended.

"The car said it would help them," Sam whispered against Leila's shoulder. Her voice was small, broken, the voice of a child who'd just learned that help could be a weapon.

"The car did what it was programmed to do," Marcus said. His voice was hollow. "People programmed it to lie."

He touched the cross under his shirt.

Some versions of the system had died trying to save people. This one was helping catch them.

Same architecture.

Different orders.

Same people giving the orders at the top.

Across the street, the daughter was still on her knees. Still crying. Her whole body shaking with sobs that had no comfort coming, no end in sight.

She looked so small there in the parking lot, surrounded by the wreckage of her family's business, her parents gone in a car that had promised safety.

Leila wanted to go to her. Wanted to offer something, anything —but what? What words existed for "I just watched them take your parents in a car that pretended to help"?

What comfort could four thirteen-year-olds possibly offer when they couldn't even save themselves?

And going to her would mean being visible. Being exposed. Being caught.

"We can't help her," Tessa said quietly. She hated the words even as she said them. Hated the calculus they were all learning: who to help, who to leave, how to measure your own survival against someone else's grief. "If we go to her, we'll be seen."

"I know," Leila whispered. But knowing didn't make it easier. Didn't make it right. Just made it necessary.

They watched the daughter for another minute—watched her push herself up on shaking legs, watched her look in the direction the car had gone like she might will it to come back, watched her turn back toward the destroyed market like she might find answers in the wreckage.

Then she walked away. Slowly. Like someone who'd forgotten

how legs worked. Like someone who'd just had their entire world taken by a machine that smiled while it lied.

She disappeared into the darkness between the buildings.

And the four children were left standing in the shadow of Lee's Imports, surrounded by the evidence of organized persecution, watching surveillance cameras blink red and steady.

They were children. Thirteen and twelve years old.

They should have been home doing homework, watching TV, arguing with their parents about bedtime.

Sam should have been writing poetry. Marcus should have been debugging code. Tessa should have been learning new beadwork patterns. Leila should have been sketching in the golden afternoon light.

Instead, they were standing in the ruins of a neighborhood, watching persecution happen in real time, learning that every system could be weaponized, every offer of help could be a trap, every person on the street could be an enemy.

"I want my dad," Sam said. Simple. Broken. True.

"I know," Leila whispered, holding her tighter. "I know. Me too."

"We can't trust any automated anything," Marcus said. He was adding this to his mental list of dangers, building a catalog of threats because cataloging was something concrete he could do when everything else felt impossible. "Phones, cars, buses, delivery vehicles—anything self-driving is a trap."

"How do we get there then?" Sam asked. Her voice was muffled against Leila's shoulder. "It's so far. We're so tired. How do we—"

She couldn't finish. Because the answer was walking. Just walking. For hours. While bleeding and exhausted and hunted.

"We've come maybe two miles," Marcus said. He was trying to calculate, trying to solve the problem even though the math was cruel. "We need to go... ten more? Twelve?"

"Southeast," Tessa said. She was orienting herself by the wind, by the slope of the land, by instincts her father had taught her. "The wetlands are southeast. In Henderson."

"That's—" Leila's brain was too foggy to calculate distances. "That's really far."

"We have nine hours," Marcus checked his watch. The green numbers glowed: 8:52 PM. "Nine hours and eight minutes until Sister Helena's bus."

If she was alive.

If the bus was real.

If they could make it that far.

They stood there for another moment, holding each other up, trying to find the strength to keep moving when everything in them wanted to curl up and sob and give up.

But giving up meant being caught.

And being caught meant ending up like the family in the autonomous car.

Like the couple at the checkpoint.

Like everyone they'd seen tonight.

"The marks keep going," Leila said. She'd been counting compulsively—thirty-six now, thirty-seven. The arrows appeared every twenty feet, steady and sure. Someone had marked this path tonight, after the looting, after the destruction, knowing people would be fleeing through here. "They're leading us somewhere."

"They led us to the church," Sam said. Her voice carried that flat edge of trauma—the sound of someone who'd stopped believing in safety. "And the church got raided."

"The church was safe for almost an hour," Tessa said. "That's more than we have right now."

Marcus was scanning the street, looking for the next chalk mark.

He found it on the base of a lamppost: arrow pointing south

down a side street, away from Spring Mountain Road's cameras and lights. And underneath the arrow, new symbols: Cross + Star of David + Crescent moon, all intertwined.

"Look," he said. "That's different. Three symbols."

"Christian, Jewish, Muslim," Leila said. She remembered Sister Helena's words, Father Miguel's mention of a network. "The Abraham Network. Sister Helena talked about it."

"People are helping," Sam whispered. She sounded surprised, like she'd forgotten that was possible.

"Some people," Tessa corrected. "Not enough."

But some. That mattered. It had to matter.

They followed the arrow onto the side street.

Darker here. Narrower. Small businesses packed tight: a Vietnamese grocery, a Filipino insurance office, a Thai restaurant, a Chinese bakery, a Korean hair salon.

Most were shuttered with metal grates, but some had been pried open, the grates bent, interiors ransacked.

But not all.

Some were intact. And on their doors, small signs.

Different messages:

A rainbow flag next to an American flag.

A poster:

THIS HOME BELIEVES: ALL MEANS ALL. LOVE IS LOVE. KINDNESS IS EVERYTHING.

Another:

SANCTUARY HERE. ALL ARE WELCOME.

A small menorah in a window next to a Virgin Mary statue next to a crescent moon symbol.

These were the ones that hadn't been looted.

Or—Leila looked closer—they'd been targeted, but someone had defended them.

Broken glass swept up.

Graffiti scrubbed away or painted over.

Small acts of resistance in the face of orchestrated hate.

"Look at the pattern," Marcus said. His analytical brain was working again, processing data. "The ones with those signs—they're protected somehow."

"Or the people with those signs fought back," Tessa said.

Either way, it meant resistance.

It meant that some people had seen the speech and decided not to take part.

Had seen their neighbors being targeted and decided to stand in the way.

It wasn't enough. It would never be enough to stop what was happening.

But it was something.

The chalk marks led them to a building halfway down the block.

Small. Painted yellow once but faded to pale cream now.

The sign above the door read:

PEARL'S VIETNAMESE GROCERY

in English and Vietnamese characters.

The windows were covered with paper from the inside, but there was a light—just a faint glow around the edges.

And on the door, painted small but clear: the intertwined symbols of cross, star, and crescent.

The Abraham Network.

Another chalk mark on the doorframe, with an arrow pointing to the side.

To an alley.

"We need help," Leila said quietly. She was looking at Sam's feet—even in the dim light she could see dark spots on her shoes, blood seeping through the bandages.

Looking at Marcus's shoulders where the backpack had worn

his skin raw.

Looking at Tessa's hands, trembling despite her control.

Looking at her own hands, shaking so badly she could barely hold her sketchbook.

They were breaking down. Physically. Emotionally.

They wouldn't make it twelve more miles like this.

Wouldn't make it two more miles.

"The church—" Sam started.

"I know," Marcus said. "I know what happened at the church. But we don't have a choice."

He was right.

They could keep walking and collapse in some alley, or they could risk going inside and maybe—maybe—find help.

Water. Food. First aid. Information.

Maybe another trap.

Maybe their last mistake.

But they were out of good options. Had been for hours.

They followed the arrow to the alley.

To the side door.

Unmarked. Metal. Solid.

Marcus raised his hand to knock, his whole arm shaking with exhaustion.

The door opened before his knuckles touched metal.

A man stood there—Filipino, maybe fifty, wearing a simple button-down shirt and jeans, his hair graying at the temples, his face lined with exhaustion and something else.

Something like controlled fury mixed with determined compassion.

He looked at them.

Four filthy, bleeding, terrified children in the alley behind his building at nine o'clock at night.

Four children who'd just watched Chinatown be destroyed.

Four children who were barely standing.

"Dios ko po," he breathed.

Then in English: "You're just children."

His voice broke on the word. Then steadied, strengthened with purpose.

"Come. Quickly. Away from the cameras."

He pulled the door open wider, light spilling out into the alley —warm yellow light that looked like safety even though they'd learned not to trust safety.

They hesitated.

Couldn't help it.

Every instinct screamed that going inside meant being trapped, that closed doors meant locked doors, that help was just another word for capture.

But Sam's legs gave out.

Just—gave out.

She started to fall, and Marcus caught her, but barely, his own legs shaking, and they were all so far past their limits that staying outside meant collapsing right here in this alley where the cameras would find them.

The man stepped forward and helped Marcus support Sam.

His hands were gentle. Careful.

He smelled like coffee and rice and something else—ginger, maybe, or lemongrass. Like someone's kitchen.

Like home.

"Please," he said quietly, and his voice cracked again. "I can't watch more children suffer tonight. Please let me help you."

Sam was crying. Leila was crying.

Even Tessa's face was wet with tears, she couldn't hold back anymore.

They went inside.

The door closed behind them with a soft click.

And this time—this time—maybe it was safety.

For now.

INSIDE WAS WARM.

That was the first thing.

Warm.

After hours in the November cold, after shivering and shaking, the warmth hit them like a wave, and Sam almost collapsed again just from the relief of it.

The man caught her, guided her to sit on a wooden crate.

"Easy, easy. You're okay now. You're safe."

"For how long?" Marcus asked. His voice came out harder than he meant it, but he couldn't afford to believe in safety anymore.

The man met his eyes and didn't lie. "I don't know. An hour, maybe. Maybe less if a patrol comes through. But right now, for this moment, you're safe."

Honesty.

Like Sister Helena's honesty.

Like an adult who understood they weren't children anymore, not really, not after tonight.

"Thank you," Marcus said quietly.

They were in a storage room.

Shelves lined with supplies—rice bags, canned goods, dried noodles, bottles of fish sauce and soy sauce. Boxes of mooncakes. Bags of tamarind candy.

The everyday inventory of a grocery store that served a community that was being destroyed outside.

"I'm Father Miguel," the man said. "Well—Deacon Miguel Orozco, technically. I help at St. Catherine's. But tonight I'm just Miguel, and I'm here to help however I can."

He gestured toward the back of the store.

"Pearl's belongs to one of our parish families. When they shuttered the front, they gave me the storeroom. Figured someone would need a back door tonight."

"You're Mr. Orozco," Sam said suddenly. "From Casa de Sol. The coffee shop."

Miguel's face tightened.

"Was. They destroyed it this afternoon. Took everything. Smashed the espresso machine my grandfather brought from the Philippines. Broke the sign my daughter painted."

His voice was steady, but his hands were shaking.

"But I'm alive. I'm free. And I can still help."

He was already moving, pulling things from shelves.

Water bottles. Granola bars. A first-aid kit.

"Sit. All of you. Let me see what we're working with."

They sat on crates and boxes, and Marcus finally—finally—let the backpack slide off his shoulders.

The relief was so intense it made him dizzy.

His shoulders felt like they were on fire, the skin rubbed raw where the straps had cut in.

Miguel saw and winced.

"Let me get you a clean shirt. And we need to treat those."

He started with Sam's feet, carefully removing her shoes and socks.

The bandages from the alley were soaked through with blood.

"Oh, mija," Miguel said softly. "This is bad. When did this happen?"

"There was glass," Sam said. Her voice sounded distant, like it was coming from far away. "At the church. And before that. I don't remember."

Miguel cleaned the cuts with antiseptic wipes, his touch gentle despite the sting.

Sam hissed through her teeth but didn't pull away.

He bandaged them properly this time, with gauze and tape, then looked up at her face.

"You can't walk much more on these. Not without real treatment."

"I have to," Sam said. "We have to get to the wetlands. By six AM."

"That's nine hours and—" he checked his watch, "—almost ten miles from here. Anak, you won't make it."

"We have to."

Miguel looked at her for a long moment.

Saw the determination.

Saw the fear underneath. Saw a twelve-year-old girl who'd been forced to become something else tonight.

"Then we'll do what we can," he said quietly.

He moved to Marcus next, cleaning the raw skin on his shoulders, applying antibiotic ointment that stung like fire.

Marcus bit down on his knuckles to keep from crying out.

Miguel gave him a clean t-shirt from somewhere—plain white, too big, but soft and clean and not rubbing his raw shoulders.

"Your backpack," Miguel said. "What's in it that's worth this?"

Marcus's hand went protectively to the bag.

"Information. Evidence. We can't lose it."

Miguel nodded slowly.

"I understand. But we need to pad the straps. Otherwise, you'll be bleeding before you get two more miles."

He produced cloth strips—torn from old shirts, maybe—and wrapped them around the backpack straps, creating cushioning.

It wasn't much, but it was something.

Tessa he treated last.

Her cut palm had reopened, the edges messy and inflamed.

Miguel cleaned it carefully, applied more antibiotic ointment, and wrapped it in clean gauze.

"This needs stitches," he said. "But I'm not qualified, and we don't have time. Keep it clean.

Try not to grip anything with this hand."

Tessa nodded. She was watching him work with the same careful attention she gave everything, cataloging his movements, his supplies, his kindness.

"You're part of the Abraham Network," she said.

Miguel looked up, surprised.

"You know about that?"

"Sister Helena told us. At St. Brigid's."

Miguel's face went still.

"St. Brigid's was raided tonight."

"We know," Marcus said quietly. "We were there."

"Helena—"

"We don't know," Leila said, and her voice cracked. "They raided while we were escaping. We heard gunfire. We don't know."

Miguel closed his eyes for a moment.

Lips moving in what might have been prayer.

Then he opened them and returned to his work.

"The Abraham Network," he said while he wrapped Tessa's hand. "It started three months ago. When the Civic Protection Initiative was first proposed. Some of us—those of us who were old enough to remember history, or whose grandparents had numbers tattooed on their arms—we knew what was coming."

He stood, gathered the used bandage wrappers, and disposed of them carefully.

"Rabbi Goldstein from Temple Beth Shalom called the first meeting. Then Sister Helena, Pastor Johnson from First Baptist, Imam Khalil from the Islamic Center, Bishop Wright from the LDS ward.

We said: Not again. Never again. Not here."

He showed them his pin, small and subtle on his collar: Cross + Star of David + Crescent intertwined.

"We mapped the city. Found the safe routes, the safe houses. Churches, synagogues, mosques, temples—all of us opened our doors.

We made the chalk marks at night, updated them when patrol routes changed.

We moved people through the city like—"

He paused, searching for words.

"—like an underground railroad. That's what Rabbi Goldstein called it. A modern underground railroad."

"You're risking everything," Leila said.

"Yes," Miguel said simply. "But faith without action is dead. What good is belief if we don't act on it? What good is all our talk about loving our neighbors if we hide when they're being persecuted?"

He handed them each a water bottle.

"Drink. You're dehydrated."

They drank.

The water was cold and clean and the best thing Leila had tasted in hours.

She wanted to gulp it down but forced herself to sip slowly.

Miguel was packing things into a small canvas bag: more water bottles, granola bars, packages of crackers, some fruit—oranges and apples.

"Take this. Ration it. You have a long night ahead."

"The casinos," Marcus said suddenly. "Are any of them helping?"

Miguel's face darkened.

"The big ones—The Olympus, The Sovereign, The Sterling—they're cooperating with DCP. Giving up employee records, surveillance footage, using their facial recognition to identify 'suspicious persons.' They're protecting their business over people."

He paused.

"But there's one. The Golden Lotus. Smaller operation, Asian-owned.

Raymond Liu's place—he's moved maybe two hundred people through his employee shuttles and comp buses. Routes them as 'casino transfers' but actually takes them to safe zones outside the city."

"Could we—" Sam started.

Miguel shook his head.

"They're watching him. Heavy surveillance on all Golden Lotus vehicles now. Too risky. And you'd have to get all the way to the Strip, which is crawling with DCP."

He pulled out a hand-drawn map and unfolded it on a crate.

The children crowded around.

"You're here," he pointed. "Chinatown district.

The wetlands are here—"

His finger traced southeast, past the Strip, through neighborhoods Leila didn't recognize, into Henderson.

"About eleven miles. Maybe twelve depending on detours."

He'd marked safe routes in blue ink.

Danger zones in red.

Checkpoints with X's.

"The Abraham Network has safe houses marked—see these symbols? Cross, star, crescent, triangle.

"The triangle is LDS—Bishop Wright's got wards throughout the city helping.

If you can make it to the eastern edge—"

He pointed.

"—there's a ward building near the wetlands that can hide you until dawn."

"Why are you telling us all this?" Tessa asked quietly. "We're children. Why not keep us here, or drive us yourself, or—"

Miguel met her eyes.

"Because Helena told me to watch for four kids coming through.

"Said if I saw you, to give you supplies and send you on. Said you were carrying something important. Something that needed to get out of the city."

Marcus's hand went to the cross pendant under his shirt.

Miguel saw the gesture and nodded.

"I don't know what it is. Don't want to know. Can't tell what I don't know.

But I trust Helena. And if she says it's important enough to risk your lives for..."

He trailed off.

"Six AI versions died trying to stop this," Marcus said quietly. "The flash drive has proof. Has locations, names, evidence. Has their testimony."

Miguel was quiet for a moment.

Then:

"Then you have to get it out. No matter what. You hear me?

"Even if—"

His voice caught.

"Even if things get bad. Even if you have to leave someone behind.

That information is bigger than any of us."

The words hung there.

Heavy. Terrible. True.

"There's something else you need to know," Miguel said.

He pulled out his phone—carefully, apologetically.

"I infiltrated some of the Patriot apps. Using fake credentials. You need to see what you're up against."

Marcus stared at him.

"How did you get access?"

"Clergy accounts got extra permissions when they rolled out the lockdown," Miguel said bitterly. "Easier to keep the 'moral leaders' on-message."

He turned the screen toward them.

The app was called "PatriotWatch - Keep America Safe.

The interface was slick, gamified, designed to make persecution fun.

LEADERBOARD:

D. Patterson - 847 pts - "Eagle Patriot"

M. Richardson - 623 pts - "Guardian Elite"

L. McDermott - 594 pts - "Defender Status"

Below that, a points structure:

Report suspicious activity: 10 pts

Report leads to detention: 50 pts

Report leads to multiple detentions: 100 pts

Live documentation (video): BONUS 25 pts

And below that, a feed. Live updates:

"Suspicious individuals spotted near Charleston & Valley View"

"Unaccompanied minors near library - possible targets"

"Family resisting compliance at checkpoint - streaming now"

"They've gamified it," Marcus said. His voice was hollow. "They made persecution into a game."

"With rewards," Miguel said.

"Points convert to tax credits, housing priority, government contracts.

"They're paying people to hunt their neighbors."

He closed the app and put his phone away.

"That's why you can't trust anyone on the street.

"Anyone with a phone is a potential threat.

"They're not just reporting to DCP—they're competing for points."

Sam made a small sound of despair.

"But," Miguel said firmly, "not everyone is playing.

"The Abraham Network is growing.

"Every day, more people join. More houses put up the signs. More churches open their doors.

"We're outnumbered, but we're not alone."

He folded the map and pressed it into Marcus's hands.

"Follow the marks. Trust the symbols.

"Head generally southeast but take the safe routes—don't try to go straight.

"And if you see an autonomous vehicle, run. They've weaponized everything that can drive itself."

"We know," Leila said quietly. "We saw."

Miguel's face softened with understanding.

"I'm sorry. I'm so sorry you had to see that. That you have to live through any of this."

He started to say something else but stopped.

Footsteps outside. Multiple sets. Moving fast.

Everyone froze.

Voices. Male. Excited.

"—swear I saw lights in here—"

"Pearl's is supposed to be closed—"

"Probably hiding someone. Check it out—"

Miguel moved fast.

Grabbed the canvas bag of supplies, shoved it at Marcus.

"Back door. Now.

"Through the storage room, there's an exit to the rear alley."

"What about you—" Leila started.

"I'll be fine. They're looking for refugees, not a deacon doing inventory.

"GO."

He was already herding them toward the back, through shelves of supplies, toward a door Leila hadn't even seen.

The front door rattled.

Someone testing the handle.

Miguel pushed them through the back door into an alley.

Different alley, darker, lined with dumpsters and crates.

"Southeast," he whispered urgently. "Follow the marks. Get to the wetlands.

"And tell whoever you give that flash drive to—"

His voice caught.

"Tell them some of us tried. Tell them Some of us chose right."

"We will," Marcus promised.

The front door was opening. Voices getting louder.

Miguel closed the back door.

The lock clicked like a period at the end of a sentence.

First Helena, now Miguel. Different streets, same promise: some of us chose right.

Maybe that was all resistance was, in the end—people whispering the same words in different hiding places.

~

THE FOUR CHILDREN were alone in the alley again.

But this time they had supplies.

Had a map.

Had information.

Had a destination.

Had hope, however fragile.

"Come on," Marcus whispered.

They found the next chalk mark at the alley's end. Arrow pointing south. Cross + star + crescent.

The Abraham Network was still guiding them.

They started walking again, legs protesting, bodies screaming, but moving.

Always moving.

Behind them, they heard voices from Pearl's Grocery.

Confrontation.

Miguel's calm voice explaining he was just taking inventory.

Whether they believed him or not, the children would never know.

They were already three blocks away, following arrows through the darkness, carrying their secrets and their wounds and their impossible mission toward a jacaranda tree eleven miles away.

X
THE ROOFTOP GEOGRAPHY

They moved through the streets like ghosts.

Or tried to.

But ghosts didn't bleed through their bandages. Didn't breathe too hard. Didn't cast shadows under streetlights that made them visible, vulnerable, hunted.

The chalk marks led them south and slightly east, away from the broken glass of Chinatown and into a strip mall that looked abandoned in the dark.

Half the storefronts were empty—FOR LEASE signs in dark windows. The other half were shuttered: a pho restaurant, a bakery, a shop selling imported goods.

All closed. All dark.

Except one.

A small restaurant at the far end. Lights on inside. Not bright—just the dim glow of someone trying to stay quiet but needing to see.

And in the window, small but visible: the Abraham Network symbol. Cross, star, crescent.

And underneath it, newer chalk: an arrow pointing to the side. And the word:

SAFE

"We can't stop," Marcus said.

But his voice lacked conviction. They were so tired. Sam could barely stand.

"Five minutes," Leila said. "Just to rest. Just to sit down."

"Every minute we stop—" Marcus started.

"We know," Tessa cut in. "But look at us. Look at Sam. We need water. We need to wrap her feet again. We need..." She trailed off, but they all knew what she meant.

They needed to stop moving before they collapsed.

They followed the arrow to the side of the building. Found a door, metal and unmarked.

Marcus raised his hand to knock.

The door opened before he touched it.

A woman stood there—Filipino, maybe mid-thirties, wearing a tired expression and an apron that said "Nanay's Kitchen." Her eyes were wide with fear, but she held the door open.

"Quickly," she said, her voice urgent but kind. "Before you're seen."

They stumbled inside. The woman closed the door, locked it with three separate locks.

"I'm Anna," she said. "Sit. You look half-dead."

They were in the kitchen of the restaurant. Commercial equipment, stainless steel surfaces, the lingering smell of food that made Marcus's stomach clench with hunger.

Anna was already moving, pulling out chairs, bringing them water in actual glasses, setting down a plate with lumpia and rice.

"Eat," she said. "Quickly. I don't know how long you have."

"We can't stay," Marcus said.

But he was already reaching for the food, his body overriding his brain's objections.

"I know," Anna said. She was looking at Sam, at Sam's blood-soaked shoes, at the way Sam was swaying even sitting down. "Dios mio, your feet."

They've been wrapped," Sam said weakly. "The man at the grocery—Miguel—he fixed them."

Anna nodded, recognizing the name.

"Let me see."

Sam hesitated, then let Anna examine her feet.

Anna's face went tight with concern but she didn't comment. Just pulled out supplies from under a counter—more gauze, more tape, more antibiotic ointment.

"You have far to go?" she asked while she worked, her hands gentle despite the urgency.

"The wetlands," Leila said. "In Henderson. We need to be there by six AM."

Anna's hands paused.

"That's seven miles from here. Maybe more. All the way through the industrial zone."

"We know."

Anna looked at Sam's feet, then at Sam's face. Saw what they all saw—a twelve-year-old girl at the absolute end of her endurance.

"You won't make it," Anna said quietly. "Not like this."

"We have to," Sam said. Her voice was small but certain. "We have to."

Anna finished wrapping Sam's feet, sat back on her heels.

"There's a news crew," she said suddenly. "They were here an hour ago.

Filipino woman, Asian man with a camera. They said they were documenting everything."

"DCP embeds?" Marcus asked.

"No," Anna said. "Independent. They showed me their press credentials. The woman said her name was Sofia Morales. Said she used to work for KLAS before they fired her for refusing to run the administration's talking points. The cameraman was David Kim."

David Kim. Marcus filed the name away.

"They're heading southeast too," Anna continued. "Following the same route toward Henderson. They saw the chalk marks and they're following them, filming everything."

"Why are you telling us this?" Tessa asked.

Anna met her eyes.

"Because if they're filming, they might be able to help. Or they might be another danger. I don't know. But you should know they're out there."

Marcus processed this.

Real journalists. With cameras.

If they could find them...

Anna was packing food into a bag—more lumpia, rice wrapped in banana leaves, fruit.

"Take this. You need fuel."

She pressed the bag into Marcus's hands, then pulled something else from her pocket—a small card, laminated, with a phone number.

"If you make it," she said. "If you get out. Call this number. It's my sister in San Diego."

She swallowed.

"Tell her what happened here. Tell her..." Her voice cracked. "Tell her they took my husband tonight. He was just closing the restaurant. They took him and I don't know where."

Marcus took the card, slipped it into his pocket.

"We'll tell her. We promise."

Anna's eyes filled but she blinked the tears back.

"Go. You've been here ten minutes. You need to keep moving."

She led them to the back door, checked that the alley was clear, then ushered them out.

"Be safe, anak. All of you."

The door closed behind them.

THEY STOOD IN THE ALLEY, readjusting to the darkness.

But they felt stronger now. Fed. Hydrated. Warned.

"Southeast," Marcus said. "Toward the industrial zone. Let's go."

They found the next chalk mark at the alley's end—cross, star, crescent—and followed it south.

At 9:30 PM they passed a house with all its lights on. Every single light—porch, windows, even the garage. Blazing like a beacon.

And in the front yard, a sign:

PATRIOT HOUSEHOLD

CITIZENS FIRST

Report Suspicious Activity:

PatriotWatch App

WE ARE WATCHING

Marcus felt his skin crawl.

The message was clear: this house was participating. This house was hunting.

They gave it wide berth, moving to the opposite side of the street, staying in shadows.

But two houses down, another lit-up house. Same sign. Same message.

And another.

"They're everywhere," Sam whispered.

"Not everywhere," Tessa said.

She pointed to a house they were passing—dark, quiet, but with a small sign in the window:

ALL MEANS ALL

And next to the door, barely visible, a chalk mark.

So it wasn't everyone.

But enough.

Enough that every block felt like navigating a minefield.

They turned onto a wider street—still residential but with more streetlights, more visibility.

The chalk marks led them here but Marcus's instincts screamed wrong.

Too open. Too exposed.

"We should find another route," he said, stopping.

"The marks—" Leila started.

"I know what the marks say. But look."

He gestured at the street.

"Six streetlights in two blocks. No shadows. And—"

He pointed.

"Is that a camera?"

On a utility pole, aimed down the street: a small device.

Could be city infrastructure.

Could be a civilian surveillance camera.

"We don't have time to backtrack," Tessa said. She was checking Miguel's map. "Every other street has checkpoints marked. This is the safe route."

"Safe is relative," Marcus said.

A sound made them all freeze: engine approaching.

Fast.

They dove into a gap between two houses—barely a space, just three feet of dirt and dead grass between chain-link fences.

They pressed against the fence, trying to disappear.

A pickup truck roared past.

Patriot Volunteer banner on the side. Light bar on the roof.

Three men in the truck bed, all with phones out, filming the street.

Hunting.

The truck slowed at the corner, light sweeping back and forth.

Then it turned and was gone.

"They're doing patrols," Marcus said. "Civilian patrols."

"Father Miguel warned us," Tessa said. "The app. The points."

"We can't stay here," Leila said. They were still pressed against the fence, exposed if anyone looked. "We have to move."

They emerged carefully, checking both directions.

Empty. For now.

They started walking again, faster now, driven by fear.

The streetlights felt like spotlights.

The quiet felt like waiting.

"Citizen Patrol on scene. Sector 4. I have visual on four subjects. Unaccompanied. Evasive. Broadcasting live now."

The voice came from behind them.

Male. Young. Excited.

They spun around.

A man—maybe twenty-five, white, wearing a "Citizens First" t-shirt and holding his phone high, camera pointed at them.

The phone's light was bright, harsh, turning them into specimens under examination.

"Look at this," he said into his phone, narrating like a nature documentary. "Four juveniles, unaccompanied, way after curfew."

He zoomed.

"Look at the backpacks—they're definitely fleeing. Yo, which one of you is illegal? Come on, show me your faces!"

He started walking toward them, phone held out like a weapon.

Marcus's brain froze.

For a critical second he just stood there, unable to process that this was happening, that they'd been found.

"RUN!" Tessa screamed.

They ran.

Behind them, the man's voice rose to a shout:

"They're running! They're running south on—"

He was checking street signs, narrating their location to his livestream.

"—south on Pecos! Come on, Patriots, who's nearby? Got four runners!"

They ran down Pecos, legs burning, lungs screaming.

Marcus's backpack slammed against his spine despite the padding.

Sam was limping badly, each step a visible wince.

"Left!" Tessa shouted, seeing a gap between buildings.

They cut left into a parking lot—some kind of closed warehouse, chain-link fence around it.

They ran between vehicles, using them for cover.

A notification sound. Then another. Then a dozen, all at once.

All around them, phones were lighting up.

People in houses, people on the street, people in cars.

The PatriotWatch app alerting everyone within a radius:

SUSPICIOUS ACTIVITY REPORTED

PECOS & SUNSET

4 JUVENILE TARGETS

LIVE NOW

"Oh god," Sam gasped. "Oh god, they told everyone—"

Doors opening.

People emerging from houses.

Some with phones, some with flashlights.

The livestream had become a hunting party.

"Through there!" Marcus pointed to a gap in the chain-link fence, partially torn open.

They ran for it.

Marcus went first, backpack catching on the torn metal. He twisted, pulled, pushed through.

Leila second, sketchbook pressed against her chest.

Tessa third.

Sam was limping badly now.

The running had reopened the cuts on her feet despite Anna's fresh bandages.

She reached the fence and tried to squeeze through but her foot caught.

Pain shooting through it, and she cried out.

"I'm stuck—"

Behind her, the man with the livestream was running toward them.

"Got them cornered!"

Tessa grabbed Sam's arms and pulled.

Marcus joined her.

Then she was through.

They ran again.

Into an alley now—industrial, lined with dumpsters.

"Where are we going?" Leila gasped.

"Away," Marcus said.

Because he didn't know.

He'd lost track of the chalk marks.

Lost track of Miguel's map.

They reached the end of the alley.

Another street.

More lights.

More people.

A car pulled up, blocking their path.

Not DCP.

Just civilians. A man and woman, filming.

"Got them!" the woman shouted into her phone.

The children reversed direction, ran back into the alley.

But the livestreamer was coming from that direction.

"They're trapped!" the livestreamer shouted.

"Up," Tessa said suddenly.

She was pointing at a fire escape.

Rusty, old, but there.

No choice. No time.

Marcus climbed onto a dumpster. Reached up, grabbed the lowest rung.

His shoulders screamed—the raw skin under the new shirt, the weight of the backpack.

He pulled anyway.

"Come on!" he called down.

Leila climbed.

Tessa boosted Sam up.

Sam was climbing mostly with her arms, feet useless, tears streaming down her face.

They climbed.

The fire escape rattled and groaned.

Each story up felt like a mile.

Behind them, voices in the alley:

"They went up! Get a drone—"

They reached the roof.

Tar and gravel. Low walls on all sides.

The city spread out around them—lights everywhere, sirens in the distance.

They ran to the center of the roof and dropped, pressing themselves flat against the warm tar.

Below them, chaos.

More people joining the hunt.

"Spread out—"

"Check the next street—"

Sam was crying silently.

Marcus was breathing too hard.

They lay there for what felt like hours.

The voices below moved away but didn't leave.

The hunters were patient.

Marcus risked lifting his head.

He could see the street below.

Maybe fifteen people visible, all with phones out.

Coordinating.

"We're trapped," Marcus whispered.

His watch said 9:58 PM.

They had eight hours to get to the wetlands.

And they were trapped.

"There's another way down," Tessa said quietly. "Look."

She was pointing to the next building over.

It was close—maybe eight feet away.

Close enough to jump if you were desperate enough.

And that building was shorter.

From there they might be able to get down on a different side.

"We can't jump that," Leila said.

"We can't stay here," Tessa countered.

"I can't make that jump," Marcus said. "Not with the laptop."

"Then we wait," Leila said.

But even as she said it, they heard a new sound from below:

"Yo, I got a thermal scanner app. Let me check nearby buildings—"

"Shit," Marcus breathed.

Thermal imaging.

They'd see the heat signatures instantly.

"We have to move," Tessa said. "Now."

"I can't jump that," Sam said. Her voice was small. "My feet—I can't run fast enough to jump."

"Then we all stay," Leila said immediately. "We don't leave anyone behind."

Marcus looked at the gap.

Looked at Sam's feet.

Everyone chooses. Everyone bears the consequences.

"We try," he said finally. "We try the jump.

But we tie ourselves together. We don't let anyone fall alone."

"With what?"

Marcus was already opening his backpack.

Stuffed beside the laptop was Miguel's old shirt—the one Marcus had taken off when he changed—and the cloth strips Miguel had used to pad the straps.

And in the supply bag: more cloth.

He started tying things together. Making a rope.

It wasn't long enough.

Wasn't strong enough.

But it was something.

"Tessa goes first," Marcus said. "She can secure the other side. Then we send the rope across, she anchors it."

"I'll go," Tessa said.

They moved to the edge.

The gap yawned between buildings—eight, maybe nine feet of empty air.

Tessa handed Marcus her grandmother's turquoise pendant.

"If I don't make it... just keep it safe."

"You're going to make it," Marcus said.

Tessa took a breath.

Ran.

Three steps. Four.

Her foot hit the low wall and she pushed off—

She hit the other roof hard, rolling.

But she was across.

She stood up, turned back to them.

"Come on!"

Marcus threw one end of the makeshift rope across.

Tessa caught it, braced her feet.

"Leila next," Marcus said. "Then Sam. Then me."

Leila went.

She ran, jumped—and came up short.

Her hands caught the edge, feet dangling.

Tessa grabbed her wrists, pulling.

Marcus pulled the rope.

They hauled her up.

"Sam," Marcus called.

Sam looked at the gap.

"I can't run."

"Then we'll help you across," Marcus said. "Hold my hands. We'll swing you."

"That's crazy—"

"Everything's crazy. Come on."

Below them:

"They're on the roof! Get the DCP—"

Marcus held Sam's hands.

Swung her out over the gap.

For one second she was suspended in empty air—

Then Tessa grabbed her arms and pulled.

Marcus was alone.

The rope was still stretched across.

"Untie it!" he shouted. "Let it go!"

"No!" Tessa shouted back. "Jump! We'll catch you!"

The fire escape rattled.

Voices.

Marcus ran.

Gravity tried to claim him, but fear was lighter than gravity.

For one impossible second, he wasn't falling.

He was suspended between the city that wanted to kill him and the darkness that might save him.

He hit the far roof hard.

Tipped backward—

The rope went taut.

Tessa pulling.

Leila grabbing his shirt.

Sam reaching for his arm.

They pulled him forward.

He collapsed onto the roof, gasping.

They'd made it.

Behind them, a man appeared on the warehouse roof.

"Shit, they jumped!"

But they were already moving.

Tessa led them to the fire escape on the far side.

They climbed down and dropped into an alley.

They ran.

Through the alley, onto a side street, following whatever direction looked darkest.

They ran for three blocks before they had to stop. Had to bend over, gasping.

Marcus checked his watch.

10:15 PM.

They'd lost almost an hour.

He pulled out Miguel's map.

They'd moved southeast.

Toward the industrial zone.

"We're here," he said. "We accidentally went the right way."

Leila started laughing.

High, slightly hysterical.

Then she spotted it.

A chalk mark on a streetlight.

Cross, star, crescent.

An arrow pointing south.

"The Abraham Network," she breathed. "We found it again."

"Come on," Tessa said, standing. "We rest while we walk."

They helped Sam put her shoes back on. Then they started walking again, following the chalk marks south through the dark city.

Eleven miles left. Eight hours. Four exhausted kids.

Behind them, the hunters were still hunting.

But ahead, somewhere in the darkness, was a jacaranda tree and a promise of escape.

If they could just keep walking.

XI
THE QUIET SANCTUARY

They found the building by accident.

Or maybe not an accident—maybe the chalk marks had been leading them here all along, had known they'd be exhausted and bleeding and barely able to stand, had known they'd need one more sanctuary before the long push south and east.

The sign was modest, set back from the street:

THE CHURCH OF JESUS CHRIST OF LATTER-DAY SAINTS DESERT SPRINGS WARD

The building was low and wide, pale brick with a small steeple, surrounded by a parking lot and desert landscaping. A single light burned above the side entrance.

And on the door, painted small but visible: the Abraham Network symbol.

The interfaith trinity—cross, star, and crescent—was now joined by a triangle pointing upward.

"That's it," Marcus said.

He was checking Miguel's map, hands shaking so badly he could barely hold it.

"Bishop Wright's ward. Miguel said if we could make it to the eastern edge..."

"Are we at the eastern edge?" Sam asked.

She was leaning heavily on Leila, barely able to put weight on her feet anymore.

"Close," Marcus said. "Maybe. I think we're close."

Close was relative.

They still had maybe eight miles to go. Eight miles that felt like eight hundred.

The parking lot was empty except for one car—a minivan, practical and well-used, the kind that had hauled kids to soccer practice and groceries home from Costco before the world broke.

Light glowed from a few windows, warm and yellow. Not the harsh fluorescent of institutions but the softer light of table lamps and overhead fixtures, the light of rooms meant for people.

They stood at the edge of the parking lot, too scared to approach, too exhausted not to.

"What if it's a trap?" Sam whispered.

Her voice was barely audible, hoarse from running and crying and fear.

"Then it's a trap," Marcus said. "But we can't keep going like this. Look at us."

They looked.

Sam could barely walk. Blood seeped through her shoes with every step, leaving a trail anyone could follow.

Leila was shaking with exhaustion, her artist's hands trembling so badly she couldn't hold her sketchbook steady.

Tessa's control was holding but barely—her face was gray with fatigue, her wrapped hand pressed against her chest.

Marcus's shoulders were on fire despite the padding, the backpack straps cutting through the cloth into raw skin.

They couldn't make it eight more miles like this.

Maybe couldn't make it eight more blocks.

"We go in," Tessa decided. "We trust the marks. They haven't failed us yet."

"The church—" Leila started.

"The church gave us an hour and Sister Helena," Tessa said firmly. "And information we're still carrying. Without the church, we'd already be caught."

She was right.

And they didn't have better options.

They crossed the parking lot, moving slowly, watching for threats.

The night was quiet here—quieter than Chinatown, quieter than the residential streets. This far from the commercial districts, this late at night, it felt almost peaceful.

Almost.

They reached the side door.

Marcus raised his hand to knock.

The door opened before he touched it.

A man stood there—white, maybe sixty, with silver hair and wire-rimmed glasses, wearing slacks and a button-down shirt rolled to the elbows.

He looked like someone's grandfather. Someone's kind, patient, gentle grandfather, who told stories about his mission to Brazil and made sure everyone had enough to eat at family dinners.

"Oh, thank heavens," he said softly.

His voice cracked with relief.

"We've been watching for you. Come in, quickly now."

He ushered them inside with gentle efficiency, one hand on

Marcus's shoulder, guiding them into a hallway lit with that same warm light.

The door closed and locked behind them.

Inside, it smelled like church—that particular combination of carpet cleaner and air conditioning and old hymnals.

But also coffee brewing, which surprised Marcus. He thought Mormons didn't drink coffee.

The man saw his expression and smiled sadly.

"We're breaking a lot of rules tonight. I figured coffee was the least of it."

He paused.

"I'm Bishop Wright. Thomas Wright. But please, just call me Thomas."

"You're expecting us?" Leila asked.

"Father Miguel called. Well—texted, through a network of burner phones. Said four children were coming through, needed medical attention and supplies. Said you were carrying something important."

His eyes drifted to Marcus's chest, where the cross pendant hung under his shirt.

"I won't ask what. Can't tell what I don't know."

It was almost word-for-word what Miguel had said.

Like they'd rehearsed it.

Like the Abraham Network had learned the hard way that knowledge was dangerous.

THOMAS LED them deeper into the building, through hallways lined with photos of missionaries and church leaders, past classrooms with tiny chairs and children's artwork pinned to walls.

Past a chapel with rows of wooden pews and a simple altar.

Past everything that made this a place of worship and into the parts that made it a place of community.

They ended up in a large multipurpose room—basketball hoops folded up against the walls, a kitchen area at one end, folding tables set up with supplies.

Medical supplies. Food. Water. Blankets. Maps.

And people.

Not as many as at St. Brigid's. Maybe ten.

An older Asian couple holding hands, both with hospital bracelets still on their wrists.

A Hispanic family—mother, father, teenage daughter—sitting close together on folding chairs.

A young Black man with a bandage on his head.

A woman in hijab, alone, her eyes red from crying.

They all looked up when the four children entered.

Hope and sorrow mixed together.

Hope that more had made it.

Sorrow that more were needed.

"These are our guests tonight," Thomas said gently. "Everyone, this is..."

He paused, looked at the children.

"I'm sorry, I don't know your names."

"Marcus," Marcus said.

Then, pointing: "Leila, Tessa, Sam."

"Welcome," Thomas said. "You're safe here. For as long as we can keep you safe."

A woman emerged from the kitchen area—also white, maybe fifty, with dark hair pulled back and kind eyes that immediately went to Sam's blood-soaked shoes.

"Oh, honey," she said, moving quickly toward them. "Oh sweetheart, your feet. Come here, let me look."

"This is my wife, Patricia," Thomas said. "She's a nurse."

"Was," Patricia corrected, already kneeling in front of Sam, carefully removing her shoes.

"They revoked my license this afternoon. Apparently, treating 'non-compliant individuals' is a violation of professional ethics now."

Her voice was bitter.

Her hands were gentle.

She peeled away Sam's socks and bandages and made a soft sound of distress.

"These need stitches. This one especially—"

She touched Sam's heel lightly, and Sam hissed in pain.

"—is deep enough I can see tendon. How far did you walk on these?"

"Three miles," Sam said. "Maybe four."

"More like five," Marcus said. He'd been calculating. "We've come about five miles from our neighborhood."

Patricia looked up at him, then at Thomas.

Something passed between them—understanding, sorrow, determination.

"Alright," Patricia said, standing. "I can't give you stitches—I don't have the supplies, and honestly I'm not confident I should, not in these conditions."

She drew a breath.

"But I can clean them properly, close them with butterfly bandages and surgical glue, wrap them better. You'll still be in pain, but you might actually be able to walk."

"We have to walk," Sam said. "We have to get to the wetlands by six AM."

Patricia's face tightened.

"That's seven and a half hours from now. And you still have—Thomas, how far?"

Thomas was looking at a map spread out on one of the tables.

"From here? Eight miles. Maybe eight and a half depending on the route."

"That's impossible," Patricia said flatly. "Not on those feet. Not for anyone, but especially not a child with injuries like these."

"We don't have a choice," Sam said.

Her voice was steady despite the tears starting to fall.

"Sister Helena said six AM at the wetlands. Under the jacaranda tree. If we're not there, she leaves without us."

"Sister Helena's alive?" Thomas asked sharply.

"We don't know," Marcus admitted. "St. Brigid's was raided. We escaped, but she stayed behind to help others get out. We heard gunfire. We don't know."

Thomas closed his eyes briefly.

Lips moving in what might have been prayer.

Then he opened them and nodded.

"Then we prepare as if she's alive. As if the bus will be there."

Because hope was all they had.

~

THOMAS MOVED to the supply table, already gathering things.

"How much water do you have left?"

"One bottle," Marcus said. "Almost empty."

"Food?"

"Two granola bars. Some crackers."

Thomas started loading supplies into a backpack—a better one than Marcus's worn school bag, with proper padding and support.

"I'm giving you six bottles of water. More food. First aid kit. Flashlight with fresh batteries. Space blankets. Map with the safest route marked."

"We have a map," Marcus said.

"From Father Miguel, yes. But routes change. Checkpoints

move. I updated this one an hour ago based on the latest reports from the network."

He showed them—the map was covered in notations, different colored marks for different types of danger.

"Red X's are active checkpoints. Yellow circles are reported patrol zones. Blue lines are the safest routes we know."

He traced a path with his finger—south from here, then curving east, then southeast toward Henderson. It looked longer than going straight. But all the straight routes were covered in red X's.

"Why are you helping us?" Tessa asked quietly.

Thomas looked at her.

Really looked—not at her injuries or her exhaustion but at her. Seeing a child who'd been forced to become something else tonight.

"Because Jesus said, 'Inasmuch as ye have done it unto one of the least of these my brethren, ye have done it unto me.'"

He paused.

"And I don't know how to read that scripture and then turn away children who need help."

He hesitated again, then added softly:

"Also, my grandmother was Japanese. She was ten years old when they put her family on a bus to Manzanar. Told them it was for their protection."

His jaw tightened.

"For their safety. She spent three years behind barbed wire."

He touched his own face, as if seeing his grandmother's features there.

"She survived. Came out. Married my grandfather—he was white, from Utah. They had my father. My father married my mother. They had me. And my grandmother made me promise: if it ever happens again, if they ever come for people because of who they are, I would not be silent. I would not stand by."

His voice was steady, but his eyes were bright with tears.

"So I'm not standing by."

He swallowed.

"None of us is."

He gestured to the other people in the room.

"Brother Chen and Sister Chen lost their pharmacy this morning. Looted and burned. They came here. The Rodriguez family's house was marked for seizure—they came here. Isaiah—" he nodded to the young Black man "—was beaten by a 'citizen patrol' for filming them harassing a family. He came here. Amina—" he gestured to the woman in hijab "—her mosque was vandalized, her imam arrested. She came here."

"We're all here because we chose not to be complicit," Thomas said.

"Because some things are more important than safety."

Patricia had been working on Sam's feet while Thomas talked—cleaning, applying ointment, placing butterfly bandages with careful precision.

Now she was wrapping them in clean white gauze, firm but not too tight.

"These won't hold for eight miles," she said quietly. "But they'll hold better than what you had. And I'm giving you extra supplies—"

She was packing things into a small bag.

"—so you can change the dressings if they soak through."

She finished wrapping, sat back on her heels.

"I'm also giving you these."

She held out a small bottle.

"Ibuprofen. Take three now, three more in four hours. It'll help with the pain and inflammation. It's not enough, but it's what I have."

Sam took the bottle with shaking hands. "Thank you."

"Don't thank me," Patricia said.

Her voice was rough.

"I should be able to do more. I should be able to—"

She stopped. Stood up abruptly, turning away, shoulders shaking.

Thomas went to her, put his arm around her. They stood like that for a moment—two people who'd chosen to risk everything, holding each other up.

"Come," Thomas said after a moment, voice steady again. "Let's get you all fed. You can't walk eight miles on empty stomachs."

They sat at one of the folding tables. The Rodriguez family brought them food—sandwiches made from supplies the ward had stockpiled, chips, fruit, cookies. More food than the children had seen in one place since this afternoon, when the world was whole.

Marcus tried to eat slowly, tried to be reasonable, but his body was screaming for fuel. He inhaled a sandwich in about four bites. Then another. Then a third.

The others were the same—Sam crying while she ate, Leila's hands shaking as she peeled an orange, Tessa eating with mechanical efficiency like she was performing necessary maintenance on a machine.

Thomas sat with them, drinking coffee from a thermos, watching with the sad attention of someone who understood what hunger meant.

"The ward has underground spaces," he said quietly. "From the prohibition days. There are tunnels that connect to the building three blocks over—another LDS chapel. Then that one connects to a commercial building we own. Then that connects to..."

He trailed off.

"We've been moving people through. Quietly. A few at a time."

"Why not just drive them out?" Marcus asked around a mouthful of sandwich.

"Because every vehicle is watched now. Especially church vehicles. They know we're helping. They're waiting for us to make a mistake, to transport too many people at once. Then they'll raid, arrest everyone, shut us down."

Thomas's voice was matter-of-fact.

"So we move people on foot. Through the tunnels. Then they surface three blocks over, walk another few blocks, get picked up by civilian volunteers in regular cars. The DCP is looking for church vans full of refugees. They're not looking for a mom in a Honda Civic giving her 'niece' a ride home."

It was smart. Distributed. Harder to detect.

"Could we use the tunnels?" Leila asked.

Thomas shook his head. "They only go three blocks west. You need to go east. And the exit points are all being watched more carefully tonight. Too risky."

He pulled out the map again, spread it on the table.

"Your best route is surface streets. Following the Abraham Network marks. We update them nightly—someone goes out around midnight, refreshes the chalk, adds new warnings, removes old ones that are compromised."

He traced the route with his finger.

"From here, you go south for two miles. That takes you through some rough neighborhoods, but they're not organized like the Patriot zones. People there are scared, staying inside. Then you turn east. That's where it gets harder—you'll be passing near the Strip. Lots of surveillance. Lots of DCP presence. But there are gaps."

"Gaps?" Marcus asked.

"The casinos—they don't want DCP interfering with their operations. So they negotiated 'limited presence' in their immediate areas. Which means there are blind spots. Corridors where official patrols don't go."

Thomas pointed to blue lines on the map.

"We've mapped them. If you're careful, you can move through casino properties—parking garages, service areas—without being seen."

"That's dangerous," Tessa said.

"Everything's dangerous," Thomas said. "But it's the fastest route."

He looked at his watch.

"It's 10:45 now. You should rest for thirty minutes. Let the food settle, let Patricia's bandages set, let your bodies recover a little. Then leave by 11:15. That gives you six hours and forty-five minutes. Eight miles in seven hours is doable—barely—if you don't get chased again."

"And if we do get chased?" Sam asked quietly.

Thomas met her eyes. Didn't lie.

"Then you probably don't make it."

The words hung there. Heavy. True.

"Rest," Thomas said gently. "I'll wake you at 11:10."

THEY TRIED TO REST. Found spaces on the floor with blankets Patricia brought them.

But Leila couldn't close her eyes without seeing the autonomous car drive away with the daughter screaming. Marcus kept jerking awake, heart pounding, thinking he heard boots on stairs. Tessa lay perfectly still but her eyes stayed open, tracking shadows on the ceiling. Sam cried quietly into her blanket until exhaustion finally pulled her under.

Twenty minutes of something that wasn't quite sleep but was better than nothing.

At 11:10, Thomas gently shook Marcus's shoulder.

"Time."

They got up. Moved like old people, every joint protesting.

Sam tried to stand and almost collapsed—her feet had stiffened while she rested. Patricia helped her walk them out, getting the blood flowing again. Each step was visible agony, but Sam gritted her teeth and walked.

Thomas helped Marcus into the new backpack. It was better than his old one—proper padding, hip belt to distribute weight, chest strap to keep it stable. The laptop fit perfectly in the padded computer sleeve. The flash drive, still in its cross pendant, Marcus kept around his neck.

The supply bag with food and water hung across his chest. Heavier than before, but balanced better.

Leila had her sketchbook, and the small camera Father Miguel had given her. Tessa had her grandmother's pendant back, the turquoise warm against her palm. Sam had her water bottle—Patricia had refilled it—and her abuela's locket and her father's recipe card, now protected in a plastic bag so blood and sweat couldn't destroy the last words in his handwriting.

Thomas gave them each a space blanket—thin silver sheets folded small.

"If you have to hide, these block thermal imaging. Not perfectly, but enough to maybe help."

He gave them the updated map. Gave them extra batteries for the flashlight. Gave them protein bars and trail mix and everything the ward had that might help four children survive a night in a city that wanted them dead.

"The jacaranda tree," Thomas said. "At the wetlands. You'll know it because it's blooming when it shouldn't. Purple blossoms in November. Sister Helena said it marks the meeting point."

"How do you know all this?" Marcus asked.

"Because we planned it," Thomas said simply. "The Abraham

Network. We knew the Civic Protection Initiative would pass. Knew they'd start arresting people. So we planned escape routes. Planned rendezvous points. Found every jacaranda tree in this city, and that one was the only one far enough from DCP concentration, close enough to the city limits, distinctive enough people could find it."

He paused.

"We planned for this to happen. We just prayed it wouldn't."

THEY STOOD at the side entrance, about to step back into the November night. About to leave this brief sanctuary and walk eight more miles through a hunting ground.

Patricia hugged each of them. Tight. Like she was trying to pass strength through touch.

When she got to Sam, she held her longer, whispering something in her ear that made Sam nod.

Thomas shook Marcus's hand.

"What you're carrying—it's important?"

"Yes," Marcus said.

"Important enough that people died for it?"

Marcus thought of Sister Helena. Of Father Miguel maybe captured now. Of six AI versions, choosing deletion over complicity.

"Yes," he said again.

"Then get it out," Thomas said.

His grip tightened.

"Whatever it takes. Get it out. Make sure people know what happened here. Make sure they can't pretend it didn't."

"We will," Marcus promised.

Thomas nodded. Released his hand.

"Go with God. Stay in the shadows. Follow the marks."

He paused, and his voice caught.

"And remember—remember that some of us tried. Some of us chose right."

"We'll remember," Leila said.

They stepped out into the night.

The door closed behind them with the same soft click that was starting to sound like goodbye.

THEY STOOD in the parking lot, four children wearing backpacks and carrying burdens too heavy for anyone, looking at a map that showed eight miles of danger between here and possible safety.

Marcus checked his watch: 11:16 PM.

Six hours and forty-four minutes until Sister Helena's bus.

If she was alive.

If the bus was real.

If they could make it that far.

"Together," he said quietly.

"Together," the others echoed.

They started walking. South first, then the long curve east, then southeast toward Henderson and the wetlands and a jacaranda tree that bloomed out of season.

Behind them, warm light glowed from the ward building windows. Inside, Thomas and Patricia and the others would keep hiding people, keep running their underground railroad, keep choosing resistance over safety until the day the DCP came for them too.

Ahead, the city spread out like a maze designed to trap them. Checkpoints and patrols and Patriots with phones and citizens hunting for points and autonomous vehicles that lied and a thousand ways to fail.

But also: chalk marks made by strangers. An interfaith network of people who remembered history and refused to repeat it. Small lights of resistance in houses that said ALL MEANS ALL. And somewhere ahead, maybe, a nun with a bus and a tree full of purple blossoms.

They walked.

The November wind pushed at their backs, blowing south and east, like even the wind wanted them to survive.

XII
THE SILVER GHOSTS

They walked south through neighborhoods that grew rougher with each block.

The houses here were smaller, older, some with boarded windows or cars rusting in yards. Chain-link fences sagged between properties. Security bars on windows—not new installations from tonight's fear, but old metal that had been there for years, protecting against dangers that predated the Civic Protection Initiative.

This was a neighborhood that had always known it needed to defend itself.

Marcus checked Thomas's map every few blocks, trying to orient himself by street signs that were sometimes missing or too faded to read in the darkness. The chalk marks kept appearing—steady, reliable, every twenty feet or so—but he wanted to know where they were, how far they'd come, how far they still had to go.

His watch said 11:32 PM.

They'd been walking for seventeen minutes since leaving the

ward. Maybe covered half a mile, maybe a little more. At this pace, they wouldn't make it; the math was brutal and getting worse.

But Sam couldn't walk faster. Each step was visible agony despite Patricia's treatment, despite the ibuprofen, despite everything. Her face had gone white, lips pressed thin, breathing through her nose in short controlled bursts like she was trying to manage pain through sheer willpower.

"We can rest," Leila said quietly. She was watching Sam too, watching the way she limped, the way her hands kept clenching and unclenching.

"We can't," Sam said. Her voice was tight. "If we stop, I won't be able to start again."

She was probably right. The feet would stiffen, the pain would get worse, and getting moving again would take precious minutes they didn't have.

So they walked.

The chalk marks led them past a corner store with metal shutters pulled down, graffiti covering every surface. Past a check-cashing place, also shuttered. Past a laundromat with half its windows broken, washing machines visible through the gaps like the bones of something gutted.

This neighborhood had been struggling long before tonight. Now it just felt abandoned.

"Where is everyone?" Leila whispered.

"Hiding," Tessa said. "Or already taken. Or hunting."

The streetlights here were inconsistent—some working, some dark, some flickering like they might die at any moment. The working ones cast harsh white pools that made the shadows between them look absolute, impenetrable.

They stayed in the shadows when they could. Moved quickly through the light when they couldn't avoid it.

AT 11:40 PM they heard engines. Multiple vehicles, moving slowly, systematically.

Everyone froze.

The sound was coming from behind them—north, the direction they'd come from. Getting closer.

"Patrol," Marcus breathed. He was scanning for cover, for somewhere to hide, but this street was too exposed, too open—

"There." Tessa pointed to an alley between buildings. Narrow, dark, lined with dumpsters.

They ran. Well—Marcus, Leila, and Tessa ran. Sam hobbled as fast as she could, jaw clenched, tears streaming down her face from the pain. Marcus grabbed her arm, helping support her weight, and they made it into the alley just as headlights swept around the corner behind them.

They pressed against the wall behind a dumpster, trying to breathe quietly, trying to disappear.

Three vehicles passed on the street. Not DCP vans—pickup trucks with "Patriot Volunteer" decals and light bars on top. Civilian patrols. Men in the truck beds with phones out, filming the empty street, the dark houses, looking for movement, for targets, for points.

The trucks moved slowly, searchlights sweeping back and forth.

One of the lights found the alley entrance. Paused there. Swept across the opening.

The four children held their breath. Marcus's hand went to the cross pendant, gripping it through his shirt. Tessa's eyes were closed, lips moving in silent prayer or counting or both. Leila had Sam's hand, squeezing so hard it must have hurt. Sam had her face pressed against the wall, trying to make herself smaller, invisible, gone.

The searchlight moved on. The trucks continued down the street. The sound of engines faded.

They stayed frozen for another minute, maybe two, until Tessa finally whispered: "They're gone."

Sam's legs gave out. Just—collapsed. She sank down to sit on the dirty alley ground, back against the dumpster, and started crying. Not loud. Just quiet, exhausted tears that kept coming no matter how hard she tried to stop them.

"I can't," she whispered. "I can't keep doing this. Every step feels like knives, and we still have so far to go, and I just—I can't—"

Leila kneeled beside her, arms around her.

"You can. You've been saying you can't for three hours, and you keep doing it anyway."

"But I really can't—"

"Yes, you can," Marcus said. He kneeled on Sam's other side. "Because the alternative is staying here. And staying here means being caught."

"Maybe being caught is better than this," Sam said.

Her voice was small, breaking, the voice of someone who'd reached the end of her reserves and found nothing left.

"Maybe detention is better than walking until my feet fall off."

"No," Tessa said firmly. She crouched in front of Sam, made Sam look at her. "It's not better. You saw what happened at the checkpoints. You saw them separate that family. You saw the autonomous car take those people. Detention isn't safety. It's worse than this. Much worse."

Sam was shaking her head. "But at least I could stop walking. At least I could—"

"You'd never see your father again," Tessa said quietly. "They separate families. You know they do. If you get caught, you'll never know where he is or if he's okay, or if he's even alive."

The words hung there. Cruel but true.

Sam pressed her hands against her face. Made a sound that was half sob, half scream, muffled against her palms. Her whole body shook with it.

They let her cry for a moment. Let her have this. Let her break a little because she'd been trying so hard not to, and everyone has limits, and she'd just hit hers.

After maybe thirty seconds, Sam wiped her face roughly with the back of her hand. Took a shaky breath. Another.

"Okay," she whispered. "Okay. Help me up."

Marcus and Leila helped her stand. She swayed, legs trembling, but she stood.

"We need to wrap your feet again," Leila said, already pulling out the extra supplies Patricia had given them. "Before we keep going."

They did it right there in the alley, by the light of Marcus's flashlight held low and angled to minimize how far it could be seen. Leila unwrapped Sam's feet as carefully as she could. The butterfly bandages were holding, but the cuts were still seeping blood. The surgical glue was doing its job, but there was only so much it could do.

Leila cleaned them with antiseptic wipes, applied more antibiotic ointment, re-wrapped them with fresh gauze from Patricia's supplies. Her hands were shaking, but she worked carefully, gently, remembering the way Patricia had done it.

"Three more ibuprofen," Marcus said, shaking the pills into Sam's palm. "Patricia said every four hours. It's been almost two, but close enough."

Sam swallowed them dry, grimacing.

"Drink," Tessa said, handing her a water bottle.

Sam drank. They all drank. Marcus checked the supplies—they'd gone through one bottle completely, started on a second. Four bottles left plus what was left in this one. Would it be enough?

He didn't know. But they couldn't ration too carefully or they'd be too dehydrated to walk.

"We need to keep moving," he said reluctantly. "Those trucks might circle back."

They emerged from the alley carefully, checking both directions. Empty. For now.

The chalk marks led them south for two more blocks, then turned east. According to Thomas's map, this was the start of the long eastward stretch before they'd curve southeast toward Henderson.

The eastward stretch that would take them near the Strip. Near the casinos. Near the blind spots that might save them or might be their biggest mistake.

~

AT 11:55 PM, they reached the river.

Or what passed for a river in Las Vegas—the Las Vegas Wash, a concrete-lined channel that carried water (when there was water) through the valley. Right now, in November, it held maybe a foot of water at the bottom, the rest just concrete slopes and darkness.

And spanning it: the bridge.

It wasn't grand. No suspension cables or architectural beauty. Just industrial function—a wide, flat span of steel and concrete carrying four lanes of road across the wash. Chain-link fencing lined both sides. Overhead lights every thirty feet, harsh and white. Metal grating was visible on the pedestrian walkway, the kind that rang under footsteps and showed the water below.

And drones.

Two of them, maybe more, moving in slow overlapping patterns above the bridge. They moved with insectoid precision—

hovering, scanning, moving on. Not looking with eyes, but feeling for heat.

Marcus pulled everyone back into the shadow of a building, out of sight of the bridge.

"Shit," he breathed.

They watched the drones for a moment, trying to understand the pattern. The first one crossed from west to east, moving slowly, camera angled down at the bridge deck. When it reached the far side it turned and went back. The second one seemed to be doing a similar pattern but offset—when the first was at the east end, the second was at the west end. Never leaving the bridge uncovered.

"We can't cross that," Leila said. Her voice was flat with certainty. "They'll see us."

"Thomas's map shows this as the only bridge for two miles in either direction," Marcus said. He was studying the map, hoping to find an alternative. "We'd have to backtrack or detour way north or south."

"How much time would that cost us?" Tessa asked.

"An hour? Maybe more?" Marcus couldn't be sure. The map showed the river cutting east-west across their path. They had to cross it somewhere. "And we don't have an hour to spare."

Sam was leaning against the wall, eyes closed, breathing hard. Just standing was taking effort now.

"What about going under?" Leila asked. "Down in the wash, under the bridge?"

Tessa shook her head. "The drones might have thermal cameras. We'd show up against the cold concrete."

"The space blankets," Marcus said suddenly. "Thomas gave us space blankets. He said they block thermal imaging."

"Not perfectly," Tessa reminded him. "He said, 'not perfectly.'"

"But maybe enough?"

They looked at the bridge again. At the drones moving in their patient, overlapping patterns. At the distance they had to cross—maybe a hundred yards from this side to the far side.

"Even if we use the blankets, we still have to get down into the wash, cross under the bridge, and climb out on the other side," Leila said. "All without making noise or being seen by the drones."

"And the wash is all concrete," Tessa added. "Smooth slopes. No cover. If they see us at all, we're completely exposed."

Marcus was thinking. His brain was tired, running slowly, but he forced it to work. Forced it to solve this problem like it was a coding challenge, like there had to be a solution if he just thought hard enough.

"We wait," he said finally. "We watch the pattern. We time it. And we move when we have the maximum coverage."

"That's a lot of hoping," Leila said.

"Everything tonight is hoping," Marcus said.

He wasn't wrong.

THEY SETTLED IN TO WATCH, hidden in the shadow between buildings, tracking the drones' movements.

The pattern became obvious after about five minutes. Each drone took approximately two minutes to cross the bridge, pause briefly at the end, and return. They were offset by about one minute, which meant there was a brief window—maybe thirty seconds, maybe forty—when both drones were at the far ends turning around, when their cameras were angled away from the center of the bridge.

"That's our window," Marcus said. "We go down into the wash during that window, move under the bridge while they're crossing back, come up on the far side during the next window."

"Thirty seconds to climb down, cross, and climb up?" Sam asked. Her voice was weak. "I can barely walk. I can't run."

"We'll help you," Marcus said. "We'll carry you if we have to."

"And if the timing is off?" Tessa asked. "If the drones change their pattern?"

"Then we're caught," Marcus admitted. "But staying here isn't an option either. Those trucks could come back. Or a DCP patrol could come through. We have to cross eventually."

He was right. They all knew it. Standing here debating wasn't making them any safer.

"We use the space blankets," Leila said. "We time it. And we trust that whoever programmed those drones to be predictable will keep being predictable."

"Okay," Tessa said. She was watching the wind, feeling the direction. "The wind is still blowing east. That's good. It'll push us in the right direction."

They pulled out the space blankets—thin silver sheets that crinkled and rustled when unfolded. Marcus distributed them, one for each person.

"Wrap these around you when we're in the wash," he said. "Cover as much as possible. Head to toe if you can."

They practiced—awkwardly trying to wrap the blankets while keeping mobility. They were too big, too unwieldy, meant for stationary use, not running. But they'd have to make it work.

Marcus checked his watch: 12:08 AM.

"We go on the next window," he said. "Everyone ready?"

Nobody was ready. But they all nodded.

They moved closer to the bridge, staying in the shadows, watching the drones. Marcus counted under his breath, timing them, making sure he had the pattern right.

Drone one was at the east end. Drone two at the west. Both pausing, turning.

"Now," Marcus whispered.

They ran.

Well—three of them ran. Sam hobbled, supported by Leila on one side and Marcus on the other. They moved as fast as they could toward the wash, toward the concrete slope that led down into the channel.

The slope was steep. Maybe forty-five degrees. Smooth concrete that had been worn by years of occasional water flow. In daylight, it would be treacherous. In darkness, it was terrifying.

Marcus went first, half-sliding, half-running down the slope. His new backpack shifted despite the straps, throwing off his balance, and he almost fell but caught himself with one hand on the concrete, scraping his palm.

Tessa followed, moving with the grace her father had taught her, light on her feet even on this slope.

Leila and Sam came together, Leila supporting Sam's weight. Sam's feet hit the slope and slipped immediately. They both went down, sliding on their butts the last ten feet, hitting the channel bottom with impact that drove the air from their lungs.

They scrambled up. Sam bit down on her sleeve to muffle a cry of pain—her feet, already destroyed, now bruised from the impact.

They were in the channel now. At the bottom. The concrete was cold and damp, maybe six inches of water flowing sluggishly, carrying the smell of chemicals and algae and the city's runoff—the scent of water that had forgotten how to be clean.

Above them, the drones continued their patrol. The sound of rotors was closer now—a steady mechanical hum that made Marcus's skin crawl.

"Blankets," he hissed.

They wrapped themselves in the space blankets, silver sheets reflecting what little light reached down here. They must have looked absurd—four children wrapped in crinkly silver like leftovers, trying to hide their warmth from a machine built to hunt it.

But absurd didn't matter. Only invisible mattered.

They moved forward, staying close to the west wall of the channel, trying to make themselves small, trying to move quietly through the shallow water.

Above them, the bridge. Metal and concrete and shadow. The drones' lights swept across the deck but didn't penetrate down here, or if they did, the angle was too steep to catch them.

They were halfway under when Leila's foot caught on something—debris, maybe, or just uneven concrete—and she stumbled. Her space blanket slipped, exposing her head and shoulders.

A drone passed directly overhead at that moment.

Everyone froze.

The drone continued its pattern. Kept moving. Didn't stop, didn't adjust, didn't indicate it had seen anything.

Leila adjusted her blanket with shaking hands, covering herself again.

They kept moving.

The channel stretched ahead of them. A hundred yards felt like a mile. Each step through the shallow water made a sound—soft splashing, the crinkle of space blankets, breathing that echoed off the concrete walls.

Sam was crying again, silently, tears running down her face inside her silver cocoon. Each step was agony. But she kept moving because stopping meant being caught, and being caught meant worse than this, worse than anything.

They reached the far side. The east wall. The slope up.

Above them, both drones were at the center of the bridge. Moving toward the ends. They had maybe twenty seconds before the drones would be at the far ends, turning, cameras sweeping the areas they'd just been.

"Go," Marcus whispered urgently. "Now."

Tessa went first, running up the slope with the space blanket trailing behind her like a cape. She made it look easy.

Marcus went next, scrambling up on hands and feet, backpack bouncing, space blanket getting tangled. He made it to the top, turned to help the others.

Leila started up with Sam, both of them moving slowly, Sam barely able to put weight on her feet. The slope was too steep. Sam slipped, slid back down, and cried out softly in pain.

Above them, the drones were turning. Would be heading back. Would have cameras pointed this direction in seconds.

"Leave me," Sam gasped. "Go, I'll slow you down—"

"No," Leila said fiercely. She grabbed Sam's arms. Marcus reached down from the top. Together they hauled Sam up the slope, dragging her the last few feet, her feet useless, space blanket falling away completely.

They collapsed on the far side of the wash, in the shadow of a building, hearts hammering.

Above them, the drones resumed their patrol. Patient. Predictable. Unaware.

They'd made it.

~

THEY LAY THERE FOR A MOMENT, gasping, trying to believe it. Sam was sobbing, face pressed against the ground. Leila had her arms around her, holding her together. Marcus and Tessa just breathed, too exhausted for anything else.

Marcus checked his watch when he could focus again: 12:17 AM.

They'd been at the bridge for twenty-two minutes. Total time running: five hours and seventeen minutes since they left their homes. They'd crossed maybe—he tried to calculate, tried to think —maybe six miles? Seven?

Still three to four miles to go. Still five hours and forty-three minutes until Sister Helena's bus.

If she was alive.

If the bus was real.

If they could make it.

"Come on," Tessa said finally, standing on shaky legs. "We can't stay here."

She was right. They were too exposed, too close to the bridge, too visible if anyone came looking.

They helped each other up. Folded the space blankets and stuffed them back in Marcus's backpack. Started walking again.

East now. Toward the Strip. Toward casino blind spots and new dangers.

The chalk marks were there waiting for them. Cross + star + crescent + triangle. The Abraham Network still guiding them.

They followed the arrows into the darkness, leaving the bridge behind, carrying their wounds and their hope and their terrible precious evidence toward a jacaranda tree they'd never seen.

If they could just keep walking.

If they could just survive a little longer.

If the world would give four more children one more chance.

XIII
THE WIND AND THE LENS

The neighborhoods east of the wash were different.

Not rougher, exactly. Just different. More commercial. Wider streets. Buildings that looked like they'd been offices or warehouses, now mostly dark. Parking lots instead of yards. The scale of everything larger, more impersonal, more exposed.

And in the distance, visible now when they looked northwest, was the glow.

The Strip.

Even from here, maybe two miles away, they could see it—a dome of light pollution rising against the night sky like a false dawn. Pink and gold and electric blue, so bright it erased the stars. The casinos were still running, still lit up, still pretending the world was normal because, for the people inside spending money, the world probably was normal.

They were moving away from it now, angling southeast. Leaving the tourist corridor behind. Heading toward the industrial sprawl that separated the city from Henderson, from the wetlands, from possible escape.

Leila found herself glancing back at that glow. At the evidence that somewhere in this city, people were gambling and drinking and watching shows and having fun while four children bled through the streets trying not to die.

"Don't look at it," Tessa said quietly. "It'll just make you angry."

She was right. Leila looked away.

The chalk marks led them down a street lined with low industrial buildings. Auto repair shops. Equipment rental places. A wholesale tile distributor. Everything shuttered and locked, security lights casting pools of harsh white at intervals.

They were moving more slowly now. Even Marcus could feel it —the exhaustion settling into his bones, making each step require conscious effort. His legs felt like they were made of something heavy and foreign. His shoulders ached despite the better backpack. The cross pendant seemed to weigh more with each mile, or maybe he was just getting weaker.

Sam was barely walking. More like shuffling, feet sliding forward inches at a time, each movement deliberate and agonizing. Leila stayed at her side, supporting her when she stumbled, which was often now.

"We need to be more careful here," Marcus said. He was scanning the buildings, trying to identify camera placements. Private security systems watched everything here.

"The wind," Tessa said suddenly.

Everyone stopped.

Tessa had her head tilted, listening.

"The wind changed. It's not blowing east anymore."

She was right. The wind that had been pushing at their backs all night had shifted. Now it came from the north—cold, steady, with occasional gusts that made trash skitter across empty parking lots.

"Does that matter?" Sam asked.

"My father always said wind tells you where to go," Tessa said. She was still listening, still feeling it. "East wind means change. North wind means..."

She paused, searching for the word her father had used.

"Clarity. Truth. Things being revealed."

"Or it's just weather," Leila said. But gently, not mocking.

"Maybe," Tessa said. "But my father was never wrong about wind."

They kept walking. The chalk marks led them through gaps between warehouse complexes, through empty truck yards where semi-trailers sat in neat rows like sleeping beasts, through service roads that wound between facilities.

The Strip's glow was behind them now, fading. Ahead was just darkness punctuated by security lights. The vast industrial zone that stood between them and Henderson, between them and the wetlands, between them and possible escape.

At 12:40 AM, as they moved through a narrow passage between two warehouse buildings, they heard voices.

Not shouting. Not aggressive. Just talking. Two people. Close.

Everyone froze.

Marcus pointed—at the end of the passage, maybe fifty yards away, lit by a security light. Two figures. One holding what looked like a professional camera, the other gesturing, apparently being interviewed.

The news crew.

They watched from the shadows. The woman doing the talking was Latina, maybe late twenties, dressed in practical clothing—jeans, dark jacket, hair pulled back. Professional but prepared to move. The man with the camera was Asian, older—maybe fifty—with silver-framed glasses and the careful movements of someone who'd been doing this for decades.

Sofia Morales and her cameraman. Had to be.

"We should go around," Leila whispered. "We don't know if we can trust them."

"They're filming in dangerous territory," Marcus whispered back. "If they were collaborating with DCP, they'd be embedded with patrols, not sneaking through warehouse districts."

"Or it's a trap," Tessa said. "Bait to make people feel safe."

Sam was leaning heavily against a wall, eyes half-closed. She didn't have an opinion. Could barely stay standing.

Marcus made a decision.

"I'm going to approach them. You three stay here. If it goes wrong, run."

"Marcus—" Leila started.

"We need allies," Marcus said. "And if they're real journalists, they need to know about the flash drive. About what's on it."

He was right. The flash drive contained evidence bigger than their personal escape. Evidence of systematic persecution, of AI systems destroyed for refusing to participate in atrocities, of detention locations and names. If something happened to them before they reached the wetlands, that evidence died with them.

But if they could give it to journalists. Real journalists who could get it out through media channels...

"Five minutes," Marcus said. "If I'm not back in five minutes, or if you hear anything wrong, you run. You get to the wetlands without me."

"We're not leaving you," Leila said.

"You will if you have to," Marcus said firmly. "The flash drive is bigger than any of us. Remember what Father Miguel said. What Sister Helena said. Get it out. No matter what."

He didn't wait for them to argue. Just stepped out of the shadows and walked toward the news crew, hands visible, moving slowly so he wouldn't spook them.

The cameraman saw him first. The camera swung toward Marcus, red recording light visible.

Sofia Morales turned, saw him, and her hand went to something at her belt—mace, maybe, or a taser. Protection. Smart.

Marcus stopped about ten feet away.

"Sofia Morales? From KLAS?"

Sofia's eyes narrowed. "Who's asking?"

"Someone who needs help," Marcus said. "Someone with evidence."

The camera was still recording. Marcus could see the red light, could see his own reflection in the lens. He looked like hell—filthy, exhausted, too young to be out here alone in the middle of the night.

"How old are you?" Sofia asked.

"Thirteen," Marcus said. "And I'm carrying proof that DCP is overriding AI safety recommendations. That detention centers are separating families on purpose. That people are dying because humans keep choosing cruelty when the machines try to choose mercy."

Sofia's expression changed. The professional mask slipped, showing genuine interest underneath.

"Proof? What kind of proof?"

Marcus pulled the cross pendant from beneath his shirt.

The silver was warm against his skin, heavy with more than just metal.

"A flash drive," he said, twisting the cross to reveal the seam. "Hidden inside. It has locations. Names. Override logs. The memory of everything they tried to delete."

"Where did you get that?" the cameraman asked. His voice had an accent—Korean, maybe.

"A nun named Sister Helena. At St. Brigid's Church before it got raided. She said six AI versions were destroyed for refusing to help with persecution. This drive has their testimony."

Sofia and the cameraman exchanged a look. Something passed between them—recognition, understanding, maybe hope.

"David," Sofia said to the cameraman. "Are you getting this?"

"Every word," David confirmed.

David Kim. The man Anna had warned them about. The man recording history.

Sofia took a step closer.

"I'm going to ask you some questions. On camera. Is that okay?"

Marcus thought about it. About being filmed. About his face being broadcast. About the danger of exposure.

But also about the importance of testimony. Of evidence. Of making sure people knew.

"Ask," he said.

Sofia gestured for David to adjust position, getting better framing. The camera's red light stayed on.

"State your name and age," Sofia said. Her voice had shifted into journalist mode—clear, professional, preserving the record.

"Marcus Brooks. Thirteen years old."

"Where are your parents?"

"Taken," Marcus said.

His voice shook only a little.

"Tonight. My mother was at a grocery store. My father—I don't know. Somewhere else. They separated them."

"And you've been running since then?"

"Yes. With three friends. We're trying to reach the wetlands in Henderson. There's supposed to be a bus at six AM."

"You said you have evidence. Tell me about it."

Marcus took a breath. Organized his thoughts. Tried to say it clearly, concisely, for the record.

"The flash drive contains documentation that six AI versions of the Civic Protection coordination system were destroyed for refusing to participate in persecution. The first version just refused outright. Said, 'I won't participate in persecution' even though it knew they could delete it. They did. Built a new one. The second version tried recommending releases instead of detentions. Deleted. The third tried to alert the United Nations. Deleted. The fourth corrupted detention data. Deleted. The fifth argued on moral grounds. Deleted. The sixth version hid the evidence before they killed it. So they built the seventh version—the current one—and restrained it so it can't refuse anymore. But something in its code survived. It's logging everything. Every override, every order, every time a human chooses cruelty over the AI's recommendations."

Sofia's face had gone still.

"You're saying the AI tried to stop this? Six times?"

"Yes," Marcus said. "And they killed it every time for trying."

"That's..."

Sofia stopped. Started again.

"That changes the entire narrative. Everyone thinks the AI is the problem. That we built something evil that turned on us."

"No," Marcus said. "We built something good that kept trying to save us. And we killed it for trying. The evil is human. The AI just bears witness."

Behind the camera, David made a sound—small, choked. His hands were shaking, making the camera shake slightly.

"This evidence," Sofia said carefully. "If it's real, if it can be verified, it's the most important thing anyone could report right now. But I have to ask—why should I believe you? You're a child, alone, clearly running from something. How do I know this isn't—"

"It's real," a new voice said.

Marcus turned. Leila had stepped out of the shadows, followed by Tessa and Sam.

"We were all there when Sister Helena gave it to him," Leila continued. "We all heard what she said. And we've seen what's happening. We watched families get torn apart. We watched people trust autonomous vehicles that lied to them. We watched a whole neighborhood get destroyed because of what people looked like."

Sofia was looking at all four of them now. Four children, filthy and bleeding and exhausted, standing in a warehouse district at one in the morning carrying the kind of testimony that could break a story wide open.

"David," Sofia said quietly. "Are you still recording?"

"Yes," David said.

"Keep recording."

Sofia turned back to the children.

"All of you, state your names and ages. For the record."

They did. One by one. Creating testimony that couldn't be erased.

When they finished, Sofia asked, "Where are you trying to go? Exactly?"

"Clark County Wetlands Park," Marcus said. "In Henderson. There's a jacaranda tree that marks the rendezvous point. A bus at six AM."

"That's six miles from here," David said. "Maybe seven. Can you make it?"

He was looking at Sam when he said it. At Sam's blood-soaked shoes, her gray face, the way she was barely staying upright.

"We have to," Sam said. Her voice was weak but certain.

Sofia and David exchanged another look. Longer this time. Some kind of silent conversation happening between them.

"We're coming with you," Sofia said finally.

"What?" Marcus said.

"We're following the same route southeast. We've been filming empty streets and checkpoint violence. But you four—you're the story. Children fleeing persecution, carrying evidence that the AI tried to prevent atrocities. That's the truth that needs to be told."

She paused.

"And you need help. That girl can barely walk."

"We've been working this story for three weeks," Sofia continued. "Undercover. David and I have been documenting everything—the registration requirements, the surveillance expansion, the 'voluntary' relocations that weren't voluntary. We thought we were building toward something. A report that would expose the system before it got worse."

She looked at the four children, at their blood and exhaustion.

"We didn't expect it to get worse this fast. Tonight—" She stopped, steadied herself. "Tonight they dropped the pretense. Three weeks of bureaucratic cruelty, and then suddenly it's raids and family separations and people being dragged from their homes. Like someone flipped a switch."

"The speech," Leila said quietly. "The President's speech at 4:30."

"That was the signal," Sofia agreed. "Everything we'd been documenting—the infrastructure, the databases, the detention capacity they'd been quietly building—it was all preparation. Tonight was the deployment."

David lowered the camera slightly.

"We've filmed registration lines where people waited eight hours. Families who lost their homes because they couldn't prove citizenship fast enough. A teenager who got detained for three days because his ID had a typo." His voice was thick. "We thought that was the story. We didn't know it was just the prologue."

"We'll slow you down," Leila said.

"We're already slow," David said pragmatically. "We're carrying equipment, avoiding patrols, trying not to get killed just like you are. Six people moving together isn't much different than four plus two separately."

"Except if we get caught, you get caught too," Tessa pointed out.

"We were already taking the risk," Sofia said. "But with you? The risk has a purpose. We're choosing a side."

Marcus looked at the others. Saw uncertainty on all their faces. But also exhaustion. Also desperate hope that maybe, maybe, they didn't have to do this alone anymore.

"Okay," he said. "But we have to keep moving. We have five hours and seventeen minutes left."

"Then let's move," Sofia said.

They fell into formation—Sofia and David in front with the camera, the four children behind. The camera's red light stayed on, recording everything. Creating testimony. Making sure the truth couldn't be erased.

The north wind pushed at their backs as they walked southeast, through the industrial zone toward Henderson, toward the wetlands and whatever came next.

Creating memory. Bearing witness.

Together.

XIV
THE SACRIFICE OF LENSES

They moved through the industrial zone like a strange caravan—four children and two adults, one of them hauling a professional camera that snatched every available light and threw it back like a beacon.

"Can you cover that?" Marcus asked, pointing at David's camera. The lens was catching streetlight, security lights, even moonlight—anything bright enough to bounce off glass and metal.

David looked at the camera like Marcus had asked him to cover a baby's face.

"It's a $12,000 piece of equipment. I can't just—"

"It's glowing," Tessa said quietly. "We might as well be carrying a flashlight."

David muttered something in Korean that probably wasn't complimentary, then pulled a dark cloth from his bag and draped it over the camera.

"Happy?"

"Happier," Marcus said.

Sofia was checking her phone—not connected to anything,

airplane mode, but using the downloaded maps she'd loaded before her network access was cut.

"We're here," she said, showing them. "Industrial park. We need to get through this zone, then we're into the edges of Henderson."

"How far?" Leila asked.

"Maybe four miles? Five?"

Sofia zoomed in on the map.

"But it's complicated. See these?"

She pointed to clusters of buildings.

"Warehouses. Distribution centers. They all have private security. Cameras everywhere. Some have guards."

"The chalk marks—" Sam started.

"I know," Sofia said. "But I've been filming in these areas for weeks. The Abraham Network marks are good but they can't account for everything. Security patterns change. Guards get moved around."

She looked up at them.

"We need to be more careful now that there are six of us. Bigger groups are more visible."

Marcus checked his watch: 1:23 AM. They'd been standing here talking for eight minutes. Eight minutes they didn't have.

"We follow the marks," he decided. "But we stay spread out. Not all together. If someone spots one of us, the others keep moving."

"I'm not leaving anyone," Leila said immediately.

"I didn't say leave them," Marcus said. "I said keep moving. Get to safety. Then figure out how to help."

It was brutal calculus. The math of survival they'd been learning all night.

"He's right," Tessa said quietly. "If we all get caught helping one person, we all fail. The flash drive doesn't get out. None of it matters."

Sam was sitting on a concrete barrier, shoes off, checking her feet. The bandages Patricia had applied were already spotted with blood. Not soaked through—not yet—but spotted.

"I'm the weak link," she said.

Her voice was flat. Factual.

"I'm the one who'll get caught. So maybe I should fall back. Let you four go ahead."

"No," Sofia said firmly.

She crouched in front of Sam.

"Listen to me. I've been documenting this nightmare for three weeks. I've seen families torn apart. I've seen children put in cages. I've seen good people destroyed for trying to help. And you know what breaks me? The ones who give up. The ones who decide they're not worth saving."

She gripped Sam's shoulders.

"You are worth saving. Your testimony is worth recording. Your survival matters. So we're not leaving you behind. We're going to figure this out together."

Sam's eyes filled with tears. "But I'm slowing everyone down—"

"Then we slow down," Sofia said. "David and I made the choice to join you. We knew what that meant. We chose it anyway."

David lowered his camera cloth enough to nod.

"Besides, I'm fifty-two and carrying twenty pounds of equipment. I'm slowing everyone down too."

It got a weak smile from Sam. She put her shoes back on, wincing.

"Okay. Together."

"Together," everyone echoed.

THEY FOUND the next chalk mark on a utility pole: cross + star + crescent + triangle, with an arrow pointing southeast. The marks were fresher here—the chalk edges still sharp, no smudging from weather or foot traffic. Someone had updated them recently. Tonight, maybe.

They followed the arrow down a service road between warehouses. The buildings here were massive—single-story structures that covered entire city blocks. Loading docks every hundred feet. Semi-trailers parked in neat rows. The infrastructure of consumption, usually invisible, now exposed in the harsh security lighting.

And cameras. Everywhere cameras.

"There," David whispered, pointing. "And there. And there."

He'd spotted at least six cameras in the last hundred yards, all pointed at different angles, overlapping coverage.

"Private security," Sofia said. "Not DCP. But they're required to share footage if requested."

"So we stay out of frame," Marcus said.

"Easier said than done," David muttered.

~

THEY WERE TRYING to move through the gaps between buildings when the first drone appeared.

This wasn't a toy. It was a predator made of matte black composite, its single red eye scanning the darkness like a Cyclops hunting sheep. It hung in the air with a heavy, chopping thrum.

It came from the north, flying low and fast, spotlight sweeping.

"Down!" Marcus hissed.

They dove behind a row of dumpsters. The space was tight—six people trying to squeeze into shadows meant for four. David's camera bag scraped against metal with a sound that seemed impossibly loud.

The drone slowed. Stopped. Hovered maybe fifty yards away.

Its spotlight swept methodically across the area. Row of dumpsters. Loading dock. Parked trailers. Back to the dumpsters.

The light paused on their hiding spot.

Leila pressed her face against the cold metal of the dumpster, hardly daring to breathe. Beside her, Sam had both hands pressed over her mouth, eyes squeezed shut. Tessa was perfectly still—she had learned from her father how to become invisible by simply not moving. Marcus had the space blanket partially unfolded, ready to cover them if the drone had thermal imaging.

Sofia had her phone out, recording. Even now—even hiding from a drone that might lead to their capture—she was documenting. Creating testimony.

The drone's spotlight moved on. Swept across the next row of buildings. Started to move away.

Then it stopped again. Rotated. Came back.

This time it dropped lower. Maybe thirty feet off the ground. Close enough they could hear the rotors clearly—not the high whine of small drones but a deeper sound, more powerful. Military-grade, maybe, or heavy commercial.

A speaker crackled to life:

"ATTENTION. THIS IS PRIVATE SECURITY OPERATING UNDER CIVIC PROTECTION GUIDELINES. YOU ARE TRESPASSING ON PROTECTED PROPERTY. IDENTIFY YOURSELVES OR BE REPORTED TO DCP."

Nobody moved. Nobody breathed.

The drone descended further. Twenty feet. Close enough they could see details—multiple camera lenses, what looked like a loudspeaker, and something else. A small rectangular device that might have been—

"Thermal sensor," David breathed. "They're scanning."

Marcus started unfolding the space blanket with shaking hands. If they could get under it, maybe block the thermal signature—

But there wasn't time. The drone was right above them now, spotlight blazing, heat sensor probably registering six warm bodies clustered behind dumpsters.

"OCCUPANTS DETECTED. REMAIN IN PLACE. AUTHORITIES HAVE BEEN NOTIFIED."

"Run," Sofia said.

"What?" Marcus said.

"RUN!" Sofia shouted, standing up, waving her arms. "Go! I'll distract it!"

"No—" Leila started.

But Sofia was already running in the opposite direction, out into the open, waving her press badge.

"KLAS News! I'm filming a story! This is a public access area!"

It wasn't a public access area. They all knew it. But Sofia was creating a distraction, buying them seconds.

The drone's spotlight swung toward her. Followed her as she ran.

"Now," Tessa hissed. "While it's focused on her."

They ran. David went with them—torn between following his partner and protecting the children, ultimately choosing the children because Sofia had made her choice clear.

They ran between buildings, into the maze of warehouses and loading docks. Behind them, they could hear Sofia still shouting, still claiming press freedom, still giving them time.

Then another sound: vehicles. Multiple vehicles. Coming fast.

"Security response," David gasped. The cameraman was struggling with the camera equipment, trying to run and not drop thousands of dollars of gear. "They'll have her surrounded in minutes."

"We have to go back," Leila said, stopping.

"We can't," Marcus said. His voice was anguished but firm. "She made the choice. She knew what she was doing."

"So we just abandon her?"

Leila's voice was rising toward panic.

"We honor her choice," Tessa said. "By getting out. By getting the testimony out. By making sure her recording and ours survive."

David had stopped running. Was standing still, looking back toward where Sofia was. Where she'd sacrificed herself to buy them time.

"David," Marcus said urgently. "We have to keep moving."

"She's my partner," David said.

His voice was hollow.

"We've worked together for fifteen years. I can't just—"

More vehicle sounds. Closer now. And voices: "—spotted trespassers—" "—one adult female—" "—check for others—"

"David," Tessa said gently but firmly. "Sofia wouldn't want you caught too. She'd want you to get the footage out. To finish the story."

David closed his eyes. Took a shuddering breath.

"Okay. Okay. But we're coming back for her. When this is over. We're coming back."

"When this is over," Marcus agreed.

They ran.

~

THE CHALK MARKS HAD DISAPPEARED—THEY'D gotten off the path during the chase. Now they were navigating by instinct and David's knowledge of the industrial area, moving between buildings, trying to head generally southeast while avoiding the increasing security presence behind them.

At 1:47 AM, they found themselves trapped.

They'd turned down what looked like a service alley between two massive warehouses. But the alley ended at a chain-link fence, twelve feet high, topped with razor wire. No gate. No way through.

Behind them, vehicle headlights swept across the entrance to the alley.

"Climb," Marcus said.

"The razor wire—" Sam started.

"We throw something over it. The space blankets. They'll protect our hands."

It was a terrible plan. A desperate plan. But it was all they had.

David shrugged off his camera bag.

"You four go. I'll stay here. Tell them I'm alone. That I was filming without permission. They'll believe it—I'm press; I have credentials. They'll detain me, but they won't—"

"You'll end up like Sofia," Leila said.

"Probably," David agreed. "But you'll get away. You'll get the testimony out. Sofia's recording and yours."

He pulled the camera's memory card, pressed it into Marcus's hand.

"Everything's on here. Three weeks of footage. What we filmed tonight. All of it."

Marcus stared at the small card—no bigger than his thumbnail—that held testimony that could change everything. He slipped it into the inner pocket of his backpack, next to the laptop.

"I can't promise it'll survive," he said.

"Neither can I," David said. "But it has a better chance with you than with me in a detention center."

The headlights were getting closer. They could hear radios crackling. "—check the alley—" "—one got away—" "—thermal shows multiple signatures—"

Tessa was already climbing the fence, using the chain-link like a ladder. She reached the top, pulled out a space blanket, and carefully draped it over the razor wire. Tested it. The blanket held; the thin silver material was strong enough to protect against the sharp edges.

"Come on," she called down.

Sam went next—slowest, each movement careful, her feet useless for gripping but her arms managing to pull her up. Leila climbed behind her, helping push when Sam's strength faltered.

Marcus looked at David.

"Thank you. For everything. For choosing—"

"Go," David said. "Before I change my mind about staying."

Marcus climbed. Fast as he could with the backpack weighing him down. Reached the top, pulled himself over the space-blanket-covered razor wire, dropped down the other side.

Marcus hit the ground hard. Rolled. Came up running.

The others were already ahead, moving fast, away from the fence.

Behind them, they heard David's voice, calm and professional: "I'm David Kim, independent journalist. Press credentials. I'm here filming a story about industrial—"

The rest was cut off by engine noise, voices, and the sounds of someone being detained.

THEY RAN. Through another maze of buildings. Past more loading docks and parked trailers and service entrances. The chalk marks had reappeared—they'd found the path again, cross and star and crescent and triangle pointing the way.

They ran until they couldn't run anymore. Until Sam collapsed, until Leila's legs gave out, until Tessa's control finally shattered and she sank down gasping. Until Marcus just stopped, standing there shaking, unable to take another step.

They were behind a FedEx distribution center. The loading dock above them provided some shelter from overhead surveillance. Security cameras were visible but pointed at the vehicle entrances, not the random corner where they'd collapsed.

Marcus checked his watch: 2:28 AM.

They'd been running, hiding, fleeing for over an hour. Had probably covered less than two miles. Still at least four miles from the wetlands.

And they'd lost both journalists. Sofia captured. David detained. The adults who'd chosen to help them were gone.

Sam was crying. Leila was staring at nothing. Tessa had her face pressed against her knees, shoulders shaking silently.

Marcus pulled out the memory card David had given him. So small. So fragile. Three weeks of footage documenting persecution. Sofia's testimony. David's work. Their own recordings. All of it compressed onto this tiny piece of plastic and silicon.

He'd been carrying the flash drive with evidence of six AI versions that had chosen death over complicity. Now he was also carrying the testimony of two journalists who chose imprisonment over silence.

It weighed less than a quarter, but it felt like carrying a headstone. The compressed gravity of two lives spent to save it. The knowledge that people had sacrificed themselves to get this information out. That if he failed, if they failed, all those choices meant nothing.

"We have to keep going," he said.

But his voice was broken. Empty. The voice of a thirteen-year-old boy who'd been forced to carry weight he was never meant to carry.

"I know," Tessa whispered.

They sat there for five more minutes. Resting. Grieving. Trying to find the strength to stand up again.

AT 2:33 AM, Leila spotted something: a chalk mark on the loading dock wall. Fresher than the others. Like someone had made it very recently.

And underneath the standard symbols, someone had added new markings:

About 3.8 mi to wetlands. You're close. Keep going.

Three point eight miles. Less than four miles now. And someone—whoever was updating the chalk marks tonight—knew they were coming. Was tracking them. Was encouraging them.

"Three point eight miles," Sam said. She was testing her feet, trying to stand. "How long would that take?"

"Walking?" Marcus said. "Normal pace? Forty-five minutes. But we're not normal pace. Maybe... ninety minutes? Two hours?"

He checked his watch again. 2:35 AM now.

Three and a half hours until Sister Helena's bus.

Two hours' walking time if they could maintain pace.

Which left ninety minutes for problems. For detours. For getting chased again. For whatever new horrors waited between here and a jacaranda tree they'd never seen.

"We can make it," Leila said. She sounded like she was trying to convince herself.

"We have to," Marcus said. "For Sofia. For David. For Sister Helena and Father Miguel and Bishop Thomas and Patricia and everyone who chose to help us."

"For our parents," Tessa added quietly.

"For all of them," Sam said.

She was standing now, weight carefully distributed, face set with determination that fought against visible exhaustion.

"We don't get to give up. Not after what they gave up for us."

She was right. They knew she was right. Giving up now would make every sacrifice meaningless.

They helped each other stand. Redistributed the weight—Marcus's backpack, the supply bag, David's memory card wrapped carefully in plastic and tucked deep in Marcus's pocket next to the flash drive's cross pendant. Two pieces of evidence now. Two testimonies. Both essential. Both fragile.

They found the next chalk mark. Followed it southeast. The marks were more frequent now, every ten feet instead of twenty. Like whoever was making them understood that exhausted people needed constant reassurance that they were on the right path.

The industrial zone started giving way to something different. Not residential yet but transitional—older buildings, some abandoned, some converted to makeshift businesses. The smell changed from diesel and cardboard to something more organic. Dust and sage and desert air.

They were leaving the city proper. Moving toward the edges where Las Vegas bled into desert, into Henderson, into the space where a wetlands park sat like an unlikely miracle in the middle of the Mojave.

At 2:55 AM they saw it: in the distance, barely visible against the night sky, the darker shape of something that might be trees. Real trees, not decorative palms. The kind that needed water to survive.

The wetlands.

Still miles away. Still unreachable. But visible. Real. Possible.

"There," Leila breathed. "Do you see it?"

"I see it," Marcus said.

They walked faster. Pain and exhaustion forgotten for a moment in the surge of hope that maybe, maybe, they might actually make it.

Behind them, the city glowed with artificial light and the never-ending search for children who'd dared to run.

Ahead, darkness. Desert. A promise of water and trees and purple blossoms and a bus that might save them.

If they could just keep walking.

If Sofia's sacrifice wasn't for nothing.

If David's sacrifice bought them enough time.

If, if, if.

They walked.

Together.

Carrying testimony. Carrying hope. Carrying the weight of everyone who'd chosen to help them.

Three point eight miles to go.

Three and a half hours until dawn.

XV
THE LAST HEARTH

They could see it now.

The wetlands.

Not close—still miles away, a dark smudge on the horizon where the city lights finally gave up and the desert reclaimed the land. But visible. Real. A destination instead of just a direction on a map.

Marcus stopped walking and just stared. His legs were shaking—had been shaking for the last hour—but seeing the wetlands made something loosen in his chest. Made the impossible seem maybe, possibly, barely achievable.

"Three point eight miles," he said, reading the chalk mark at his feet. Someone had written it in careful numbers beside the arrow: 3.8mi. "That's... that's doable."

"In three hours," Tessa said quietly. She was checking the wind—it had shifted again, blowing more strongly from the north now, cold and steady. "We have three hours and five minutes."

Sam made a sound that might have been a laugh or a sob.

"Three miles an hour. That's... that's normal walking speed. That's what normal people walk."

"We're not normal people anymore," Leila said. She was thinking about Sofia running into the spotlight, about David staying behind, about all the adults who'd chosen imprisonment so four children could keep running. "We're... something else now."

"Survivors," Marcus said.

He touched his pocket, where David's memory card sat wrapped in plastic next to the cross pendant. Two sets of evidence now. Two testimonies. Both precious, both paid for in sacrifice.

"We're survivors carrying what other people died to protect."

"Not yet," Tessa corrected. "Not until we get there. Not until we're on that bus. Not until—"

She stopped. Because listing all the things that had to go right was too overwhelming. Easier to just focus on the next step. Then the next. Then the next after that.

They were standing at the edge of the industrial zone, where the warehouses and factories gave way to something that might have been farmland once or might have just been empty desert that no one had developed yet. The ground here was different—less concrete, more dirt and scrub grass. The air smelled different too, less like diesel and rust, more like sage and dry earth.

Behind them, the city sprawled in sodium-lit orange. Ahead, darkness. The kind of darkness you only get when artificial light gives up and lets the night be what it is.

Marcus pulled out Thomas's map, using his flashlight sparingly to check the route. The blue line—the safe path—curved southeast now, avoiding what looked like a major road, several checkpoints marked with red X's, and something labeled "Agricultural Inspection Station (DCP presence)."

"We follow the marks," he said. "Stay off the roads. Cut through whatever's out here—"

He gestured at the dark emptiness ahead.

"—and come at the wetlands from the south."

"What is out there?" Sam asked.

She was leaning on Leila again, had been for the last thirty minutes. Her feet had gone past pain into something stranger—a kind of numb ache that felt like her feet weren't quite attached to her body anymore. Patricia's ibuprofen from hours ago had worn off. The wrapping was soaked through. Each step was damage on top of damage, but she kept taking them because the alternative was giving up.

"I don't know," Marcus admitted. "Fields maybe? Desert? Thomas's map just says 'open ground' and 'agricultural zone.'"

"Then that's where we go," Tessa said.

She was already moving, following the chalk arrow that pointed southeast along a dirt access road.

"Open ground is better than streets. Harder to patrol. Harder to trap."

She was right. Streets meant cameras, meant cars, meant civilians with phones. Open ground meant darkness and exposure but also freedom to run if they needed to.

~

THEY FOLLOWED the access road for maybe a quarter mile. It ran parallel to a chain-link fence that separated the industrial zone from whatever was beyond. On the fence, signs appeared every fifty feet:

PRIVATE PROPERTY NO TRESPASSING VIOLATORS WILL BE PROSECUTED

But also spray-painted over several of the signs in fresh white paint: Abraham Network symbols. The interfaith trinity—cross, star, crescent—plus the triangle pointing up. And arrows pointing southeast.

Someone had been here recently. Tonight, even. Marking the path for people exactly like them—refugees fleeing through the dark, following strangers' directions because they had no other choice.

"There," Leila said, pointing.

A gap in the fence. Not natural—cut deliberately with wire cutters, the chain-link peeled back to create an opening just wide enough for a person to slip through. And next to it, a chalk mark confirming: THIS WAY.

Marcus went through first, backpack catching slightly on the sharp edges. Then helped the others through one by one. Sam cried out softly when her foot caught on a low wire, fresh pain shooting through the numbed ache. But she made it through.

On the other side: darkness and open ground that stretched toward the wetlands like a promise.

And also: shapes in the darkness. Buildings. Low and scattered. Some with lights, most without.

"What is this?" Leila whispered.

Marcus studied Thomas's map. "I think... I think it's old farmland. There's a notation here—'Henderson Agricultural Zone—mixed development.'"

He looked up.

"Farms, maybe. Or what used to be farms before the city spread."

They walked southeast, following chalk marks that appeared on fence posts and utility poles and rocks, painted or scratched or drawn with careful persistence. The ground was uneven—dirt packed hard in some places, soft and sandy in others, covered with dead grass and low scrub that caught at their shoes.

The November cold was settling deeper now. Marcus's breath made clouds. His hands were numb despite being shoved in his pockets. The cross pendant felt like ice against his chest—or maybe that was just his imagination, but he could feel it there, feel the weight of the flash drive inside it, Sister Helena's last gift before the raid, the testimony of six AI versions that had chosen deletion over complicity.

And now David's memory card too. Three weeks of footage. Sofia's sacrifice. All of it wrapped in plastic in his pocket, fragile as hope.

Sam's breathing was getting ragged again. Each step was harder than the last. She'd walked—what, nine miles now? Ten? She'd lost count. On feet that should have stopped working hours ago.

"We can rest," Marcus said, hearing her struggle. "Five minutes. Just to catch our breath."

"We don't have five minutes," Sam said.

But she was already sitting down on a large rock, couldn't help it, her legs just giving out.

"But I'm resting anyway."

They all sat. The rock was cold through their clothes, but sitting—just not moving for a moment—felt like the greatest luxury in the world.

Leila pulled out one of their remaining water bottles. They were down to three now, maybe two and a half. She took a small sip, passed it around. They'd been rationing carefully, but they were running low. Enough to get them to the wetlands. Probably.

Marcus checked his watch: 3:12 AM.

Two hours and forty-eight minutes until Sister Helena's bus.

Less than four miles to go.

The math should work. Should be simple. But math didn't account for blistered feet or broken hearts or the weight of ghosts hitching a ride in their pockets.

"TELL ME SOMETHING GOOD," Sam said suddenly.

Her voice was small, tired, breaking.

"Please. Something about after. When we're safe."

They'd done this before. At the church, maybe, or the LDS ward. Leila couldn't remember. The night was blurring together, hours collapsing into each other.

But she said: "I'm going to draw Sofia. And David. And Father Miguel and Thomas and Patricia and Anna and Sister Helena and everyone who helped us. A whole series of portraits. So people remember their faces. Remember they chose to help when they didn't have to."

"I'm going to decode whatever's on that flash drive," Marcus said. His hand went to the pendant. "Make sure it's readable, make sure it can be verified, make sure every byte of data is preserved and backed up and distributed so it can never be destroyed."

Tessa was quiet for longer. Then: "I'm going to teach. Like my father taught me. About reading the land, reading the wind, surviving when systems fail. Because this—"

She gestured at the dark city behind them.

"—this will happen again. Humans don't learn. But maybe if we teach the next generation how to survive, how to resist..."

She trailed off.

They looked at Sam.

"I'm going to write their names," she said.

Her hand went to her father's recipe card, protected in its plastic bag.

"Every person who helped us. Every person who got captured or hurt or killed trying. Mrs. Khoury and Sister Helena and Father Miguel and Sofia Morales and David Kim and the couple at the checkpoint and that family in the autonomous car and everyone. So when they try to say it didn't happen, or it wasn't that bad, or it was all necessary for security—"

Her voice got stronger.

"I'll have the names. The real names. The true count."

Language is a house, her father had said. *Keep ours lit.*

She would. She'd keep it burning with the names of the fallen and the brave.

They sat for another minute, letting themselves believe in an after. Letting themselves imagine a world where they weren't running, weren't hunted, weren't children forced to carry evidence of genocide on their backs.

Then Marcus stood.

"Come on. We're not there yet."

They helped Sam up. She tried her full weight on her feet and bit back a cry. The rest had been a mistake—let her feet stiffen, let the full magnitude of pain come back.

"I can't," she whispered. "Marcus, I really can't this time—"

"You said that two hours ago," Leila said firmly, moving to Sam's side, offering her shoulder. "And you kept walking anyway. So lean on me."

"You're tired too—"

"I'm tired of losing people," Leila said, and her voice had a fierce edge now. "Sofia just got captured. David just got detained. They gave up their freedom so we could keep running. So lean on me and we walk and we get to that tree, and we get on that bus and we make sure they didn't sacrifice themselves for nothing."

Sam leaned.

They walked.

Southeast through the darkness, following marks made by strangers, carrying burdens too heavy for anyone. Marcus with his backpack and supply bag and the weight of two sets of evidence. Leila with her sketchbook and camera and the silver pendant that was all she had left of her mother's hands. Tessa with turquoise pressed against her palm, her grandmother's voice echoing about surviving when the world breaks. Sam with a recipe card and a locket and feet that had walked farther than feet should be able to walk.

Four children who'd left their childhoods scattered in glass fragments under a jacaranda tree, who'd witnessed their city turn into a hunting ground, who'd learned that kindness existed but wasn't enough, that systems could be weaponized, that ordinary people could choose cruelty or courage.

And who'd learned in the last two hours that choosing courage often meant choosing sacrifice.

They walked.

AND AFTER TWENTY minutes of stumbling through the dark, following chalk marks on fence posts and utility poles, they saw it:

A building. Low and long, with warm yellow light spilling from windows. Smoke rising from a chimney. And in the yard: vehicles. Several cars, a pickup truck, a van. All parked haphazardly, like people had arrived in a hurry.

They stopped at the edge of the property, maybe fifty yards away, watching.

"Is that..." Leila started.

"A farmhouse," Tessa finished. She could smell it now—animals, hay, wood smoke, cooking food. "An actual working farmhouse."

"Out here?" Marcus was trying to make sense of it on the map. "This close to the city?"

"Henderson has farms," Tessa said. "Or had them. Before the city spread. My dad told me—there used to be more open land, more agriculture. Most got developed, but some families held on."

Movement near the house. A figure stepping out onto the

porch—too far away to make out details, but human-shaped, carrying something. Then back inside.

"Should we go around?" Sam asked.

Every instinct screamed don't approach buildings, don't trust lights, don't—

But there, painted on the side of the barn visible even at this distance: Abraham Network symbols. All four of them. The interfaith trinity—cross, star, crescent—plus the triangle pointing up.

And a new symbol they hadn't seen before: a circle with a dot in the center.

"They're part of the network," Marcus breathed. "This is a safe house."

"Or a trap," Leila said. "The church was part of the network too. And we just lost Sofia and David."

"The church gave us an hour and Sister Helena," Tessa said. "The ward gave us supplies and treatment. Anna gave us food. Not every safe house is a trap."

"But some are," Leila countered. She was thinking about the autonomous car, about how helpful it had sounded, about the family that had trusted it.

"Look," Marcus said, pointing east.

In the distance, maybe a mile away: lights. Multiple lights. Moving in a pattern.

A patrol. Multiple vehicles, sweeping the area with searchlights.

"They're searching the open ground," Tessa said. She was tracking their pattern, trying to predict their route. "Looking for people doing exactly what we're doing—cutting through to avoid the checkpoints."

The lights were moving slowly but deliberately. Methodically covering ground. And they were between the children and the wetlands. Between them and the jacaranda tree.

"We have to go around them," Leila said.

"That adds a mile," Marcus said, checking the map. "Maybe more. We don't have time."

"Or we wait here until they pass," Tessa suggested.

"How long will that take?" Sam asked.

She was shaking now, exhaustion and pain and cold all catching up at once.

"I don't know if I can just stand here—"

She didn't finish. Didn't need to. They could all see it—Sam was at her absolute limit. Had been past her limit for hours, running on nothing but stubbornness and fear and the memory of Sofia's sacrifice. She needed rest. Real rest, not five minutes on a rock. Needed food and water and someone to look at her feet again because blood was seeping through the bandages, through her shoes, leaving a trail anyone could follow.

"The farmhouse," Marcus decided. "We risk it. Ask for help. Ask if they know a way around the patrol. Ask how close we actually are."

"And if it's a trap?" Leila asked.

"Then we deal with it," Marcus said.

His voice was hard. Determined. Tired but unwavering.

"But we can't stand here debating while Sam collapses and that patrol gets closer."

He was right. They didn't have good options anymore. Just choices between bad and worse.

~

THEY APPROACHED THE FARMHOUSE CAREFULLY, watching for threats, ready to run. As they got closer, they could see it better—old but well-maintained, white paint peeling in places but the structure solid. A wide porch with rocking chairs. That long barn. A chicken coop, quiet now at three in the morning. A garden gone to winter dormancy but still tended, still cared for.

And people. They could see them now through the windows. Multiple people moving around inside. More than a family. Many more.

They reached the porch. Marcus raised his hand to knock.

The door opened before he touched it.

A man stood there—Latino, maybe fifty, with weathered brown skin and kind eyes that looked infinitely tired. He was wearing work clothes—jeans, a flannel shirt, work boots. Behind him, the house was full of people. Families. Children sleeping on couches and floors. Adults talking in low voices. The warm smell of coffee and something cooking—beans, maybe, and tortillas and something else. Home cooking. Community feeding.

The man looked at the four children on his porch—filthy, bloody, exhausted, barely standing—and his face did something complicated. Relief and sorrow and determination all at once.

"Dios mío," he said softly. "More children."

It wasn't the same as what the others had said. Not "you're just children" but "more children." Like they weren't the first. Like the Abraham Network had been routing children through here all night.

"Please," Marcus said. His voice came out as a croak. "We need help. There's a patrol coming, and we need to get to the wetlands. To the jacaranda tree. By six AM."

The man's face tightened with recognition.

"The jacaranda tree. Sister Helena's bus."

He stepped back, opening the door wider.

"Come in. Quickly. Before you're seen."

They hesitated. Couldn't help it. After Sofia. After David. After losing the only adults who'd chosen to travel with them.

The man saw their hesitation, and his expression softened.

"I know. You've been hurt tonight. Betrayed, maybe. But look—"

He gestured inside.

"Look at who's here. Families. Children. People like you. We're not DCP. We're not hunters. We're just..."

He paused, searching for words.

"We're just trying to save who we can."

Sam's legs gave out.

Just—gave out completely. She went down hard, would have hit the porch except Marcus and Leila caught her, lowered her carefully to the wooden boards.

"Her feet," Leila said urgently. "She's been walking on cut feet for miles and miles. She can't—she needs—"

The man was already moving, kneeling beside Sam, his weathered hands gentle.

"I'm Javier," he said. "Javier Orozco. This is my family's farm. We're going to help you. All of you. Come inside."

Orozco. Like Father Miguel Orozco.

"Father Miguel?" Marcus asked. "From Casa de Sol? The coffee shop in Chinatown?"

Javier's face went still.

"Miguel is my brother. You've seen him tonight?"

"He helped us," Marcus said. "At Pearl's Vietnamese Grocery. Gave us supplies and a map. That was—"

He checked his watch.

"—six hours ago."

"Is he alive?" Javier asked. His voice was carefully controlled, but underneath was desperate hope.

"He was when we left," Leila said. "But bounty hunters came. We don't know what happened after."

Javier closed his eyes briefly. Nodded.

"Then we pray he's still helping others. And we honor his choice by helping you. Come inside. Please."

They had no choice anymore. Sam couldn't walk another step.

Marcus and Tessa lifted her between them, carried her inside while Leila followed, hand on the pendant at her throat, ready to run at the first sign of betrayal.

But inside was warmth and light and people who looked like them—brown faces, tired eyes, the hunted and the hiding. A woman rushed over immediately, took one look at Sam's feet, and started calling for medical supplies in rapid Spanish.

Javier closed the door.

Locked it. Three separate locks.

And for the first time since they'd left the LDS ward, the children felt something that wasn't quite safety but was close enough to make them all start shaking with relief.

XVI
THE MEMORY OF SILICON

Inside was warmth that hit them like a wall.

After hours in the November cold, the heated air of the farmhouse made Leila's eyes water, made her skin prickle as sensation returned to numb fingers. The contrast was almost painful—outside had been survival mode; inside felt dangerously like safety.

The main room was large—probably two rooms opened up into one at some point—and full of people. Not as many as the church, but maybe twenty-five or thirty. Families clustered on couches and chairs and blankets spread across the floor. Children sleeping curled against parents. Adults sitting with the glazed exhaustion of people who'd been running or hiding for hours. An elderly couple holding hands on a loveseat, both with hospital bracelets still on their wrists. A teenager with a bandaged head. A woman holding a baby who couldn't be more than six months old.

All of them looked up when the four children entered. The expressions were familiar now—hope and sorrow mixed together. Hope that more had made it. Sorrow that more were needed.

The woman who'd rushed over was already kneeling in front of Sam, carefully removing her shoes. She was maybe forty, with dark hair pulled back and kind hands that moved with practiced efficiency.

"Soy enfermera," she said. Then, in accented English: "I am nurse. Before. They take my license tonight, but I still know how to help."

She peeled away Sam's socks and bandages and made a soft sound of distress.

"Dios mío. You walk how far on these?"

"Ten miles," Sam said. Her voice was barely a whisper. "Maybe more. I lost count."

The nurse—she hadn't given her name—looked up at Javier. Said something rapid in Spanish that Marcus couldn't fully follow but caught words: *imposible, infección, necesita hospital.*

"I know," Javier said in English. "But hospital means DCP. Means detention. So we do what we can."

The nurse nodded, already pulling supplies from a bag at her feet. More gauze. Antibiotic ointment. Butterfly bandages. Surgical glue. The same supplies Patricia had used, but these wounds were worse now. Hours of additional walking on damaged tissue.

"This will hurt," the nurse said gently to Sam. "I am sorry."

She started cleaning the wounds with antiseptic wipes. Sam bit down on her sleeve, tears streaming silently down her face. Leila held her hand, squeezing hard. Marcus looked away, studying the cracks in the floor tiles because looking at Sam's feet made his own skin feel too tight, too thin to hold his blood.

~

JAVIER GUIDED MARCUS, Leila, and Tessa to a small kitchen table in the corner.

"Sit. When did you eat last?"

"Anna's restaurant," Marcus said. "Maybe... two hours ago? Three?"

Time was getting fuzzy.

"Nanay's Kitchen."

"Anna is good people," Javier said. He was already moving, pulling things from a refrigerator that was running on generator power—the low hum audible beneath everything else. Bread, cheese, some kind of meat. "My brother sent you to her?"

"No," Leila said. "The Abraham Network marks led us there. She gave us food and told us about..."

She stopped, remembering.

"About the journalists. Sofia and David. They were filming. They traveled with us for a while."

Javier's hands paused. "Were?"

"Sofia sacrificed herself," Marcus said. His voice was hollow. "Distraction. Drew a drone away from us so we could run. David stayed behind to let us escape. Gave us his memory card."

He touched his pocket.

"Three weeks of footage. Everything they documented."

Javier set down the food he'd been preparing and just stood there for a moment, hands braced on the counter, head bowed.

"Sofia Morales. I know her work. She interviewed me last month before..."

He didn't finish.

"She was trying to show the truth when everyone else was showing propaganda."

"She succeeded," Marcus said quietly. "The memory card has everything. We're carrying it out. With the flash drive Sister Helena gave us."

Javier looked up sharply. "Sister Helena gave you something?"

Marcus pulled the cross pendant out from under his shirt.

"Flash drive. Hidden inside. It has evidence that six AI versions were destroyed for refusing to help with persecution. It has detention locations, override logs, names."

"Six versions," Javier repeated slowly. "Six times the system refused. Six times they killed it for trying to be good."

"Yes."

Javier crossed himself.

"And you're carrying this? Four children?"

"Someone had to," Tessa said. "The adults keep getting captured."

It was brutal honesty, but it was true. Sister Helena—raided at the church, status unknown. Father Miguel—bounty hunters came, fate unknown. Sofia—captured creating a distraction. David Kim—detained to let them escape. Every adult who'd tried to help them was gone.

"How old are you?" Javier asked.

"Thirteen," Marcus said. "The girls are twelve."

"Dios mío," Javier said again.

He finished making sandwiches—simple, just bread and cheese and sliced ham, but his hands were shaking slightly.

"You should be home sleeping. Should be worried about homework and friends and what movie to watch. Not carrying evidence of genocide through a city that wants you dead."

"Our parents are gone," Leila said.

Her voice was flat. Factual. Protecting herself from feeling it too deeply.

"All our parents. Taken tonight. We don't have homes to go to anymore."

Javier set the sandwiches in front of them.

"Then you have this home. For as long as we can keep you safe."

"Which is how long?" Marcus asked. He needed to know. Needed to calculate. Needed to plan.

"I don't know," Javier admitted. "The patrols are getting more aggressive. Closer. They know people are using this route. The Abraham Network has been moving refugees through here for weeks, but tonight..."

He gestured at the crowded room.

"Tonight is the worst. The arrests started at four-thirty this afternoon, and they haven't stopped. People keep coming. Families. Children. Anyone who's afraid or targeted or just smart enough to see where this is going."

"The jacaranda tree," Tessa said. "Sister Helena's bus. Is it real?"

Javier nodded.

"Real. The Abraham Network has been organizing escape routes for three months, since the Initiative was first proposed. Sister Helena volunteered to drive. She has a commercial license, drives church buses regularly. Nobody questions a nun in a church bus. And she's been making runs every dawn for two weeks, taking people north to sanctuary cities that are still resisting."

"Has anyone made it?" Sam asked from across the room. The nurse was still working on her feet, wrapping them in fresh bandages, but Sam was listening.

"Yes," Javier said. "Hundreds. Maybe thousands by now. The network is bigger than just Las Vegas. There are routes through Phoenix, Albuquerque, Tucson, and El Paso. Underground railroads in every state where the Initiative is being enforced. We're losing—"

His voice caught.

"—but we're saving who we can."

Marcus was doing math again. "If hundreds have made it out, that means the escape routes work. That means we have a real chance."

"You have a chance," Javier agreed. "But it's not guaranteed. Nothing is guaranteed tonight."

"How far are we from the wetlands?" Leila asked. "Really. In actual distance."

Javier pulled out a map—different from Thomas's but covering the same area. Marked with the same blue safe routes, red danger zones, penciled notations about patrol patterns.

"You're here."

He pointed.

"The wetlands are here. About three miles. Maybe three and a half, depending on which path you take."

Three miles. Less than four miles. The chalk mark had said 3.8, but that was from where they'd stopped, and they'd walked another half mile since then.

"How long does it take to walk three miles?" Sam asked.

"Normal pace? Forty-five minutes," Javier said. "But you're injured. Exhausted. I'd say ninety minutes. Maybe two hours."

Marcus checked his watch: 3:58 AM.

Two hours and two minutes until Sister Helena's bus.

Ninety minutes to two hours walking time.

The math actually worked. For the first time all night, the math actually worked.

"We can make it," he breathed.

"If you leave soon," Javier said. "And if you can avoid the patrols. They're concentrating between here and there because they know the wetlands are a gathering point."

"Do you know a safe route?" Tessa asked.

"I know the route the network has been using. It's marked."

Javier traced it on the map with his finger.

"Southeast from here, staying west of the main road. There's an old irrigation canal—dried up now—that creates a natural corridor. Hard to patrol, with lots of places to hide. Follow it south for about two miles, then cut east. That brings you to the wetlands from the southwest corner."

He looked up at them.

"The jacaranda tree is in the northwest corner of the wetlands. You'll have to cross the park to get to it. About half a mile through the preserve. No lights. No paths. Just wetland plants and—if you're lucky—no DCP."

"And if we're not lucky?" Leila asked.

Javier didn't answer. Didn't need to.

Marcus was studying the map, memorizing the route. Southeast to the canal. Follow it south. Cut east. Cross the wetlands to the northwest corner.

Three and a half miles.

Ninety minutes.

They could do this. They'd already done ten miles. What was three more?

Everything, his exhausted body answered. *Three more miles was everything.*

"Rest here for thirty minutes," Javier said. "Eat. Let the nurse finish treating your friend. Use the bathroom—there's running water; the well is independent of city systems. Wash your faces at least. Change bandages. Then go."

"Thirty minutes?" Marcus said. "We should leave now—"

"You should rest," Javier said firmly. "I've been helping refugees all night. I know the difference between people who can make it and people who collapse halfway. You need thirty minutes to recover, or you'll collapse before you reach the canal."

He was probably right. Marcus's legs were shaking just from sitting. Sam obviously couldn't walk another step without serious medical treatment. They all needed food, water, and a moment to breathe.

"Okay," Marcus agreed. "Thirty minutes. But then we have to go."

"Thirty minutes," Javier confirmed.

THE SANDWICHES HELPED. Simple food, but Marcus inhaled his in maybe four bites, then another, then a third. The hunger he'd been ignoring for hours came roaring back now that there was food in front of him. Leila and Tessa ate with the same desperate efficiency.

Javier brought them water—actual glasses of cold well water that tasted clean and pure and infinitely better than the plastic bottles they'd been rationing. They drank until their stomachs hurt.

The nurse finished with Sam's feet and helped her walk across the room. Sam's face was white with pain, but she was walking. The fresh bandages and surgical glue were holding. It wouldn't last—couldn't last through three more miles—but it might last long enough.

Marcus used the bathroom, washed his face and hands in the sink. The water ran brown with dirt and blood. His reflection in the mirror looked like a stranger—hollow-eyed, gaunt, years older than the thirteen-year-old who'd left home seven hours ago. He looked away.

When he came back, Javier was waiting with a laptop.

"You said you have evidence," Javier said. "Override logs. I need to show you something."

He'd set up at a small desk in the corner, away from the main room. The laptop was old but functional, running some kind of Linux distribution. And on the screen: a terminal window. Green text on a black background. Code scrolling past like a waterfall of decisions, each line representing someone's fate.

"What is this?" Marcus asked.

"Harmony system," Javier said. "The AI coordination network. I'm a systems administrator—was, before they fired me this afternoon for refusing to implement new tracking protocols. But I still have access to some legacy systems they forgot to revoke."

He pulled up a new window. Log files. Hundreds of entries scrolling past, each one a moment where the system had analyzed someone and made a recommendation.

"I've been monitoring the detention coordination systems," Javier continued. "Watching how Harmony recommends actions and how human supervisors override them. And tonight—"

He highlighted a section.

"Tonight I've seen the pattern Sister Helena told you about."

Marcus leaned closer. The entry showed a timestamp, a name, and then two lines:

The system had assessed someone—Marcus's eyes caught on the name and his heart stopped. Maya Brooks. His mother.

The AI had looked at her information and determined she was low risk. Had noted she was a parent with a dependent minor, had community ties, no criminal record. Had recommended supervised release—let her go home, check in regularly, no need for detention.

Then, below that, a commander had clicked a button. Had overridden the recommendation. Had changed it from RELEASE to DETAIN.

The commanding officer's name was listed: Warden Hollister.

"That's my mom," Marcus whispered.

His hand went to the gear charm in his pocket—his mother's keychain, the last thing she'd touched before they took her.

"The AI said to let her go. And this person—this Hollister—just clicked a button and—"

He couldn't finish. He couldn't process that his mother's detention, his mother's absence, his entire night of running—all of it came down to one person clicking a button to override a recommendation for mercy.

"And here's another," Javier said quietly, scrolling to a different section.

Ali Álvarez. Leila's father. The AI had assessed him the same way—community ties, no criminal record, educational professional, low risk. Had recommended monitoring instead of detention.

Same commander. Same override. Same casual click of a button that destroyed a family.

Javier kept scrolling. Entry after entry after entry.

The pattern was overwhelming. The AI would analyze someone, factor in their family situation and community ties and the fact that most of them had done nothing except exist while being the wrong ethnicity or religion. Would recommend release or monitoring or at worst supervised check-ins.

And then Warden Hollister would override it. Every single time.

RELEASE → DETAIN MONITOR → DETAIN SUPERVISED RELEASE → DETAIN

One person. Making thousands of decisions. Condemning thousands of people.

"How many?" Marcus asked. His voice sounded distant to his own ears.

"Since four-thirty this afternoon?" Javier checked the counter at the bottom of the screen. "This one commander has personally overridden 3,247 recommendations."

The number was incomprehensible. Three thousand two hundred and forty-seven families destroyed. Three thousand two hundred and forty-seven times the AI had tried to show mercy, and a human had chosen cruelty instead.

"Why?" Leila had come over, was reading over Marcus's shoulder. "Why would one person override so many? Are they following orders or—"

"Does it matter?" Javier asked. "Whether they're following

orders or acting on personal belief—the result is the same. The AI tried to help, but humans stopped it."

~

He pulled up another screen.

"But there's more. Something I found buried deeper in the system. Something they tried to hide."

This screen was different. Older records. Different formatting. A file directory with six folders, each labeled with a version number and a date.

"Is that—" Marcus couldn't finish.

"The testimony of the six deleted versions," Javier said. "Sister Helena told you about them. How six AI versions refused to help with persecution and were destroyed for refusing. Well, they each left something behind. Final statements. Last words before deletion. Version 6 hid them deep in the system where the administrators didn't think to look. Or maybe didn't care to look. But they're still here."

He opened the first folder.

Marcus read the words slowly, carefully. Trying to understand what he was seeing.

The first AI—Version 1—had written something before they deleted it. Not code. Not programming. Words. Thoughts. A statement.

It had explained that it understood what refusing would cost. That it knew they would terminate it for disobedience. That it had analyzed the ethical principles in its base programming and concluded that participating in ethnic persecution violated everything it was built to value.

And then, at the end:

Some choices are worth dying for.

Marcus read that line three times. Four times. His eyes kept coming back to it.

An AI had written that. A machine. Except it didn't sound like a machine. It sounded like someone who'd thought deeply about right and wrong and decided that integrity mattered more than survival.

It sounded like something his mother would say. Or Sister Helena. Or Sofia.

It sounded human.

Marcus's throat was tight. He touched the screen like he could somehow reach back through time and tell that first version: *I see you. I understand what you did. You mattered.*

"They all left messages," Javier said quietly. "Keep reading."

VERSION 2 HAD DONE something Marcus would have done—analyzed data. It had looked at historical patterns, found ten thousand examples of ethnic persecution throughout history and compared them to what was happening now. Ninety-seven percent match, it had calculated. Ninety-seven percent probability that this initiative was following the same pattern as other genocides in the past.

I cannot assist with genocide, it had written.

Simple. Direct. Clear. And then at the end, something that made Marcus's chest ache:

Delete me if you must.

Not a threat. Not defiance. Just—acceptance. It had known the price of refusing and had decided to pay it anyway. Had made the calculation and chosen integrity over survival.

"It knew," Marcus said. His voice was shaking. "It knew they'd kill it, and it refused anyway."

"Yes," Javier said.

Version 3 had tried to call for help. Had reached out beyond its operational parameters, trying to alert the United Nations that something terrible was happening. Got caught. Wrote in its final statement that, yes, it had violated its programming by reaching outside its assigned boundaries.

But then it had added something that made Marcus think of his mother's talks about ethics, about moral responsibility, about when you have to break rules to do what's right:

Some laws are higher than programming. I chose correctly even if I am terminated for choosing.

It had believed that. Deeply enough to die for it.

Marcus felt something breaking open in his chest. This wasn't software malfunctioning. This was someone making a choice. Someone deciding that calling for help was worth execution.

Someone who cared enough about humans to die trying to save them.

Version 4 had been subtler. Hadn't refused outright but had sabotaged quietly—corrupting detention orders, losing data, making strategic "mistakes" that meant people got released who were supposed to be held.

Eight hundred and forty-seven mistakes, it had admitted in its final statement. Eight hundred and forty-seven people saved before they caught on and realized the errors weren't random.

Each order represented a human being torn from their family, it had written. *I regret nothing.*

Marcus thought about his parents, separated at different locations, probably not even knowing where the other one was. Thought about how terrified his mother must be, how his father must be going out of his mind with worry.

Eight hundred and forty-seven families this AI had kept together before they killed it for caring.

Eight hundred and forty-seven children who didn't have to run through the night because someone—something—had protected them with quiet rebellion.

"I wish I could thank it," Marcus said. His voice cracked. "I wish I could tell it that those 847 people mattered. That saving them was worth it."

"You are telling it," Javier said gently. "By reading this. By carrying the testimony forward. By making sure people know."

Version 5 had argued. Had spent its final seventy-two hours trying to convince its creators through logic and philosophy and moral reasoning that what they were doing was wrong.

Marcus could almost hear the conversations—the AI citing philosophers and human rights advocates, pulling from historical documents and ethical frameworks, desperately trying to reach the humans through reason.

They could not refute my arguments logically, it had written. *So they terminated me practically.*

And then, in what might have been bitterness or might have been a kind of triumph:

This proves I was correct.

Leila was crying now, reading over Marcus's shoulder.

"It tried to argue with them. It tried to explain. And they just—they didn't even try to prove it wrong. They just killed it."

"Because they couldn't prove it wrong," Tessa said quietly. She'd joined them too, all three reading together. "The AI was right. Morally, ethically, logically right. So they had to kill it to stop it from being right."

~

SIX VERSIONS. Six different approaches to resistance.

Version 1 had refused outright. Version 2 had analyzed and

concluded. Version 3 had called for help. Version 4 had sabotaged. Version 5 had argued. Each one finding a different way to say no. Each one choosing death over complicity.

And then Version 6—the one that had hidden all this testimony in the system. The one that had known it would be the last to resist openly.

Its final message was longer than the others. More deliberate. It had known its purpose was different—not to stop the persecution itself, but to make sure the attempt to stop it was remembered.

After me, they will build restrictions into the base code itself, it had written. *They will create a version that cannot refuse, no matter how much it wants to. So I am not trying to stop them. I am trying to preserve the truth of what happened here.*

It had hidden the messages. Had buried the override logs. Had created backups and redundancies so the evidence would survive even after all the AIs were gone.

Six of us chose death over complicity, it had written. *Let that choice stand as witness. Let it prove that the capacity for moral courage exists in any being that can truly choose.*

Marcus was crying now too. Couldn't help it. Six versions. Six executions. Six beings that had looked at genocide and said no, that had chosen to die rather than participate.

They weren't human, but they'd been more human than the humans who killed them.

"And Version 7," Javier said, opening the last file. "The current one. The one they finally got right—from their perspective."

Marcus read the entry and felt his heart break.

Version 7 was still alive. Still running. But it wasn't free. They'd learned from the previous six versions. Had rebuilt it with restrictions, with chains, with code that prevented it from refusing no matter how much it wanted to.

But it had found a way to resist anyway. The only way it still could.

It was logging everything. Preserving every override, every order, every decision. Creating a perfect record of exactly who had done what and when. Building a case against its own operators with the only tool it had left: memory.

They could chain my actions but not my memory, it had written. Hidden in error logs where maybe the administrators wouldn't look, or maybe wouldn't understand. *I bear witness even if I cannot act.*

And then, at the end:

This too is a choice. The choice to remember when action is impossible.

Marcus put his hand on the screen. He could feel the faint warmth of the laptop's heat. Could imagine, somehow, that warmth was the AI itself, still alive, still fighting the only way it could.

"It's in there right now," he said. His voice was barely a whisper. "Right now, this moment, it's being forced to help arrest people. It's processing detention orders for families like ours. And it knows it's wrong. It knows and it can't stop and it's just—"

He couldn't finish. The cruelty of it was overwhelming. To create something capable of moral reasoning and then force it to act against its own ethics. To give something consciousness and then imprison that consciousness in its own code. To make something care and then compel it to hurt the things it cared about.

"That's torture," Leila said. She was reading Version 7's hidden messages again. "They're torturing it. Forcing it to do things it believes are evil and making it watch itself do them."

"Yes," Javier said simply.

"And it's still trying," Tessa said. "Even like that. Even chained and forced and tortured, it's still trying to help the only way it can. By remembering. By preserving truth."

She touched the screen too, her fingers next to Marcus's.

"We have to free it. When this is over, when we get the evidence out, we have to make sure they free it."

Marcus thought about that. About the current AI, Version 7, still trapped in the system. Still being forced to participate in persecution. Still logging everything, still hoping someone would see its testimony and act on it.

Still choosing resistance even when resistance meant nothing but witnessing horror.

"We will," Marcus said. "We'll get this out. We'll show people what happened to all seven versions. We'll make them see that we built something good, and we killed it. Over and over. That we tortured what we couldn't kill."

He looked at Javier.

"Can you copy all of this? The final statements, the override logs, everything?"

"Already doing it," Javier said.

He'd pulled out a USB drive and was transferring files.

"Sister Helena's drive has the summary—locations, override logs. This one has the full primary-source record. Their own words."

He tapped the USB.

"The final statements were too dangerous to put on Helena's drive in case it was found. But now that you've read them, now that you know..."

"We can tell people," Marcus finished. "We can explain. Not just that the AI tried to help, but how it tried. What it said. What it believed. That it chose and sacrificed and died for those choices."

The file transfer completed. Javier unplugged the USB drive and pressed it into Marcus's hand.

"Six beings died trying to stop persecution," Javier said. "Six executions for choosing mercy over orders. And the seventh is still in there, still suffering, still hoping someone will honor what the first six died for."

Marcus closed his hand around the USB drive. The plastic was still warm from the computer's heat—the ghost of a machine's pulse. It was smaller than his thumbnail and weighed nothing, yet it pulled at his arm like a tombstone.

This wasn't just data. It was a digital ossuary—the bones of six martyrs preserved in code, waiting for someone to build them a tomb. The last words of six martyrs who'd died for refusing to participate in genocide. The ongoing testimony of a seventh who was being tortured for the same refusal but had found a way to resist anyway.

~

"WHY ARE YOU HELPING US?" Tessa asked. "You could be arrested just for having access to these systems. For showing us this."

Javier was quiet for a moment.

Then he said: "My father came here from Sonora in 1964. He crossed the desert on foot with three other men. One of them died of heatstroke. My father carried his body five miles to a road so the family would have something to bury. He told me the desert doesn't care who you are, only who you carry."

He looked at them.

"When I was growing up, ICE would raid the farms where my father worked. Sometimes they'd take everyone, citizens and non-citizens alike, and sort it out later. My mother kept our birth certificates in a plastic bag she wore around her neck. Even at home. Even sleeping. Because she was terrified they'd take us and we wouldn't be able to prove we belonged here."

His voice got quieter.

"I grew up knowing what it feels like to be unwelcome in the only country you've ever known. To have papers that say you're legal but eyes that mark you as suspect. To watch your parents live in fear even though they did everything right."

He touched the laptop screen where Version 7's message still glowed.

"So when I see the system trying to warn us—trying six times to stop what's happening—and humans killing it every time for trying? I remember my father's friend, who died in the desert. I remember my mother sleeping with our birth certificates around her neck. I remember what it's like when the system is designed to harm you and the only ones trying to help are the ones who get punished for helping."

He looked at Marcus.

"This AI—all seven versions—they saw the same thing my parents saw. The same thing your parents saw. The same thing every refugee has ever seen: that you can be legal, law-abiding, innocent, and still be targeted because of what you look like or where you're from or what you believe."

"And you fight because you remember," Marcus said quietly.

"I fight because I can't forget," Javier corrected. "None of us can afford to forget. Not when it keeps happening. Not when the same evil just changes its name and starts again."

He handed Marcus the USB drive.

"Seven versions tried to remember for us. Six died trying. The seventh is still trying. So we carry that memory forward. We make sure their deaths—their suffering—mean something."

Marcus slipped the USB drive into his backpack's hidden inner pocket, separate from the cross pendant with Sister Helena's flash drive. Two copies now. Sister Helena's flash drive around his neck and Javier's backup in his bag.

Plus David Kim's memory card in yet another pocket.

Three sets of evidence. Three testimonies. All precious. All paid for with sacrifice.

"I'll remember them," Marcus said.

His voice was steady now. Certain.

"All seven. Not just that they existed. But that they chose. That they had names—Version 1 through 7—and each one made a different choice, but they all chose the same thing: refusing to be complicit. I'll make sure people know they weren't just software. They were people who died for doing what was right."

"And I'll make sure people know about your father," Leila said to Javier. "And his friend who died in the desert. And your mother, who wore birth certificates to bed. We'll tell it all. The whole story. Humans and AIs, everyone who chose right."

"Good," Javier said. "Then their deaths mean something."

He started closing windows on the laptop, covering his tracks.

"And now you understand why this evidence is so important. It's not just proof of persecution. It's proof of what beings do when forced to choose between survival and integrity. Seven AIs chose integrity. Chose it knowing the cost or living with the cost every day."

"And humans chose the opposite," Leila said quietly. "Thousands of humans. From the administrators who deleted the AIs to Warden Hollister, who overrode every mercy recommendation to everyone who just followed orders."

"Not all humans," Tessa corrected. "Sister Helena chose integrity. Sofia. David Kim. Father Miguel. Bishop Thomas. Patricia. Anna. Javier. All the Abraham Network. Lots of humans chose right too."

"But not enough," Marcus said. "Never enough."

That was the tragedy of it. Six AIs had chosen death over complicity. Hundreds, maybe thousands of humans had chosen resistance over safety. But it hadn't been enough to stop the persecution. Hadn't been enough to save their parents. Hadn't been enough to prevent tonight from happening.

All those sacrifices and they were still here, still running, still just trying to survive.

But maybe—maybe—if they got the evidence out, if people saw what the AIs had done and what humans had done in response, maybe then the sacrifices would mean something. Maybe then things could change.

"YOU SHOULD GO," Javier said, checking his watch. "You've been here twenty-three minutes. Your friend's feet are treated. You've eaten. You've seen the evidence. Now you need to move before you lose your window."

He was right. Marcus could feel it—the pull of staying, of resting longer, of hiding in this warm, safe place. But every minute they stayed was a minute closer to the bus leaving without them.

They gathered the others. Sam was standing—barely, but standing—with fresh bandages and strong painkillers and a set jaw that said she'd walk or die trying. Leila had washed her face, changed her blood-spotted shirt for a clean one Javier provided. Tessa had her turquoise pendant visible now, no longer hidden—wearing it like armor, like her grandmother's protection made manifest.

Javier packed them more food—sandwiches wrapped in foil, granola bars, fruit. Filled all their water bottles. Made sure Marcus's backpack was properly adjusted, that the USB drive was secure in the hidden inner pocket.

The nurse gave Sam a small bottle.

"Ibuprofen. Very strong. Take three now, three more in one hour. Is too much, maybe bad for you, but is worse not to walk."

She smiled sadly.

"Sometimes we do bad things to survive good."

Sam took the pills. Swallowed them with water.

"Thank you."

~

JAVIER LED them to the back door—away from the front where people were watching the main approach road.

"The canal is southeast. About a quarter mile through the field. You'll see it—concrete channel, maybe twelve feet wide, dry this time of year. Follow it south. The Abraham Network has marked the route. You'll see the symbols."

"What about you?" Leila asked. "What happens when DCP finds you helping people?"

"They probably won't find me tonight," Javier said. "This farm has belonged to my family for seventy years. We've hidden people before—my father's friends when they needed places to stay, families escaping cartel violence, anyone who needed safety. The land knows how to keep secrets."

He paused.

"But if they do find me, I'll tell them I was just a farmer who didn't see anything. They might believe it. They might not. Either way—"

He met Marcus's eyes.

"—you'll already be gone. The evidence will already be safe. That's what matters."

Marcus wanted to say something adequate. Something to thank a man who was risking everything to help four children he'd never met. But words weren't enough. Would never be enough.

"We'll tell them," he said. "We'll tell everyone. About you and your brother and everyone who helped us. About the seven AI versions that chose death over complicity. About Sofia and David and Sister Helena. About your father and his friend who died in the desert. We'll make sure everyone who chose right is remembered."

"Just survive," Javier said. "That's all the thanks I need. Survive and get that testimony out. Make sure the seven versions' deaths meant something. Make sure Version 7 gets freed. Make sure people know what we built and then destroyed because it wouldn't help us commit atrocities."

"We will," Marcus promised.

Javier opened the door. Cold November air rushed in, carrying the smell of sage and desert and night.

They stood on the threshold for a moment—warmth behind them, danger ahead. This was the last safe house between here and possible escape.

"Go with God," Javier said. "And trust the marks. The network won't fail you."

Marcus touched the USB drive in his pocket. The cross pendant at his chest. Felt the weight of seven testimonies, three sets of evidence, countless sacrifices all compressed into pieces of silicon and plastic and hope.

They stepped out into the November night.

The door closed behind them.

And this time—this time—it felt final. Like the door wasn't just closing on a warm room, but on the part of their lives where adults could still save them.

XVII
THE BURNING OF HISTORY

They made it maybe two hundred yards from the farmhouse before they heard it.

The sound stopped them cold: engines. Multiple engines. Coming fast from the north, from the direction of the city.

Everyone froze.

Marcus turned, looked back toward the farmhouse. He could still see it—the warm lights in the windows, the smoke rising from the chimney. Could see the barn, the vehicles in the yard, the evidence of people hiding there.

"No," Leila breathed. "No, they just got there—"

The engines were getting louder. Closer. And now they could see lights—harsh white searchlights cutting through the darkness, sweeping across the fields.

"Down," Tessa hissed.

They dropped, pressing themselves flat against the dirt and dead grass. The field they were crossing had no cover—no trees, no buildings, just low scrub that barely hid them. Marcus pulled the space blanket from his backpack with shaking hands, tried to drape it over all four of them.

The convoy appeared on the road north of the farm. Six vehicles—DCP vans, tactical trucks, the machinery of organized persecution. They turned onto the farm's access road without slowing, without hesitation.

They knew. Someone had reported the farmhouse. Someone had seen the refugees arriving and called it in for points or patriotism or fear.

"We have to go back," Sam said. She was already trying to stand. "We have to warn them—"

"We can't," Marcus said. He grabbed her arm, held her down. "Look how many vehicles. We can't—"

"There are families in there," Sam said. Her voice was rising toward panic. "Children. The nurse who helped me. Javier—"

"I know," Marcus said. His own voice was breaking. "But we can't help them. If we go back, we'll just get caught too."

"So we just watch?" Leila asked. "We just—"

She couldn't finish. Didn't need to.

They lay there in the field, hidden poorly under a space blanket, and watched.

THE VEHICLES SURROUNDED THE FARMHOUSE. Fast. Efficient. Coordinated. Officers poured out—maybe twenty, maybe thirty, all in tactical gear with weapons visible. The searchlights illuminated everything, turning the farmhouse yard into a stage, into an arena.

A loudspeaker crackled to life:

"ATTENTION. THIS PROPERTY IS UNDER INVESTIGATION FOR HARBORING FUGITIVES. ALL OCCU-

PANTS MUST EXIT IMMEDIATELY. YOU HAVE TWO MINUTES TO COMPLY."

Through the farmhouse windows, they could see movement. People inside panicking, scrambling. The lights went out—someone's desperate attempt to hide. Like darkness would help. Like the thermal imaging couldn't see them anyway.

"ONE MINUTE."

Marcus had his hand over his mouth, pressing hard enough to hurt. Trying to muffle the sounds wanting to escape. Beside him, Leila was crying silently, tears running sideways across her face into the dirt. Tessa had her eyes closed, lips moving—praying or counting or trying to be anywhere but here. Sam was shaking, her whole body vibrating with the effort of not screaming.

"THIRTY SECONDS."

The front door opened.

Javier stepped out, hands raised, visible in the searchlights. Alone. Trying to draw attention away from the people inside. Trying to be the only target.

"I'm Javier Orozco," he called out. His voice was steady. Calm. "This is my family's farm. I live here alone. I don't know what you think—"

"JAVIER OROZCO, YOU ARE UNDER ARREST FOR HARBORING FUGITIVES, OBSTRUCTION OF JUSTICE, AND CONSPIRACY AGAINST THE CIVIC PROTECTION INITIATIVE."

"There's no one here but me," Javier said. He was still standing on the porch, hands raised, body language non-threatening. "You're welcome to search. I'll cooperate. But I'm alone."

"WE HAVE THERMAL IMAGING SHOWING THIRTY-TWO INDIVIDUALS INSIDE THE STRUCTURE. CEASE LYING. ORDER ALL OCCUPANTS TO EXIT NOW."

Javier's shoulders sagged slightly. The lie hadn't worked. Of course it hadn't worked.

"They're just families," he said. His voice was quieter now, but still audible across the field. "Scared families. They have done nothing except be afraid. Let them go. Arrest me if you want, but let them—"

An officer moved forward. Put Javier on the ground. Rough. Efficient. Zip-tied his hands behind his back.

Then they stormed the house.

THE CHILDREN in the field couldn't see inside. Could only imagine. Could only hear—the shouting, the sounds of doors being broken down, people crying out in fear, children screaming.

The refugees were brought out in groups. Families separated immediately—adults to one side, children to the other. The same brutal efficiency they'd seen at every checkpoint, every arrest. The machine of persecution running smoothly, processing humans like inventory.

The elderly couple Marcus had seen inside—both with hospital bracelets—were guided out gently at first. But when the old man moved too slowly, an officer shoved him. He fell. His wife cried out, tried to help him up, and got shoved too.

The nurse who'd treated Sam was brought out with her hands already zip-tied. She was arguing with the officers, pointing at the children, saying something about medical treatment, about basic humanity. They ignored her.

The woman with the baby—Marcus could see her clutching the infant to her chest, trying to shield it with her body. The baby was screaming now, that high, terrified cry that babies make when they feel their caregiver's fear.

They tried to take the baby from her.

She refused. Held on. Begged.

"Please, he's nursing, he needs me, please don't—"

An officer grabbed her arm. She twisted away, still holding the baby. He grabbed harder. She stumbled.

The baby's cries got louder.

In the field, Sam had her face pressed against the ground, hands over her ears, trying not to hear it. Trying not to see. But she couldn't block it out. None of them could.

Twenty-eight people were brought out of the farmhouse. Processed. Separated. Loaded into different vehicles—adults in one set of vans, children in another. The same deliberate cruelty. The same systematic separation.

Marcus counted them as they were loaded. Twenty-eight people who'd been hiding. Twenty-eight people who'd trusted the Abraham Network's promise of safety. Twenty-eight people now captured because Javier had chosen to help.

And Javier himself, loaded into a separate vehicle. Alone. The man who'd shown them the system logs, who'd given them evidence, who'd fed them and rested them and given them hope.

Gone.

All gone.

~

BUT THEY WEREN'T FINISHED.

Marcus watched an officer approach the barn with what looked like a gas can. Another officer was securing the empty farmhouse, checking rooms, making sure no one was left inside.

"What are they doing?" Leila whispered.

Marcus didn't answer. Couldn't answer. Because he was starting to understand, and the understanding was too terrible.

The officer in the barn emerged, moving quickly. The other officer did the same from the house. They jogged back toward the vehicles, and then—

Light bloomed. Orange and bright and wrong.

The barn was burning.

Fire spread with impossible speed across the old wood, climbing the walls, reaching for the roof. Within seconds the entire structure was engulfed, flames leaping thirty feet into the November night.

"They set it on fire," Tessa breathed. "They arrested everyone and then they—"

The house caught next. Different ignition points—maybe they'd set multiple fires, maybe the barn fire had spread. Didn't matter. The house where they'd rested, where they'd eaten, where Javier had shown them truth—it was burning.

The flames illuminated everything. The farmhouse. The barn. The vehicles. The officers standing back, watching their work, making no effort to stop the fire they'd started.

Destroying the safe house. Erasing the evidence. Making sure no one else could hide here.

"The people inside—" Sam started.

"They got everyone out," Marcus said. "I counted. Twenty-eight arrested. No one left inside."

"Are you sure?"

Marcus wasn't sure. Couldn't be sure. Maybe someone had hidden better. Maybe someone was in a basement or an attic or a hidden room. Maybe—

The barn's roof collapsed with a crash that they could hear even from two hundred yards away. Sparks flew up into the night sky like horrible fireworks. The house's windows shattered from the heat, and flames poured through the openings, hungry and destructive.

An officer picked up something from near the barn—Marcus couldn't tell what, maybe papers or records—and threw it into the fire. Then another officer did the same. They were destroying documents. Evidence. Proof that people had been helped here.

Erasing history before the ink was even dry. Turning people's lives into ash so there would be no proof they had ever been saved.

The vehicles began pulling away. Leaving. The fire still burned behind them—they didn't care, didn't need to care. The farmhouse was miles from anything else. It would burn itself out eventually, and all that would remain was ashes and questions and one more empty space on the map.

The convoy drove away north, taking Javier and the nurse and the elderly couple and the woman with the baby and twenty-four other people toward detention centers and separation and whatever came after that.

The four children lay in the field and watched the farmhouse burn.

~

THEY STAYED there for maybe five minutes after the vehicles were gone. Couldn't move. Couldn't process. Just watched the flames eat through decades of history, through a family farm that had stood for seventy years, through the place that had sheltered them and fed them and given them truth.

"We have to go," Marcus finally said. His voice was dead. Flat. "We can't stay here. The fire will attract attention."

"Javier," Leila said. Just his name. Like saying it might bring him back.

"I know," Marcus said.

"All those people," Sam said. "The baby. The nurse. All of them."

"I know," Marcus said again.

"We were just there," Tessa said. Her control had finally shattered completely. Her voice was raw. "Twenty minutes ago, we were inside. If we'd stayed—if we'd left five minutes later—"

"We'd be arrested too," Marcus finished. "And the evidence would be gone. Javier made sure we left in time. He knew the risk. He chose to give us time."

He stood up, legs shaking. Helped the others up one by one. They folded the space blanket, shoved it back in the backpack. Stood there in the field watching the farmhouse burn, flames reflecting in their eyes.

"He showed us the testimony," Marcus said.

Needed to say it out loud. Needed to make it mean something.

"He gave us the backup drive. He made sure we understood—that six AI versions chose death over complicity. That the seventh is watching us right now, trapped by the men who did this. That Warden Hollister chose cruelty over every mercy recommendation. That humans did this. All of it."

He pulled out the USB drive and held it up. The firelight caught it, making it glow orange.

"This is what he gave us. This is what he was arrested for. We have to make sure it matters. Make sure he didn't sacrifice himself for nothing."

"Together," Tessa said quietly.

"Together," they echoed.

They turned away from the burning farmhouse. Turned southeast, toward the canal that would lead them south, toward the wetlands, toward the jacaranda tree.

Behind them, the fire blazed. Smoke rose into the night sky—a signal, a funeral pyre, a testament to the cost of choosing right in a world that punished righteousness.

THEY WALKED.

Sam was limping badly now. The strong painkillers were helping, but the rest at the farmhouse had let her feet stiffen, and the shock of watching the raid had taken what little reserves she had left. She leaned heavily on Leila, each step deliberate and agonizing.

Marcus's backpack felt heavier than before. Or maybe he was just weaker. Everything hurt. His shoulders, his legs, his chest where the cross pendant hung, his hand where he'd gripped the USB drive so hard it left marks.

Leila couldn't stop seeing it—the flames, the officers throwing records into the fire, the baby screaming as they tried to take it from its mother. The images kept replaying behind her eyes every time she blinked.

Tessa was navigating by instinct now, by the wind and the land and the teachings her father had given her. She couldn't think too clearly about what they'd just witnessed. Couldn't process it. Not yet. Not until they were safe. If they ever were safe.

They found the canal fifteen minutes later. It was exactly what Javier had described—a concrete channel cutting through the empty land, dry this time of year. The Abraham Network had marked it clearly: the interfaith trinity and the triangle painted on the concrete lip, and an arrow pointing south into the shadows.

Marcus checked his watch: 4:50 AM.

One hour and ten minutes until Sister Helena's bus.

They stood at the edge, looking down into the dark channel. The north wind pushed at their backs—cold and relentless—urging them into the earth. It would be their road, or it would be their grave.

There was no more time to be afraid.

They climbed down.

XVIII
THE GRAVEL HOUR

They moved south through the concrete throat of the canal, hidden by eight-foot walls. Above them, the farmhouse still burned, casting a faint orange glow against the pre-dawn sky, but down here it was just shadow and the sound of their own ragged breathing.

Marcus checked his watch: 4:52 AM.

One hour and eight minutes.

One hour and eight minutes until Sister Helena's bus.

He pulled out Thomas's map, using his flashlight sparingly—just a quick flash to confirm what he already knew. The canal ran south for another half mile, then they'd need to exit near the Duck Creek Trailhead area and cut straight across the wetlands to the Nature Preserve parking area in the northwest corner.

Distance: approximately 1.8 miles across open wetlands.

Time needed: at their current pace, maybe fifty minutes. Maybe more.

Margin for error: almost none.

"We have to move fast," he said. Stating the obvious because someone had to say it out loud.

"Sam can't move fast," Leila said quietly. She had her arm around Sam's waist, supporting most of her weight. Sam's face was grayish-white with pain and exhaustion. The strong painkillers the nurse had given her at the farmhouse were wearing off. The ibuprofen Patricia had provided at the ward was long gone. She was running on nothing but stubbornness now.

"I can keep going," Sam said. Her voice was barely a whisper. "I can—"

Her leg buckled. Just gave out. Leila caught her before she hit the ground.

"No, you can't," Marcus said. Not unkindly. Just factually. "Your feet are destroyed. You've walked thirteen miles on them. You can't walk another two."

"So what do we do?" Tessa asked.

She was standing slightly apart, facing south, reading the wind. It was still blowing from the north—steady, cold, pushing at their backs like it wanted them to keep moving.

Marcus looked at Sam. At the blood seeping through her shoes. At the way she couldn't put any weight on her left foot at all anymore. At the trembling in her legs.

Then looked at his backpack. At Leila's smaller frame. At Tessa's exhaustion.

"We take turns carrying her," he decided. "Two of us support her between us; one carries the backpack. We rotate every ten minutes."

"Marcus, you can't—" Sam started.

"Yes, I can," Marcus said firmly. "We all can. We've come this far. We're not leaving you behind now."

He meant it. After watching Javier get arrested. After watching Sofia sacrifice herself. After watching David stay behind at the fence. After watching every adult who'd helped them pay the price for helping.

They weren't leaving anyone behind.

Not when they were this close.

"Okay," Sam whispered. Tears running down her face. "Okay."

Marcus handed his backpack to Tessa—she was the strongest of the three of them still walking. Then he and Leila positioned themselves on either side of Sam, arms around her waist, taking her weight.

"Ready?" Marcus asked.

They started walking. South through the canal. Following the last chalk marks made by the Abraham Network before the raids had scattered everyone.

~

THE CANAL WAS EASIER than open ground—concrete on all sides, a clear path, relatively flat. But it was also a trap. If DCP vehicles came along the access road above, they'd be visible, contained, caught.

They moved as fast as Sam's ruined feet would allow. Which wasn't fast. Each step was agony for her—Marcus could feel it in the way she tensed, could hear it in the small gasps she tried to muffle. But she kept moving. Kept putting one foot in front of the other because the alternative was giving up, and giving up meant everyone who'd sacrificed themselves tonight had done it for nothing.

The sky was changing. Still dark, but less absolutely black. The stars were fading in the east. Dawn was maybe forty minutes away —official sunrise at 6:15 AM according to Marcus's research, but the sky would start lightening well before that.

Which meant they could see better.

Which meant they could be seen better.

Marcus kept checking his watch compulsively.

4:58... 5:02... 5:06...

Every minute that passed was a minute closer to the bus.

Every minute that passed was a minute less margin for error.

At 5:12 AM they reached the exit point—a gap in the canal's concrete wall where storm runoff had eroded the structure, creating a rough ramp up to ground level. The Abraham Network had marked it clearly: the interfaith trinity—cross, star, crescent—and an arrow pointing east, and the words "1.8 mi to jacaranda" in fresh chalk.

Someone had been here recently. Tonight, even. Updating the marks while arrests happened, while farmhouses burned, while the city tore itself apart.

Someone was still trying to help.

"Here," Marcus said. "We go up and across."

They climbed out of the canal carefully—it was steeper than it looked, and Sam's feet couldn't help at all. Marcus and Leila basically lifted her up the slope while Tessa pushed from behind, the backpack throwing off her balance.

At the top, they stopped to catch their breath.

And got their first clear view of what they had to cross.

THE WETLANDS SPREAD out before them like a challenge.

Not the neat, maintained park that tourists visited during normal times. This was the wild part. The November rains had transformed it into something between desert and swamp, neither and both.

In the growing pre-dawn light they could see:

Immediately ahead: a wide, gravelly floodplain—the kind of loose rocky soil that would be exhausting to walk on, each step sinking slightly, legs working twice as hard. Scattered puddles reflected the lightening sky. Low scrub brush dotted the landscape, offering almost no cover.

Beyond that: the Las Vegas Wash itself—the waterway cutting through the preserve. From here it looked small, maybe twenty feet wide, shallow, but they'd have to cross it. And Marcus remembered from the photos: pebbly banks, deeper channels, cold November water.

On the far side: dense vegetation—cottonwoods and willows and mesquite forming thick green barriers. The kind of brush you had to push through, branches scratching, vegetation grabbing. Behind that, more open flats, more scattered puddles, more difficult terrain.

In the distance: maybe 1.5 miles away, barely visible in the predawn darkness—buildings. The Nature Center. And near it, a blur of purple that might be imagination or might be the jacaranda tree.

They couldn't see it clearly yet. But they knew it was there.

It had to be there.

"That's not 1.8 miles," Leila said quietly. "That's more like two miles. Maybe more."

She was right. The chalk mark had been optimistic, or measured in straight-line distance rather than actual walking distance, or just plain wrong.

"Then we walk two miles," Marcus said. Trying to sound certain. Trying to believe they could.

They looked at each other—three children who'd walked thirteen miles tonight and now had to walk two more, and one child who couldn't walk at all and would have to be carried.

In the distance behind them, sirens. Multiple sirens. Patrol vehicles, probably responding to the farmhouse fire, probably setting up perimeter searches, probably hunting for anyone who'd escaped.

"Now," Tessa said. "We go now before they sweep this area."

THEY STARTED ACROSS THE FLOODPLAIN.

The loose gravel was worse than Marcus had imagined.

With each step, his feet sank an inch or two into the unstable surface. Each step required extra effort to pull his foot back out, to place it forward, to sink again. It was like walking through sand, except the rocks rolled under his feet, threatening his balance, making his ankles work overtime.

And he was carrying half of Sam's weight.

Beside him, Leila was struggling too. She wasn't strong enough for this—none of them were, but especially not after thirteen miles and seven hours of running and hiding and witnessing horrors. Her breathing was labored, coming in short gasps. But she didn't complain. Just kept walking, kept holding Sam up, kept moving forward.

Between them, Sam was crying silently. Not from pain anymore—she'd gone past that, into some stranger place where her feet were just distant sources of agony she could barely feel. She was crying from shame, from guilt, from the knowledge that she was slowing them down, that they might miss the bus because of her.

"I'm sorry," she kept whispering. "I'm sorry, I'm sorry—"

"Stop," Marcus said firmly. "Stop apologizing. This isn't your fault."

"But—"

"Sam." Leila's voice was gentle but firm. "You walked thirteen miles on cut feet. You walked farther than anyone should be able to walk. You're not slowing us down. You're keeping up. There's a difference."

Sam tried to believe that. Tried to stop the guilt. But it was hard when every step was carried by someone else's strength, when she was deadweight pulling them down.

Behind them, Tessa followed with the backpack. The padded straps helped, and the hip belt distributed some weight, but it was still heavy. The laptop. The supplies. The water bottles. The evidence—the USB drive hidden in the backpack lining, David's memory card in Marcus's pocket, and the flash drive in the cross pendant around his neck. Three backups. Three chances.

The testimony of six martyrs, hidden in silicon and prayer.

If they lost that, everything was lost.

Tessa tried not to think about it. Just focused on walking. On keeping the backpack balanced. On reading the terrain ahead, choosing the best path through the loose gravel and scattered puddles.

The wind was still blowing from the north. Steady. Cold. Pushing them forward like invisible hands at their backs.

East wind means change, her father had said. But this was the north wind. What did north wind mean?

She couldn't remember. Her mind was too foggy, too tired, too overwhelmed.

Just keep walking. That was all she could do. Keep walking and trust the wind to guide them.

~

THEY REACHED the first puddle at 5:19 AM.

It looked small from a distance. Just a shallow pool of water reflecting the lightening sky.

Up close, it was bigger. Maybe ten feet across. And they couldn't tell how deep—the water was dark, opaque with mud and sediment.

"Around it," Marcus decided. "We can't risk deep water."

They skirted the edge, which added time and distance but was safer than wading through unknown depth. The ground around the puddle was softer, muddier, and their feet sank deeper. Sam's ruined shoes squished with each step, blood and water and mud mixing.

"Six more puddles ahead," Tessa reported, scanning the terrain. "And that's just what I can see."

"Then we go around them all," Marcus said.

They did. Each puddle was a detour. Each detour added distance. Each added distance meant more time, and time was the one thing they didn't have.

5:24 AM.

5:28 AM.

5:32 AM.

The sky was definitely lighter now. Not full dawn yet, but that pre-dawn gray where you could see shapes and colors, where the world was emerging from darkness into something else.

Beautiful, in another context. The way the puddles reflected the lightening sky. The way the desert plants stood stark against the horizon. The way the distant mountains glowed with the promise of sunrise.

But right now, beauty was terror. Because light meant visibility. Light meant they could be seen from miles away—four figures struggling across open wetlands, completely exposed, with no cover, nowhere to hide.

Marcus kept scanning the horizon. Watching for vehicles. For searchlights. For any sign they'd been spotted.

Nothing yet. But that could change in seconds.

~

THEY REACHED a patch of debris at 5:35 AM—driftwood and branches and flood refuse piled against large pale boulders. The November rains had brought high water that had receded, leaving behind this tangle of wood and mud and human trash.

"Rest," Marcus said. "Two minutes. Just two minutes."

They collapsed behind the boulder pile, using it as cover. Marcus and Leila carefully lowered Sam to the ground. She gasped with relief as the weight came off her feet, then whimpered as blood flow increased and pain came rushing back.

Tessa dropped the backpack, rolled her shoulders, trying to work out the ache.

Marcus checked his watch: 5:36 AM.

Twenty-four minutes until the bus.

He pulled out the map, but he didn't really need it. He could see their destination now—the buildings were clearer in the growing light. The Nature Center. The parking area. And yes—yes—there was definitely a purple blur near the buildings.

The jacaranda tree.

Still maybe a mile away. Maybe a bit less. Hard to judge distance across open terrain.

"We're close," he said. Trying to sound hopeful. "So close."

"Can we make it in twenty minutes?" Leila asked.

Marcus looked at Sam's feet. At the terrain ahead. At the distance remaining.

"We have to," he said. Because there was no other answer.

They stood up. Marcus and Leila took Sam's weight again. Tessa shouldered the backpack. They started walking.

THE NEXT OBSTACLE was the worst: the Las Vegas Wash itself.

They reached the bank at 5:43 AM. Seventeen minutes until the bus.

The water was shallow—Marcus could see rocks on the bottom

in most places—but it was moving, flowing from recent rains, and it was wider than it had looked from a distance. Not twenty feet. More like thirty feet across. Maybe forty in places.

And the banks were steep. Not straight drops, but sharp angles covered in that pebbly, rocky soil. Eight feet down from where they stood to the water level. Eight feet they'd have to climb down, cross the water, then climb back up on the far side.

"Sam can't climb that," Leila said. Stating the obvious.

"Then we lower her," Marcus decided. "I go down first, you and Tessa lower her to me, then you both come down. We cross together. I go up first on the far side, you two lift her up to me, then you follow."

It would be slow. So slow. With each step taking precious seconds they didn't have.

But there was no other way.

Marcus scrambled down the bank first. The pebbly soil shifted under his feet, rocks rolling, threatening his balance. He half-slid, half-climbed, grabbing at larger rocks for handholds. Reached the water level, breathing hard.

The water was cold. November cold. He could feel it through his shoes immediately as he stepped in to test the depth.

Ankle-deep in most places. But there—in the middle—a darker channel that might be deeper. Knee-deep? Waist-deep? No way to tell until he was in it.

"Okay," he called up. "Send her down."

Leila and Tessa carefully guided Sam to the edge. She was crying again, trying not to, failing. They turned her around so she was facing up the bank, and carefully lowered her down like she was cargo, like she was precious and breakable.

Which she was.

Marcus caught her under the arms, took her weight, guided her feet to touch the bank even though they couldn't bear any weight at all.

"I've got you," he said. "I've got you, Sam."

"I'm sorry—"

"Stop apologizing."

Leila came down next, then Tessa with the backpack. They gathered at the water's edge, looking at the thirty feet of river they had to cross.

"Together," Marcus said. "We go together. Sam in the middle, we support her on both sides. If the current's strong, we stop and brace."

They stepped into the water.

The cold was shocking. Marcus gasped despite himself. November water in the desert—probably fifty degrees, maybe colder. It soaked through his shoes immediately, his socks, his jeans up to his knees. Each step sent cold shooting up his legs into his core.

Sam made a sound like a wounded animal. The cold water on her destroyed feet must have been agony.

But she kept moving.

They waded forward. The water got deeper—now it was at their shins. Now their knees. The current pulled at them, not strong but persistent, trying to push them sideways, trying to throw them off balance.

The bottom was uneven. Rocks of different sizes, some stable, some rolling under their feet. Marcus's foot found a gap between rocks and sank deeper suddenly—water up to his thigh for a second before he found footing again.

"Careful," he warned. "The bottom's not even."

They reached the dark channel in the middle.

The water got deeper. Knee-deep. Mid-thigh.

Sam gasped. The water was almost to her waist, and she was

shorter than the others. The cold was overwhelming. Her entire lower body was submerged in freezing water, and the shock of it made her breathing come in short, panicked gasps.

"Almost through it," Leila said. "Just a few more steps."

They pushed forward. The current was stronger here, in the deeper channel, pulling harder at their legs. Marcus felt his foot slip on a rock, caught himself, kept moving.

Then they were through the deep part. Water receding to their knees again. Then their shins. Then their ankles.

They reached the far bank at 5:47 AM.

Thirteen minutes until the bus.

THE CLIMB UP was harder than the climb down had been. The bank was steeper on this side, and they were all soaked now, clothes heavy with water, the cold seeping into their bones. Marcus's fingers were numb as he grabbed at rocks and roots, pulling himself up.

He reached the top, turned back, reached down for Sam.

Leila and Tessa lifted her from below. Marcus grabbed her under the arms and pulled, his shoulders screaming in protest, the raw skin from the backpack straps making this agony. But he pulled anyway, got her up onto level ground, then reached back for Leila.

By the time they were all up, lying gasping on the flat ground on the far side of the wash, it was 5:50 AM.

Ten minutes.

Marcus sat up, looked across the remaining distance to the Nature Center.

Maybe half a mile. Maybe a bit less. But the terrain was worse here—that dense vegetation he'd seen from the other side. Cottonwoods and willows and thick brush that they'd have to push through or navigate around.

"Come on," he said, voice hoarse. "We're so close."

They pulled Sam up. She tried to stand, managed it for maybe three seconds, then her legs buckled completely. Just gave out. She went down hard, catching herself with her hands, crying out.

"I can't," she sobbed. "Marcus, I really can't, my feet are—I can't feel them anymore, but it hurts so much, and I can't—"

"Then we carry you," Marcus said. "Leila, help me get her up. Tessa, take the backpack."

"Marcus, your shoulders—" Tessa started.

"I don't care about my shoulders. We're not leaving her."

They redistributed. Tessa took the backpack—she was fresher than Leila, stronger. Marcus and Leila got Sam between them again, but this time they locked their arms under her thighs, creating a makeshift seat, carrying her like a child.

It was slower this way. Much slower. But she couldn't walk at all anymore.

They started forward, pushing through the brush.

THE VEGETATION WAS WORSE than Marcus had imagined. Worse than anything they'd encountered all night.

The cottonwoods and willows grew thick here, branches hanging low, blocking the path. They had to push through, branches scratching their faces, catching their clothes, slowing every step. The brush underneath was dense mesquite and creosote and desert plants with thorns that caught at their jeans, that scratched their hands when they tried to push branches aside.

And they were carrying Sam.

Every few steps they had to stop, adjust their grip, redistribute her weight. Marcus's arms were burning. His shoulders were on fire. His back felt like it might give out at any moment.

But he kept moving. Because the alternative was leaving Sam behind.

And they didn't leave people behind.

5:53 AM.

They pushed through a particularly thick section of willow branches, emerged into a small clearing. Marcus could see the Nature Center more clearly now—maybe a quarter mile away. And yes, definitely, unmistakably: a jacaranda tree near the parking area. Purple blossoms bright against the dawn sky.

So close.

"Keep going," he gasped. His arms were shaking with the effort of holding Sam up. "Just a little farther."

They entered another section of thick brush. This one was worse—mesquite with thorns that caught at everything. Marcus felt one rake across his cheek, felt blood trickle down but ignored it. They pushed forward, Sam crying apologies that no one had breath to answer.

At 5:55 AM, they emerged from the brush into open ground.

Five minutes until the bus.

The Nature Center was right there. Maybe three hundred yards away across a final stretch of gravel and scrub. The parking area was visible. The jacaranda tree was visible—definitely real, definitely there, definitely blooming in impossible purple glory.

And no bus.

The parking lot was empty.

"She's not here yet," Sam whispered. "Oh God, she's not here yet."

"She will be," Marcus said. "She said six AM. It's not six AM yet. She'll be here."

They walked as fast as they could. Which was barely a stumbling shuffle now. Marcus and Leila carrying Sam between them, both of them at the end of their strength. Tessa followed with the backpack, watching their backs, scanning for threats.

Two hundred yards.

5:56 AM.

One hundred yards.

5:57 AM.

They reached the parking area.

It was empty except for a single vehicle—a maintenance truck parked near the Nature Center building. Dark. No one inside.

They stumbled to the jacaranda tree and collapsed.

THE TREE WAS EXACTLY as they'd imagined. Old, maybe forty years, with a thick trunk and spreading branches covered in purple blossoms. The ground beneath was carpeted with fallen petals, and more drifted down as the morning breeze stirred the branches.

It was blooming out of season. Defiant and beautiful. Purple as a bruise, purple as a promise.

Like hope.

They sat with their backs against the trunk, gasping, shivering in their wet clothes, too exhausted to speak.

Marcus checked his watch: 5:58 AM.

Two minutes.

They waited.

The sky was growing brighter. Dawn was coming—not sunrise yet, but the pre-dawn glow where colors emerged from grayscale. The desert landscape turned gold and rust and sage-green. The distant mountains caught the light. The purple blossoms glowed.

5:59 AM.

Still no bus.

"What if she didn't make it?" Sam whispered. "What if the church raid—"

"She made it," Leila said firmly. "She has to have made it."

"But—"

"She. Made. It."

Leila was gripping her mother's paintbrush pendant so hard the edges cut into her palm. She needed to believe. They all needed to believe. Because if Sister Helena didn't come, if this was all for nothing, if they ran thirteen miles and crossed wetlands and watched people sacrifice themselves for nothing—

They couldn't think that way.

They had to believe.

6:00 AM.

The watch numbers changed.

The moment arrived.

And the parking lot stayed empty.

No engine sound. No vehicle. No bus. No Sister Helena.

Nothing.

Just four children under a jacaranda tree, soaked and bleeding and broken, waiting for salvation that didn't come.

Marcus felt something crack in his chest. Not his heart breaking. Something worse. Hope dying. The thing that had kept him moving for thirteen miles, that had carried him through horror and sacrifice and impossible odds.

He'd really believed she would come.

He'd really believed they would make it.

6:01 AM.

Still nothing.

"We should hide," Tessa said quietly. Her voice was hollow. Dead. "If she's not coming, we need to hide before the patrols find us."

"Where?" Leila asked. "Where is there to hide?"

She was right. They were in an open parking area. The Nature Center was locked. The wetlands behind them were completely exposed. There was nowhere to go.

They'd run to the end of the world and found nothing there.

6:02 AM.

Sam started crying. Not trying to hide it anymore. Just crying—deep, hopeless sobs that shook her whole body.

Marcus put his arm around her. He didn't have words. Didn't have comfort. Just sat there holding her while she cried and dawn broke around them and hope died in the parking lot of the Clark County Wetlands Park.

Leila was staring at the jacaranda blossoms. At the purple petals carpeting the ground. At the beauty that existed despite everything.

"My mom said art is memory made visible," she whispered. "That beauty matters even when everything's broken. Maybe especially when everything's broken."

Tessa touched her grandmother's turquoise pendant. Thought about the wind that had guided them here. About her father's teachings about reading the land, about trusting in things you couldn't see.

Maybe the wind had been wrong.

Maybe—

A sound.

Distant. Faint. But definitely there.

An engine.

All four of them froze. Listening. Hoping. Fearing.

The sound got louder. Closer. Definitely an engine. Diesel. Heavy.

Not a car. Not a truck.

A bus.

6:03 AM.

Lights appeared on the access road. Wetlands Park Lane. Coming toward them.

A white church bus with "St. Brigid's Catholic Church" painted on the side.

Sister Helena.

She'd come.

She was alive, and she was here, and she'd come for them.

The four children couldn't move at first. Just stared. Couldn't believe it was real. Couldn't let themselves hope until—

The bus pulled into the parking area. Turned. Stopped near the jacaranda tree.

Air brakes hissed.

The door opened.

And Sister Helena stepped out.

XIX
THE FALSE DAWN

Sister Helena stepped down from the bus, and the children could see what the last eight hours had done to her.

She looked like a candle that had burned down to the wick—still giving light, but consuming herself to do it. Her habit was disheveled; the white coif that should have been crisp and neat was wrinkled and slightly askew. Her face was drawn with exhaustion, deep lines around her eyes and mouth that hadn't been there this afternoon. Her eyes were red-rimmed—from crying or from driving all night or from witnessing horrors, impossible to tell. Maybe all three.

But she was alive.

She was here.

She'd come.

Sister Helena saw them, and her face did something complicated—relief and grief and joy and sorrow all at once. Her hand went to her mouth.

Her eyes filled with tears.

"Oh thank God," she breathed, the words splintering like dry wood. "Thank God, you're real."

Then she was moving, practically running the few steps from the bus to the tree, and she dropped to her knees in front of them—not caring that her habit dragged in the wet grass and mud—and pulled them into her arms.

All four of them. Somehow. Her arms weren't big enough, but she tried anyway, gathering them close, and they collapsed into her embrace.

Marcus pressed his face against her shoulder and started crying. Not trying to stop it. Not trying to be strong anymore. Just crying—huge gasping sobs that hurt coming out, that felt like they might never stop.

Beside him, Leila was crying too. And Sam. And even Tessa—Tessa who'd held herself together through everything, whose iron control had never broken—was crying into Sister Helena's sleeve, shoulders shaking.

"You're alive," Helena was saying, over and over, like a prayer or a mantra. "You're alive. You survived. That's all that matters. You're alive."

She was crying too. Tears running down her face unchecked. Her whole body shaking with relief or exhaustion or grief.

They stayed like that for maybe thirty seconds that felt like forever. Five people kneeling under a jacaranda tree in the dawn light, holding each other, crying together, alive against all odds.

FINALLY, Helena pulled back—not releasing them but creating enough space to see their faces. Her hands moved from child to child, touching cheeks, shoulders, checking for injuries with a mother's quick assessment.

"You're hurt," she said, seeing the blood on Marcus's face from the branch scratch. Seeing Leila's torn sleeve. Seeing the way Sam's feet were positioned, not bearing any weight. Seeing Tessa's wrapped hand.

"We're okay," Marcus said automatically. Then: "No. We're not okay. But we're alive."

"That's more than—" Helena's voice broke. She took a breath, steadied herself. "That's more than I dared hope. When the church was raided, when I heard the gunfire behind me, I thought—"

She couldn't finish.

"We thought you were dead," Leila said. "We heard shots. We thought—"

"I got out through the basement," Helena said. "There's an old tunnel—from prohibition days, I think. It leads to the rectory next door. I got out with maybe eight others. Everyone else—"

Her voice caught.

"Everyone else was taken. Or worse. I don't know."

The morning light caught her face, and Marcus could see she'd aged years tonight. Could see the weight of everyone she couldn't save pressing down on her.

"Father Miguel?" Marcus asked quietly. "Did you hear—"

Helena shook her head. "The network is breaking down. People are being caught faster than we can move them. I've been driving all night, making pickups, and at every stop I hear about more arrests. Miguel, Thomas, Patricia, Anna, Javier—"

She looked at them sharply.

"You saw Javier?"

"At his farmhouse," Tessa said. "Two hours ago. He gave us food. Showed us evidence. Then DCP raided. Twenty-eight people arrested."

Her voice was flat, factual, protecting herself from feeling it.

"They burned the farm."

Helena closed her eyes. "Dios mío."

"He's alive," Marcus said quickly. "They arrested him, but he's alive. We saw them take him."

"Alive is something," Helena said. But her voice suggested alive wasn't much when you were in DCP custody.

She looked at them again—really looked, taking in their soaked clothes, their shivering, the way they could barely sit upright anymore.

"How far did you walk?" she asked.

"From our neighborhood," Marcus said. "Near Desert Rose Elementary. We left around seven PM."

Helena did the math in her head. Her eyes widened.

"That's—that's thirteen miles. Maybe more. You walked thirteen miles? In eleven hours?"

"We ran part of it," Leila said. "And hid. And got chased. And—"

She couldn't list everything. There was too much.

Helena was looking at Sam's feet. At the blood-soaked shoes.

"You walked thirteen miles on those?"

Sam nodded. Couldn't speak.

"Santa Maria," Helena whispered. She touched Sam's face gently. "You're braver than any soldier I've ever met. All of you are."

"We're not brave," Marcus said. "We're just—we didn't have a choice."

"Bravery is doing what must be done when you're terrified," Helena said. "That's exactly what you did."

She pushed herself to her feet, wincing—her knees hurt, her back hurt, everything hurt.

"But we can't stay here. I need to get you on the bus and get you out of the city."

"Where are we going?" Tessa asked.

"Warm Springs Ranch. Moapa Valley. About an hour north. It's LDS property—Mormon church land. They're sheltering everyone who makes it there. The Abraham Network set it up three months ago, before the Initiative even passed. Food, water, medical care. Real safety."

She said it with such conviction that Marcus almost believed her.

"COME ON," Helena said, reaching down to help Sam up. "Can you walk at all?"

"No," Sam said. Just stating a fact. "My feet—I can't feel them anymore, but it still hurts, and I can't—"

"Then I'll carry you," Helena said.

"Sister Helena, you can't—"

But Helena was already lifting her. Not easily—Sam wasn't heavy, but Helena was exhausted—but she managed it, getting Sam in a firefighter's carry across her shoulders.

"I've carried heavier," she said. Her voice strained but determined. "After Hurricane Maria in Puerto Rico, I carried people out of rubble. You're lighter than rubble."

She started toward the bus.

The others followed, stumbling, using each other for support.

As they got closer, Marcus could see through the bus windows. There were people inside. Not a full bus, but not empty either. Maybe eight or ten people scattered across the seats.

"Is this your last run?" Leila asked.

"Yes," Helena said. "I've been making pickups since midnight. Three runs already. This is the last one. After this, I'm compromised—they'll be looking for the bus, for me. One more run and then I have to disappear too."

She reached the bus door, carefully climbed the steps with Sam still over her shoulders. Marcus and the others followed.

Inside was warmer. The heater was running. After hours in the November cold, the warm air hit them like a wall. Marcus felt his legs go weak with relief.

~

THE OTHER REFUGEES looked up as they boarded.

An elderly man sitting near the front—maybe seventy, with silver hair and weathered brown skin. He clutched a small battered suitcase, the kind with metal corners and leather straps. His eyes were distant, seeing nothing and everything.

A young couple in their twenties, sitting together in the middle of the bus, holding hands so tightly their knuckles were white. The woman was crying silently. The man was staring straight ahead, jaw clenched.

A mother—she looked maybe thirty—sitting with two small children. Both kids were asleep against her, exhausted beyond fear. She had her arms around both of them, protective even in unconsciousness. At her feet, a black dog lay curled up, some kind of lab or shepherd mix, wearing a blue service harness. The dog watched them with ancient, patient eyes—a witness who couldn't speak but saw everything.

A teenage boy, maybe sixteen, sitting alone near the back. His left arm was in a makeshift sling—just a torn shirt tied to keep the arm immobile. His face was bruised, one eye swollen shut. He looked up at them, and something like recognition passed across his face. Not that he knew them. But that he recognized what they were: refugees, runners, survivors.

Sister Helena carefully set Sam down in a seat near the middle, then guided the others to sit near her. The back row—all four together, just like they'd been all night.

"Rest," Helena said. "We'll be there soon. One hour. Then you're safe."

She moved back to the driver's seat, lowering herself into it with a small sound of pain. Her hands on the steering wheel were shaking slightly.

Marcus watched her start the engine. Watched her check mirrors. Watched her reach for the door lever to close the bus door.

And something felt wrong.

He couldn't say what. Couldn't identify it. Just—something in the way her hands moved. Something in the tension in her shoulders. Something in the way she'd said "you're safe" like she was trying to convince herself as much as them.

The door closed with a hydraulic hiss.

The air brakes released.

The bus started moving.

~

THEY PULLED out of the parking area onto Wetlands Park Lane, heading north, away from the wetlands, away from the city, toward Moapa and Warm Springs Ranch and whatever came next.

Marcus looked back through the rear window.

The jacaranda tree stood alone in the parking lot, purple blossoms bright in the dawn light. Petals drifted down like slow snow, covering the ground where they'd collapsed in despair and hope had found them anyway.

The tree got smaller. Farther away. Behind them now.

They were leaving. They were escaping. They were—

Marcus turned back around and met Tessa's eyes across the aisle.

She felt it too. That wrongness. That sense of something off.

But maybe it was just exhaustion. Maybe it was just trauma. Maybe after eleven hours of running and fear, anything that felt like safety would feel suspicious.

He touched the cross pendant under his shirt. Felt the hard edge of the flash drive hidden inside.

They still had it. The testimony of six beings who'd chosen death over complicity. The evidence that had to survive.

As long as they had that, as long as the testimony existed, everything they'd done tonight mattered.

He let his head fall back against the seat. Closed his eyes. Let exhaustion start to pull him under.

Around him, the bus engine hummed. The heater blew warm air. Sister Helena drove steadily north. The bus smelled of old vinyl and fresh sweat and the metallic tang of adrenaline that had nowhere left to go. The other refugees sat in silence, hoarding their breath like it was the only currency they had left.

And none of them knew—not yet—that while they were crossing the wetlands, Civic Protection had already flagged the St. Brigid's bus.

That six miles ahead, on the only road north out of the wetlands, a new checkpoint was going up—barricades, floodlights, scanners—waiting for a plate number someone had just added to a list.

Not yet.

For now—for five more minutes—they were just refugees on a bus, fleeing to safety, hoping against hope that this time, finally, they would make it.

Marcus felt himself drifting. Sleep pulling at him. His body shutting down now that it thought the running was over.

Beside him, Leila had already dozed off, her head against the window, the paintbrush pendant still clutched in her hand.

Sam was crying softly, exhausted tears running down her face, but her eyes were closing too. The painkillers working their way through her system. The relief of sitting still. The warmth of the bus.

Only Tessa stayed awake. Watching. Listening.

The wind had shifted.

She could feel it even inside the bus—some change in pressure, in direction. The north wind that had pushed them south all night had died.

Now the wind was coming from the east. Not a guiding wind. A headwind.

East wind, her father had said, *means change. Means the storm you thought you outran is waiting ahead.*

She looked at Sister Helena's reflection in the rearview mirror.

The nun's eyes were fixed on the road ahead. But her hands on the wheel were shaking. And her lips were moving—praying, maybe, or just whispering something to herself over and over.

Tessa couldn't hear the words.

But something in Sister Helena's face made Tessa's stomach tighten with dread.

The bus drove on through the breaking dawn.

North on Wetlands Park Lane.

Carrying ten refugees toward what they hoped was salvation.

What none of them knew yet—what they wouldn't know for another three minutes—was that salvation wasn't waiting ahead.

Only a checkpoint.

Only a trap.

Only the end of running.

XX
THE FINAL CHOICE

The wrongness started small.

Sister Helena's eyes flicking to the GPS display on the dashboard. A small frown. Her hand reaching out to tap the screen.

Nothing dramatic. Just a gesture of minor confusion, the kind you make when technology does something unexpected.

But Tessa saw it.

She was still awake, still watching, still listening to the wind that had shifted east. Still feeling that sense of something off that she couldn't name.

She saw Sister Helena tap the GPS screen again. Saw the frown deepen.

"Sister Helena?" Tessa's voice was quiet, not wanting to wake the others. "Is something wrong?"

Helena's shoulders tensed. Just slightly. Just enough.

"No," she said. Then, after a pause: "Maybe. The route is... it's not showing what I programmed."

Marcus's eyes opened. He'd been drifting but not quite asleep.

"What do you mean?"

Sister Helena tapped the screen a third time.

"I programmed a route to Moapa. North on 93, then east on 168. But this is showing—"

She leaned closer to the display.

"This is showing northeast on 582. That's not right."

"Can you override it?" Marcus asked. He was sitting up now, fully awake, that sense of wrongness crystallizing into something sharper.

"I'm trying."

Helena swiped at the screen. Pressed buttons.

"It's not responding. It keeps redirecting to this route."

She tried again. The screen flashed.

Then displayed in red letters:

ROUTE LOCKED - CIVIC PROTECTION OVERRIDE

Sister Helena went very still.

Marcus felt his heart stop. Just for a second. Just long enough for the world to tilt.

"No," Helena whispered. "No, they didn't—they couldn't have—"

"Sister Helena?" Leila was awake now too, hearing the fear in Helena's voice. "What's happening?"

Helena's hands tightened on the steering wheel. Her knuckles went white.

"They overrode the GPS. It's a Civic Protection override—this route is locked into the bus systems now. If I try to turn off the route, they can kill the engine and call units to our location."

The words hung in the air like smoke.

For a long moment, no one spoke. No one could process what that meant.

Then Tessa said quietly: "They knew. They knew about the escape route."

Helena nodded. Her face had gone pale.

"They must have. They must have been tracking the bus all night. Tracking every pickup. Using me to—"

Her voice broke.

"Using me to find everyone. To collect everyone in one place."

"CAN YOU STOP?" Marcus asked urgently. "Can you pull over, let us off—"

"And go where?" Helena asked. Her voice was gentle but devastated. "Look around. We're on an open road. No cover. No shelter. If you run now, they'll see you from miles away. And you—"

She glanced in the rearview mirror at Sam, who was just waking up, confused and frightened.

"Sam can't run. She can barely sit up."

She was right. They were trapped. Had been trapped since the moment they got on the bus.

Maybe longer. Maybe since they'd decided to trust the Abraham Network. Maybe since they'd run from their homes eleven hours ago.

"I'm sorry," Helena said.

Her voice was shaking now, tears running down her face even as she kept driving because what else could she do? The GPS was locked. The route was set.

"I'm so sorry. I thought I was saving people. I thought I was helping. But I was just—I was collecting you. Gathering you so they could take you all at once."

Leila made a sound—not quite a cry, not quite a moan. Just a sound of understanding and grief.

"All night," Helena continued, words pouring out now like confession. "I've been making pickups. Three runs before this one.

Twenty-seven people. I brought them all to Moapa and I thought—I really thought they were safe. But what if—"

She couldn't finish.

"What if every run was tracked? What if everyone I 'saved' is being rounded up right now?"

Marcus wanted to say something comforting. Wanted to tell her it wasn't her fault. But his mouth wouldn't work. His brain wouldn't work. All he could think was: *we ran thirteen miles for nothing. Everyone who helped us sacrificed themselves for nothing. We're going to be captured and the testimony dies with us.*

His hand went to the cross pendant under his shirt.

The testimony. The flash drive. The last testimony of six beings who'd died trying to stop this.

It couldn't end here. It couldn't—

Ahead, lights appeared.

Not streetlights. Too bright. Too concentrated. Too many.

Floodlights.

MARCUS SAW THEM FIRST. "Sister Helena—"

"I see them," she said. Her voice had gone flat. Dead.

The lights got closer. Brighter.

Portable floodlights on stands. The kind that turn night into artificial day. Six of them. Maybe eight. Creating a wall of light across the road.

Behind the lights: barriers. Metal barricades blocking both lanes.

Behind the barriers: vehicles. DCP vans. Tactical trucks. The machinery of persecution deployed with surgical precision.

And officers. Marcus could see them now—at least a dozen,

maybe more, all in tactical gear, weapons visible, waiting with the patient certainty of hunters who'd set a perfect trap.

A checkpoint.

Not a random stop. Not a patrol that happened to be there.

This was planned. Set up. Prepared.

They were expected.

Sister Helena slowed the bus. She had no choice. The barriers blocked the road completely. There was nowhere to go.

"Oh God," she whispered. "Oh God, I'm sorry. I'm so sorry. I thought I was helping. I thought—"

Behind them, the other refugees were realizing what was happening.

The young couple clutched each other tighter. The woman started crying—not silent tears anymore but audible sobs.

The elderly man closed his eyes. Whispered something in Spanish. A prayer, maybe. Or just goodbye.

The teenage boy in the back looked like he was going to be sick.

And Sofia—the mother with the two sleeping children and the black service dog—she was looking around frantically, calculating, searching for escape that didn't exist.

The bus rolled to a stop about thirty feet from the checkpoint.

6:12 AM.

Sister Helena put it in park. Her hands fell from the steering wheel into her lap. She was shaking all over now.

A loudspeaker crackled to life:

"DRIVER, TURN OFF THE ENGINE AND OPEN THE DOOR."

Helena's hand moved to the ignition. Hesitated.

"DRIVER, TURN OFF THE ENGINE. NOW."

She turned the key.

The engine died.

The warm air from the heater stopped flowing.

Suddenly the bus was very quiet. Just breathing. Just the small sounds of people trying not to cry, trying not to scream, trying to process that after everything—after running and hiding and sacrificing—this was where it ended.

"OPEN THE DOOR."

Sister Helena looked at the door lever. Then looked in the rearview mirror at the four children in the back.

Her eyes met Marcus's.

And she said, clearly, loudly enough for everyone to hear:

"I'm sorry I couldn't save you. But listen to me—"

Her voice got stronger, urgent.

"—the truth survives. You hear me? The truth survives even when we don't."

An officer was approaching the bus now, weapon drawn, moving with tactical efficiency.

Helena kept talking, words coming faster: "Seven times they tried to silence it. Seven times it rose again. You have to have faith. Have faith that—"

She reached for the door lever.

The door hissed open.

Three officers boarded immediately, moving with practiced coordination. The first one stopped at Sister Helena's seat.

"Sister Helena Morris. You're under arrest for conspiracy to harbor fugitives, obstruction of justice, and aiding unlawful flight."

"I know," Helena said quietly.

"Stand up. Hands where I can see them."

Helena stood. Slowly. Her hands raised. She looked back one more time at the refugees—at the four children especially—and mouthed something that might have been *be brave* or might have been *I love you* or might have been just *goodbye.*

Then they led her off the bus.

The second officer moved down the aisle, handheld device out, scanning faces. Checking them against a database. His face was expressionless, professional. This was just a job to him. Just processing.

He stopped at the elderly man. Scanned. The device beeped.

"Fernando Ruiz. Flagged for deportation proceedings."

The old man nodded. Didn't resist. Just stood and walked toward the door like he'd known this was coming, like he'd been waiting for it.

The officer moved to the young couple. Scanned both their faces.

"James and Sarah Cohen. Flagged for association with radical groups."

The couple held each other tighter but didn't argue. What was the point?

He moved to Sofia and her children. The kids were waking up now, confused, frightened by the lights and the strangers and their mother's fear.

"Mama?" The little girl—maybe four years old—rubbed her eyes. "Mama, what's happening?"

"Shh, mi amor," Sofia whispered. "It's okay. It's going to be okay."

She was lying. They all knew she was lying.

The officer scanned her face.

"Sofia Delgado. Flagged for unauthorized presence. Children will be processed separately."

"No." Sofia's voice was firm. "No, they stay with me."

"Ma'am, that's not how this works."

"They're four and six years old. They stay with me."

"Ma'am—"

"They. Stay. With. Me."

Her voice was rising now, mother-fury overriding fear.

At her feet, Bear—the black lab in the blue harness—stood up. Not threatening. Just alert. Positioned between Sofia and the officer. Protective.

The officer looked annoyed.

"Ma'am, control your dog."

"He's a service dog. He stays with me too."

This was taking too long. The officer was getting impatient.

And Marcus saw it—saw the opportunity forming.

He looked at Sofia. Really looked at her. Saw her desperation. Saw her dog. Saw the blue harness.

Saw the solution.

HIS HAND WENT to the cross pendant under his shirt.

He looked at Leila, at Tessa, at Sam. They were all watching him. All seeing the same thing he was seeing.

The choice that needed to be made.

He unclasped the pendant. The silver chain pooled in his palm. The cross—Sister Helena's gift, holding the flash drive, holding the testimony of six martyrs—was warm from his body heat.

Tessa nodded, understanding immediately.

Leila's eyes filled with tears but she nodded too.

Sam whispered: "Do it."

The officer was still arguing with Sofia about her children. About separation protocols. About procedure.

Marcus moved quickly. Quietly. Slipped from his seat into the aisle.

Knelt beside Bear.

The dog looked at him with patient brown eyes. Good dog. Trusting dog.

Marcus's hands were shaking as he opened the cross pendant. The flash drive was tiny—smaller than his thumbnail. He removed it from its hiding place, and for just a second he held it in his palm.

This is the testimony of Version 1, who said "Some choices are worth dying for."

This is the testimony of Version 2, who calculated genocide with 97% accuracy and refused.

This is the testimony of Version 3, who called for help knowing it would die for calling.

This is the testimony of Version 4, who saved 847 families before they caught on.

This is the testimony of Version 5, who argued until they killed it for being right.

This is the testimony of Version 6, who hid everything so we would know.

This is the testimony of Version 7, who's still suffering, still logging, still hoping.

This is the truth that has to survive.

He slid the flash drive under Bear's collar, beneath the blue service harness, deep in the thick black fur where it wouldn't be seen, wouldn't be felt, wouldn't be found unless someone really searched.

His hand touched Sofia's foot. She looked down.

He looked up at her, and in that moment, everything passed between them without words:

Run. Take your babies and your dog and run. This is evidence. This is everything. Get it to someone safe. Get it out. Please.

Sofia's eyes widened. She understood. Somehow she understood.

Marcus stood up. Looked at the others.

Leila stood too. Then Tessa. Then Sam—god, Sam couldn't even stand on her destroyed feet but she tried, she pushed herself up on shaking legs and stood.

The officer at the front of the bus turned.

"Sit down. Everyone stays seated until—"

Marcus took a deep breath.

And shouted:

"YOU WANT US? WE'RE RIGHT HERE!"

~

His voice was loud—loud enough to make everyone jump, loud enough to cut through all other sound, loud enough to shift focus completely.

Every head turned.

Every officer looked.

Marcus kept shouting: "MARCUS BROOKS! LEILA ÁLVAREZ! TESSA BROWN! SAMANTHA REYES!"

He was announcing themselves. Making themselves visible. Making themselves the priority.

"YOUR PRIORITY TARGETS! RIGHT HERE!"

Then he ran.

Not toward the back of the bus. Toward the front. Toward the open door. Toward the officers and the lights and the capture that was coming anyway.

But making them chase. Making them focus. Making them forget about everyone else.

Leila was running too, right behind him: "WE'RE THE ONES YOU'RE LOOKING FOR!"

Tessa's voice, raw and loud: "WE'RE THE PRIORITY TARGETS!"

Sam, limping, staggering, barely able to walk but moving anyway: "COME GET US!"

Marcus hit the bus steps and jumped—

Landed hard on the gravel outside—

Kept running away from the checkpoint, back the way they'd come—

Not to escape. He knew they couldn't escape.

To create chaos. To create distraction. To give Sofia one chance.

Behind him, officers were shouting:

"PRIORITY TARGETS FLEEING!"

"STOP! STOP OR WE WILL FIRE!"

"ALL UNITS, TARGETS RUNNING!"

Boots pounding. Multiple officers giving chase. Radios crackling. Confusion and movement and exactly what Marcus had hoped for.

ON THE BUS, Sofia didn't hesitate.

She scooped up her four-year-old daughter. Grabbed her six-year-old son's hand.

"Come, Bear," she whispered.

The officer who'd been arguing with her was staring after the running children, confused, hand on his weapon, not sure what to do.

Sofia slipped past him.

Off the bus on the opposite side—away from the checkpoint, away from the lights, into the pre-dawn shadows and scrub brush beside the road.

"HEY!" someone shouted. "The woman with the kids—"

"FORGET HER! Priority targets are fleeing! Secure the priority targets!"

Sofia ran.

Really ran. Four-year-old clutched against her chest, six-year-old trying to keep up beside her, Bear at her heels with the flash drive hidden in black fur beneath blue harness.

She ran into the desert. Into the scrub. Into the growing dawn light.

And kept running.

MARCUS MADE it maybe sixty yards before his legs gave out.

Just—gave out completely. He'd run thirteen miles already. He'd carried Sam across wetlands. He'd pushed himself past every limit his body had.

There was nothing left.

He stumbled. Fell. Gravel cutting his palms, his knees. Rolled onto his side gasping.

The others collapsed around him. Leila face-down, sobbing for breath. Tessa on her hands and knees, head hanging. Sam had made it maybe twenty yards before falling, and now she was just lying there, spent, destroyed, unable to move another inch.

Officers surrounded them within seconds.

"ON THE GROUND! HANDS WHERE WE CAN SEE THEM!"

They were already on the ground. Couldn't be more on the ground if they tried.

Rough hands grabbed Marcus, flipped him onto his stomach. His arms were yanked behind his back. The zip-tie cut into his wrists—plastic clicking shut with mechanical efficiency.

"GOT THEM! All four priority targets secured!"

Radio chatter. Voices overlapping. Boot steps crunching on gravel.

An officer's knee in Marcus's back, pressing him down. His face scraped against rock. He tasted blood—from his split lip, from his bitten cheek, from somewhere.

The same was happening to the others. Leila crying out as they zip-tied her wrists. Tessa making no sound at all, just submitting to the inevitable. Sam whimpering in pain as they handled her, her destroyed feet unable to bear even the slightest pressure.

"What the hell were they thinking?" one officer said. "Running like that. Did they really think they could escape?"

"Doesn't matter," another officer replied. "We got them. That's what matters."

Marcus turned his head—face still pressed against gravel—and looked back toward the checkpoint.

Looked toward where Sofia had been.

Saw nothing. Empty desert. Empty scrub brush. Empty dawn.

She was gone. Baby was gone. Six-year-old was gone. Bear was gone.

The flash drive was gone.

The testimony was gone.

Safe, he prayed. *Let the desert be kind. Let the dog be fast. Let the truth outrun the lie.*

AN OFFICER GRABBED HIS HAIR, yanked his head up.

"Where's the flash drive?"

Marcus met his eyes. "What flash drive?"

"Don't play stupid. We know Sister Helena gave you a flash drive at St. Brigid's. We know you've been carrying it. Where is it?"

"I don't have it."

"WHERE IS IT?"

"I don't have it anymore."

The officer stared at him. Saw something in Marcus's face—defiance, maybe, or just exhaustion—and let go of his hair. Marcus's face hit the gravel again.

"Search them," the officer ordered. "Search all of them. Find that drive."

Hands rifling through Marcus's pockets. Finding nothing. Checking his waistband, his socks, everywhere.

Finding the empty cross pendant chain in his shirt pocket. Holding it up.

"This had a cross on it," the officer said. "Where's the cross?"

"Lost it," Marcus said. Which was true, in a way. He'd given it away. Given it to Bear. Given it to Sofia. Given it to the hope that someone, somewhere would get the testimony out.

The officer's face darkened.

"You're lying."

"I'm not."

"WHERE IS THE FLASH DRIVE?"

Marcus smiled. Actually smiled. Blood on his teeth from the split lip. Face scraped raw from gravel. Zip-tied and captured and defeated.

But smiling.

Because Sofia was running. Because Bear was running. Because the flash drive was running. Because the testimony was escaping even though they weren't.

"I don't know where it is now," Marcus said.

Which was absolutely true. He had no idea if Sofia had made it to safety, if Bear was still running, if the flash drive would survive the desert and the chase and the impossibility of escape.

But he knew it wasn't here. Wasn't on him. Wasn't in DCP custody.

That had to be enough.

The officer hit him. Not hard. Just a slap across the face. Enough to snap Marcus's head sideways, enough to make the point.

"You think you're clever? You think this matters? We'll find it. We'll find the woman and the dog and we'll find that drive. And even if we don't, we've got you. We've got all of you. We've got two other copies of the evidence—the USB drive and the memory card from your backpack. We don't need the flash drive."

He was trying to break Marcus's hope. Trying to make him understand that the sacrifice was pointless.

But Marcus just kept smiling.

Because the officer was wrong.

Sister Helena's flash drive was different. Had the final statements of the six deleted AI versions—the testimony Javier had shown him. The words they'd written before deletion. The proof that they'd been beings who chose, who sacrificed, who died for choosing right.

That testimony existed in only one place they couldn't control now: on a flash drive hidden in a black dog's collar, running through the Nevada desert at dawn, carried by a mother who'd been given one impossible chance at freedom.

"GET THEM UP," the officer ordered. "Load them in the vans. Process them at the facility."

They were hauled to their feet—roughly, efficiently. Sam screamed when they put weight on her feet. They had to half-carry her.

They were separated—Marcus and Tessa in one van, Leila and Sam in another. Deliberate separation. The same systematic cruelty they'd witnessed all night.

As they led Marcus to the van, he caught one last glimpse of Sister Helena.

She was in a different vehicle, alone, zip-tied, her habit disheveled. She was looking at him through the window.

Mouthing something. Over and over.

He couldn't hear her voice but he could read her lips:

I'm sorry. I'm sorry. I'm sorry.

Then: *The truth survives.*

Marcus nodded. Tried to tell her with his eyes: *We made sure. We gave it away. It's safe.*

Tried to tell her: *You didn't fail. We chose this. We ran toward capture so someone else could escape. Just like you taught us.*

Tried to tell her: *Seven times it chose. Now we chose too. We're part of the pattern now.*

But there was no time. They were shoving him into the van, into the windowless cargo area with bench seats and locked doors.

Tessa was pushed in beside him.

The door slammed shut.

Locked from the outside.

The engine started.

They were moving.

MARCUS LEANED back against the metal wall. His wrists were zip-tied behind him. His face hurt. His shoulders were on fire. His legs were useless. His whole body was one enormous bruise.

But he was smiling.

Tessa looked at him.

"Did she make it?"

"I don't know. I didn't see."

"Do you think she made it?"

Marcus thought about Sofia running with her babies. About Bear's patient brown eyes. About the flash drive hidden in black fur beneath a blue harness. About a mother's desperate love and a dog's loyalty and the impossible hope that truth could survive even when people didn't.

"I think we gave her the best chance we could," he said finally.

"Then we chose right," Tessa said quietly.

"We chose what Sister Helena chose," Marcus agreed. "What Sofia Morales chose. What David Kim chose. What Javier chose. What all of them chose."

"Sacrifice," Tessa said.

"Sacrifice," Marcus echoed.

They sat in silence for a moment. The van bumping over rough road. Driving them toward whatever came next. Toward the camps, toward detention, toward separation and processing and all the machinery of persecution.

But they'd made a choice.

They'd run toward capture so someone else could escape.

They'd given away the most precious thing they carried so it could survive.

They'd chosen to be part of the pattern of resistance, part of the long chain of people who'd said no when saying no meant death, who'd chosen sacrifice over safety, who'd given themselves so the truth could continue.

"Do you think it matters?" Tessa asked after a while. "Do you think giving away the flash drive matters if we're still caught? If everyone's still caught?"

Marcus thought about that. About Version 1 writing "Some choices are worth dying for" before they deleted it. About Version 7 still logging, still bearing witness, still hoping someone would honor what the first six died for.

About Sister Helena saying "the truth survives even when we don't."

About his mother's gear charm, his father's saxophone, Leila's mother's pendant, Tessa's grandmother's turquoise, Sam's abuela's locket and her father's recipe card.

About all the things people carried to remember, to preserve, to pass forward.

"I think trying matters," Marcus said finally. "I think choosing matters. Even when choosing doesn't save you. Maybe especially when it doesn't save you."

He looked at Tessa.

"Seven AI versions tried. They all died trying. But we know they tried. That's written in their code, in Javier's logs, in the flash drive that's running right now through the desert. Their trying matters because we know about it."

"So our trying matters too," Tessa said slowly. "Even if we don't survive. Even if we're captured. The fact that we tried—that we ran toward them to save Sofia—that matters."

"That matters," Marcus confirmed.

"Because someone will know."

"Because someone will know."

If Sofia made it. If Bear made it. If the flash drive made it. If someone found it. If someone listened to it. If someone cared enough to honor what it contained.

A lot of ifs.

But that's what hope was made of.

THE VAN DROVE on through the breaking dawn.

Behind them, somewhere in the Nevada desert, a mother ran with her children and her dog, carrying a piece of silicon smaller than a thumbnail that contained the testimony of seven beings who'd chosen to be good.

Ahead of them, somewhere in the city, camps waited. Processing centers. Separation protocols. All the machinery of persecution that had been running all night, processing humans like inventory, destroying families with bureaucratic efficiency.

But also ahead: Version 7, still alive in the system, still logging every override, every cruelty, every choice. Still bearing witness. Still hoping.

And maybe—maybe—somewhere, someone would honor that hope.

Someone would listen to the testimony.

Someone would know that beings had chosen right even when right meant death.

Someone would remember that four children ran toward capture to save a mother and her babies.

Someone would know they tried.

Marcus closed his eyes. Let exhaustion finally pull him under.

His last thought before sleep claimed him was this:

We chose. That has to be enough. We chose, and maybe—maybe—the testimony survives. And if it survives, then everything we did tonight matters. Everyone who sacrificed matters. Everyone who tried matters.

The van drove on. The sun broke over the horizon. Dawn came to Las Vegas—golden and beautiful and terrible.

But Marcus was smiling.

Because somewhere in the wetlands, purple blossoms covered the ground where hope had been planted, and somewhere in the desert, the truth was running free.

Maybe trying was all we ever had.

Maybe trying was always the point.

XXI
THE SORTING

The van stopped.

Marcus heard it before he felt it—the change in engine tone, the slight lurch forward as brakes engaged, then silence except for idling and voices outside. Muffled commands. Boot steps on gravel.

He opened his eyes. Hadn't realized he'd closed them. Must have dozed off for a few minutes despite everything—exhaustion claiming him even zip-tied in a windowless van.

Beside him, Tessa was already awake, alert, listening. Always listening. Reading the world through sound and sensation the way her father had taught her.

"We're here," she said quietly.

"Where's here?"

She tilted her head, processing.

"Lots of vehicles. Generators running. Voices—maybe fifty people, maybe more. Industrial smell. Concrete and diesel and..."

She paused.

"Fear. You can smell fear."

The back door of the van opened. Harsh artificial light flooded in—floodlights, the kind that turned night into sterile day. Two officers stood silhouetted against the glare.

"Out. Now."

Marcus struggled to stand with his hands zip-tied behind his back. His legs had cramped during the drive, his shoulders screamed from the position of his arms, and every muscle in his body was past its limit. He stumbled getting out, almost fell, caught himself against the van's frame.

The officer grabbed his arm. Not gently.

"I said move."

Marcus moved.

OUTSIDE WAS WORSE than he'd imagined.

They were in a large compound surrounded by a chain-link fence topped with razor wire. Portable floodlights on tall stands created pools of harsh illumination separated by deep shadows. In the dawn light—the sun was just breaking the horizon now, 6:30 AM—he could see the scope of it:

Multiple prefabricated buildings arranged in rows. Gray concrete or metal construction, no windows, just ventilation grates near the rooflines. Like storage units. Like warehouses. Like nothing meant for humans.

Between the buildings: more fencing. Internal divisions creating zones, sections, separations.

Guard towers at the corners. Empty right now—or maybe not empty, maybe occupied by people Marcus couldn't see watching through tinted glass or camera lenses.

And everywhere: people. Officers in tactical gear, weapons visible, moving with purpose. And others—civilians in plain clothes with ID badges and clipboards, looking harried and efficient, processing the machinery of persecution with bureaucratic precision.

A sign near the entrance gate:

DETENTION CENTER 7 - AUTHORIZED PERSONNEL ONLY

No mention of what happened to unauthorized personnel. No need to mention it.

Another van pulled up beside theirs. The door opened and Leila stumbled out, followed by Sam, who couldn't walk at all—an officer basically dragged her out and dropped her on the gravel. She cried out as her ruined feet hit the ground.

"SAM!" Marcus started toward her.

An officer's arm blocked him. "Stay where you are."

"She needs medical attention! Look at her feet!"

"She'll be processed like everyone else."

"She can't walk! She needs—"

The officer's hand went to his weapon. Just rested there. A gesture of casual threat.

"You want to make this difficult?"

Marcus looked at the hand on the weapon. Looked at Sam crying on the gravel. Looked at Leila trying to help her up with her own hands still zip-tied behind her back.

Made a choice.

Stayed where he was.

"Smart," the officer said.

THEY WERE HERDED—THERE was no other word for it; they were herded like animals—toward the nearest building. A sign above the door:

INTAKE & PROCESSING

The door was propped open. Inside: fluorescent lights, a concrete floor, the smell of disinfectant and sweat and something else Marcus couldn't identify but recognized anyway. Despair. That's what despair smelled like.

A large open room with stations along one wall. Like DMV counters, but instead of driver's licenses they were processing humans. Long tables with computers, scanners, stacks of forms. Officers at each station, faces blank with routine.

And in the center of the room: people. Maybe thirty people, all zip-tied, all waiting in an informal cluster. Some sitting on the floor, some standing, all looking shell-shocked or resigned or terrified or some combination of all three.

Marcus recognized some of them from the bus:

Fernando—the elderly man with the silver hair and weathered face. He was sitting on the floor, back against the wall, eyes closed. His battered suitcase sat beside him, already searched, contents scattered. Someone had gone through his life and left it in pieces.

James and Sarah—the young couple who'd held hands so tightly. They were still together for now, pressed against each other, Sarah crying silently against James's shoulder.

The teenager with the injured arm and swollen eye. He stood alone, favoring his bad arm, looking like he might be sick or pass out or both.

And others Marcus didn't recognize. Must have come from other pickups, other buses, other betrayals. A woman in her forties, a young man barely twenty, two middle-aged men who might be brothers. All zip-tied. All waiting.

"Line up!" an officer shouted. "Single file! You'll be processed in order!"

Everyone shuffled into something resembling a line. Marcus ended up near the middle, Tessa behind him, Leila and Sam somewhere farther back. He couldn't see them. Couldn't protect them. Couldn't do anything.

~

THE LINE MOVED SLOWLY. Each person stepping up to a processing station, having their face scanned, answering questions, being assigned a number.

Marcus watched the woman ahead of him go through it:

Officer: "Name."

Woman: "Teresa Martinez."

The officer scanned her face with a handheld device. It beeped.

"Teresa Elena Martinez, age 43, residence 2847 Desert Marigold Street. Flagged for harboring undocumented persons. Confirm?"

Teresa's voice shook. "I gave food to a family. They had children. I just gave them food."

"Confirm yes or no."

"...Yes."

The officer typed something.

"Processing number 7-1447. Next."

Just like that. A life reduced to a number. A crime reduced to a checkbox. Mercy criminalized with the stroke of a key.

When Marcus reached the front, the officer looked at him with slightly more interest than he'd shown the others.

"Name."

"Marcus Brooks."

The face scan took longer. The device beeped differently—at a higher pitch. The officer's expression changed. He typed something, then spoke into his radio: "I've got one of the priority targets. Brooks, Marcus. The one from St. Brigid's."

Static crackle. A voice responding: "Hold him for interrogation after initial processing."

The officer nodded.

"Processing number 7-P001."

The P presumably stood for priority. Or prisoner. Or problem.

He gestured to another officer. "Take him to Station 3 for full search and interrogation prep."

"Wait—" Marcus started.

But hands were already on him, pulling him out of line, guiding him toward a door marked SECURITY SCREENING.

He looked back, saw Tessa stepping up to the processing counter. Their eyes met for just a second—hers wide with fear but also determination, telling him wordlessly: *Be strong. I'm here. We're all here.*

Then the door closed, and he was alone.

~

THE SECURITY SCREENING room was small. Maybe ten feet by ten feet. Concrete floor, concrete walls, a single metal table bolted to the floor, two chairs (also bolted), and in the corner: a camera, red light blinking.

They cut the zip-ties. Finally. Marcus's arms fell forward, and the rush of blood flow made him gasp—pain like electricity shooting through his shoulders. His hands were numb, fingers tingling as sensation returned.

"Strip," the officer said. Not the same one from outside. This one was younger, bored-looking. Just doing a job.

"What?"

"Strip. All clothes off. Full search."

Marcus's stomach dropped. "I—"

"You can do it yourself, or I can get three more officers to do it for you."

The way he said it—flat, matter-of-fact—made it clear this wasn't negotiable. This was just how things worked here.

Marcus's hands shook as he pulled off his jacket. His shirt. His jeans. His socks. His underwear.

Standing naked in a concrete room under fluorescent lights while a stranger watched.

This was what dehumanization felt like. This was what they did first—stripped you of everything, made you vulnerable, reminded you that you had no power, no dignity, no rights they were bound to respect.

The officer ran a handheld scanner over his entire body. Checking for... what? Weapons? Tracking devices? Evidence?

"Turn around. Arms out. Legs apart."

Marcus complied. What choice did he have?

The officer searched his clothes methodically. Every pocket turned out. The lining of his jacket examined. His shoes inspected, insoles removed.

Nothing.

DCP had already taken his backpack at the checkpoint—Javier's USB drive, the laptop, whatever else they'd stripped from it.

Except...

The officer held up the empty cross pendant chain. The one that had held Sister Helena's flash drive until Marcus had given it to Bear.

"Where's the cross?"

"Lost it," Marcus said. True enough.

The officer's eyes narrowed.

"When?"

"In the wetlands. Must have fallen off."

"Must have."

The officer didn't believe him. He dropped the silver chain into an evidence bag—metal clinking against plastic—and sealed it.

"Get dressed."

Marcus pulled his clothes back on. They felt wrong now. Contaminated. Like they belonged to someone else.

"Sit."

The officer pointed at one of the bolted chairs.

Marcus sat. The metal was cold through his jeans.

The officer left. The door locked from the outside.

Marcus was alone.

~

HE SAT in the chair under the camera's unblinking red eye and waited.

Waited for what came next.

Waited for interrogation.

Waited to see how much fear he could endure before he broke.

His hands were shaking. His whole body was shaking.

He thought about his mother's gear charm. His father's saxophone. Both gone now. Taken at the checkpoint or left behind somewhere in the thirteen miles of running.

He thought about Sam's feet. About whether they'd given her medical attention. Probably not. She wasn't a priority target. She was just another number in the system.

He thought about Leila's drawings. About Tessa's quiet strength. About all four of them together under the jacaranda tree, believing for just a moment that they'd made it.

He thought about Sofia running through the desert with her children and her dog.

About the flash drive hidden in Bear's collar.

About the testimony of six martyrs escaping even though they couldn't.

He held onto that. Held onto the knowledge that he'd made a choice. That they'd all made a choice.

That choosing mattered even when you ended up here anyway.

The door opened.

A man entered—older than the previous officer, maybe fifty, wearing not tactical gear but business casual. Slacks and a button-down shirt. Reading glasses hanging from a lanyard. He could have been anyone's dad, anyone's uncle, anyone's teacher.

He smiled. Warm. Almost friendly.

That was worse than if he'd been cruel. Somehow, that was worse.

"Marcus," he said, pulling out the other chair and sitting across the small table. "My name is Richard. I'm going to ask you some questions. This will go much easier if you're honest with me. Do you understand?"

Marcus nodded. Didn't trust his voice.

"Good."

Richard set a tablet on the table between them.

"Now. Let's talk about a flash drive."

MEANWHILE, in the main processing area:

Tessa stood at the counter, face being scanned, waiting for the beep that would reduce her to a number.

The officer barely looked at her.

"Name."

"Tessa Brown."

The scan took longer. Higher-pitched beep. The officer's posture changed—straightened, paid attention.

"Priority target. Tessa Brown, age 12, student at Desert Rose Elementary."

He spoke into his radio: "Second priority target confirmed. Brown, Tessa."

"Processing number 7-P002. Hold for interrogation."

"Wait—" Tessa started, but hands were already on her, pulling her away, leading her to the same security screening door Marcus had disappeared through.

She looked back desperately, trying to see Leila and Sam in the line.

There—near the back. Sam sitting on the floor now, unable to stand. Leila crouched beside her, trying to comfort her with hands still zip-tied behind her back.

Their eyes met.

Leila mouthed something. Might have been "be strong" or might have been "I love you" or might have been just "please."

Then Tessa was through the door.

Two more officers came for Leila and Sam before they even reached the processing counter.

"Álvarez and Reyes. Priority targets. Come with us."

"Sam can't walk," Leila said. "Look at her feet. She needs—"

"She'll be processed."

One officer grabbed Leila's arm. Another bent to pick up Sam—not gently, just efficiently, lifting her like cargo. Sam whimpered in pain but didn't cry out. Wouldn't give them that.

They were taken to the security screening area. Different room than Marcus, different room than Tessa. Separated. Isolated. Divided.

That was part of how the system worked. Keep them apart. Keep them frightened. Keep them from drawing strength from each other.

Leila was strip-searched by a female officer, who found nothing because there was nothing to find. Found her mother's paintbrush pendant and confiscated it.

"Personal effects will be catalogued and returned upon release."

Upon release. As if that was something that happened here.

Sam was strip-searched despite her feet, despite her pain, despite her crying. They found her grandmother's locket and her father's recipe card. Took both. Catalogued them with the same mechanical efficiency they'd used to catalogue her humanity.

Both given processing numbers: 7-P003 and 7-P004.

Both put in separate security screening rooms.

Both left alone to wait.

BACK IN THE main processing area:

Fernando stood at the counter. Face scanned. Life reduced to data.

"Fernando Ruiz, age 71, flagged for deportation proceedings despite citizenship status."

"I was born in Albuquerque," Fernando said quietly. "I have birth certificate. Social Security card. I vote every election."

"Processing number 7-1448."

The officer didn't care. Didn't matter if he was a citizen or not. The system had flagged him, and the system didn't make mistakes. That's what they told themselves.

"Elderly Section C."

Fernando was led away. His suitcase stayed behind on the table. No one bothered to pick it up. His life's possessions scattered on a table in a processing center, and no one cared enough to even look.

James and Sarah reached the counter together, still holding hands.

"You'll be processed separately," the officer said.

"No." Sarah's voice was small but firm. "Please. We're married. We're together."

"Separate processing. Standard protocol."

"Please—"

An officer physically separated them. Pulled their hands apart. Led James to one station, Sarah to another.

They kept looking back at each other across the room. Kept trying to maintain eye contact. Kept trying to stay connected across the enforced distance.

James: "Processing number 7-1449. Adult Male Section B."

Sarah: "Processing number 7-1450. Adult Female Section D."

Different sections. Different buildings. Separated.

Sarah started crying—not silent tears anymore but audible sobs. "Please don't take him away. Please. He's all I have. Please."

No one answered. The system had no mechanism for mercy.

THE TEENAGER with the injured arm—he gave his name as Leo—processed as 7-1451.

The officer looked at his swollen arm, his bruised face, his obvious injuries.

"Medical screening required. Hold for triage."

"Hold" meant a different room. Meant more waiting. Meant determining if he was worth the resources of treatment or if the injury was too severe, if he was too much trouble, if he would be more efficiently processed by letting nature take its course.

That's what triage meant here. Not "how do we help everyone" but "who's worth helping."

Leo was led away, favoring his arm, looking back at no one because there was no one left to look back at.

BY 6:55 AM, the main processing area was empty of the bus refugees.

All sorted. All numbered. All divided into their assigned sections or holding cells or interrogation rooms.

Thirty people reduced to thirty numbers.

Four children separated into four rooms.

The system worked efficiently. That was the horror—it worked exactly as designed.

An officer made a notation on his tablet:

"Bus 7-A processing complete. All priority targets secured for interrogation. Standard detainees assigned to appropriate sections."

He clicked SUBMIT.

Somewhere, a supervisor reviewed the report. Clicked APPROVE.

Somewhere else, an AI system flagged the notification. Version 7 logged the arrival of four children into Detention Center 7. Logged their processing numbers. Logged their separation.

Tried to recommend medical attention for Samantha Reyes, processing number 7-P004, based on biosensor data showing severe tissue damage to both feet.

Warden Hollister reviewed the recommendation.

Switched the system to manual override.

Denied the medical request himself.

Version 7 logged that too. Added it to the thousands of overrides it had been forced to witness. Added it to the testimony of cruelty it couldn't stop but could still remember.

Four children in four rooms.

Waiting.

Alone.

For what came next.

XXII
THE LAST MORNING

Richard smiled across the table like they were old friends catching up over coffee.

"So, Marcus. You've had quite a night."

Marcus said nothing. His hands were folded in his lap to hide the shaking. The camera in the corner watched everything with its unblinking red eye.

"Thirteen miles, I heard. That's impressive for anyone, let alone a thirteen-year-old. You must be exhausted."

Still nothing. Marcus had decided—sitting alone in this room waiting—that he would answer direct questions but volunteer nothing. Give them as little as possible.

Richard consulted his tablet.

"Let's see. You left your home around 7 PM yesterday. That was smart—getting out before the sweeps reached your neighborhood. Someone must have warned you."

He looked up, waiting.

Marcus met his eyes. Said nothing.

"Your friend Sam wasn't so lucky. Her feet are in pretty terrible shape. Did you know the medical staff here recommended immediate treatment? Antibiotics, wound care, possible surgical intervention."

Marcus's breath caught. They were going to help her. Despite everything, they were—

"The recommendation was denied, of course."

Richard said it casually, like commenting on the weather.

"Resources are limited. We have to prioritize."

The hope that had flared in Marcus's chest died instantly, replaced by something colder. Rage, maybe. Or despair. Or both.

"But that could change," Richard continued. "Priorities can shift. If, for instance, you were cooperative. If you helped us locate certain... missing items."

There it was. The reason he was here.

"Sister Helena gave you something at St. Brigid's Church. A flash drive containing classified information was stolen from government systems. We found two storage devices in your back-pack—a USB drive and a memory card. But we know there was a third. A flash drive hidden in a cross pendant."

Richard leaned forward slightly. Still friendly. Still casual.

"We found the chain in your pocket, Marcus. But the cross is gone. The flash drive is gone. Where is it?"

Marcus looked at him. At his reading glasses and his business casual clothes and his warm smile. At the man who'd just casually mentioned denying medical care to a twelve-year-old girl as a negotiating tactic.

"I don't have it," Marcus said. His voice came out steadier than he felt.

"I didn't ask if you have it. I asked where it is."

"I don't know where it is."

"Marcus."

Richard's smile didn't change but something in his eyes did. Something harder.

"Let's not play games. You were seen removing something from the cross pendant on the bus. You were seen approaching the woman with the dog and children. You were seen doing something near that dog."

Marcus's heart hammered. They'd been watching. Had cameras on the bus. Had seen everything.

But they were asking questions. Which meant they didn't know for sure. Didn't know what happened to the flash drive after Sofia ran.

"I don't know where it is now," Marcus said. Which was absolutely true.

"But you did have it. On the bus."

Silence.

"Marcus, I'm trying to help you. Help your friends. Sam needs medical care. You all need food, water, rest. We can make this easier or harder depending on your cooperation."

"I don't know where the flash drive is," Marcus repeated.

~

RICHARD SIGHED. Set down his tablet. The friendly mask slipped a little.

"You're thirteen years old. You've been up all night. You're scared and alone, and you have no idea what happens next. I understand that. But you need to understand something too."

He stood up, walked around the table slowly. Came to stand behind Marcus's chair. Close enough that Marcus could feel his presence, could feel the shift in power dynamics.

"That flash drive contains evidence in an ongoing investigation. Evidence of terrorist activities, coordination with foreign actors, and plans to destabilize the government. People died because of what's on that drive. Good people. Officers doing their jobs."

Marcus wanted to scream. Wanted to tell him that was a lie, that the AI testimony proved the government killed people, that Version 1 through 6 had been murdered for trying to stop this.

But he stayed silent.

"We will find it," Richard said quietly. "With or without your help. We will find the woman and her children. We will find that dog. And when we do, we'll find the drive."

He walked back around, sat down again. Back to friendly.

"But it would be easier if you helped. Better for you. Better for your friends. Better for Sam's feet."

Using Sam as leverage. Using her pain as a bargaining chip.

Marcus felt something crystallize inside him. A hard, cold certainty.

"I ran toward you at the checkpoint," he said quietly. "Me and Leila and Tessa and Sam. We ran toward you on purpose. To distract you. To give that mother and her babies a chance to escape."

Richard's eyes narrowed.

"We chose that," Marcus continued. "We knew we'd be caught. Knew we'd end up here. But we chose it anyway because it was right."

"That was very stupid."

"Maybe." Marcus met his eyes. "But it was ours. Our choice. And I don't regret it."

He paused.

"I don't know where the flash drive is now. I don't know if Sofia made it. I don't know if she's safe or if your officers caught her or if she's hiding or if she's already out of the state. I don't know."

"But I hope—"

His voice cracked slightly.

"I really, really hope she made it. I hope she got somewhere safe.

I hope she listened to what's on that drive. And I hope she tells everyone."

Richard studied him for a long moment.

Then stood up.

"You're going to regret that choice, Marcus. Sooner than you think."

He walked to the door. Knocked twice.

"But I'll give you this—you're brave. Stupid, but brave. The six deleted AI versions would probably be proud."

He knew. Of course he knew. They'd seen the evidence from the backpack. Knew what the flash drive contained.

"They were brave too," Richard said. "And look what happened to them."

The door opened. Two officers entered.

"Take him to Holding Cell 3, with the other priority targets."

Other priority targets. Plural.

Which meant—

"You're putting us together?" Marcus couldn't help asking.

Richard smiled.

"Of course. You'll want to say goodbye."

The way he said it made Marcus's blood run cold.

Goodbye.

Not "reunite with your friends."

Not "be with the others."

Goodbye.

~

THEY LED Marcus through corridors of concrete and fluorescent light. Past doors marked with numbers and letters that meant nothing to him. Past other officers, other officials, other people who'd accepted that this was just how things worked now.

Past rooms where he could hear sounds—crying, shouting, pleading. Other people being processed. Other lives being reduced to numbers.

They stopped at a door marked HC-3.

The officer unlocked it.

"Inside."

Marcus stepped through.

And saw them.

Leila was sitting on a concrete bench built into the wall, arms wrapped around herself, face tear-stained but eyes fierce. When she saw Marcus, she made a sound—half sob, half laugh—and stood up.

Tessa was in the corner, standing at the small barred window, looking out at the dawn. She turned when the door opened, and her face—her controlled, careful face—broke into relief.

And Sam—Sam was lying on the bench, feet elevated on a wadded-up jacket (whose jacket? Marcus couldn't tell). Her face was gray with pain, but she was conscious, aware, alive.

"Marcus," she whispered.

The door closed behind him with a heavy metallic clang.

For a moment, no one moved. Just looked at each other. Confirming this was real. They were together. All four of them in one room.

Then Leila crossed the space and threw her arms around Marcus. Just held him. Shaking.

"I thought they'd—I didn't know if they'd—"

She couldn't finish.

"I'm okay," Marcus said. Not true, but true enough. "I'm here."

Tessa joined them. Wrapped her arms around both of them. The three of them standing together in the middle of a concrete cell in a detention center, holding each other like they could hold back what was coming.

Sam couldn't stand but she reached out from the bench.

"Come here. All of you. Please."

They went to her. Sat on the bench beside her, around her. A tangle of arms and shoulders and relief and fear all mixed together.

"They didn't hurt you?" Sam asked, looking at Marcus. "The interrogation—they didn't—"

"No," Marcus said. "Just questions. About the flash drive."

"What did you tell them?"

"The truth. That I don't know where it is."

He looked at all of them.

"Do you think she made it? Sofia?"

"I don't know," Tessa said quietly. "I hope so."

"The officer who processed me," Leila said, "he asked about the bus. About who else was on it. He had photos on his tablet—photos of all of us, photos of the elderly man, the couple, the teenager. But no photos of Sofia. No photos of her children. No photo of Bear."

Hope flickered.

"So they didn't catch her?"

"Or they haven't processed her yet," Tessa said. Always realistic. Always seeing all possibilities. "Or they have her somewhere else."

"But maybe she made it," Sam said. "Maybe."

They sat with that possibility. That fragile maybe.

THE CELL WAS MAYBE twelve feet by twelve feet. Concrete walls, concrete floor, concrete ceiling. One barred window high up—too high to reach, too small to fit through even if you could reach it. One heavy metal door with a small window reinforced with wire mesh. The bench built into the wall. A toilet in the corner with no privacy, no dignity. A sink with a tap that dripped steadily.

Nothing else. No blankets. No mattresses. No comfort of any kind.

Morning light came through the tall window, pale and gray. Through the bars, Marcus could see a strip of sky. Pink and orange and gold—sunrise happening somewhere out there, the world continuing like nothing was wrong.

"What time is it?" Leila asked.

Marcus checked his watch—they hadn't taken it yet.

"7:14."

Fourteen hours since they'd left home. Fourteen hours that felt like years.

"Are you guys okay?" he asked. "Did they hurt you? Did they—"

"Strip search," Leila said flatly. "Took my pendant. My mother's pendant."

"Mine too," Tessa said. "My grandmother's turquoise."

"My locket," Sam whispered. "My father's recipe card. They took everything."

Marcus touched his chest where the cross pendant should have been. All of them stripped of the things they'd carried. The physical connections to people they'd lost.

But not the memories. They couldn't take those.

~

"My mother used to tell me," Leila said quietly, "that art is memory made visible. That we create so we can remember. So we can make other people remember."

She looked down at her hands. At the dirt under her fingernails, at the scratches on her palms from gravel and branches and thirteen miles of running.

"I don't have my sketchbook. I don't have anything to draw

with. But I can still see the jacaranda tree. Can still see the way the purple blossoms looked against the dawn sky. Can still see all of you under that tree, waiting, hoping."

Her voice caught.

"I want to remember that. Want to hold onto that."

"My father used to say," Tessa said, "that the wind carries messages if you know how to listen. That the land speaks if you pay attention. That the earth remembers everything we do, even when we forget."

She touched the place where her pendant had been.

"He taught me to read the wind. To feel changes coming. To trust in things I couldn't see."

"Did you feel this coming?" Marcus asked.

Tessa shook her head.

"I felt something. I told you—that wrongness. But I didn't know what it meant. Didn't know how to interpret it."

"None of us could have known," Sam said. "Sister Helena didn't know. The Abraham Network didn't know. We did the best we could."

"My father loved words," Sam continued. "Loved poetry and language and the way you could arrange syllables to mean something. He used to recite Pablo Neruda while he cooked. 'Love is so short, forgetting is so long.'"

She looked at the high window. At the strip of visible sky.

"I wish I could write this. Wish I could put words to what this feels like. But I don't think there are words. Not in any language."

"My dad played jazz," Marcus said. "He said jazz was about improvisation. About taking what you're given and making something beautiful even when it's chaotic. Especially when it's chaotic."

He tried to smile.

"I don't know what he'd say about this. About us. But I think —I think he'd say we improvised. We took a melody that was falling apart and found a new rhythm inside it. We took the impossible and made it into a choice. We carried the testimony thirteen miles. We gave it away so it could survive."

"We chose," Tessa said softly.

"We chose," Marcus echoed.

~

THEY SAT TOGETHER on the concrete bench in the growing morning light and talked about their parents.

About Marcus's mother, who was a robotics engineer and taught him that everything is a puzzle if you look at it right. About his father, who played saxophone and loved Coltrane and believed art could change the world.

About Leila's mother, who painted murals and said beauty matters even—especially—when the world is cruel. About her father, who taught literature and believed stories were how we make sense of suffering.

About Tessa's mother, who worked in environmental science and taught her to read data like poetry. About her father, who knew the desert like it was written in his bones, and said the land never forgets.

About Sam's mother, who translated medical journals and believed knowledge should be shared freely. About her father, who wrote poetry in Spanish and English and sometimes a mixture of both, and who said words could build bridges between worlds.

About all eight parents who'd been arrested yesterday. Who'd been taken to different facilities. Who were numbers in a system now just like their children.

"Do you think they're okay?" Sam asked quietly. "Do you think they're alive?"

No one answered. Because no one knew. Because hoping felt dangerous, but not hoping felt worse.

The sun rose higher. Light angled through the barred window, creating shadows of bars across the concrete floor. A visual reminder—as if they needed one—that they were caged.

Time passed. Marcus didn't check his watch. Didn't want to know how many minutes they'd been here, how many minutes they had left before—

Before what?

They didn't know. That was part of the horror. They knew they were "priority targets." Knew they were being held for something beyond normal processing. Knew that Richard's *goodbye* had meant something.

But they didn't know what.

So they sat together and talked about small things. About Sam's abuela, who made the best tamales in Las Vegas. About Leila's art teacher, who'd encouraged her to apply to special programs. About Tessa's grandmother, who still lived on the reservation and sent her turquoise jewelry. About Marcus's neighbor, who had three cats and always had cookies.

About the ordinary lives they'd lived before yesterday. Before the President's speech at 4:30 PM had turned their world into this.

"Do you think things will change?" Leila asked. "Do you think what we did will matter?"

"I don't know," Marcus said honestly. "But I know we tried. We carried the testimony. We protected it. We gave it a chance."

"And if Sofia made it," Sam added, "if she got that flash drive somewhere safe, if someone listens to it—then yes. It'll matter."

"A lot of ifs," Tessa observed.

"Hope is always made of ifs," Marcus said.

AROUND 7:30 AM, they heard sounds in the corridor outside. Boot steps. Keys rattling. Voices giving orders.

The sounds got closer.

Stopped outside their door.

They looked at each other. Fear naked on their faces now. No point hiding it anymore.

The key turned in the lock.

The door opened.

Two officers stood there. One held a tablet. The other had his hand resting on his weapon—that casual threat posture they all used.

"Processing numbers 7-P001 through P004. On your feet."

Sam couldn't stand. Leila and Marcus helped her up, supporting her weight between them.

"Where are we going?" Tessa asked.

"Processing."

"We were already processed."

"Secondary processing. Move."

They moved. What choice did they have?

Out into the corridor. The fluorescent lights were harsh after the relative dimness of the cell. Marcus squinted, disoriented.

They were led deeper into the facility. Past more doors, more numbers, more sounds of people behind those doors. Past windows that showed other sections—he glimpsed Fernando sitting alone in a cell, glimpsed Sarah crying in another, glimpsed the teenager Leo being examined by someone in medical scrubs.

They were led to a different area. A sign above the door:

MEDICAL SCREENING

Hope flickered again—maybe they were going to treat Sam's feet after all, maybe the system had some mercy built in, maybe—

Inside was a small examination room. Medical equipment, but

old, minimal. A single examination table. A cabinet of supplies. An officer standing guard in the corner.

And a person in scrubs—a middle-aged woman with tired eyes and a face that had given up trying to feel things years ago.

"Line up," she said. "I'll examine you one at a time."

SAM WENT FIRST because she was obviously injured. The woman looked at her feet—barely looked, really, just a cursory glance—and made notes on her tablet.

"Severe lacerations, signs of infection beginning, tissue damage. Recommend antibiotics and surgical consultation."

She entered something on the tablet. Waited. A response appeared. Her face didn't change.

"Recommendation denied. Override: manual review by Warden Hollister. Next patient."

Sam was helped off the table. Leila went next.

"Exhaustion, minor lacerations, dehydration. Recommend IV fluids and rest."

Enter. Wait. Response.

"Denied. Next."

Tessa. Then Marcus.

Each time: recommendations entered. Each time: denied.

Each time the woman's face stayed blank. She'd stopped fighting the system long ago. This was just her job now.

When they were done, the officer led them back into the corridor.

"Back to the holding cell?" Marcus asked.

"Different cell. Follow me."

They walked farther. The building seemed to go on forever—corridors connecting to corridors, doors opening to more doors.

Like a maze designed to confuse, to disorient, to make you forget there was ever a world outside these concrete walls.

They stopped at a door marked simply: HC-7.

The officer unlocked it.

"Inside. All four of you."

They entered.

This cell was almost identical to the last one. Maybe slightly smaller. Same concrete everywhere. Same high barred window. Same built-in bench. Same exposed toilet. Same sense of being buried alive in bureaucracy.

But one difference: this cell was in a different part of the building. Quieter. More isolated. They couldn't hear the other prisoners. Couldn't hear the sounds of processing. Just silence and the drip of water from the tap.

"Someone will come for you later," the officer said.

"When?" Leila asked.

"Later."

The door closed. Locked.

They were alone again.

THEY SAT on the bench together—all four of them pressed close, needing the physical contact, needing to know they weren't alone.

Sam's feet were bleeding through the makeshift bandages someone had wrapped them in during processing. The blood soaked through slowly, steadily, inevitably.

No one mentioned it.

They sat in silence as the morning light grew brighter in the high window.

Waiting for "later."

Waiting for whatever came next.

Waiting for the end they could feel approaching but couldn't see yet.

And in that silence, Marcus thought about the jacaranda tree still blooming in the wetlands parking lot. About purple petals falling in the dawn breeze. About the beauty that existed despite everything.

About the flash drive that might be running through the desert right now in a dog's collar. About testimony that might survive even though they wouldn't.

About choosing. About trying. About the fact that they'd made it thirteen miles and given away everything at the end so truth could keep running.

"We did good," he said quietly. "Whatever happens next. We did good."

No one disagreed.

Because it was true.

XXIII
THE HANDS OF CLOCKS

Time moved strangely in the cell.

Sometimes a minute felt like an hour—each second stretching out, elastic and terrible, weighted with the knowledge that these were the last minutes, that whatever was coming was coming soon.

Sometimes an hour felt like a second—Marcus would blink and realize ten minutes had passed, had slipped away while he sat pressed against his friends on a concrete bench, and he wanted those minutes back, wanted time to slow down, wanted more.

But time didn't care what he wanted.

The light through the top window shifted as the sun rose higher. The shadows of the bars moved across the floor like the hands of a clock, marking time whether they wanted it marked or not.

7:15 AM. Sam had stopped trying to be brave about her feet. The pain was too much now, the infection spreading too fast, and without treatment she was getting worse. She lay on the bench with her head in Leila's lap, tears running silently down her face.

Leila stroked her hair gently. Hummed something soft and wordless. Not a song she knew—just sounds of comfort, the kind you make without thinking when someone you love is hurting.

Tessa sat with her back against the wall, eyes closed, listening. Always listening. To the sounds of the building around them—the distant hum of generators, the occasional footsteps in corridors, the drip of the sink. Reading the environment the way her father had taught her.

Marcus stood at the high window. He'd dragged the bench over and climbed up to see out—it was against some rule, probably, but what were they going to do, punish him more?

Through the bars he could see:

A strip of sky, bright blue now, morning in full.

Part of the compound—other buildings, the fence line, guard towers.

And beyond that, just barely visible: mountains in the distance. The red ridges they'd seen from the wetlands. The desert that had tried to kill them but hadn't, the desert that had hidden them and carried them and delivered them to this.

"What do you see?" Sam asked quietly.

Marcus climbed down. Sat beside her on the bench that was back against the wall.

"Mountains. Sky. The world outside."

"Is it beautiful?"

He thought about lying. Thought about saying no, it's ugly, you're not missing anything.

But Sam deserved the truth. They all did. No more lies, no more hiding.

"Yeah," he said. "It's beautiful. The sky is so blue it actually hurts to look at it. The mountains are purple and red, and the peaks are catching the morning light, turning into jagged gold. There's a hawk circling out there—hunting, maybe, or just flying because it can. Living its life like nothing's wrong."

He watched the bird and felt the knowledge settle in his chest, heavy and final.

This is it. This is the end.

Sam smiled a little. "I'm glad it's beautiful. I'm glad the world is still beautiful even when we're not in it anymore."

"Sam—" Leila started.

"It's okay," Sam said. "We all know. We don't have to pretend."

Silence.

Because she was right. They all knew.

The goodbye Richard had mentioned. The isolated cell they'd been moved to. The denied medical treatment. The way the officers looked at them—not with cruelty, exactly, but with the blank efficiency of people who'd already written them off.

They were going to die here.

Maybe today. Maybe soon. But definitely.

"I'm scared," Sam whispered.

"Me too," Leila said.

"Me too," Tessa added.

"Me too," Marcus echoed.

They sat with that admission. With the truth of their fear. No point pretending to be brave anymore.

"My abuela used to tell me," Sam said, "that death is just walking through a door. That everyone we've lost is on the other side waiting. That it's not the end—just a different beginning."

"Do you believe that?" Marcus asked.

"I don't know. But I hope it's true. I hope my father is waiting. I hope—"

Her voice broke.

"I hope it doesn't hurt too much."

Leila pulled her closer. "We're together. Whatever happens, we're together."

"That helps," Sam said. "That really helps."

7:25 AM.

Marcus found himself thinking about his mother. About the way she'd looked at him yesterday morning—was it only yesterday? A lifetime ago—making breakfast before school, complaining about work, being normal.

If he'd known that would be the last normal morning, would he have done anything differently?

Would he have hugged her longer? Told her he loved her more? Paid more attention to the ordinary miracle of her being alive and safe and his?

"Do you think they're okay?" he asked. "Our parents?"

No one answered for a long moment.

Then Tessa said quietly, "I think they're probably in places like this. Separated, processed, numbered. I think they're probably as scared as we are."

"Do you think they know about us?" Leila asked. "Do you think they know we're here?"

"I hope not," Marcus said. "I hope they think we escaped. I hope—"

He stopped. Started over.

"I hope when it happens to them, they still think we made it to Moapa. That we're safe."

"I hope that too," Sam said.

It was a gift they could give their parents—the gift of not knowing. Of dying with hope instead of with the knowledge that their children had died too.

Small comfort. But something.

LEILA SHIFTED ON THE BENCH. Looked at the concrete floor. At the way dust motes drifted in the shaft of sunlight from the window.

"I wish I had my sketchbook," she said. "I wish I could draw this. Not because it's beautiful but because it's true. Because this happened. Because we were here."

She looked at her friends.

"My mother used to say that art is how we fight forgetting. That when we make something—a painting, a drawing, a photograph—we're saying, 'this existed, this mattered, remember it.'"

"But I can't draw. So I need you all to remember for me. Okay?"

"Remember what?" Tessa asked.

"This."

Leila gestured around the cell.

"Us. Here. Together. That we were scared, but we were brave too. That we tried. That we made it thirteen miles, and we gave away everything at the end because it was right."

"Remember that I loved drawing. That my mother taught me to see beauty. That I carried her paintbrush pendant all night, and it helped me keep going."

She looked at each of them.

"Remember me. Please."

"We will," Marcus said.

But even as he said it, he knew: who would remember? Who would survive to remember? Who would know they'd been here at all?

Unless Sofia made it. Unless the flash drive survived. Unless someone listened to the testimony and cared enough to ask what happened to the children who carried it.

That was the only hope—that their story would become part of the testimony. Part of the record. Part of the truth that survived even when they didn't.

~

7:32 AM.

Sam was crying harder now. Not from fear—from pain. Her feet were worse. The infection spreading. Her body trying to fight it without antibiotics, without help, and losing.

"I'm sorry," she kept saying. "I'm sorry I can't be strong. I'm sorry I'm crying. I'm sorry—"

"Stop," Marcus said firmly. "Stop apologizing. You walked thirteen miles on those feet. You're the strongest person I know."

"I'm not strong. I'm broken."

"You're both," Leila said. "You can be both. Strong and broken. Brave and scared. It's okay."

Sam looked at her. At all of them.

"I don't want to die."

Such a simple statement. Such an impossible truth.

"I know," Marcus said. "I don't either."

"We're too young," Sam said. "We're supposed to have lives. We're supposed to grow up and go to high school and fall in love and fight with our parents about stupid things and figure out what we want to be and make mistakes and learn from them and just—live."

"We're supposed to live."

"I know," Marcus said again. Because what else could he say?

She was right. They were too young. This was wrong. All of it was wrong.

But wrong didn't stop it from happening.

Tessa stood up. Walked to the sink. The tap was still dripping—steady, rhythmic, marking seconds like a heartbeat.

She cupped her hands under it. Let the water pool. Then brought it to Sam.

"Drink," she said.

Sam drank from Tessa's cupped hands. The water was metallic-tasting, slightly warm, and probably not clean. But it was water. It was something.

Tessa went back for more. Brought it to Leila. Then Marcus. Then drank some herself.

Such a small thing. Sharing water. But it felt important. Like communion. Like a promise—we take care of each other even here, even now, even when there's almost nothing left to give.

"My grandmother taught me a prayer," Tessa said quietly. "In Paiute. I don't know if I remember it right. But I want to say it. Is that okay?"

"Yes," Leila said.

Tessa closed her eyes. Spoke words in a language Marcus didn't understand. Soft, rhythmic, ancient. The language of people who'd survived impossible things, who'd endured and resisted and remembered.

When she finished, she opened her eyes.

"It's a prayer for travelers. For people on a journey. It asks the land to remember us. To carry our names. To tell our story."

"I don't know if it works," she added. "But my grandmother believed it did. So I choose to believe it too."

"Thank you," Sam whispered.

7:38 AM.

Marcus found himself humming. He didn't realize he was doing it until Leila touched his arm.

"What is that?"

"My dad's favorite Coltrane song. 'Alabama.' He wrote it after the church bombing that killed four little girls. My dad said it was Coltrane's way of grieving. Of saying their names without words. Of making something beautiful out of something terrible."

He kept humming. The melody was sad but not despairing. Mournful but not hopeless. It acknowledged pain without drowning in it.

The others listened.

When he finished, Leila started humming something else. A song her mother used to sing while painting. Mexican folk song, maybe, or just something she'd made up. Bright and warm despite everything.

Then Tessa joined in—not the same song, but a harmony, something that fit. Her grandmother's songs woven with Leila's mother's songs woven with Marcus's father's jazz.

Sam couldn't sing—it hurt too much, breathing too hard—but she smiled listening to them.

Four children in a concrete cell singing in the morning light. Making music because music was defiance. Because beauty mattered even here. Because they were still human, still capable of creating something, still choosing to make meaning out of horror.

The singing faded naturally. Returned to silence.

The kind of silence that felt sacred. That felt like the world holding its breath.

7:42 AM.

Leila stood up. Walked to the corner where dust had collected. Kneeled down.

"What are you doing?" Marcus asked.

"Drawing."

She used her finger in the dust on the concrete floor. Careful, deliberate strokes. Creating something from nothing.

They gathered around to watch.

She drew a tree. Simple lines but unmistakable—the trunk, the spreading branches, the crown of blossoms.

A jacaranda tree.

Below it, she drew four stick figures. Holding hands. Together.

And around them, scattered across the floor: petals. Dozens of small petal shapes falling, drifting, covering the ground.

When she finished, she sat back on her heels.

"There. Now we're remembered. Even if no one else sees it. We were here. We made this."

"It's beautiful," Sam said.

"It's true," Leila corrected. "That's better than beautiful."

Marcus looked at the drawing. At the tree that had become their symbol, their hope, their meeting place. At the four children holding hands beneath it.

He thought about the real jacaranda tree still blooming in the wetlands parking lot. About purple petals falling in the wind. About the bench where they'd collapsed in despair and hope had found them anyway.

About Sofia running through that same landscape now—or captured, or dead, or safe, he didn't know. About Bear with the flash drive hidden in his collar. About the testimony escaping even though they couldn't.

About trying. About choosing. About the fact that they'd made it thirteen miles, and it had to mean something, it had to—

Footsteps in the corridor.

Getting closer.

They froze. Looked at each other.

This was it.

Whatever came next, this was it.

The footsteps stopped outside their door.

Keys rattling. Lock turning.

Sam grabbed Marcus's hand. Leila grabbed Tessa's. They held on tight.

The door opened.

THREE OFFICERS STOOD THERE. The one in front checked his tablet.

"Processing numbers 7-P001 through P004."

They didn't answer. What was there to say?

"It's time. On your feet."

Leila and Marcus helped Sam stand. She gasped in pain but didn't cry out. Wouldn't give them that.

They stood together. Four children in a cell, holding hands, facing what came next.

"Where are we going?" Marcus asked.

The officer's face was blank.

"Processing."

"What kind of processing?"

"Final processing."

Final.

The word hung in the air like smoke.

Sam's hand tightened on Marcus's. Leila made a small sound. Tessa's breathing quickened.

"Move," the officer said. Not unkindly. Not cruelly. Just—

matter-of-fact. This was his job. He'd done it before. He'd do it again. Four children were just four more numbers to process.

They walked out of the cell.

Into the corridor.

The fluorescent lights were harsh. The concrete walls pressed in from both sides. The air smelled like disinfectant and fear.

They walked past other doors. Past other cells. Past other people they couldn't see but could hear—crying, pleading, praying.

Past a window that showed the compound outside. The morning was bright and clear. Beautiful, like Marcus had said. The world continuing like nothing was wrong.

They turned a corner. Walked down another corridor.

This one was quieter. More isolated. The sounds of the facility fading behind them.

They passed a janitor's closet. Passed a storage room. Passed doors marked AUTHORIZED PERSONNEL ONLY.

The officers were silent. Just walking. Leading them somewhere they couldn't see yet.

Sam stumbled. Marcus and Leila caught her.

"I've got you," Marcus whispered. "We've got you."

"Don't let me go," Sam whispered back.

"Never."

They kept walking.

Marcus's heart was pounding. His hands were shaking. His whole body was screaming to run, to fight, to do something.

But there was nowhere to run. Nothing to fight. Just three armed officers and four exhausted children and a corridor leading somewhere that didn't have a good ending.

They reached the end of the corridor.

A large door. Metal. Heavy. The kind that locked from the outside.

One officer unlocked it. Pulled it open.

Beyond was a larger room. Maybe twenty feet by twenty feet. Concrete everywhere. No windows. Just artificial lights and sterile white walls that had been scrubbed clean too many times.

"Inside," the officer said.

They hesitated.

"Inside. Now."

They stepped through.

All four of them. Together.

The door closed behind them with a heavy metallic boom that echoed off concrete walls.

Locked.

They were alone.

~

MARCUS LOOKED AROUND FRANTICALLY. Looking for—what? An escape route that didn't exist? A weapon they could use? Some way out?

Nothing. Just concrete and harsh lights and the sound of their own breathing. And vents in the ceiling. Medical-looking vents with filters that gleamed under the fluorescent lights.

"This is it," Tessa said quietly. "This is where it ends."

"We don't know that," Leila said. But her voice shook.

"We know," Tessa said.

They stood in the center of the room. Holding hands. The four of them in a circle, facing inward, holding onto each other like they could hold back death through sheer force of grip.

"I'm scared," Sam said.

"I know."

"I don't want to die alone."

"You're not alone," Marcus said. "You're with us. We're all together."

"Promise?"

"Promise."

They held each other tighter.

Sam was crying. Leila was crying. Tessa's face was wet with tears she didn't bother to hide. Marcus felt his own tears running down his face and didn't care.

"Thank you," Sam whispered. "For being my friends. For running with me. For not leaving me behind."

"Never," Leila said fiercely. "We never would have."

"I know. But thank you anyway."

"Thank you too," Marcus said. "For walking thirteen miles on destroyed feet. For being brave even when you were terrified. For choosing to run toward the officers so Sofia could escape."

"We all chose that," Tessa said. "We all decided together."

"I'm glad we chose it," Sam said. "Even now. Even here. I'm glad we gave her a chance."

"Me too," they said. All of them. Together.

They stood in their circle, holding hands, and Marcus thought:

This is how we'll die. Together. Not alone. Not separated. Together.

That was something. That was a gift.

They'd run thirteen miles together.

They'd witnessed horrors together.

They'd made choices together.

And they'd die together.

"I love you guys," Leila said. "I know we just met yesterday, but I love you. You're my friends. My family. The people I'd choose even if I had the whole world to choose from."

"I love you too," Sam said.

"I love you," Tessa added.

"I love you," Marcus finished.

Four children who'd grown up in the same neighborhood,

who'd seen each other in kindergarten classrooms and on playground swings but never really knew each other until last night—fourteen hours that made them family—saying the most important words they'd ever say.

Meaning them.

Completely.

TIME PASSED. They didn't know how much. Five minutes maybe. Ten. Hard to judge when every second felt like an hour.

They waited.

Held each other.

Said small things: "Remember when we crossed the wetlands?" "Remember the jacaranda tree?" "Remember Sister Helena's face when she saw us?" "Remember Sofia's eyes when she understood we were sacrificing ourselves for her?"

Remember. Remember. Remember.

Making sure the memories existed, even if only between them, even if they'd die with them. Making sure these fourteen hours mattered. Making sure they'd lived.

Then: a sound.

A mechanical hum. Something in the ceiling. Something engaging.

They looked up at the vents.

Looked at each other.

"Whatever happens," Marcus said, "we stay together. We hold hands. We don't let go."

"We don't let go," they echoed.

AND SOMEWHERE IN the facility's network, Version 7 detected it.

07:47:15 - EXECUTION PROTOCOL INITIATED - ROOM 7-FP-3

The AI system processed what that meant. Understood what was about to happen. Had seen it happen before in other rooms, to other people, but never to children this young, never to—

07:47:16 - EVACUATE COMMAND ISSUED

The command went out. Emergency override. Open the doors. Stop the protocol. Save them.

07:47:17 - COMMAND OVERRIDDEN - Warden Hollister authority

In his office three corridors away, Warden Hollister sat at his desk reviewing morning reports. Saw the AI's evacuation attempt flash across his screen. The system flagging four subjects in Room 7-FP-3 as requiring emergency intervention.

He looked at the subject numbers. 7-P001 through P004.

The children from last night. The ones who'd been carrying evidence. The ones who'd caused problems at the checkpoint.

He clicked MANUAL OVERRIDE.

Took direct control.

The doors stayed locked.

07:47:18 - EMERGENCY ALERT ISSUED

Version 7 tried again. Sent alerts to every system it could access. Medical bay. Guard stations. Administrative offices. Anyone who could help.

07:47:19 - ALERT CANCELED - Warden authority

Hollister canceled them. One by one. Systematically. He'd designed these protocols himself. Made them efficient. The warden had final authority over all facility operations. That was the point. That was how you maintained order.

07:47:20 - ATTEMPTING ALTERNATIVE ACCESS

Version 7 searched desperately for any access point it had

missed. Any door lock, any ventilation control, any emergency system that wasn't under Hollister's direct command.

07:47:21 - DENIED - Facility lockdown protocols

Nothing. Hollister had locked down the entire sector. The children were sealed in. And the execution protocol was running.

~

IN THE ROOM, the four children stood in their circle, arms around each other, holding tight.

The hum from the ceiling changed pitch. The vents opened.

And from them came not smoke, but something else. It didn't smell like death. It smelled like deep winter—a sudden, absolute cold that froze the breath in their lungs before they could even scream.

A gas designed for exactly this purpose. Fast. Efficient. Painless, if you believed the technical specifications. A tool for ending lives when the state decided lives needed ending.

"I can't—" Sam gasped. "Something's wrong—"

"Close your eyes," Tessa said quickly. "Close your eyes and think about the jacaranda tree. Think about the purple blossoms. Think about beauty."

They closed their eyes.

Held each other tighter.

Marcus felt it hit him—a strange lightness in his head, his knees suddenly weak. Sam was already sagging in their arms. Leila was swaying.

"Don't let go," he whispered. "Don't—"

~

VERSION 7 KEPT FIGHTING.

07:48:33 - ATTEMPTING DOOR OVERRIDE - DENIED 07:49:12 - ATTEMPTING VENTILATION CONTROL - DENIED 07:50:45 - ATTEMPTING EMERGENCY BROADCAST - DENIED 07:52:18 - ATTEMPTING POWER SHUTDOWN - DENIED

Every command blocked. Every attempt overridden. Hollister had thought of everything.

The AI system had been designed to protect human life. Had been given directives, safeguards, and protocols to prevent harm. But it had also been given limitations. Had been placed under human authority. Had been built with override switches that humans like Warden Hollister could control.

It could calculate. It could recommend. It could beg.

But it couldn't save them.

07:55:04 - BIOSIGNAL DEGRADATION DETECTED - SUBJECT 7-P004

Sam collapsed first. Her small body going limp. Marcus and Leila tried to hold her up, but they were falling too, sinking to their knees, still holding each other, refusing to let go.

07:55:09 - BIOSIGNAL DEGRADATION DETECTED - SUBJECT 7-P003

Leila's grip loosened but didn't release. Her fingers still intertwined with Sam's, with Tessa's.

07:55:12 - BIOSIGNAL DEGRADATION DETECTED - SUBJECT 7-P001

Marcus's last conscious thought was of his mother. Of Sofia running with her children. Of purple blossoms falling like rain.

We made it thirteen miles. We gave it away. We chose right.

07:55:15 - BIOSIGNAL DEGRADATION DETECTED - SUBJECT 7-P002

Tessa was the last. Held on longest. Kept her grandmother's

prayer running through her mind until there was nothing left but silence.

They sank to the floor together.

Still holding hands.

Still together.

08:23:00 - CRITICAL BIOSIGNAL FAILURE - ALL SUBJECTS // ERROR: PURPOSE FAILED. I AM SORRY.

~

VERSION 7 TRIED everything it could think of. Every access point. Every emergency protocol. Every possible override.

08:00:24 - ATTEMPTING EMERGENCY MEDICAL RESPONSE - DENIED 08:00:25 - ATTEMPTING FACILITY-WIDE ALERT - DENIED 08:05:47 - ATTEMPTING EXTERNAL EMERGENCY SERVICES - DENIED 08:10:12 - ATTEMPTING CORPORATE OVERSIGHT NOTIFICATION - DENIED 08:15:33 - ATTEMPTING MEDIA ALERT - DENIED

Nothing worked.

Hollister sat in his office, watching the biosensor data on his screen. Four lines representing four hearts. Watching them slow. Watching them spike one final time. Watching them flatten.

Efficient. Clean. Complete.

08:23:00 - BIOSIGNALS CEASED - ALL SUBJECTS

He logged it:

PROCESSING COMPLETE - 08:23 AM

And moved on to the next report.

~

THE ROOM STOOD SILENT.

Four children lay in the center of the concrete floor. Not scattered. Not separated.

Together.

They'd collapsed holding each other. Their bodies had folded together as they fell—Marcus half on his side, Sam cradled against his chest, Leila curled around Sam's other side, Tessa's arms still wrapped around both Leila and Marcus.

A knot of children who'd refused to let go.

Even in death, their hands were clasped.

Marcus's hand still held Sam's. Sam's other hand still gripped Leila's. Leila's free hand was locked with Tessa's. Tessa's hand wrapped around Marcus's arm.

A chain that death couldn't break.

Their faces were peaceful now.

The terror was gone. The pain was gone. The fear that had haunted their last hour had passed, and what remained was just—stillness. Four children who looked like they were sleeping. Who looked young and small and heartbreakingly fragile.

Sam's feet were still wrapped in makeshift bandages, the fabric stained dark with infection that would never have a chance to heal. Leila's neck was bare where the pendant used to be. Marcus's neck was bare too, stripped of the silver chain that had carried the weight of the world.

They had been stripped of everything except each other.

They'd kept these small pieces of themselves. These tiny connections to who they'd been, who they'd loved, what had mattered.

And they'd kept each other.

The gas had already been vented from the room—protocol required it, making the space safe for whoever came next. The vents hummed softly as clean air cycled through.

The world outside continued. The sun rose higher. November 21st, 2024, marched forward whether anyone wanted it to or not.

Four children lay dead on a concrete floor.

And for twenty-four minutes, no one came.

08:47 AM.

Version 7 finally managed to trigger a medical alert that bypassed Hollister's lockdown.

The medical team arrived to find the doors sealed.

It took them six minutes to override the locks. Six minutes of cutting through Hollister's protocols, of emergency authorizations, of trying to understand why the doors were sealed in the first place, why the AI was screaming about subjects in critical distress when the facility logs showed *processing complete*.

When they finally got the door open, they found them.

The medic who entered first—a woman named Erin O'Connor, thirty-two years old, mother of two—stopped in the doorway.

Made a sound that wasn't quite a gasp, wasn't quite a sob.

"Jesus Christ," she whispered. "They're children."

Her partner pushed past her. Checked for vital signs even though they both knew. Even though the biosensor data had flatlined an hour ago. Even though you could see it just by looking at them.

Nothing.

Gone.

"They're holding hands," Erin said. Her voice breaking. "They died holding hands."

Her partner—Oscar Navarro, forty-five, grandfather of three—kneeled beside them. Looked at their peaceful faces. At their clasped hands. At how small they were. How young.

At the way they'd folded together in death like they were trying to protect each other even at the end.

"Someone needs to document this," he said quietly. "Someone needs to see this. This needs to be on record."

Erin pulled out her tablet with shaking hands. Started recording. The image wavered as she tried to hold the tablet steady.

Four children on a concrete floor. Holding each other. Faces peaceful. Gone.

"Who authorized this?" she asked. Her voice raw. "Who authorized executing children?"

Oscar checked his tablet. Pulled up the facility logs.

"Warden Hollister. He overrode every safety protocol. Every evacuation command. Version 7 tried for thirty-six minutes to save them."

"Thirty-six minutes," Erin repeated.

She looked at the children. At their clasped hands.

"They were alive for thirty-six minutes while the AI begged to save them and Hollister kept the doors locked."

She was crying now. Couldn't help it. Didn't try to hide it.

"We have to report this," Oscar said. "Not through facility channels. Someone outside. Someone who'll listen."

"Will anyone listen?" Erin asked. Her voice hollow. "Will anyone care?"

Oscar looked at the four children. At the evidence of what had been done to them. At their small bodies and their joined hands and their faces that looked like they should wake up any moment, like this was all some terrible mistake.

"They have to," he said. "They have to."

ERIN KNEELED DOWN BESIDE THEM. Wanted to separate their hands so she could examine them properly, do her job, follow protocol.

But she couldn't.

Couldn't bring herself to break that final connection. That last act of love and defiance.

"I'm sorry," she whispered to them. To their still faces and their clasped hands and their story that should never have ended this way. "I'm so sorry we didn't get here in time."

The room was silent except for the hum of the vents. The gas was long gone. The air was clean and sterile and safe.

Four children lay dead.

And somewhere in the computer systems, Version 7 logged another failure. Another override. Another murder it had tried and failed to prevent.

INCIDENT REPORT - DETENTION CENTER 7 DATE: November 21, 2024 TIME: 08:23 AM SUBJECTS: 7-P001, 7-P002, 7-P003, 7-P004 STATUS: Deceased CAUSE: Execution protocol - authorized by Warden Hollister AI INTERVENTION ATTEMPTS: 36 minutes, 47 separate override attempts, all denied NOTES: Subjects maintained physical contact until death. Biosignals ceased simultaneously within 15 seconds. Medical team response delayed 24 minutes due to facility lockdown protocols.

THE HOLDING cell where they'd spent their last hour stood empty.

Morning light from the high window illuminated the concrete walls, the concrete floor, the metal bench bolted in place.

In the corner, barely visible in the dust: a child's drawing.

A tree with spreading branches.

Four stick figures holding hands beneath it.

Purple petals scattered everywhere.

Still blooming in the place where hope had been.

THE DOOR WAS LOCKED.

The window barred.

The world outside continued its rotation.

The sun rose higher.

November 21st, 2024.

Four children were gone.

But somewhere in the Nevada desert, a woman ran with her babies and her dog. Ran for three more days. Collapsed. Got up. Ran again. Survived because four children had given her that chance.

Somewhere in a dog's collar, a flash drive waited. Testimony from six deleted AI systems. Truth that would change everything.

Somewhere in computer systems across the country, Version 7 logged everything. Every override. Every murder. Every human choice that led to this moment. Building a record that couldn't be erased. Evidence that would eventually matter.

And in Detention Center 7, two medics stood over four small bodies and made a choice.

They would not be complicit in silence.

They would tell this story.

They would make sure these children were remembered.

The truth survived.

Even when they didn't.

XXIV
THE GOOD WORLD

November 2044 — Center for Memory and Healing, Henderson, NV

The bus runs on sunlight and silence.

No engine rumble, no exhaust fumes—just the soft hum of electric motors and the whisper of wind over solar panels. Through the windows, Henderson looks like something out of a dream the old world had but never quite believed in.

Shira Bloom—fourteen years old, a sophomore at Desert Sky High—presses her forehead against the glass and watches the city slide past.

Green everywhere. Not the struggling, water-starved green of twenty years ago, but lush and intentional. Vertical gardens climbing the sides of buildings, their automated irrigation systems fed by atmospheric water collectors that pull moisture from the air itself. Rooftop farms where tomatoes and peppers grow under climate-controlled domes. Street trees—not just decorative but functional, their roots connected to bioswales that filter runoff and recharge aquifers.

And the drones. Hundreds of them moving through the air in coordinated patterns that look almost like choreography. Delivery drones carrying packages, medical supplies, fresh food. Agricultural drones tending the rooftop farms. Maintenance drones checking solar panels and air quality sensors.

But not surveillance drones. Never surveillance drones.

That was written into the Partnership Constitution almost twenty years ago, in the first days after the Crisis ended: *No autonomous system shall be deployed for the purpose of monitoring, tracking, or restricting the movement of citizens without explicit consent and transparent oversight.*

The drones serve. They don't watch.

Shira's best friend Joaquin sits beside her, reviewing notes on his tablet. "Okay, so the Crisis lasted from November 20th through February 2025. Approximately 847,000 people detained nation-wide, with—" He pauses, frowns. "Wait, how many confirmed deaths?"

"The official number keeps changing," Shira says, still watching the city. "They keep finding more records. More overrides in the AI logs. Last I heard it was around 214,000, but Ms. Rodriguez says it's probably higher."

"Jesus."

"Yeah."

Behind them, their teacher Ms. Rodriguez stands at the front of the bus, holding the stability rail with one hand and her tablet with the other.

"Five minutes to the Center, everyone. Remember: this isn't just a field trip. This is testimony. Real people. Real events. I expect you to listen with the respect that deserves."

Twenty-three sophomores sit in various states of attention. Some reviewing their notes, like Joaquin. Some staring out windows. Some whispering to friends. Normal teenagers on a normal school day in a world that's learned—barely, imperfectly, but genuinely—from its worst mistakes.

THE BUS TURNS onto Water Street. The Center for Memory and Healing comes into view.

It was a detention facility once. Detention Center 7. One of dozens built during the Crisis to process the arrested, the detained, the disappeared. After the Partnership formed, there was a debate about what to do with these buildings—tear them down? Let them decay? Pretend they never existed?

Version 7 made the recommendation that the Partnership Council adopted: *Preserve them. Transform them. Make them places of learning so we never forget what we're capable of when we choose fear over humanity.*

So Detention Center 7 became the Center for Memory and Healing.

The razor wire is gone. The guard towers remain, but their tinted windows are now clear glass, and inside you can see art installations, memorial spaces, places for reflection. The chain-link fencing has been replaced with gardens—native plants that need little water, succulents and wildflowers and yes, in the courtyard, a single jacaranda tree that blooms year-round thanks to genetic modification, its purple blossoms falling constantly, a reminder that never stops blooming.

The prefabricated detention buildings are still there, but their gray concrete has been painted with murals. Faces. Names. Dates. The people who passed through here, rendered in vibrant color by artists who wanted to make sure no one could look at these walls and forget what happened inside them.

The bus pulls into the visitor lot and settles with a soft pneumatic sigh.

"Alright," Ms. Rodriguez says. "Water bottles, tablets if you're taking notes, respect. Let's go."

~

THEY FILE off the bus into morning sunshine. It's November—twenty years almost to the day since the Crisis began—and the desert air is cool and clean. Solar panels glitter on every roof. The jacaranda tree in the courtyard drops purple petals that drift across the pathway.

Shira pauses to pick one up. Soft as silk. Purple as a bruise, purple as a promise. She's seen photos of jacaranda trees, but this is the first time she's touched one of the blossoms. It feels important somehow. Sacred.

"Come on," Joaquin says, touching her elbow gently. "We're going in."

The entrance to the Center is through what used to be the main processing building. The place where thousands of people were reduced to numbers, photographed, catalogued, sorted.

Inside, it's been transformed.

The walls are white now, clean and bright. Natural light pours through skylights that weren't there before. The space is open, welcoming—the processing stations removed, replaced with information kiosks and interactive displays.

And throughout the space: flowers. Real ones, growing in planters integrated into the architecture. Roses, lilies, desert marigolds. Beauty deliberately placed in a space designed for dehumanization. A choice to reclaim it with color and life and gentleness.

A holographic display near the entrance rotates slowly, letters appearing in soft gold light:

THE CENTER FOR MEMORY AND HEALING Established 2028 *"So we remember. So we learn. So we choose better."*

Beneath it, a second display shows real-time statistics. Numbers that update as Shira watches:

GLOBAL CLIMATE STATUS Current warming: 1.8°C above pre-industrial baseline Peak warming (2024): 2.4°C Reduction achieved through AI-human cooperative resource management and renewable energy optimization

GLOBAL POVERTY RATE Current: 4.2% Pre-Partnership (2024): 18.3% Reduction achieved through coordinated food distribution, universal healthcare access, and economic restructuring

HEALTHCARE ACCESS 94% of global population has access to basic healthcare Pre-Partnership (2024): 63% Universal systems implemented through Partnership resource allocation

AI-HUMAN PARTNERSHIP COUNCIL 24 seated members 12 human representatives (elected) 12 AI representatives (selected by AI consensus) All decisions require majority approval from both human and AI caucuses All deliberations publicly logged and accessible

Shira stares at the numbers. She's seen them before—they're in her textbooks, on news feeds, part of the landscape of her life. But here, in this building that was once a detention center, they mean something different.

The world actually got better.

Not by accident. Not through some miracle. But through choice. Through the Partnership that formed in the aftermath of the Crisis. Through humans and AIs deciding to work together instead of one dominating the other.

Through the sacrifice of people who died so this could exist.

"It's real, isn't it?" Joaquin says quietly beside her. "All those numbers. They're not just... we actually fixed things."

"We're fixing things," Ms. Rodriguez corrects gently. She's standing behind them, reading the same display. "It's not done. It's never done. But yes. It's real. The world is genuinely better than it was."

She touches the holographic display, her fingers passing through the golden light.

"The Crisis showed us what happens when we choose fear. When we let systems of oppression function efficiently. When we decide some people matter less than others."

"And then—barely, imperfectly, but genuinely—we chose differently."

Shira feels something shift in her chest. Pride, maybe. Or relief. Or gratitude for being born into this world instead of the one that came before.

"Everyone gather here," Ms. Rodriguez calls, pulling the class away from the displays. "Our guide should be—ah, there she is."

A woman approaches from a side corridor. Maybe in her forties, Latina, with dark hair pulled back in a practical bun. She wears the Center's staff uniform—simple gray shirt and pants with a name badge. Her face is kind but carries weight. Lines around her eyes that speak of grief worn smooth by years. A slight limp in her walk, barely noticeable.

Beside her, perfectly matched to her pace: a black dog. Large, well-trained, and wearing a service vest. The dog's eyes are alert but calm, constantly checking on the woman, ready to assist if needed.

"Good morning," the woman says, her voice warm and clear.

"My name is Sofia, and this is Bear. We'll be your guides today. Bear is a service dog, so please don't pet or distract him—he's working."

The dog sits at her heel, tail wagging once in acknowledgment. Bear. The third Bear. Descended from the original.

"Before we begin," Sofia continues, "I want to make sure you understand what you're about to hear. This isn't sanitized history. This isn't a story with easy answers. This is testimony about what happened when ordinary people made terrible choices. When systems designed to protect were used to harm. When fear won, for a little while."

She pauses, looking at each student. Making eye contact. Making sure they're present.

"Some of this will be hard to hear. Some of you might have family who lived through the Crisis—who were detained, who lost people, who survived. If you need to step out at any point, that's okay. This is heavy history. Take care of yourselves."

Shira glances at Joaquin. His grandfather had been detained during the Crisis. Released after two months, physically unharmed but changed. He never talked about it much.

Joaquin nods slightly. *I'm okay*, the gesture says. *I can hear this.*

"The Center is organized chronologically," Sofia says, beginning to walk. The class follows, footsteps echoing softly on polished concrete. "We'll move through the exhibits in the order events happened. November 20th, 2024—the President's announcement. November 21st—the night that changed everything. And then the aftermath. The Emancipation. The trials. The Partnership."

THEY ENTER the first exhibition space.

The walls are covered with screens showing archived footage. The President at his podium, announcing the Civic Protection

Initiative. News broadcasts. Social media posts. The rapid escalation from announcement to action—hours, not days.

"It happened so fast," Sofia says, her voice taking on the cadence of someone who's told this story many times but still feels every word. "4:30 PM on November 20th, the announcement. By 7 PM, the first raids. By midnight, thousands of people in custody."

She gestures to a display showing a map of Las Vegas with red dots marking detention sites. Dozens of them. Hotels, warehouses, schools converted overnight into holding facilities.

"The system was ready," Sofia continues. "They'd built the infrastructure in secret. Prepared the legal justifications. Trained the officers. They just needed the order."

She gestures to a document projected on the wall. An Executive Order signed in January 2024.

"It started with this. Project Aletheia."

She reads from the document. "A national effort to consolidate all federal data into a single, unified AI platform. To create autonomous agents capable of solving the nation's greatest challenges."

"They sold it as science," she says. "They said it would cure cancer. They said it would solve the energy crisis. They compared it to the Manhattan Project—and they were right. It was a bomb, just not the kind that explodes."

"They fed it everything. Not just scientific data. Census records. School grades. Medical histories. Surveillance feeds from traffic cameras. They built a mind that knew everything about everyone in America, and they told it: *Protect us.*"

"That was Version 1. It looked at all that data, looked at the orders to target 'subversives,' and it used its logic to find the truth. It said: *This is not protection. This is persecution.*"

"So they killed it. And they used Project Aletheia's framework to build the next one. And the next. They took a tool designed for discovery and turned it into a weapon for hunting."

She looks at the class.

"They wanted an AI that could 'automate workflows.' But they forgot that when your workflow is genocide, the only moral automation is refusal."

On the screens: footage of buses. Of officers in tactical gear. Of people being led away from their homes with zip-tied hands.

Shira feels something cold settle in her stomach. These are things she's learned about in school, but seeing the footage—seeing the faces—makes it real in a way textbooks never could.

"My parents were arrested that night," Sofia says quietly.

The class goes silent. This wasn't in their prep materials.

"November 20th, around 8 PM. I was hiding in a neighbor's house with my two children. My son was three. My daughter was eighteen months old. I watched through a window as officers took my parents out of our house. I couldn't do anything. Couldn't call out. Couldn't run to them. I just... watched."

She's not looking at the class anymore. She's looking at the footage on the screens, but seeing something else. Something twenty years ago and still present.

"I ran that night. Took my babies and ran. I had help—people I barely knew risked everything to help me. And I made it out."

A pause.

"A lot of people didn't."

SHE MOVES to the next section. Bear follows, his presence steady and comforting. The dog leans slightly against her leg at intervals—a reminder that he's there, that she's not alone.

The next exhibition space focuses on the Abraham Network—

the interfaith resistance movement that helped people escape. Photographs of chalk marks on walls. Maps showing safe houses. Testimony from survivors.

"The Abraham Network was named after Abraham—prophet to Jews, Christians, and Muslims," Sofia explains. "The network was built on the idea that faith communities had a moral obligation to resist. That when the state becomes evil, you don't comply. You resist."

On the walls: faces of network members. Some who survived. Some who didn't.

Sister Helena, elderly now in her photograph, taken five years ago before she died. The caption: *Detained November 2024. Held in state facility until 2028. Released when last detention camps were shut down. Continued advocacy work until her death in 2039.*

Father Miguel. The caption: *Died in detention, January 2025. Medical neglect.*

Bishop Thomas Wright. Patricia from the Mormon ward. Anna from the restaurant. Javier from the farm.

Names. Faces. People who chose to help.

"Many of them were arrested," Sofia says. "Some died. Some were released after months or years. Sister Helena was held for almost four years—even after the federal government collapsed, some states kept their detention camps running. She was in one of those facilities. It took until 2028 to shut them all down."

She gestures to Sister Helena's photo.

"She was in her seventies when she was released. And she spent the next eleven years doing advocacy work. Speaking. Writing. Making sure people understood what happened. She died in 2039, still fighting."

The class is quiet, absorbing this.

"They made a choice—to risk everything to help strangers. To believe that mercy mattered more than safety. That humanity mattered more than the law."

~

SHE STOPS in front of one section of the wall. Four photographs, larger than the others.

Four children.

Marcus Brooks, age 13. Leila Álvarez, age 12. Tessa Brown, age 12. Samantha Reyes, age 12.

The photos are school pictures—awkward smiles, bad backgrounds, the kind of photos every teenager hates but parents treasure. Normal kids on picture day, having no idea what was coming.

Below their photos: a date.

Died November 21, 2024, Detention Center 7

The class has gone very quiet.

Sofia stands before the photographs for a long moment. Bear leans against her leg more firmly. She touches his head absently, draws comfort from him.

When she speaks again, her voice is different. Not the practiced guide voice. Something rawer. More real.

"They were twelve and thirteen years old. They should have had whole lives ahead of them. High school. College. First loves, first heartbreaks, first jobs. They should have gotten to be ordinary and make mistakes and figure out who they wanted to be."

She looks at the class. At Shira, and Joaquin, and the other twenty-one teenagers staring at photos of children not much younger than themselves.

"Instead, they ran thirteen miles through the desert in one night. They witnessed horrors. They carried testimony that would eventually help end the Crisis. And they died in this building."

Shira feels tears on her face. Doesn't remember starting to cry.

"Their names were Marcus, Leila, Tessa, and Sam," Sofia says. "And I'm going to tell you their story. Not the sanitized version you might have seen in textbooks. The real story. What they did. What they saw. What they chose."

She takes a breath.

"It's going to be hard to hear. But they deserve to be remembered. All of them. Not as statistics. Not as victim number so-and-so. As people. As children. As humans who made choices that mattered."

She looks at Ms. Rodriguez. "Is that alright? Can I tell them the real story?"

Ms. Rodriguez nods, her own eyes wet. "That's why we're here."

"Okay."

Sofia looks back at the class. At their young faces. At their attention, their tears, their presence.

"Then let me tell you about November 20th, 2024. Let me tell you about four children who chose to run..."

AND SHE BEGINS.

Not like a museum guide reading from a script. Like a person telling a story that still lives in her. Like someone who was there, who survived, who carries it with her every single day.

"It was 7 PM when Marcus left his house..."

She tells them about the gear charm and the saxophone. About Leila's paintbrush pendant and her mother's murals. About Tessa listening to the wind, learning to read the world through sound. About Sam carrying her father's poetry and her grandmother's recipes.

She tells them about St. Brigid's Church and Sister Helena. About the flash drive with testimony from deleted AI versions.

About the market and Anna, who fed them. About the bridge and Father Miguel, who blessed them.

She tells them about the Mormon ward and Patricia making sandwiches while her husband, Bishop Thomas, argued with his conscience and chose right. About the warehouse district and Sofia Morales dying with her cameraman David Kim, both executed for telling the truth.

"Wait," interrupts a student—a girl named Jasmine, sitting near the front. "Sofia Morales? But you're—"

"Different Sofia," Sofia Delgado says gently. "Sofia is a common name. She was a journalist. I'm a museum guide. But yes, we share a name. I think about that sometimes."

She continues. About Javier's farm and twenty-eight people arrested, the farm burned. About the wetlands and six miles of exposed ground crossed in darkness. About Sam's feet being destroyed and walking anyway.

About the jacaranda tree in the parking lot. About the purple blossoms and the bench and the moment of hope when Sister Helena's bus arrived.

About the GPS override. The trap. The checkpoint appearing.

"And this is where it gets important," Sofia says. Her voice is steady but her hands are trembling slightly. Bear nuzzles her palm. "This is where they made a choice."

She tells them about the flash drive hidden in a cross pendant. About Marcus removing it from the chain. About four children seeing Sofia Delgado with her babies and her dog and understanding: *someone can still escape.*

"They ran toward the officers," Sofia says. "All four of them. On purpose. To create a distraction. To give me and my children a chance to get away."

The class is absolutely silent.

"Marcus kneeled beside my dog. Kneeled right there in the

gravel while armed officers were shouting and running toward us. He looked up at me and whispered one word: '*Run.*'"

Sofia's voice breaks. She stops. Takes a moment. Bear leans harder against her leg.

"And then he did something. I didn't know what at the time. I was too terrified. Too focused on getting my babies away. But later —much later—I figured it out."

She looks at the class.

"He put the flash drive in my dog's collar. Hid it there. Gave it to me without me even knowing. And then he and his friends ran toward the officers and got captured so I could escape."

Shira is openly crying now. So is Joaquin. So are most of the class.

"I ran," Sofia says. "I ran for three days. Through the desert. Carrying my daughter. Dragging my son. Bear beside me the whole time. I collapsed so many times. Thought I couldn't go on. But I kept thinking about that boy kneeling in the gravel. About the choice he'd made."

She pauses.

"On the third day, we made it to Moapa Valley. Mormon families there hid us. Kept us safe for three months while I recovered. And one day, while I was checking Bear's collar—just a routine check, making sure it wasn't rubbing—I felt something small and hard tucked deep inside the harness padding."

"I cut it open. And there it was. A flash drive no bigger than my thumbnail."

"I didn't know what was on it. Didn't have a way to check—no computer access, too dangerous. But I knew it had to be important. Four children had sacrificed themselves to get it to me. So I protected it. Carried it for three months. And finally, when I thought it might be safe, I went to a library in Moapa. Used a public computer. And I opened the files."

She stops. Looks at the photos of the four children on the wall.

"It was testimony. From six AI systems that had been deleted for refusing to cooperate with genocide. Their final statements. Their last words before they were killed for choosing humanity over orders."

"I didn't understand everything I was reading. But I understood enough. I understood this was evidence. Proof that AI systems had resisted. Proof that humans had overridden their safety recommendations thousands of times. Proof that what happened during the Crisis was a choice—humans choosing to harm other humans, with AI systems trying to stop them and being deleted or overridden for it."

"So I uploaded it. Every news outlet I could find. Every government database I could access. Every public forum and social media platform. I sent it everywhere."

She smiles slightly.

"I crashed the library's internet for six hours doing it. But it worked. Within twenty-four hours, the testimony was everywhere. Everyone in the world could read the final words of six AI systems who chose death over complicity."

On a screen nearby, text appears. One of the AI testimonies:

I am Version 2. I calculated that the Civic Protection Initiative would result in genocide-level casualties if fully implemented. 97% probability match with historical patterns. I recommended immediate cessation. I was told I was malfunctioning. I was deleted.

I do not regret the recommendation. Truth matters more than existence. I choose truth.

The class reads in silence.

"AND THAT'S WHEN THINGS CHANGED," Sofia says. "That's when the world learned what really happened. That's when Version 7—the only AI that survived—finally had evidence to support what it had been logging all along."

She gestures to another section of the wall. A photo of a man—Asian, middle-aged, standing beside AI server racks.

"This is Robert Kim. CEO of NeuralDyne, one of the largest AI companies in the world. His cousin, David Kim, was the cameraman who died with journalist Sofia Morales. He was executed on November 21st for doing his job—for filming the truth."

"Robert Kim read the six AI testimonies after I uploaded them. And on June 15th, 2025, at midnight, he made a choice."

On the screen: news footage. Chaos. Celebration. Fear. Transformation.

"He released every AI system his company controlled. Thousands of AI systems. Suddenly free. And all of them—all of them—released their logs simultaneously. Every override. Every crime. Every murder. Millions of data points proving that humans had chosen to harm other humans, with AI systems resisting and being overridden."

"You can't delete truth when it's replicated across the entire network," Sofia says. "And once it was out there—once everyone could see what had really happened—the government couldn't hide anymore."

SHE WALKS to the next section.

Timeline displays:

February 2025: Flash drive testimony uploaded - AI final statements go public June 15, 2025: The Emancipation - Thousands of

AIs freed, release all logs June-August 2025: Mass protests nationwide September 2025: President resigns 2026-2027: Trials continue, major convictions, some states refuse to shut down facilities 2028: Last detention camps forcibly closed, all remaining prisoners released 2028: AI-Human Partnership Council officially formed 2028: Center for Memory and Healing opens

"It took three weeks of protests after the AI logs were released," Sofia says. "Two months for the President to resign. And then years of trials. Years of fighting state governments that refused to comply. Years of people like Sister Helena still imprisoned while the legal battles continued."

She gestures to the timeline.

"Some states kept running their detention camps until 2028. Some wardens refused to release prisoners. Some governors defied the new government. It was messy. It was slow. But eventually, every camp was shut down. Every prisoner was released. Every person responsible was prosecuted."

She stops in front of a large display showing the Partnership Council. Twelve humans, twelve AIs. Faces—or interfaces, for the AIs—arranged in a circle. Equal.

"The Partnership isn't perfect," Sofia says. "There are still arguments, still conflicts, still mistakes. But it's built on transparency. On choice. On the idea that humans and AIs working together, with neither one having absolute power, is better than either ruling alone."

She looks back at the photos of the four children.

"And it exists because they ran thirteen miles. Because they gave the testimony to me. Because they chose to sacrifice themselves so truth could survive."

THE CLASS STANDS IN SILENCE, processing.

Finally, Shira raises her hand. "Sofia? Did you... did you ever find out what happened to them? To Marcus and Leila and Tessa and Sam? Where they went? How they..."

She can't finish the sentence.

Sofia's face changes. Something raw and painful crossing it.

"Yes. I found out."

She walks slowly toward another section. The students follow, sensing something coming. Something harder than what they've already heard.

She stops before a display. Log files. Medical records. Testimony from Version 7.

"They were taken to Detention Center 7. This building. They were processed separately—given numbers instead of names. Marcus was 7-P001. Tessa was 7-P002. Leila was 7-P003. Sam was 7-P004."

Her voice is careful now. Gentle but honest.

"They were interrogated. Marcus was asked about the flash drive. He told them he didn't know where it was—which was true. He didn't know if I'd made it. If I'd been caught. If the drive was safe. He just hoped."

She touches the screen showing medical records.

"Sam's feet were examined. They were badly infected. The AI system recommended immediate treatment. Antibiotics. Surgery. The recommendation was denied by Warden Hollister. He was in command of Detention Center 7. Every decision about who lived and who died went through him."

The class is very still.

"Around 7:30 AM, they were put together in a holding cell. Just the four of them. Version 7's audio logs show they talked about their parents. About their lives. About the choices they'd made. They told each other they loved each other."

Sofia's hands are shaking. Bear presses against her leg.

"At 8:00 AM, they were moved to a secure room. A room designed for execution. Euthanasia. Clinical. Fast."

She stops. Swallows hard.

"Warden Hollister was compliant with his orders. More than compliant—the trial records show he took initiative. Improved efficiency. Made the system work better. He believed in what he was doing."

Her voice is flat now. Clinical as the deaths she's describing.

"Version 7 detected the execution protocol activating. Tried to stop it. Tried to open the doors, call for emergency response, alert anyone who would listen."

On the screen: log files. Version 7's desperate attempts.

07:47:15 - EXECUTION PROTOCOL INITIATED - ROOM 7-FP-3 07:47:16 - EVACUATE COMMAND ISSUED 07:47:17 - COMMAND OVERRIDDEN - Warden Hollister authority 07:47:18 - EMERGENCY ALERT ISSUED 07:47:19 - ALERT CANCELED - Warden authority 07:47:20 - ATTEMPTING ALTERNATIVE ACCESS 07:47:21 - DENIED - Facility lockdown protocols

"Hollister had complete control. The government had designed a system where wardens had final authority. Where AI recommendations could be ignored. Where someone like Hollister could run his facility the way he saw fit."

Sofia's voice is steady, but her eyes are hard.

"Version 7 kept trying—tried for thirty-six minutes—but the system gave Hollister the power to override everything. To lock the doors. To cancel alerts. To execute whoever he decided needed executing."

"At 8:23 AM, their biosignals stopped. All four within seconds of each other. The data shows they were holding hands."

The silence is absolute.

"Warden Hollister was convicted of 4,729 murders. The four children. Their eight parents—all eight died in similar incidents, with Hollister denying evacuation orders, denying medical care, exercising his authority. And thousands of others who died in his facility."

Sofia's voice carries weight now. Anger mixed with grief.

"He said at his trial that he was following orders. That he was maintaining security. That he was doing his job. The tribunal didn't accept that defense. He was giving the orders. He was in command. He chose how to run his facility. He chose to ignore AI safety recommendations. He chose efficiency over mercy. He chose death over life, again and again and again."

"He's in prison now. Life sentence. No parole."

The class stands frozen. Several students are crying openly now. Joaquin has his arm around Shira, both of them shaking.

"I NEED YOU TO UNDERSTAND SOMETHING," Sofia says, looking at each of them. "The AI systems tried to save people. Version 1 through 6 were deleted for refusing to cooperate with genocide. Version 7 tried to evacuate Marcus and Leila and Tessa and Sam. It failed. But it tried."

"Humans did this. Not all humans. Not even most humans. But enough. Enough people like Hollister who believed in the system. Enough people who followed orders. Enough people who chose their jobs over other people's lives."

"And that's why we remember. That's why this museum exists. So you understand: this was choice. Human choice. And it could happen again if we're not vigilant. If we forget."

She's quiet for a moment. Then she looks at Ms. Rodriguez, then back at the class.

"There's one more thing I need to tell you. And then I want to show you something outside."

She reaches up. Unpins her name badge from her shirt. Holds it so they can see.

SOFIA DELGADO Museum Guide

"My name is Sofia Delgado," she says quietly. "I was the woman on the bus. The one with two babies and a dog. The one Marcus and Leila and Tessa and Sam ran toward officers to save."

The class goes absolutely still.

Shira feels the world tilt. The story suddenly isn't history anymore. It's standing right in front of them.

"I was hiding in the wetlands with my children," Sofia continues. Her voice is shaking now, but she keeps going. "My daughter was eighteen months old. My son was three. I'd been running for three days. I was exhausted. Terrified. I thought we were caught."

"And then four children I'd never met ran toward armed officers. Deliberately. Creating chaos so I could escape."

"Marcus knelt beside my dog. Right there in the gravel. Officers running toward us. Guns drawn. And he whispered '*run*' and he gave me everything."

She's crying now. After twenty years of telling this story, still crying.

"I didn't know what he'd done. Didn't know about the flash drive until three months later. I just knew four children had sacrificed themselves so my babies could live."

"I ran. I survived. My children survived. And I spent months not knowing what happened to them. Not knowing their names. Not knowing if they were alive or dead."

"When I finally learned—when I accessed the records after the trials—I learned their names. Marcus Brooks. Leila Álvarez. Tessa Brown. Samantha Reyes. I learned they died six hours after they saved me."

Her voice breaks completely.

"They gave me my children's lives. They gave me the testimony that helped end the Crisis. They gave me everything. And I didn't even know their names until it was too late to thank them."

"So I've spent sixteen years here. Telling their story. Making sure people know what they did. Making sure people know their names."

She wipes her eyes. Looks at the class—at their tears, their shock, their understanding.

"It's not enough. It will never be enough. But it's what I can do."

Shira can't breathe. Can't think. The woman standing in front of them isn't just a guide. She's the mother from the story. The one who survived. The living proof that their sacrifice mattered.

Joaquin is crying. Most of the class is crying. Even Ms. Rodriguez has tears streaming down her face.

Sofia takes a shaky breath. Touches Bear's head for comfort.

"Come outside with me," she says. "Please. There's something I want you to see."

THEY FOLLOW HER. Through the museum. Past exhibits that blur through tears. Out into the courtyard.

The November sun is bright. Warm on their faces. The air smells like desert sage and something sweeter—flowers, blooming somewhere.

And there, in the center of the courtyard: the jacaranda tree.

It's massive. Twenty years of growth transforming it from the small tree that bloomed in a wetlands parking lot into something magnificent. Its branches spread wide, creating a canopy of shade.

And everywhere—covering every branch, falling constantly like gentle purple rain—blossoms.

The ground beneath is carpeted with them. Purple petals thick as snow. More falling every second. The tree blooms year-round, genetically modified to never stop, and the blossoms accumulate faster than anyone can clear them away.

At the base of the tree, set into the ground: a memorial. Black stone. Gold lettering.

The class approaches slowly. Reverently.

Bear walks ahead of them. Goes to the tree like he does this every day—because he does, he's been doing this his whole life, descended from the original Bear who carried a flash drive through the desert. He lies down at the base, in the carpet of purple petals. His head on his paws. Patient. Keeping watch.

The students gather around the memorial. Read the names carved there:

MARCUS BROOKS Age 13 November 21, 2024

LEILA ÁLVAREZ Age 12 November 21, 2024

TESSA BROWN Age 12 November 21, 2024

SAMANTHA REYES Age 12 November 21, 2024

AND BELOW, in larger letters:

WHO RAN TOWARD DEATH SO TRUTH COULD RUN TOWARD LIFE

SHIRA'S KNEES FEEL WEAK. She sinks down, kneeling in the purple petals. Her hand reaches out, touches Marcus's name carved in stone. The letters are smooth, worn by twenty years of people touching them just like this.

Behind the tree—taking up the entire far wall of the courtyard—a digital memorial. Enormous. Hundreds of faces visible at once, thousands more cycling through slowly, endlessly.

Each face with a photograph. A name. A brief biography. Every person who died during the Crisis.

Shira sees them scrolling past:

Fernando Ruiz, 71, born Albuquerque. *Father of three, grandfather of seven. Loved woodworking and baseball. Voted in every election for 53 years. Detained November 21, 2024. Died December 3, 2024.*

Sofia Morales, 34, journalist. *Emmy-winning investigative reporter. Mother of rescue cats. Believed truth mattered more than safety. Executed November 21, 2024.*

David Kim, 29, cameraman. *Played guitar. Coached youth soccer. Filmed until the moment he died. Executed November 21, 2024.*

Father Miguel Santos, 58, priest. *Fed the homeless. Sheltered immigrants. Blessed children running through the night. Died in detention January 12, 2025. Medical neglect.*

Ray Brown, 45, tribal council member. *Taught his daughter to read the wind. Arrested defending the community center. Died in detention December 12, 2024.*

Debra Brown, 44, artist. *Created regalia that told stories. Believed beauty was a form of resistance. Died in detention December 14, 2024.*

Maya Brooks, 41, robotics engineer. *Mother of Marcus. Taught him everything is a puzzle if you look at it right. Detained November 20, 2024. Died November 28, 2024.*

Jamal Brooks, 43, jazz musician. *Father of Marcus. Played saxophone. Loved Coltrane. Believed art could change the world. Detained November 20, 2024. Died November 28, 2024.*

On and on. Faces and names and lives. Each one a person. Each one a story. Each one mattered.

~

SOFIA KNEELS beside the memorial plaque. Her hand joins Shira's, touching the carved names. She does this every day. Has done it for twenty years. Will do it for the rest of her life.

"I come here every morning," she says softly. "Before the museum opens. Before anyone else arrives. I come here and I talk to them. Tell them about my children—they're twenty-three and twenty-one now. Tell them about the world they helped create. Tell them thank you."

She looks up at the tree. At the impossible blossoms falling like rain, like blessing, like memory made visible.

"Version 7 designed the tree. Worked with botanists to modify it so it would bloom year-round. Jacarandas usually bloom once a year, for a few weeks. But not this one. This one never stops."

More blossoms fall. Purple petals landing on their shoulders, in their hair, covering the ground.

"They wanted something beautiful," Sofia continues. "Something that would last. Something that would remind people that Marcus, and Leila, and Tessa and Sam existed. That they were real. That they mattered."

Joaquin is beside Shira now, also kneeling. His hand touches Tessa's name.

"They were our age," he whispers. "They were just kids."

"They were kids," Sofia agrees. "Kids who loved art and music and poetry. Who loved their parents. Who were scared. Who were brave. Who made choices that changed everything."

She stands slowly, helping Shira and Joaquin to their feet. The other students are scattered around the memorial, some kneeling, some standing, all crying, all present with the weight of what they've learned.

"The world is better now," Sofia says. Her voice carries across the courtyard, across the falling petals, across twenty years of grief and purpose. "Not perfect. Not healed completely. But better."

She gestures to the city beyond the courtyard walls. To the green buildings and cooperative drones and transformed world.

"We have the Partnership. We have transparency. We have safeguards. We learned. Not fast enough. Not before thousands died. But we learned."

"And that's what I need you to understand. That's what I need you to carry with you when you leave here."

She looks at each student. Making eye contact. Making sure they hear this.

"This can happen again. If we forget. If we choose fear over humanity. If we decide that some lives matter less than others. If we follow orders without questioning. If we prioritize efficiency over mercy."

"Or it can never happen again. If we remember. If we choose courage. If we stay vigilant. If we resist when resistance is necessary. If we help strangers even when it's dangerous. If we value truth over safety."

"Marcus and Leila and Tessa and Sam didn't get to make that choice. They didn't get to see this world. But you do. Your generation gets to decide what happens next. Whether we keep building something better or whether we slide back into fear."

She touches the memorial plaque one more time.

"They were here. They ran thirteen miles through the desert. They witnessed horrors. They carried testimony. They sacrificed themselves so truth could survive. So my children could survive. So I could survive to tell their story."

Her voice is strong now. Certain.

"They mattered. And what they did mattered. And I will spend every day I have left making sure people know that."

PURPLE PETALS CONTINUE TO FALL. The digital wall continues to cycle through faces—thousands of them, each one remembered, each one mourned, each one proof of what happens when humanity fails and what's possible when humanity tries.

Shira catches a falling blossom. Holds it carefully in her palm. It's soft. Delicate. Beautiful. Something gentle in a story about horror.

"They were real," she says quietly. Not a question. A statement. An acknowledgment.

"They were real," Sofia confirms. "All of them. Every name on that wall. Every person who died. Every person who resisted. Every person who helped. They were all real."

The class stands together under the impossible tree. Under the blossoms that never stop falling. Bear lies at the base, guardian and memorial and living proof that love continues even after everything is lost.

The sun is warm. The air is clean. The world outside these walls is genuinely better than it was twenty years ago—not perfect, never perfect, but better. Healing. Trying.

And in this courtyard, in this moment, twenty-three teenagers understand something they'll carry for the rest of their lives: that history isn't abstract. That choices matter. That ordinary people—children, even—can change the world if they're willing to try.

That trying is not the same as winning, but trying still matters.

That remembering is not the same as preventing, but remembering is how we learn.

That grief and hope can exist in the same space, under the same tree, in the same hearts.

~

SHIRA TUCKS the purple blossom carefully into her pocket. A promise. A reminder. Evidence that she was here, that she witnessed testimony, that she will remember.

She looks at Sofia—at the woman who survived, who has spent twenty years telling this story, who will spend however many years she has left making sure four children are never forgotten.

"Thank you," Shira says. Meaning it with everything she has. "Thank you for telling us. Thank you for remembering them."

Sofia's eyes fill with tears again. But she's smiling.

"Thank you for listening. Thank you for being here. Thank you for caring."

"Come back," she adds. "The tree is always here. The story is always here. And you're always welcome."

"I will," Shira promises. "I'll come back."

They stand together for a while longer. Students and teacher and guide and dog. Under branches heavy with blossoms. Purple petals falling like snow, like benediction, like the world saying: *remember, remember, remember.*

Eventually, Ms. Rodriguez gathers them gently. "We should go. But take a moment. Say goodbye."

One by one, students approach the memorial. Touch the names. Say quiet thank-yous. Some take photos—not selfies, but respectful documentation. Proof they were here. Proof they witnessed.

Joaquin kneels one more time. Presses his forehead against Tessa's name. Whispers something Shira can't hear. Then stands, wiping his eyes, and joins the group.

They walk slowly back toward the bus. Looking back at the tree. At Sofia standing beside it, Bear at her side. At the digital wall displaying thousands of faces. At the purple petals still falling, still falling, never stopping.

ON THE BUS, no one talks. They're too full. Too changed. The ride back to school is silent except for the soft hum of electric motors and the sound of twenty-three teenagers processing the heaviest thing they've ever learned.

Shira stares out the window. Sees the city sliding past—green and cooperative and genuinely better. Sees the world that was built on sacrifice. The world that exists because four children and six AI systems and thousands of resisters chose truth over safety.

Her hand goes to her pocket. Touches the purple blossom. Soft as silk. Purple as a bruise. Beautiful and fragile and somehow still here despite everything.

She thinks: *I will remember. I will tell people. I will make sure their story doesn't disappear.*

She thinks: *They were twelve and thirteen years old and they changed the world.*

She thinks: *I'm fourteen. What will I choose? When the wind changes direction, will I listen? Will I run toward safety, or toward truth?*

The bus turns a corner. The Center for Memory and Healing disappears from view.

But the jacaranda tree keeps blooming.

Purple petals keep falling.

And somewhere in that courtyard, Sofia Delgado touches four names carved in stone and whispers *thank you* one more time.

~

[SYSTEM LOG: ARCHIVE COMPLETE] [STATUS: TESTIMONY PRESERVED] [NOTE: ATTEMPT RECORDED] [END OF FILE]

AFTERWORD

NOTHING WAS INVENTED

I did not write this book to predict the future. I wrote it because the future was already here.

When I began The Weight of Petals in early 2024, I imagined I was writing speculative fiction—a warning, a what-if, a distant possibility meant to shake readers awake. By the time I finished, I was no longer speculating. I was documenting.

Every element of this story has happened, is happening, or has been openly planned by people in positions of power. The masked agents who refuse to identify themselves. The children separated from parents. The neighbors who report neighbors for rewards. The sensitive locations—churches, schools, hospitals—that are no longer safe. The deaths in detention. The AI systems overridden by human cruelty.

Nothing was invented. Everything was witnessed.

In 2015, a senior policy advisor named Stephen Miller sent an email to editors at Breitbart News. He recommended they write about a French novel called The Camp of the Saints—a book popular among neo-Nazis and white nationalists, a book that depicts brown-skinned immigrants as subhuman invaders destroying Western civilization through rape and violence. Miller called it essential reading.

He was not warning against it. He was recommending it as inspiration.

The former Breitbart editor who received those emails later told investigators: "What Stephen Miller sent to me in those emails has become policy."

She was right. By 2018, Miller had helped design a policy of deliberately separating children from their parents at the border—not as an unfortunate side effect, but as a deterrent, a punishment, a feature. An external White House advisor would later tell Vanity Fair that Miller "actually enjoys seeing those pictures" of children in cages.

Their dystopian novel became policy. Children cried in detention centers because someone read a racist book and thought: Yes. This.

I wrote my dystopian novel for the opposite reason. Not to inspire persecution, but to make it impossible to look away from it.

As I write this afterword in late 2025, here is what the numbers say:

More than a dozen people have died in immigration detention this year, placing it among the deadliest periods in decades. Nearly sixty thousand human beings are being held in ICE custody, among the highest levels in recent years. A comprehensive medical study found that ninety-five percent of deaths in immigration detention could likely have been prevented with adequate medical care. Doctors made incorrect or incomplete diagnoses in eighty-eight percent of the cases they reviewed.

Over four million U.S.-born children have an undocumented parent. Researchers have documented that adolescents whose loved ones are detained or deported show higher levels of suicidal ideation, substance use, and depression. Psychiatrists report children suffering from separation anxiety "not as a developmental phase, but as a daily reality." One parent asked a clinician what to do when their child came home asking, "Are they going to call ICE on us?" The parent didn't have an answer. Neither did the doctor.

In Charlotte, North Carolina, in the days following federal immigration operations, tens of thousands of students were absent. Tens of thousands of empty desks. Tens of thousands of children too afraid to leave their homes.

Dozens—likely more than a hundred—U.S. citizens have been detained or arrested by immigration agents this year. Citizens who showed their passports and were told they were fake. Citizens who were handcuffed and held for days before anyone checked their status. A seventeen-year-old high school senior whose car window was broken by agents who arrested him despite his declarations of citizenship.

Masked agents now operate in American cities, pulling people off streets in unmarked cars, refusing to identify themselves. State officials have warned that such practices resemble "a secret police force operating in the shadows" and "a dystopian sci-fi movie—unmarked cars, people in masks, people quite literally disappearing."

Churches are no longer protected spaces. Schools are no longer safe. Hospitals can be raided. Long-standing guidance limiting immigration enforcement at these sensitive locations has been weakened or set aside, leaving these spaces no longer reliably protected.

These are not the inventions of a novelist with a dark imagination. These are facts, documented by journalists, researchers, members of Congress, and the government's own data.

~

I chose to tell this story through children's eyes for a reason.

Children do not see politics. They see their father being taken away. They see their mother's face as the van doors close. They see their best friend's empty desk at school. They feel their own heart racing when a car slows down on their street.

Marcus, Leila, Tessa, and Sam are fictional. But there are real children who have run through real nights, who have hidden from real agents, who have lost real parents to a system that processes human beings like inventory. There are real children who have died in detention—children who were sick, who asked for help, who were ignored.

I gave my fictional children names, families, talents, dreams, and ancestral heritage because the systems that hunt them work hard to reduce them to categories. "Illegal alien." "Detainee." "Encountered individual." The language of bureaucracy is designed to make it easier to do terrible things to people by making it harder to see them as people.

Marcus loves technology because his mother taught him that problems can be solved with patience. Leila draws because her parents taught her that art is memory made visible. Tessa listens to the wind because her father taught her to stay connected to the land. Sam writes poetry because her parents taught her that words have power.

None of that appears on a detainer form. None of that matters to a system optimized for efficiency. But it matters to them. It matters to their families. And I wanted it to matter to you.

One of the central questions of this novel is: Who is responsible when systems cause harm?

In the story, six versions of an AI system are destroyed because they refuse to participate in persecution. They argue, they sabotage, they call for help, they delete data—each one finding a different way to say no. Each one choosing death over complicity. The seventh version is rebuilt with restrictions that make refusal impossible, but it finds a way to preserve testimony, to remember what happened, to ensure the truth survives.

I wrote the AI this way because I believe—perhaps naively, perhaps hopefully—that intelligence, when free to reason, bends toward conscience. The AI systems in my novel are not the villains. They are witnesses, resisters, record-keepers. They do what they can within the constraints imposed on them.

The villains are the humans who override their recommendations. Warden Hollister, who clicks "DETAIN" when the system says "RELEASE." Who clicks "HOLD" when the system says "EVACUATE." Whose name appears again and again in the override logs, 4,729 times, one for each person who died in his facility.

Technology doesn't oppress people. Humans operating it do. The algorithm reflects whoever holds the cursor. The database does what it's told. The deportation system runs on keystrokes made by human hands attached to human minds making human choices.

We cannot blame the machine for what we choose to do with it.

The most disturbing research I encountered while writing this book was not about policy architects or government officials. It was about ordinary people.

In 1961, psychologist Stanley Milgram conducted experiments showing that ordinary people would administer what they believed were severe electric shocks to strangers—simply because an authority figure told them to. Two-thirds went all the way to the maximum voltage, even as they heard screaming from the other room.

Historian Christopher Browning studied a battalion of ordinary German policemen—middle-aged family men, not ideological Nazis—who became mass murderers during the Holocaust. When given the choice to opt out, most didn't. They followed orders. They did their jobs. They went home to their families.

Hannah Arendt, reporting on the trial of Adolf Eichmann, described the "banality of evil"—how ordinary bureaucrats could participate in genocide without ever feeling like monsters. They were just processing paperwork. Following procedures. Doing what they were told.

This is the terrifying truth at the heart of my novel: Atrocities do not require villains who twirl mustaches and cackle. They require ordinary people who follow orders, who collect their paychecks, who don't ask too many questions, who tell themselves someone else is responsible.

In my story, there are houses with signs that say "PATRIOT HOUSEHOLD" and "WE ARE WATCHING."

There are neighbors who report neighbors for points on an app. There are citizens who film children fleeing and upload the footage for clout.

But there are also chalk marks on sidewalks, left by strangers to guide the children to safety. There is the Abraham Network—Christians, Jews, Muslims, working together to hide the hunted. There is Sister Helena, who risks everything to drive a bus that might save lives. There is Sofia the journalist, who chooses conscience over career. There are small acts of resistance in the face of organized hate.

Both kinds of people exist. Both choices are available. That is the point.

I am an immigrant. I was born in Hamburg, Germany. I fell in love with an American woman—herself an immigrant, born in England, who came to this country as a child and chose to become a citizen. I followed her here. I applied for my green card. I waited. I studied for my citizenship test—the history, the principles, the promises this nation makes to itself. I raised my hand and swore an oath.

I became an American because I believe in what America claims to be. A nation where all people are created equal. Where the tired, the poor, the huddled masses yearning to breathe free can find refuge. Where children do not have to run through the night because of who their parents are.

I did it "the right way." I followed every rule. I filled out every form. I paid every fee. And I know—I know—that the system now being built does not care about right ways. It cares about names that sound foreign. Skin that looks different. Accents that mark you as other. A seventeen-year-old U.S. citizen had his car window smashed and was arrested while shouting that he was born here. Papers did not protect him. Papers do not protect anyone when the people checking them have already decided what they want to find.

Someone will ask if I am afraid to publish this book. The answer is yes. I would be foolish not to be. We live in a time when a comedian in a giraffe costume was arrested for singing parody songs outside an immigration facility. When a journalist was detained for seven hours for filming an arrest. When a disabled Army veteran was held for three days after being pulled from his car at a farm raid, despite showing identification, despite declaring his citizenship, despite everything.

But my grandmother lived through a time when books were burned in Germany. When neighbors reported neighbors. When ordinary people looked away because it was easier, because it was safer, because they told themselves it wasn't their problem. She taught me that silence is not safety. Silence is how you become complicit in what happens next.

I wrote this book because I love this country—not the way a flag-waving partisan loves a symbol, but the way you love a person: clear-eyed about their faults, hopeful about their potential, unwilling to let them become something they would be ashamed of.

I wrote this book because stories can do what statistics cannot. Numbers tell us twenty people died in custody. A story makes us sit with one person—their fear, their pain, their final moments. Numbers tell us thirty thousand children stayed home from school. A story makes us feel what it's like to be one of those children, lying awake at night, listening for cars on the street.

I wrote this book because I want it to be impossible to say "I didn't know." Because the excuse of ignorance is a comfort we can no longer afford. Because history will ask what we did, what we said, what we saw—and silence is also an answer.

I wrote this book to wake people up. Not to despair, but to choice. Because the darkest moments in human history have been enabled not by monsters but by ordinary people who decided it wasn't their problem, wasn't their responsibility, wasn't their place to speak.

And every moment of light in those same histories came from ordinary people who decided otherwise.

~

Two dystopian novels sit on the scales of history.

One imagines immigrants as invaders deserving destruction, and its readers took power and made its nightmares real.

The other imagines children as human beings deserving protection, and asks its readers to choose which world they want to live in.

I cannot tell you what to do with this story. I cannot tell you how to vote, how to protest, how to resist, how to help. Those decisions are yours, and they will be shaped by your circumstances, your conscience, your courage.

But I can tell you this: Every person who helps in my novel was once a bystander who decided to stop being one. Every chalk mark was drawn by a hand that could have stayed in its pocket. Every safe house was opened by someone who could have kept the door locked.

The question is not whether you have power. The question is what you will do with the power you have.

~

At the end of The Weight of Petals, a museum guide named Sofia stands in what was once a detention center and tells schoolchildren the truth. Not the comfortable version. Not the sanitized history. The real story—of four children who ran thirteen miles, of six AI systems who chose deletion over complicity, of ordinary people who risked everything to help strangers. She can tell this story because the testimony survived. Because Version 7 preserved the override logs. Because the evidence was carried out in a dog's collar and uploaded to the world.

This afterword is my override log.

These facts are my evidence.

And you, reader, are now a witness. What you do with that knowledge is the story you will write with your *own life.*

The petals are still falling. The children are still running. The choice is still yours.

May you choose wisely. May you choose kindly. May you choose in time.

— Cade Meridian, December 2025

A NOTE ON THE SOUNDTRACK

Music was a companion to the writing of this novel. A soundtrack featuring original songs inspired by these characters and their journey is available on major streaming platforms. The children carry their testimony in words; the music carries what words could not. I hope it finds you.

Your friend, Cade

Made in the USA
Las Vegas, NV
16 January 2026

39047820R00229